EVERMORE ACADEMY: SPRING

YEAR TWO

AUDREY GREY

STARFALL PRESS

Book cover design by Jay R. Villalobos

For my husband and partner in life (and crime), Chris

"Summer Solstice, I need to see you running so hard your heels are tapping your mortal ass!" Eclipsa orders from her purple and yellow leopard printed hammock chair, where she's been overseeing my run around the Lake of Sorrows for the last forty minutes.

"Yeah, tap that ass!" Ruby cheers from her perch on my shoulder. "Tap it so hard the prince will have to ice it down later."

Oh. My. God. My friends have no idea how dirty they sound.

I would laugh—*would*, if I wasn't getting my butt kicked five ways from Sunday. Pumping my arms, I burst through a patch of dandelions, my legs disturbing the wispy white seeds into the air.

"I'm . . . trying," I pant, glaring at the Lunar Court assassin turned sadistic torturer. Her moon-white hair is pulled back in a high ponytail, her lithe body poured into metallic silver-blue yoga pants and a sports bra, showing off the lunar tattoos cresting her ripped abdomen. The half-moon jewels over her brow glimmer beneath the afternoon sun.

I'm pretty sure she added a couple jewels, which means the Fae assassin killed again.

Eclipsa summoned me to the Everwilde a week early to train. I think she *thinks* I should be appreciative—and I am, I suppose—but that's in between my near constant pity party.

When I round the final leg of the run, I sprint across the meadowscape, the bright pink Nike trainers Eclipsa loaned me skipping over hyacinth flowers and daisies, and collapse at the finish line in front of her.

Six freaking miles. And I just sprinted every single one of them like a boss. Thank Queen Titania I kept up my training during the summer. My routine was grueling. Mornings I ran the paths around our land. Afternoons I practiced my yoga regimen. And nights were spent squatting, deadlifting, and planking my way into the best shape of my life.

This was going to be my year. Winter could suck it.

Yet, none of it prepared me for Eclipsa's brutal punishment.

Eclipsa glances over the neon green stopwatch in her hand. "You shaved two seconds off your time."

"Yeah I did," I boast, winking at Ruby.

"Okay, badass. Now stop gloating and get up."

"More torture? You can't be serious."

She cuts her dark eyes at me. "Why? Is today special or something?"

Nope, it's just my birthday. But I don't say that. Who knows how the Fae celebrate birthdays, or if they even do, considering their long lifespans?

Groaning, I drag myself to my feet, hands on my head, and suck in giant gulps of the sweet spring air. Around us, a vibrant tapestry of color unfurls. Wildflowers in every hue imaginable blanket the campus grounds, contrasted against an ocean of tranquil blue. Pink trees bloom like fireworks, their buds so large they look like cotton candy caught in the branches.

It's hard to believe this is the same academy I left three months ago.

Ruby buzzes toward the side table, her magenta hair smudging the air, and wraps her tiny arms around the dark gray hydroflask Mack sent me as an early birthday present. The hot pink words, *Property of the WP*, are engraved into the steel.

Mack's idea of a joke. *Hardy har.*

The spell my BFF paid to make the words only visible to me must have cost a pretty penny.

"Look at you," I tease, "being all useful."

Ruby hands off the water and bows, her shimmery wings flapping so fast they're a blur. "With what that savage is about to put you through, you'll need every drop."

Holy Fae. I throw a pleading look at Eclipsa. "Please not burpees. Anything but those."

Eclipsa springs from the hammock chair. Every muscle in her abdomen flickers, the moon cycle tats rippling as if alive. I'm pretty sure she does sit ups in her sleep.

"That's right, beotch." Eclipsa grins. "Prepare for an epic beat down."

That's when I notice one hand is behind her back.

Squealing, she thrusts her arm out, a sparkly silver-wrapped gift in her hand. "How dare you not tell me it's your birthday."

"Ruby!" I scold. "You little snitch."

"What?" Ruby grins. "She bribed me with sugar drops."

Eclipsa stuffs the gift into my Puma gym bag. "Open this later, okay?"

I nod as Ruby flits up level with my face, holding out a half-chewed Charms lollipop. "Here you go, Kid."

"Thanks." I take her gross birthday offering, still wet with slobber, and glance at Eclipsa, suddenly hopeful. "Does this mean no more trying to kill me today?"

Eclipsa's eyes light up, and she waves her hand through the air. "Who said anything about taking it easy on you?"

A translucent golden portal just large enough to step through appears in front of her.

Crap. The last time she sent me through a portal for training, I ended up fighting two orcs. Granted, they were a miniature variety, and not fully grown . . . but still.

I glare at Eclipsa.

She grins back. "After you, Princess."

With Ruby resettled on my shoulder, I jump through the portal, ready for anything.

Anything except . . . Mack's Manhattan apartment? I recognize the luxurious penthouse immediately, my gaze flicking from the white marble and abstract paintings to Mack's beaming face.

"Surprise!" she screams.

Like some birthday nightmare come to life, silver and blue balloons and confetti fall from the air. Mack's parents, Nick and Sebastian, flip on the lights and jump from the kitchen, waving their hands.

When I see Aunt Zinnia appear behind them, wearing the apron with the cats, her frizzy blonde hair haloing her head, stupid tears spring to my eyes. Aunt Vi waits a little ways behind her sister, wringing her hands. She stands ramrod straight, her mouth a stern line, refusing to move, as if Fae magic lurks in the opulent modern steel countertops and appliances.

Maybe it does.

Mack throws her arms around me. "Happy birthday, Beezy!"

My heart swells. We haven't seen each other in a month.

We tried Facetiming, but the internet in our area crapped out recently.

"How's the academy?" Mack asks as she guides me from the kitchen to the dining room.

"Colorful," I say, sweeping my gaze over the elaborate setup piled over the long mahogany table. "Everything smells like flowers, the birds are really loud, and I'm still getting used to actual sunlight."

"You're so lucky." She sighs, as if getting an extra week of getting her ass kicked is her idea of heaven. "I would die to train with Eclipsa. I can't wait until you meet up with Reina this year."

"Our turn!" Mack's dads rush over, and before I can escape, I'm locked into a group hug.

"Okay, okay," Mack says, swatting at both men. "Personal space, remember?"

Her dads back off, and it's Zinnia and Vi's turn. I hug them both, surprised and a little overwhelmed that they would venture into the Untouched Zone for me.

Just getting Vi here was a miracle in and of itself. I can't imagine the effort it took to convince her, plus managing the travel visas and then talking Vi into using a portal.

I owe Mack's dads big time.

Zinnia pinches my cheeks. "Sweet girl, we're so proud of you. Now, look what I found you."

She holds up an opened, near-empty bag of Zapps sweet southern heat barbeque chips.

Vi rolls her eyes. "The old cow ate nearly the entire bag."

"You can't just have one chip, Vi!" Zinnia protests. "Those things are like crack in a bag."

Before the two can get into an all-out brawl in front of Mack's dads, I take the present Vi is holding. "What's this?"

"I thought, since we can't be at the academy to protect you . . ."

"She got you a knife," Zinnia clarifies, clicking her tongue.

My mouth hangs open as I rip off the red wrapping paper to reveal the wood-handled hunting knife inside.

"It's made with iron," Vi clarifies, throwing a not-so-subtle glance at Eclipsa, who's posted up near the french doors leading to the balcony, watching everything with mild curiosity.

Oh, God. This must have cost them a fortune.

Sebastian frowns at the blade while Nick rushes over. "The academy is perfectly safe. We both attended and survived."

Aunt Vi doesn't argue, at least, not with words. But her mouth goes hard, and her hands, weathered by years of gardening in the Texas sun, flutter over her chest.

That's when I notice the four dark red furrows ridging her collarbone. "What is that?"

Vi and Zinnia exchange glances, and then Zinnia says, "There was an attack recently."

My stomach hollows out. "Darkling?"

Zinnia nods. "They reopened the farmer's market near Willowbark Lake, and Vi convinced me to help her sell her canned jams and homemade soaps. The darklings . . . there were so many of them."

My chest pinches with fear. Normal darkling incidents in the Tainted Zone involve one darkling, usually newly trans-formed. But a pack of darklings?

I try to hide my growing panic. If they know I'm worried, they'll try to conceal the true extent of the danger. "Are the attacks getting worse?"

The grooves etched into Vi's forehead deepen, and she and Zinnia share a glance.

"You don't need to worry over such things, sweet child," Zinnia says.

Oberon's beard. It's worse than I thought. "How did you get away?"

"Nothing old Betsy and some iron buckshot couldn't handle," Vi remarks, using her nickname for the 12-gauge shotgun she keeps near the door. She waves her hand as if the entire ordeal is unimportant. "Enough crass talk. We might be from the country, but we have manners, after all."

Mack's dads look horrified at the prospect of a darkling attack. I remind myself that here, in the Untouched Zone, they don't have to worry about such things.

Nick scrambles to redirect the conversation. He takes my aunts on a quick tour of the penthouse. Unfortunately, his efforts backfire. The more Aunt Vi takes in this new world, the more agitated she becomes.

I follow her suspicious stare to a picture frame on the wall above the couch. The *moving* picture. Mack stands between Nick and Sebastian, all three trying to floss. The image plays over and over, each time a little bit different.

Note to self: get more video footage of Mack's dancing skills for future blackmail.

It's hilarious—and also very much imbued with magic.

As are other items, like the centerpiece of white tulips on the table. Each perfect flower blooms while giving off a perfume too strong to be real. And golden candles sparkle with magic from a three-tiered strawberry cake.

Vi's critical gaze whips back to Ruby as she descends on a silver tray full of white chocolate truffles. "Summer, is that . . . the *thing* you told us about?"

"Yes." I glance at Ruby, praying she's on her best behavior. "Her name's Ruby, and she's not a thing, she's a sprite."

Unaware she's being assessed, Ruby smashes a truffle bigger than her head into her mouth, lets out a loud belch, and breaks into a bizarre dance.

Vi's eyes narrow. "Charming."

Before Ruby can devour the second truffle, wild

screeching draws my focus to the two blue-skinned sprites perched on the contemporary bronze light fixture above.

What the Fae hell?

The creatures dive bomb Ruby, and the three tumble together in battle. China shatters, tulip petals explode in the air, and my cake gets knocked to the delicate Angora rug below.

"Lily Pad. Dew Drop. No!" Nick scolds, rushing to stamp out the candles smoldering on the rug.

Vi's mouth has fallen open in horror. "What are . . . those horrid little creatures?"

"Sebastian!" Nick glares at his husband. "I thought you locked them up."

Sebastian frowns. "I *did*."

Mack leans over and whispers, "Sebastian recently bought Nick two pet sprites to help with his anxiety while I'm gone. But they're wicked, half-feral beasts, and they can't find the black-market trader to return them."

Eclipsa laughs. "Did the dealer not explain to you those are water sprites? Their habitat includes bogs and lakes, not high-rises and antique china. Without water, they become violent and deranged."

Nick shoots Sebastian an I-told-you-so look.

Meanwhile, the fight between Ruby and the water sprites moves to the living room, quickly laying waste to a very expensive looking glass lamp and a pink phallic sculpture.

I would find Ruby's predicament hilarious, if Aunt Vi didn't look two seconds away from murdering everyone with the cake knife to her left.

Ugh. All my work over the summer break trying to make Vi accept the Fae world and it's unraveling before my eyes. How will she ever accept that *I'm* a Fae if she hates everything about their world?

2

*Z*innia takes one look at the worry on my face and jumps into action. "Vi, let's get some fresh air. Lookie"—Zinnia waggles a half-empty pack of slims in front of her—"I brought your slims."

Vi nods, clutching Zinnia's hand, her shocked gaze never leaving the sprites as she lets Zinnia guide her toward the glass doors leading to the sweeping balcony. Nick, who knows everything about our family, thanks to his long gabfests with Zinnia, quickly whips up a martini for my aunt and rushes to follow.

Eclipsa begins some sort of spell to calm the sprites. While she and Sebastian circle the battling creatures, Mack drags me down the hall.

"Sorry this turned into such a shitshow," she says. "But I stashed a couple cans of emergency frosting in my room."

From the other end of the corridor, Sebastian screams, "Not the Neiman Marcus drapes!"

As soon as I cross into her room, my jaw goes slack. "Holy Fae ears, your lady-cave is bigger than our entire house in Texas."

She waltzes across the floor, flips on some music, and says in Gaelic, "*Mo taigh, do taigh.*"

My house, your house.

The space is an open concept, with a zebra printed leather loveseat, curtained off reading nook, bathroom with a claw-footed tub, and a mini-fridge stocked full of Mountain Dew and orange Fanta. Her sprawling king-sized bed rests above on the loft, the railing decorated with flashing Faerie lights.

A skylight paints the hardwood floor in golden light, and neon orange and teal butterflies dive in the sunbeam like giant dust motes, their magic impossible to ignore. A slight breeze ruffles white lace curtains framing the open balcony door.

A floor-to-ceiling mirror hangs to my right. My reflection catches me off guard, and I briefly inspect the woman staring back.

My thick, wavy blonde hair is pulled into a high ponytail, streaks of sun-bleached platinum catching the light. Long, lean arms tanned from my daily runs give me a surfer girl vibe. The only makeup I wear is a thick sweep of eyeliner that makes my hazel eyes—more gold than green at the moment —appear larger than normal.

I spin, taking it all in. Myself. The room. The buttery light from the bajillion windows. "I don't see how you ever leave this room."

Mack's grin is practically blinding. "I didn't bring you here to talk about my room. And I have something waiting for you that's even better than eating frosting by the spoonful."

I snort. "Wrong. There's literally nothing better than—"

That's when I feel it. Feel *him*. Like a shock of electricity straight to my core.

Valerian.

The Winter Prince is leaned against the stone balcony railing, looking panty-dropping gorgeous in a fitted black tee and dark skinny-jeans. Despite the summer heat, snowflakes swirl around him. The wind tousles his wavy inky-blue hair to one side, showing off its thickness, and I immediately imagine running my fingers through it.

His lips tug into a smirk.

Dammit. So much better than frosting.

My belly tightens as his dark gaze drops to the tight curve of my black athletic pants. He drinks me in, slowly, and I find myself drawn into his icy orbit. Pulled along by some stupid, invisible thread that grows stronger by the day.

Double dammit.

"Have fun with the ILB," Mack teases, the psycho, before she busies herself in her bathroom.

ILB: Instant lady boner. Our favorite nickname for the Winter Prince. Since we can't say his name aloud, and we chat about him a lot, he's developed quite a few nicknames and acronyms.

SOAS: Sex on a stick. PESG: Pointy-eared sex god. FBD: Future baby daddy. Mack gets all the credit for that last one.

His dark stare draws me from my thoughts, and I peer at him behind my lashes, surprised by the intense swirl of emotions raging inside me.

Just like Mack, I haven't seen Valerian for weeks. I thought, or maybe hoped, having him out of my life would lessen the attraction between us. He spent the last month hunting down the Fae responsible for nearly killing him in the Wild Hunt. Cal was a dead end.

Whoever Cal reports to, he's been spelled with powerful magic not to tell.

Not that Valerian didn't torture him anyway, just to be sure.

The phone Valerian sent me to keep in touch buzzes in my

pocket. Grinning, I pull the iPhone out and stare at the message.

Valerian's gorgeous face peers from my phone, along with the words, *Happy birthday, Princess.*

Pausing by a giant Andy Warhol style portrait of Mack, I type back, *Someone figured out how to use the camera option.*

Valerian's court frowns on mortal trappings like technology. In fact, if his father knew he had a phone, he would probably flip.

My screen lights up in response. *Why are you walking so slow?*

Maybe I want to give you a show.

Holy crap. I stare at my words. *Yes, idiot, you just said that.*

I swore when I left school that Valerian was off limits, that the soulbond between us was too dangerous to accept—at least, until I can figure out what I want.

But here I am, flirting like a deranged sex addict.

I shove the phone into my pocket, resolve to control myself, and march toward him, only swaying my hips a little bit. But as soon as I slip onto the balcony, the heat of the New York summer gives way to delicious cold, and something inside my heart—where I feel the bond between us the most —jerks taut.

Whoa. I'd forgotten how intense that is.

My breath frosts out in a crystalline cloud, highlighting the space between us. Each inch feels like a mile.

What would it feel like to finally accept this thing? The one and only time we let ourselves give into it, the experience was beyond anything I've ever felt. Like, toe-curling, soul-leaving-my-body, mind-melting pleasure.

I shake the thought from my head. Giving in now, even once, would be like Zinnia opening that bag of barbeque chips.

Once I had one taste of Valerian, I'd lose all reason, all control.

Once I give in, I won't be able to quit him.

The thought is terrifying.

The walking Fae potato chip smiles at me, his grin practically a weapon. "Hello, Princess. How does it feel to be so . . . young?"

"Technically, I'm your age," I point out. Thanks to Eclipsa's lessons over the break, I know as the reincarnated princess from the Summer Court, my soul is actually over hundreds and hundreds of years old.

"Right. How does it feel to be ancient, then?"

That silky, teasing voice reaches inside me, each word that leaves those beautiful lips a spark warming my middle. Smoldering that intense attraction I keep deeply hidden.

Don't open the bag, Summer. Don't. Open. The. Beautiful. Sexy. Bag.

"I prefer perfectly aged," I say, skirting around him to peer out across the New York skyline. "So, did you find the Fae responsible for the attack during the Wild Hunt?"

Whoever used Valerian's name to bind his power and then set darklings on us is still out there.

In my periphery, I see him shake his head. "Not yet."

"Eclipsa said you suspect someone in your own court?"

"Perhaps."

His caginess only piques my curiosity.

"What about Cal?" Just mentioning the Fae changeling's name makes me shudder. "You couldn't get anything out of him?"

"Whoever he answers to glamoured him into secrecy. There are ways to break past a glamour that powerful, but most would result in his death, and Cal's father is a high-ranking general in the Winter Court." Valerian runs a finger over the sharp tip of his ear. "Back home, our lands are increasingly under attack from the darkling scourge, and we need the general more than ever. Still, if it were up to me and not my father, I would have punished him *appropriately*."

I shiver. I know exactly what appropriately means, and it involves the dark side of Fae justice.

Not that Cal wouldn't deserve to be murdered in the most creative ways imaginable. But . . . still. It's just another reminder of how different the Fae and the human world is, and all the problems that arise from merging them.

To my left, near a wrought iron set of patio furniture, movement catches my eye. A blur wavers in the air. Once my eyes pierce the glamour, my lips stretch into a grin.

"Hey, Asher!" I call.

The dragon shifter blinks at me with those huge moss-green eyes, his black-tipped gray wings pulled tight to his back. Sunlight swims along the leathery wings, illuminating delicate green markings. "Hey, Summer."

"Mack's inside, if you . . . you know, maybe want to say hi?"

He frowns, tugging at his shoulder-length brown hair, pulled back into a man-bun only Asher could pull off. "I'm on duty."

Right. Now that someone knows Valerian's name, it's only a matter of time before they strike again.

I glance around, searching the premises for the other guards Eclipsa assigned to Valerian when she's not available. But she chose well, and not a single one gives up their position.

Unable to keep finding things to distract myself from Valerian, I turn to my mate. His eyes fall to my lips, but he tears his gaze away, hands me a small, thin present wrapped in ice-blue wrapping paper and ivory ribbon, and says, "Eclipsa said mortals celebrate their birth dates with presents, so . . . this is for you."

The moment I strip the last shred of paper from the gift and spy the delicate silver frame, heavy and cold against my fingers, I know *who's* inside.

My stomach somersaults as I stare at the three figures. "Valerian, where did you get this?"

"I visited the Summer realm a few weeks ago." He shrugs, the cavalier gesture shifting his black tee to reveal the pale skin of his upper chest. "The wards around the Summer Court palace have grown weak. I was able to break into your old room and steal the miniature portrait. Thought you might want it."

"You could have started a war." Even during the best of times, the Summer Court and the Winter Court are one incident away from full-blown battle.

"Being able to give you a piece of your stolen history is totally worth the risk."

I turn the picture over in my hand, my mind reeling.

Summer, meet your parents and dead self.

My little pep talk falls flat. The people inside—my real parents—feel like strangers. My mother, the Fae Summer Queen, wears a sumptuous green and gold brocade gown, her red hair teased into a thick net that's pulled up in a spiderweb of green ribbons and pinned with gold-and-black butterflies. The Summer King, my father and also the man who killed me, sits proudly in a matching green and gold jacket.

And the girl that sits on a throne between them, wearing the crown of ivy, poppies, and bellflowers—

I flip the picture facedown, unable to bear looking at it anymore. "Thanks. Really."

"You don't like it?"

"No, the opposite. It's the best birthday gift anyone's ever given me. It's just . . . a lot to take in."

Another pause. The tension between us grows. I stare at

the ice prince, the Fae male I'm tied to by soulmagic and fate's terrible sense of humor, and wonder if there's a way to bridge our differences.

No matter how my body responds to him, my mind still warns that he—and the world he represents—is dangerous.

Is it possible to love someone you can't be with? To want them in every possible way, knowing giving in to that desire could destroy you completely?

I catch Asher gesturing something to Valerian, but the prince's expression is unreadable as he ignores the dragon shifter, his focus never wavering from me.

His normally silver-blue irises are like mercury in the bright sun, and they regard me for what feels like an eternity, shaded by a thick blue fan of eyelashes.

Finally, he reaches out. I freeze as I feel his hands slide over my hips, his fingertips pressing deep into my flesh. Reminding me of when he touched me once before.

Slowly, as if letting our bodies get used to each other, he pulls me to him.

3

Titania save me, I want to devour Valerian whole. His scent—juniper and balsam and cedar—his devilishly bowed lips, that intoxicating familiarity I've never felt with anyone else . . . all of it threatens to undo me.

"Summer," he breathes, hardly daring to move as he stares into my eyes, "I know you asked for time, and I'm giving it to you. But tell me you won't fight our bond forever. As long as I know there's hope, I can deal with the agony of not being able to have you. To claim you the way every cell in my body demands."

I bristle at that word, *claim*, even as my traitorous body begs for it. To be claimed, possessed, devoured whole. I want to sink into him. To inhale him like he's a Bath & Body Works store during clearance. I want to kiss him until my lips are numb with cold and my belly smolders with heat and I can no longer remember my name.

Bad, Summer. Bad!

Biting the inside of my lip, I stand my ground. "You talk

like I'm something to be possessed and used up, but that's not love."

A wry smile plays over his lips. "Love?"

For the Evermore, who live for thousands of years, love is antiquated. A naive emotion that fades quickly and serves very little purpose, except perhaps to trick and entrap.

I square my chin and look him in the eye. "Yes, love. You may not like it, but a part of me is mortal, and we expect the whole shebang. The sappy courting, the over-priced chocolates and roses, the Hallmark cards where you underline words like love and forever, the milestone like the first fight over who ate the last ice cream sandwich or forgot to throw the wet clothes into the dryer and now they're all mildewed and . . ."

Why am I even trying? This is the part he will never understand. The boring, mundane parts of a relationship we humans need.

He blinks, a divot appearing between his eyebrows. "I don't understand half of what you're saying, but you and I did have something like that once."

Right. The girl inside the picture. The Fae Evermore whose parents I don't remember, whose life I can't recall, whose emotions are a mystery to me.

"You say that, but I don't even know what you like. What's your favorite type of music? Your favorite food? Favorite color? Do you prefer briefs or boxers or—"

"Pretty sure you know that one," he adds, a dark grin spreading across his handsome face and reminding me why my favorite nickname for him is ILB.

When I go to protest, he adds, "I like *you*, Summer. What does it matter about colors or food or anything else?"

"It just does." I cross my arms, pretending my body doesn't react to the throaty purr in his voice. "You don't get it. How can I give myself to a stranger?"

18

A near-imperceptible flinch ripples across his countenance. Never taking his gaze off my lips, he drags his knuckles gently across my jaw. "Then get to know me, Princess. *All* of me."

Fae ears, everything about him—from his voice to his smoldering eyes to the way his fingers press into my flesh—drips sex and desire.

Which is exactly why I can't trust my feelings around him.

I exhale, trying to break the spell his presence has over me. "What about your father? I thought he would get suspicious if we're together."

"I'll take care of him." His sharp features harden with determination. Whoa, he's sexy when he's serious—

I clear my throat. "And the school?"

"Everyone thinks I'm still with Inara."

Oh, that. Of all the reasons—plural—falling for the Winter Prince is a bad idea, his pretend relationship with Inara is the worst. Both let the ruse that they're still together play out, although for very different reasons.

Inara refuses because her ego can't handle publicly losing him. And Valerian goes along with the rumor that they're still together for my safety. Because as long as his father and all the other courts think their engagement is still on, no one will pay any attention to his interest in me.

"I could be expelled," I remind him.

He smiles, the grin so arrogant that I'm reminded how much power he commands. "No, you couldn't. One word from me and the headmistress won't touch you."

"Okay. What about what happened to Evelyn?" A blush creeps over my cheeks at the thought.

"You mean, what if you became pregnant?" he asks softly. "There are herbs to prevent pregnancy as well as spells. What happened to your friend was a tragedy, but that won't happen to you—if you choose to give yourself to me."

Give myself to him? Like a shiny present ready to be unwrapped? I shiver, a pulse of warmth hitting me square in the chest as I imagine his deft fingers slowly undressing me—

No, Summer. We all know where that road leads—darkling city. So unless you enjoy being a zombie who dines on Fae flesh, knock it off.

As if he can hear my thoughts, he leans forward, his wavy ink-colored hair sweeping over his forehead, and brushes his mouth over mine. "What we share will never be simple. It's always going to be messy and complicated and dangerous."

The second our lips meet, a wave of need rushes over me, so thick I can't breathe.

"But screw easy. Easy's boring." He nips at my bottom lip. "You can't tell me this isn't worth fighting for."

I want so badly to let him kiss me. My body practically thrums as one of his hands lazily runs up and down my back, stroking, reminding me how he once lavished that same gentle, meticulous attention on my thighs, and other places.

He must feel the shiver that slams through my core, because he chuckles.

Not fair. "Is there a way to inactivate the, you know, mating bond, once we . . . turn it on?"

His fingers slide up my neck, take hold of my jaw, and gently tilt my head back. His eyes dance with amusement and something else, something more primal. "You mean, once we make love and the magic binding your soul to mine reaches its full power?"

I nod, my throat suddenly dry. "Yeah, that."

Another wolfish smile. *Shimmer save me.* "No, there's no turning it off. Our soulbond isn't a light switch, Summer. It's a rare gift from Queen Titania, one that every Evermore in existence would kill for. Once the powerful magic is finalized it's permanent."

"Permanent," I repeat, breathless, my throat choked with emotion.

I still struggle to commit to my sock color every morning; I'm definitely not ready to activate some magical bond thingy that locks me with a Fae male for the rest of eternity. Especially considering Vi's reaction today.

Over the summer, I let myself believe she would warm up to the Fae world, given enough time. I ignored the rancor in her voice whenever I brought up anything academy related. Overlooked the horrified way she would stare at the prince's brand on my arm when she thought I wasn't looking.

Speaking of . . .

"And when do I get this removed?" I hold up my arm, moving it so that his metallic gold swirls glint softly. Admittedly, a part of me relished having something of the prince during his absence. At the same time, having a tattoo that marks me as someone's property goes against everything I believe.

His gaze shifts to the mark, the corners of his mouth hardening. "You know I can't remove my claim on you, Summer. As long as it darkens your flesh, you're protected."

That all sounds fine in theory, but . . .

Sighing, I retreat from his embrace.

A muscle ticks in his temple. His sensual lips purse, as if he has a thousand things he wants to say, but then he nods. Swallows.

"If you need to get to know me before you make your decision, I respect that." He reaches for me, purposefully brushing his fingertips lightly over my waist just so I'll squirm at his touch. "You can get to know as *much* of me as you want."

My eyes widen. Titania restrain me, he knows exactly how dirty that sounds.

"Just be aware," he continues, teasing me with that gravelly voice, "I don't fight fair when it comes to getting what I want. So from now on, I'll be helping Eclipsa train you. We'll be in close contact every single day, giving you countless opportunities to discover what sort of . . . underwear I prefer."

This mofo came to play. Against my will, a rush of excitement surges through me at the thought of seeing Valerian every day. The physical contact, the adrenaline of the fight. That sex-on-a-stick Fae body slick with sweat—

Get. Ahold. Of. Your. Thirsty. Self.

I brush off my enthusiasm with a cool shrug. "Okay."

From the corner of my eyes, I see Asher waving and mouthing something, but Valerian ignores him. "See you at the academy?"

"Yep." I force a cool smile. "I'll be there, ready to kick some ass."

An arched dark blue eyebrow lifts, a devilish look overtaking his face. "Good. Because as my shadow, I don't plan on showing you any mercy."

Mack pops her head out the door, pink strawberry frosting rimming her lips. "Sorry to interrupt this love fest"— she waggles her eyebrows at me when she says this—"but Nick sent the doorman out for another cake, and they're all ready to sing happy birthday to you." Her gaze skips from Valerian to Asher, her lips curving upward. "You guys are welcome to join us."

A smile stretches across the dragon shifter's square jaw, but Valerian shakes his head. "Thanks for the offer of what I'm sure are delicious mortal treats, but we were just about to leave."

As I watch Valerian create his portal, the snowflakes drifting into that rainbow oval and disappearing, a part of me aches for him to stay.

He catches my gaze, gives a dark smile, and disappears along with a sullen Asher before I can say anything.

Mack squeezes my shoulder, concern welling inside her corn-flower blue eyes. "What did he do? Do I need to murder him? I will, you know. I'll make the ice prince my bitch."

"Now *that* I would love to see," Eclipsa drawls from the doorway. She has a death-grip on the now empty bag of Zapp's potato chips, and she's licking the last bit of spice from her baby-blue fingernails.

Frick, how does she sneak up like that?

"The prince didn't do anything," I assure them both. "In fact, he was actually pretty decent."

Which is super annoying because this would all be so much easier if he switched back to dickhead mode.

Eclipsa raises a silver eyebrow, causing the jewels above to sparkle. "The Winter Prince, decent? Has the seven Fae hells frozen over?"

I shake my head, just as confused as she is.

"Oberon's beard, I never thought I'd see the day. The Winter Prince, tamed by a mortal." Eclipsa finishes licking her fingers and jerks her head toward the door. "You have to come back in there with me. I thought the tension between the Summer and Winter Courts was bad, but that room—"

I hold up my hand. "Coming. Just keep my aunt away from any weapons until then, okay?"

As soon as Eclipsa disappears, Mack wraps her arm in mine. "Pfft, how dare the Winter Prince be nice to you. Now, let's go drown your sorrows in grocery-bought cake frosting before the tiny terrorists ruin that one too."

I roll out my shoulders. "Mackenzie Fairchild, I don't deserve you."

She laughs. "Just wait until you open my gift. Then you really won't deserve me."

We spend the next two hours doing just that. Opening my

presents and eating ourselves into a sugar coma. When it's time to return to the academy, I check my phone, annoyed at how my heart leaps when I see Valerian's text.

Silk briefs are my favorite . . . if you're still curious.

I smile at the winky face emoji he added before my grin falters.

Summer Solstice, you're so epically screwed.

4

The first day of school starts off completely different than last time. First, I'm not freezing my lady balls off. Second, I actually fill out the hunter green shorts and white tank top, and my arms ripple with muscles. Third, thanks to the highly complicated espresso machine Mack's dads gifted her for the first day, a latte warms my fingers. The rich coffee aroma, intermingled with the perfume of tulips and lilies drifting in the air, makes me grin like a maniac.

If victory had a smell, it would be this. *And* my day doesn't start with swimming for my life, performing CPR, and then being ogled and fought over.

The only downside is not getting to punch Reina in her surgically enhanced nose—but the day is young.

I take a sip of my latte and sigh. "This year is going to be my year, Mack. I can feel it."

"Correction, it's going to be *our* year."

Mack tucks a strand of her chocolate shoulder-length hair behind her ear. It's longer than the last time I saw her, and she must have had it straightened, large chunks dyed pink and yellow. No doubt to expertly match the tulips lining the path to school.

A flower print romper and brown leather booties make her even more adorable than usual.

Her sprite, Thornilia, flies just above her. Thornilia lists off Mack's class schedule, which she's already memorized, the showoff, and reminds Mack which books she needs for the first period.

Somehow, Thornilia also carries Mack's triple almond-milk latte.

Ruby, on the other hand, hasn't even woken up. She's nestled on top of my backpack, snoring in my ear.

My new phone buzzes in my short's pocket. I grin as I pull it out, ignoring Mack's knowing look.

Valerian's message pops onto the screen. *Sorry I can't be there for your first day. Want me to send Asher back, just in case?*

I release a breath. Eclipsa told me this morning during training that she was accompanying him to the Winter Court, but in her typical cryptic fashion, left out why. I gathered from her grumpier than usual morning mood that it was pretty serious.

If Valerian is taking both the dragon shifter and the lunar assassin with him, it's really bad.

No way will I leave him unprotected.

Besides, what have I been training for this entire time if I can't survive the first day of school?

No, I one-handedly text back, *I'm a badass now, remember?*

An eternity passes as he types out a response, and I grin imagining him searching for the right letters, erasing, and grumbling. He's the absolute worst at texting, or technology in general.

Stay out of trouble. The snowflake emojis punctuate the command.

Smiling, I hurriedly type back, *Too bad you're not here tho. Mack and I thought it would be funny to sneak in a couple baby orcs on the first day.*

Funny. I look forward to bribing your way out of detention. Be thinking of ways to repay me.

I send him little angel emojis and then slip the phone back into my pocket.

Mack hip checks me. "Just friends, huh?"

I erase the humor from my face and sigh. "Just friends."

"You lying little B. There is no 'just friends' with the ILB."

As we near the wide steps leading up to the main courtyard, second year shadows Jace, Layla, and Richard join us.

Jace grins, his handsome face brightening, and tips his head. "Ladies."

Richard stares glumly forward, his fingers clenched tightly around his backpack straps.

A pang of sympathy threatens to darken my happy mood. I can't imagine what he's feeling after Evelyn's transformation to a darkling. Especially considering what caused her change.

She was pregnant with a Fae child, what both Fae and mortals cruelly call a dirty-blood.

Evelyn never once mentioned dating a Fae or even *liking* one.

We enter the courtyard, and I search the throng of students. Each time I find a Fae male, I scour them for signs that they fathered Evelyn's child.

Which is dumb. It's not like the Fae who impregnated Evelyn is going to be wearing a shirt that says, *Baby Daddy*, on it.

"Fae's teeth, is that for . . . us?" Mack asks.

I follow her wide-eyed stare to linen-draped tables brimming with trays of food and refreshments. Shadows have already started tentatively filling their plates.

Jace groans. "Oh, God, I smell real coffee. Could it be a trick?"

"It's definitely a trick, right?" I swallow, remembering the hazing from last year. This feels wrong, somehow. There's no way the Fae are suddenly being nice to us.

"It's because of her," Richard points out, nodding to a woman standing near the tables, clipboard in hand. The woman has a pinched face, frosted blonde hair in need of a touch-up, and a dark suit. "She's a censor from The CMH. They're everywhere on campus."

I'd nearly forgotten that the Council for the Mistreatment of Humans opened an investigation into the school. Perhaps with the added scrutiny, no one will die this year.

The skeptical shrew inside me cackles at this absurd idea, but . . . the promise of spending our second year with access to basic human rights lingers.

As Mack sends Thornilia off with her backpack to organize her locker, we line up behind the others, all of us chattering excitedly.

Two plates of chocolate croissants later, I slide in next to Mack at a picnic table. Richard, Jace, Layla, and a few others crowd in next to us.

Mack eyes my mountain of deliciousness. "Afraid they'd run out or something?"

I snort, taking in her measly banana and tiny bowl of oatmeal before offering her a croissant. "Here, your mouth will thank me."

I prepare for an epic response, like that's what she said. Instead, Mack's lips press together. "No, thanks."

Jace arches an eyebrow as we share a look.

"You can eat that stuff because you're tall and burning like a zillion calories in your extra workouts," she adds with a pout, "but some of us can't afford to."

"Afford to? Since when do you care about that?"

Jace snatches the pastry I was offering Mack and takes a bite. "Since we became second years. That's when they start measuring us."

"Measuring what? Students?" I nearly spit out my mouthful of yum, sure I misheard him. "Like cattle?"

"Darling, we're part of an elite group of mortals who represent the most beautiful creatures in existence. That responsibility comes with impossibly high standards. Didn't you have to fill out your measurements on the application along with your picture?"

And . . . that explains why everyone here is abnormally gorgeous. I stare at my hands, covered in chocolate, unsure how to answer.

I forget sometimes that not everyone knows my enrollment story. Which is way darker than the rags-to-riches tale the academy peddles.

Mack drags her stare away from my plate and sighs. "I had to lie on my application. Only a few inches but you don't get into Evermore Academy with these curves."

And just when I thought I couldn't possibly hate the Fae any more.

Mack was promised to the Fae since birth, part of the bargain her dads made when they used Fae magic to influence her adoption.

I shudder, thinking about what would have happened if she hadn't been accepted.

Mack's tough, but even she wouldn't survive long fighting the darklings in the scourge lands.

"Screw their standards." I shove one of the mini chocolate orgasms into my mouth. I angry-chew my way through two more before pushing the tray away.

Someone as kind and amazing as Mack should never feel less than because her body doesn't fit a certain made-up ideal.

The Fae watch us while we gorge ourselves, high on sugar and the promise of humane treatment.

At some point, I catch sight of Rhaegar Moorland standing in the shadow of the nearest awning, and a chill dampens my mood.

He's watching me, nostrils flared, not even trying to hide his simmering hatred.

Does he know Valerian is gone? The food in my stomach threatens to come back up at the thought.

Refusing to cower, I stare right back, surprised by how much he's changed.

No longer the bright, handsome Summer Court Fae I remember, there's something raw and wounded about him, like a wolf who was caught in a steel trap and healed, but will never quite be the same.

His once bright green eyes appear dark, almost muddy, his once glorious reddish gold hair now faded, shaggy, and unkempt. But it goes beyond his outer beauty.

Like autumn leaves after they've fallen from their branches, their stunning colors bleeding away into rot, his inner vibrancy has withered into something ugly.

Ugh. I drag my focus from the Summer Court Evermore and will myself to pick up another croissant. No way in Fae hell am I going to let Rhaegar, or anyone else, ruin this moment.

I've barely taken a bite when I feel Ruby rustle from her slumber behind me. She sniffs the air. "What is that smell?"

"Ruby, meet croissant." I hold my barely-touched pastry up in the air. "Want one?"

Hissing, she rips the treat from my fingers and tosses it across the courtyard, hitting a third year shadow in the back of the head. "Want one? That thing is swimming with glamour magic!"

The second the words leave her tiny red lips, my stomach flutters strangely. A wave of euphoria rushes through my veins.

Crap on a stick.

A quick check of the courtyard reveals the censor is gone.

Nonono—

"Stand up, you dull little mortals," a horribly familiar female voice orders. "It's time for a game."

Inara Winterspell. Any hope I have left that we're not totally screwed dies a quick death at the sound of her cruel voice. The entire courtyard full of shadows jumps to their feet at the exact same time, including me.

"Ruby," I call. "What's happening? Why didn't my necklace protect me?"

"Sorry, Kid." The concern in her voice scares me. "Your soulstone can't protect you when you willingly consume the magic."

"It will be okay," Mack assures me, but I don't fully believe her. Nothing's ever okay where the Fae are concerned.

Inara strolls through the tables, shadowed by what's left of the Elite Six. Kimber wears a black veil against the spring sun that partially obscures the vampire's feline golden eyes and chin-length black hair. Lyra, positioned to Inara's left, looks both ferocious and stunning, her caramel mane of hair falling over tawny, athletic arms.

Only Inara could make both a lycan and a vampire submit to her command.

While Reina and her twin boy toys stroll around filming, Inara's twin, Bane, busies himself toying with the mortal shadows.

My blood boils as I watch him pick up a plate of pink frosted donuts and force a first year shadow girl to shove them down her throat until she pukes. All the while, his face is transforming into monstrous faces meant to terrify the first years, who haven't yet been told about his creepy gift.

The only silver lining to this whole situation is that I can't move. Otherwise, I would have already throat punched Bane and earned myself the Six's attention.

Not that I'm deluded enough to think they've forgotten about me . . . but a girl can dream.

"What?" Inara purrs. "Did you really think we couldn't control one human censor? That you were safe now?" Her unnerving frost-colored eyes sift through the crowd until they find me, and freezing fingernails scrape down my spine. "Dance, monkeys, dance!"

I glance down at my arms and legs, both awed and horrified as I watch them twist and leap like some drunken Faerie.

Mack's eyes are huge as they meet mine. The terror in her expression contrasts against the joyful way she spins and sways. Our bodies collide as we move faster. Spinning and spinning and spinning—

"Stop." Inara's command freezes us in place. I'm breathing hard, sweat pasting my tank top to my ribcage. It feels like my heart will beat right out of my chest.

The wolf pendant burns against my flesh, powerless to help me.

Inara's focus hones in on me. *Oh, goody.*

I can tell by the murderous anger in her eyes that she hasn't forgotten about me.

If anything, our months apart have only stoked her hatred to the next level.

What's the saying? Absence makes the heart grow more stabby?

Her seven-inch crystal heels spear the grass between the cobblestones as she stalks this way. It's like a repeat of last year, only now—despite all my training—I'm at her absolute mercy.

Frustration slams into me. I try to ball my hands into fists, to move even an inch, just enough to look intimidating, but I'm frozen mid-dance—arms out like I'm about to fly.

As soon as Inara nears, the others smell blood and converge. Inara smiles sweetly at me. Her hair seems bluer somehow, a dark ultramarine that's pulled into a high bun, and her skin shimmers with ice crystals, as if she's literally made from snow.

Blinding frost-white teeth flash as she smirks. "Wow, so brave to come back after your humiliation last year. Or, wait. Did you think your little prince would save you?"

I glare at her, my tongue loading up curse words that my frozen lips fail to deliver.

Dammit!

"What?" Inara continues. "Darkling got your tongue?"

Reina and the others laugh at Inara's stupid joke. Everyone except Kimber, who's feline gold eyes watch me through her veil. Once upon a time, I thought she and I could be friends.

She looks away from my pleading stare, making it clear how naive that notion was.

Inara nods at Mack. "Aw, look. It's your bestie." Inara's focus flickers over Reina. "Is this the girl you told me about? The one who was rude to you?"

Reina nods, a gleeful smirk lifting her cheeks.

Anger and fear darken my heart. If they hurt Mack, I'll gut them.

Every. Single. One. Of. Them.

Relief loosens my shoulders as Inara's cruel focus drifts back to me. "It's hot, isn't it?" she asks. "Why don't you take off your shirt and shorts?"

No. I refuse. Hell no . . .

Looking down, I watch in horror as my fingers curl under my shirt and tug up up up—

A cold breeze ripples over my bare stomach and chest as I lift the shirt over my head and chuck it to the ground. My shorts are next. When I'm done, only my gray underwear and black sports bra cover me.

I know none of this is my fault. I know I'm not in control. But shame fills me anyway.

A deep, raw, overwhelming shame.

"Pathetic." Inara looks me up and down. "What? Did you think you could force your way back into the academy with that stunt last semester and escape punishment?" She glances around, her blue lips curled in derision. "As long as Summer is enrolled in the academy, I will punish all of you. But I'm not without mercy." She flashes an icy smile to prove her point. "The first shadow responsible for making Summer flunk out or be expelled will not only have my favor, but you'll receive a fourth year's stipend."

By fourth year, shadows actually earn a wage for their services. It's not much, but considering our work conditions now, being paid anything is like winning the lottery.

The morning air felt pleasant moments ago, but now it seems to slip right through my flesh and into my bones. I shiver, unable to move, to speak, to do anything but watch as Inara orders the students to come forward.

"Let's remind this mortal of what she really is: trash."

A few seem to enjoy the spectacle, but most shadows' eyes are apologetic as, one by one, they dump their plates and cups over my head.

Hot coffee. Cool orange juice. Greasy eggs. Still-warm biscuits sticky with blackberry jam. A veritable feast cascades over me.

Stay strong. Inara can only hurt you if you let her.

But each time I feel someone's breakfast fall around my shoulders, each time sticky apple juice soaks my hair and wets my bra—the one I carefully wash every night because it's the only bra I own—a piece of my dignity gets chipped away.

When it's Mack's turn, tears clump the eyelashes framing her soft blue eyes. Tears I know she won't shed because she's strong, and we prepared for this possibility.

It's not your fault, I think, trying to will my thoughts across the air between us.

After she's through dumping her latte and bowl of oatmeal over my head, Inara dismisses her.

Grinning, Inara waves her fingers in front of my face. My lips soften; the magic muzzle preventing me from speaking falls away.

"Ready to leave the academy?" she asks. "I promise, you don't want this to escalate."

It's hard to summon dignity when you're half-naked and covered in other people's breakfast, but hell if I'm not going to try.

I refuse to let her break me.

I. Fricking. Refuse.

Holding her stare, I lick a glob of chocolate from the side of my cheek and grin. "Thanks. I was starving."

That's right, you snowflake psycho. You can't break me.

Reina's grin falters. She lowers the camera. Kimber and Lyra exchange surprised looks. There might be a sliver of respect in Kimber's face . . . or she might simply find me more appealing as a mortal snack when I'm lathered in sugary pastries.

But the emotion beneath Bane's icy features is one hundred percent rage. "Are you going to let her talk to you like that?"

Inara's expression is terrifyingly blank as she laughs, a

35

sharp, murderous sound. "We're just playing a game, that's all. Rhaegar, come here."

In my periphery, Rhaegar eagerly follows her command. My stomach lurches. I know I've gone too far, embarrassing her in front of the Six. Goose bumps prickle my exposed skin, my chest tight with dread.

Basil is behind Rhaegar, whispering heatedly in his ear. With a growl, Rhaegar shoves the poor fawn, sending him tumbling into a trio of planters. Blue ceramic, soil, and cotton-candy pink pansies go flying.

"Here." Inara gives a dismissive wave in my direction, as if I truly am trash to be discarded. "She's yours for the day. Do whatever you'd like with her."

My stomach lurches. All my dreams of thriving at school, of graduating and doing something good with my life, disintegrate.

Fae like Inara and Rhaegar will never let that happen.

Walling off my emotions, I grit my teeth, ready to face whatever happens next.

I'm so wrapped up in my anger that I don't notice the scent. Not at first. Not until the others are already falling back, their sneers transforming into confusion.

Rhaegar's head snaps up, his nostrils flaring as he inhales.

Alarm flickers inside his eyes. Like a wolf suddenly scared off by a larger predator, he darts away.

All at once, the perfume fills my nostrils, a potent, overwhelming bouquet of floral scents. As if lilies, roses, jasmine, and honeysuckle all got busy and had a giant flower baby.

Inara screams. At the same time, the courtyard trembles. Flowering vines surge from the ground, exploding from the small fissures between the cobblestones.

The crack of stone rends the air.

Before Inara can move, the ropy green vines snake up her long legs, up her torso, twisting over her arms. I watch in shock as the vines lift my tormentor into the air like a rag doll.

Inch-long thorns pierce her pale flesh, drawing out beads of metallic silver blood.

Her lips peel open in another scream, but she makes strangled, gurgling noises. Something white sprouts inside the chasm of her mouth—a humongous magnolia flower.

Her eyes stretch wide. She's . . . *choking*.

The air stirs with creatures. A swarm of bees appears, darkening the sky above as they descend on the Fae. Blue jays and robins dive bomb my tormentors, picking at their flesh and adding to the confusion. Giant red wasps buzz by my head as they violently attack the others.

This is a whole lot of nope. Whatever new Fae horror I've stumbled into, I want nothing to do with it. The moment my magical binds spring free, I jump into action.

For some idiotic reason, the first thing I do is gather my clothes and slip them on.

Even here, in the middle of all this chaos, Aunt Vi's lessons on modesty supersede my survival instincts.

Mack rushes to my side and begins to drag me away. At the same moment, Ruby tugs on my earlobe, hard. "Run, Kid, while the maniac is distracted!"

Except I don't think Inara's distracted—unless distracted is a new word for actively *dying*.

Her face has turned a sickly blue, her eyes glossy with raw fear. Ducking the stinger of the biggest hornet I've ever seen, Bane throws spears of ice at the tendrils trapping his sister, while Kimber uses her inhuman strength to hold onto Inara legs, and Lyra shreds her claws over the plants.

But there's too many vines and creatures. In less than a minute, the entire Elite Six is caught in a nightmarish display, each Fae trapped and bound by sentient vines, at the mercy of whoever is attacking them.

Pushing my curiosity aside, I let Ruby and Mack shove me away from the murderous scene. As I sprint across campus toward the main hall, I can't help but look at the beautiful landscape with a newfound fear.

By the powerful display of magic, I know an Evermore just saved me. I also know that thinking this new, terrifying Fae is my friend is dangerous.

If I've learned anything in my short, traumatizing time here, it's that an Evermore never does anything for free. Meaning I now owe a debt I have no means to pay.

"Who the Shimmer was that?" I pant as we round the last hall and the second year lockers appear. What I wouldn't give for a freaking shower right now. Every part of me is covered in breakfast, and the ankle socks inside my sneakers squish with orange juice.

Ruby, perched on my shoulder, plucks a piece of frosted donut from my hair, shoves it in her mouth, and glances up at me. "*That* was the Spring Court Prince and heir."

I have no idea who that is, but by the way Mack's mouth hangs open, it must be bad.

"Prince Hellebore attends Whitehall Academy," Mack protests.

It's my turn to gape. "There's another academy?"

Both look at me as if I should know this. "Centuries ago," Mack explains, "there was an incident. After that, the royals from the Spring Court decided to create their own academy. It's not officially recognized by the Unseelie Courts or the council."

We find our lockers and quickly throw our books inside.

"But there are Spring Court Evermore here," I insist, my brain refusing to believe two places like this could exist.

"That's because Whitehall Academy is uber elite, so most Spring Evermore don't get accepted. Only the highest ranking Seelie Evermore attend, usually royals, and it's located in Spring Court territory instead of neutral territory."

"Oh." I ignore the stare from a female shadow rushing by us in the hall. I can't even imagine *what* I look like. "So the Spring Court prince just randomly decided to attend here?"

Ruby shrugs. "Kid, all I know is that magic was powerful enough to take down Inara Winterspell and the Six. All because of you. And being the center of any powerful Evermore's attention—other than lover boy—is a wonderful way to shorten your already tiny mortal lifespan."

I shut my locker, sling my backpack over my shoulder, and grin. "I hope they got *that* on video. Now, off to . . ."

I look to Ruby for a reminder of my first period, but she just shrugs and goes back to licking the syrup from a tangled strand of my hair.

Mack frowns. "Summer, go shower. I'll explain to your teacher what happened—"

"No." I cross my arms, cringing as they stick together. "If I miss my first class, they win. It proves that I can't handle being here. I'm already on thin ice after my expulsion last semester, and now, with Inara's incentive to get me kicked out . . ."

"I'll never understand why some people have to be such dickwads," Mack mutters.

Ruby sighs. "Evermore like Inara are broken and shattered inside, and they're only happy when they make others feel the same way they do."

The profoundness of Ruby's statement nearly makes me drop my backpack.

Mack slams her locker shut with a loud clang, drawing a

few questioning stares from the nearest shadows. "That's no excuse for her awfulness. I hope the Spring Prince left her there to squirm for a while."

That makes two of us.

Mack gives me one last look. "You got this, Summer. Take Ruby for support. Second years are allowed to bring their sprites to class if they need them for note taking or . . . whatever."

Normally I would refuse. Even on her best of days, Ruby is a distraction more than a help. But facing a class full of people rooting for me to fail might just be a bit more bearable with someone I care about nearby.

I pat my shoulder. "Alright, Ruby, ready to be my emotional support sprite?"

"Ready as a broke stripper at a bachelor party."

"*O-kay.* I'll take that as a yes."

As I sprint down the stairs to my first class, Ruby scraping bits of bacon and eggs from my collarbone, I cheer myself up with lies.

It's fine. This is fine. You're fine.

But my gut disagrees, making nervous gurgles. If the first day is any indication of how the rest of the year will go, I'm epically screwed.

---

*D*espite my efforts, I'm tardy first period. My Faerie Courts and History teacher, Professor Hawthorne, raises an eyebrow when Ruby and I slip into the room. Thankfully, the towering, jade-skinned Fae is too busy trying to work the new projector screen to publicly remark on my lateness, or the fact that I smell like an IHOP.

As I slip into a seat in the back, Reina laughs. "Who ordered breakfast?"

I've already decided my plan of attack this year will be ignoring the insults. Rise above and all that crap.

But Ruby didn't get the memo on my new, dignified strategy, and she bares her tiny needle-like teeth at Reina. "Who ordered murder? Oh, right. You did if you keep talking smack, mortal harlot."

Welp, that escalated quickly.

I have no idea what the classroom rules state about threatening death against another student, but thankfully Reina loses interest, and Ruby falls asleep the moment the room darkens and the projector flashes across the wall.

After class ends, I rush to second period, praying Reina isn't there. But of course she is. In some horrible cosmic twist of fate, I share *every* class with Inara's shadow.

The rest of the day goes exactly how I expect. Snickers. Stares. Uninspired jokes. Ruby handing out death threats like a serial killer hands out candy. Professors pretending I'm *not* covered in syrup and bacon so they don't have to address *why* I'm a walking buffet.

At one point between classes, as I unsuccessfully scrub at the stains on my clothes with paper towels in the bathroom, the woman from the CMH strolls in. She glances at my hair, my clothes, frowns, and walks away.

So much for that protection.

A few human shadows afford me looks of pity, but that's almost worse than being gaped and laughed at.

Somehow, I endure all of it with steely resolve.

Ruby's rare words of wisdom were right: Inara wants to hurt me until my insides resemble hers. But that can't happen unless I give her permission to wound me so badly that I shatter.

Now that I know my purpose in life is to protect humans from the Fae, it's going to take a hell of a lot more than covering me in breakfast to break me.

When it's time for lunch, I rush back to the dorm to shower and change. A new super cute white crop top and navy blue Nike jogging pants later, I've recovered the dregs of my dignity, enough at least to hold my head high.

I glance in the dressing mirror.

Summer, you badass bitch, show them your lady balls are made of Teflon.

Emboldened by my little speech, I wrangle my wet hair into a messy top-knot and sprint back to campus. The fuzzy dandelion seeds that swarm this place stick to my damp skin. I make it back just in time to meet Mack and the others at the picnic tables near the lake.

She tosses me an apple and a cheese stick. "Hurry, they're cutting lunch short for a mandatory announcement in the main courtyard."

A dramatic sigh bursts from my chest. "I was just there this morning and look how great that turned out."

Richard, Jace, and Layla find something else to stare at. A part of me wonders if just by sitting with me, they're making themselves targets of Inara's rage.

Once again, I'm radioactive.

Have you accidentally been exposed to Summer Solstice? I think in my best TV lawyer impression. *Symptoms may include random bullying, higher risk of death, and social suicide.*

Eff my life.

As if Valerian can feel my spirit sagging, my cell buzzes in my pocket. Thank the Shimmer one of Mack's birthday gifts was a protective case or it would have been fried during my orange juice bath.

Shoving the cheese stick into my mouth, I quickly scan the short text. ***Eclipsa's on her way.***

My shoulders sag. The last thing I wanted was for Valerian to feel like he has to protect me.

Before I can reply, another text pops up. *Want me to come back and talk to Inara?*

Yes, I type, *can you murder her please and thank you?* I stare at my words before hitting delete and writing, **No, I can handle it.**

As much as I'd love to watch Valerian *talk* to Inara, I can't let him fight my battles. Plus, someone already did that . . .

Little dots flash as he writes. *I can't stop thinking about what you'd taste like covered in syrup.*

Heat barrels through my core just as Mack yanks my phone away. "Fae tits! What are you, a pancake?"

Her fingers fly over my phone screen as she sends him a barrage of pancake gifs.

Yes—yes I am, I don't say. *A confused, lonely, radioactive pancake.*

She shakes her head, sending her silky, multi-colored hair swaying around her face. "If only you could let him butter your pancake, just once, and get him out of your system."

Water nearly sprays from my nose as I laugh. "There is no *just once* with him. He's like . . . like the Ebola virus. The second I let him inside, he'll infect every cell, every molecule of my being until he owns me."

Richard and Jace exchange weird looks, while Layla flashes a sympathetic smile. They have no idea who we're talking about, thankfully.

Jace finishes off his ham sandwich and shoots me a pitying stare. "Not that I'm one for sage relationship advice, but If you're comparing romance to an infection, you're probably doing it wrong."

Shrugging, I shove my phone deep into my pocket. Obviously Jace has never experienced the delicious agony that is Valerian Sylverfrost.

6

We've barely started toward the courtyard with the others before Eclipsa appears across campus, near a collection of bright green sculpted hedges. I know she's furious by the way she marches, her long legs stabbing the lush lawn, arms pumping. She's dressed for battle in a dark gray leather ensemble fitted with enough knives to take out a small country.

Alarm prickles my skin. Dressed like that, with that many weapons . . .

What is Valerian not telling me?

If I thought I was notorious before, when the infamous Lunar Fae assassin makes a bee-line straight for me, the other human shadows around us gape before scattering like the dandelions swirling in the wind.

"What happened?" she demands, wrapping me in a quick hug.

"Inara happened."

"You should know better than to eat any food not procured in the comm or the cafeteria, Summer."

I glare at my shoes. No matter how much I cleaned them, I

couldn't erase the dark coffee stain that mars the white laces and stitching. "There were chocolate croissants."

Her expression is less than amused.

"Fine. Lesson learned."

"I'll have a word with her—"

"No." I shake my head. "I can't have you or the prince fighting my battles. If I'm going to live in this world, I have to prove I can handle myself."

"Okay." The twitch of her lips tells me she respects my decision.

"So, are you going to divulge what's going on in the Winter Court?"

She flicks a narrow-eyed gaze my way. "Fae politics. Nothing you need to worry about."

"Is he . . . in danger?" I prod, a strange flutter dancing in my chest.

One of her hands hovers over her favorite dagger, a curved white moonstone blade set in a jade handle. "Nothing he can't handle."

I blink as the invisible wires constricting my heart tighten. *Does she think that's supposed to be comforting?*

We clear the courtyard steps. A dais sits near the back, white cherry blossoms blowing from the nearby trees and scattering across the stage. The main building rises in the background, the pale stone walls tinged green with ivy.

Wisteria and jasmine tangle over the windows and balcony railings, filling the air with their cloying scent.

I peer at the huge crowd. The entire school is here, from faculty to shadows and Evermore. Even the ancillary staff is in attendance. I spot Magus and wave, but the kind centaur with the beautiful red mane doesn't see me.

Sprites buzz above our heads, while gnomes, fauns, and other types of lower Fae work in the fragrant gardens around us.

Headmistress Luna Lepidonis takes the stage. Giant gray moths wings with green dots unfurl behind her. Their powdery softness is in stark contrast to her sharp, almost severe features. The entire staff stands behind her.

"Students of Evermore Academy," she begins. "I have some special news. Because of the darklings continued attacks near the Spring borders, the students from Whitehall Academy have chosen to transfer here for the year."

A collective gasp travels through the crowd. Beside me, Eclipsa sucks air through her teeth. "Impossible."

I guess someone didn't hear what happened *after* Inara's stunt this morning.

"As you're all aware, the highest ranking Evermore of the reigning season traditionally gives a speech at the beginning of each year. Please give a warm welcome to the Spring Court Prince, Hellebore Narcissus."

I look to Eclipsa, prepared to pepper her with a million questions—

She's frozen, mouth twisted into what could either be shock or rage or something rawer.

What the frick? I've never seen her look so . . . unnerved. Her nostrils flare, her dark eyes unblinking, mouth parted slightly as she glares at the stage.

I follow her death stare to the Evermore male ascending the dais, expecting the pageantry I'm used to for high ranking Evermore.

Instead, I'm met with an alarmingly handsome blond male wearing fashionably frayed dark-wash jeans and a salmon-pink shirt that's just tight enough to flaunt his heavenly abs and muscular chest. His hair is the color of aged honey. Styled to be edgy, the thick strands are cropped short on one side and fall to the tip of his ear on the other.

A male sprite with spiky platinum locks and delicate black wings flits just above him.

It's rare to see a male sprite at the academy. Because males possess stronger venom, they're typically used as guardians to royal Evermore babies in the nurseries.

On my shoulder, I feel Ruby sit up and suddenly take interest.

I slide my focus back to the Spring Prince. He's not bulky like Rhaegar, whose strength is marked by his size, nor does he possess Valerian's lupine strength.

No, there's something dangerously magnetic about him, like a filthy rich bad boy who knows his money, power, and charm can buy him almost anything.

His I'm-special-just-because aura is nauseating. Especially as he casually rests his hands in his pockets, looks at the crowd, and curls his lips into a sensual smile.

And, whoa, that grin is like watching a flower bloom. Even the teachers seem to melt a little, male and female.

"Sweet baby Faeries," Ruby whispers into my ear. "That boy can water my garden any day."

Before I can help myself, a laugh trickles from my throat.

Prince Hellebore's blue eyes slide to meet mine. They linger just long enough to ignite my insides before sweeping over the crowd.

"Students of Evermore Academy." The arrogant, syrupy drawl is exactly what you'd expect from a spoiled Spring Court prince. "Thank you for opening your school to the students of Whitehall. I know, in the past, we've been adversaries, but I think we can all agree the darkling infestation is a common enemy."

Growling, Eclipsa storms off, the violence seething from her willowy figure sending the nearest Evermore careening back, as far away from the enraged assassin as possible.

I watch her rip open a portal and disappear. There's definitely a story there. Resolved to ask her about it later, I search the crowd for Inara and her deranged crew, but they're missing.

Maybe the prince killed them after all. A girl can hope.

I take another, harder look at the Spring Court Prince, trying to reconcile the charming, laidback male on the podium with someone who could single-handedly disarm the Six. Full sleeve tats cover both forearms, an intricate pattern of vining flowers that must have taken weeks to create.

On any other male, flowers would look ridiculous, but not on Prince Hellebore. He possesses the natural beauty of the Fae. Large, seductive sky-blue eyes. Sharp, elegant features. Full, entirely too-kissable lips.

Every detail is constructed like plants in a garden to work harmoniously together to . . . what?

Lure people in? Disarm them?

For some reason, I think about Valerian. Whereas the ice prince's beauty is disconcerting, almost overwhelming, Helle-bore's is soothing, Venus flytrap style.

He reminds me of the tale of the Fae who appears near the Shimmer and lures mortal girls away with his promise of love only to cage them in glass, like butterflies pinned to a board.

"For the most part," Prince Hellebore continues, "I want to honor your traditions. But, considering the incident with the shadow who turned darkling, I'm implementing a few . . . changes."

Again, his near-turquoise eyes alight on me, their unnat-ural brightness unnerving. Is he seriously staring at me again?

The subtle tick of his lips confirms my paranoia that he is, in fact, speaking directly to me. "At Whitehall Academy, shadows are expected to meet the highest of standards. But, more importantly, they are supposed to know their place. What I've witnessed implies the opposite. Your shadows are defiant. Untrained. Undisciplined. A few even managed to bypass the rigorous acceptance standards to gain a coveted spot here."

Whoa. Now there's no doubt he's talking about me. His gaze lingers, long enough for whispers to grow and my cheeks to flame with embarrassment.

Mother trucker.

"From this day forward, shadows must earn their spot in a series of trials."

Dread fills my veins as I look at Mack. Her face is pinched, mirroring my growing worry.

Yells erupt as the Evermore students react to that bombshell. Most are, if not fond of their shadows, used to us and the many benefits we bring.

"What gives you the right to come here and make new rules?" a dark haired Unseelie quips. I recognize her as one of Inara's friends.

Hellebore doesn't even look at the girl as he says, "The laws of your academy, actually. Right, Headmistress Lepidonis?"

The Headmistress gives a pained nod. "The covenants say the ruling Evermore of the current season can make changes to the academy, as long as they do not go against the bylaws or unduly favor their court."

My stomach clenches . . . then plummets as he returns his focus to me, his lips twitching cruelly at the corners. "Another thing. Shadows caught sleeping with the Evermore for favors will be branded a Fae whore and treated as such."

My mouth goes paper dry. The options for a shadow after being labeled a Fae whore are cringy at best. Most end up on the front lines, used to entertain the Fae soldiers, or in the Winter King's clubs after he buys out their contracts.

I don't know which option is worse. Moreover, I can't understand why the human world would even entertain letting creatures like the Fae reside in their cities when such travesties still happen.

I have to think most of the human world doesn't know. They tried to erase my memories of this place when I was expelled, so they probably do that to most human Shadows that survive.

That explains why Nick and Sebastian never really worry about Mack. If they truly remembered all the awful things that transpired, they would have moved heaven and earth to buy off her Fae contract somehow.

The human world has no idea how cruel the Fae really are.

"That's not a new rule," a male Dusk Court Fae calls.

I blink, pulling myself out of my ragey thoughts to see the spring bastard's stare still parked on me.

"No," Prince Hellebore admits. "But up until now, it hasn't been enforced."

My forehead furrows as I scowl. *Ugh. Why are you singling me out, jerkwad?*

I clench and unclench my fists as the murmurs and stares grow. Mack tries to grab my hand, but I gently pull away.

I don't want her tainted by association with me.

"Now that we're clear on how shadows are to behave, let's discuss the trials. At Whitehall, we ensure only the best shadows attend beside us by holding three gauntlets. These trials are meant not to simply cull the deserving from the undeserving, but to remind them of their place in Everwilde. They are beneath us. Slaves bound by magic to do our bidding and enhance all of Faerie."

They. He's talking about us like we're not here. Like we're non-entities.

I thought there was no one I could despise more than Inara.

I was so fricking wrong.

"Because of its mortality rate, the final gauntlet is required for fourth years only," Hellebore adds, as if this somehow makes him a hero.

The Unseelie Evermore Courts look rather ambivalent about the whole speech. As long as their favorite form of entertainment—watching us die—is still in place, they don't seem to care one way or another who's in charge. The Seelie Courts glance around, shocked but not exactly disappointed.

Prince Hellebore is a Seelie Fae, after all.

"One last thing." Prince Hellebore smiles. "Fail any of the gauntlets and you'll be expelled from the academy and sent to fight the scourge."

Well, crap.

In one sentence, this Spring Court jerkwad just jeopardized my entire future.

My hand flutters to my throat where a giant lump forms. Expelled? Sent to an almost certain death fighting the scourge?

That can never happen.

7

T he rest of the school day passes in a blur of nervous chatter as everyone scrambles to learn what they can about the Spring Court gauntlets. Even the fourth years are worried.

What sort of contest will the trials be? How dangerous are they? How many students pass, on average?

No one seems to know anything, but I can't help assuming the worst. All my plans, all my grand ambitions for my future, and this Spring Court pretty boy dickwad comes and ruins everything.

If the contest was fair, I would pull my crap together and do whatever it took to succeed. But after Inara's threat, everyone has a vested interest in seeing me fail.

The only bright spot in my day is that Mack shares every class after lunch with me. Since the last four periods are when shadows attend school with the Evermore, I prepare myself for more hazing, but Inara and her homicidal gang don't show up until the last class, Advanced Properties of Magic.

I can't help but grin as I watch Inara, Kimber, and Lyra

slip quietly into the auditorium right as Professor Lambert begins to talk. Rhaegar and Basil follow.

All of them file into the back row, subdued, missing their usual arrogant I-own-the-school grins.

No one even notices them. The entire classroom's focus is riveted on Hellebore and the girl he sits next to. Like him, she's dressed casually in black leggings and an oversized gray tee, artfully ripped at the shoulders and frayed in the hem. Her hair is a shade lighter than his, the uneven ends tinted pastel purple, making her gray eyes pop.

Tapping her pencil on her desk, Mack leans over. "That's his sister, Freesia Narcissus. She's a first year."

Mack tilts her MacBook Pro so I can see the screen. She's pulled up the Whitehall Academy website dedicated to the most powerful Evermore students. The screen is split in half, Hellebore's insanely photogenic face on one side and his sister's on the other.

I enlarge Prince Hellebore's bio and quickly run through his long-ass list of attributes. Top Whitehall student two years running. Champion sprite-ball player. Head of the Seelie Fae for Integration club. Rising star at Narcissus Asset Management, a real estate conglomerate run by his aunt, the Spring Court Queen.

The list of achievements goes on and on until I want to gag.

Geez. Did he write this himself?

"Who the frick is this guy trying to impress?" I whisper, sneaking a look at the teacher. The last thing I need is to be called out by Professor Lambert for talking on the first day.

Mack's eyes sparkle as she looks over Hellebore's bio. "He's like a Fae male version of me. Overachieving bastard. I hate him."

I peer at the photo, strangely intrigued. "What are his powers?"

"Beyond what we saw today? I don't know. Whitehall students don't have to declare their powers third year like Evermore, so we can only guess. But I heard a rumor."

I arch an eyebrow. "Spill."

Her eyes light up. She's definitely going to make me work for it.

"Mack," I whisper-growl.

Grinning, she jerks her chin toward Hellebore and his sister. "Don't you wonder why their seats are set away from the others?"

I shrug. "Because they're too good to sit with the rest of the peasants?"

"Well that. But also, the prince is rumored to have some sort of carnal powers of persuasion."

"I don't even know what that means."

Wagging her chocolate eyebrows, she runs her tongue over her lips, looking more like she's seizing than trying to be sexy. Lord help her if that's how she flirts. "Supposedly, with a single touch, he can make you wild with desire. I heard that they only accepted him here after he agreed to wear some spelled jewelry that prevents him from touching a mortal without their permission."

Only the Fae could turn desire into a weapon.

I peer at the prince's photo again. If what Mack says is true, humans are even more screwed than I thought. As if the Fae don't already have an advantage with their flawless looks and cunning nature, now they can use magic to seduce us at will?

In what world is that fair?

A sudden idea has me screenshotting the page. Enlarging the photo capture, I quickly edit it. When I'm done, I flip the masterpiece for Mack's viewing pleasure.

She claps a hand over her mouth as she takes in the arrows pointing to his piercing blue eyes with the words, *shoots laser beams of lust.* For his mouth, I've written, *weapons of mass destruction.*

His ears are the best. *Small ears=small you know what.*

When she gets to the revised achievements section, she doubles over with suppressed laughter.

1. Self-proclaimed winner of the hottest douche canoe contest.
2. Lifetime achievements include staring at his reflection the longest, filling out his overly expensive jeans, taking selfies in exotic places, and filming his workouts.
3. Once voted most in love with himself.
4. Won the award for best spray tan two years in a row.
5. Head of many organizations including his own fan club.

"Miss Solstice, Miss Fairchild." Professor Lambert's voice drags me from my joke and square into reality. Crap. "Care to share with the class what's more important than my lesson?"

"No." Heart smashing itself against my ribs, I shake my head, to the laughter of the room. "I mean . . ." *Crapcrapcrap.* "If that's an option?"

In answer, a burst of lilies and copper fills the air as Professor Lambert sends his magic hurtling across the students toward us. I go to slam the laptop shut, but the professor's magic is too powerful and it whips the MacBook into the air.

Whelp. I'm screwed.

Mack and I watch in horror as the laptop floats toward Lambert and settles on his desk.

Without even looking at the content on the screen, he plugs an adapter into the port, hits a button, and projects

Hellebore's new and *improved* picture and bio onto the huge white projector screen.

As Prince Hellebore's giant face comes into focus along with my *edits*, the classroom erupts in snickers.

Someone kill me.

Embarrassment sizzles across my cheeks. Ugh. I fight the urge to hide my face in my hands. Or worse. Sneak a glance at Hellebore and his sister.

Groaning, Mack ducks low, her face the color of one of Vi's prize winning tomatoes.

Professor Lambert clicks his tongue. "Ah, I think I understand why you two were laughing." He sighs, fixing both of us with a stern look. "In my classroom, I expect your full attention. Don't make me use glamour to get it. Understood?"

Mack and I nod in unison.

"Good." Relief shoots through me as he shifts his intense focus to Hellebore. Reluctantly, I follow the teacher's stare.

The Spring Prince is leaned back in his seat, long legs stretched out in front of him, a lazy smirk curving his lips. As if he knows how dang kissable they are, he taps the stylus pencil against his lower lip, ignoring the sudden shift in attention.

Only Hellebore could ignore an entire auditorium full of students laser-focused on him.

He tilts his head to the side as he reads his new biography. Did one side of his lips curl with amusement? Or maybe that's his murder tell.

Everyone freezes as he chuckles, like his voice alone has the power to paralyze the room. Dropping his stylus onto his desk, he performs a slow clap.

The sound cuts through the auditorium in tandem with my galloping heart. "Whoever wrote this forgot one thing," he drawls, as if whoever wrote this isn't right *here*, twenty feet away. "I was voted most eligible Evermore bachelor by the

New York Fae Times. That should be added. It really was a marvelous accomplishment."

Is that even true? One look around the room at all the females gazing at the Spring Prince like he's a glazed donut on cheat day tells me, yes.

It's absolutely true.

"Ah, I see you have a sense of humor," Professor Lambert jokes, but he wipes his palms nervously on his slacks.

Is that . . . fear on the professor's face?

The teacher quickly turns off the screen and shuts Mack's laptop. *Yep, he's definitely afraid of the prince.*

"So, Prince Hellebore," the teacher continues, a tight smile plastered over his face. "How are you finding our academy thus far?"

Hellebore shares an arrogant look with his sister before finally deigning to acknowledge the professor. The way he flicks that bored gaze at him boils my blood. "Thus far, I would say . . . I now understand why Whitehall has beaten Evermore at the Tournament of Cups for the last ten centuries. And *counting*."

The professor's eyebrows gather. "Hmm. A bold assessment after less than a day."

"Yes, well," Hellebore tucks a strand of his pale honey hair behind his pointed ear, much to the delight of the closest females, who watch his every move, "if the skill of your Shadows are any indication, I foresee another victory for Whitehall very soon."

This time, when his gaze drifts my way, there's no denying it's on purpose.

Mother. Trucker. I will mess you up. I glare at him until Mack has the sense to pinch my leg, forcing me into reality.

"Summer," she hisses. "Do you have a death wish?"

Ruby, who's literally been asleep atop the nest she made inside my backpack, groggily flutters in the air. Her shiny wings are crinkled from napping, and she makes lopsided pirouettes before crash landing on my desk. "What? Who's dying?"

Mack glares at me. "Summer just murder-eyed the Spring Prince."

"Murder what?" Ruby mutters before understanding lights up her face. She winks at me. "Oh. I get it." Wobbling like a drunken hobo, Ruby picks up my pencil and begins to . . . to . . .

"Holy crap, is your sprite humping your pencil?" Mack snorts.

I rip my pencil from Ruby's dirty little fingers and shove it into the front pocket of my backpack. "Ruby, no! That's not what I meant and—never mind. Just never do that again."

A rattling sound draws my attention to my phone vibrating on my desk. Valerian!

I'm so desperate to connect with him that I don't even check who the text is from until it's already open.

I gape at the picture, blinking, trying to reconcile my hope and excitement with the gut punch I feel staring at the girl on the screen.

Me. In my underwear and sports bra, no less. Shivering and pissed. This is from . . . today, at breakfast.

Just like I edited the prince's photo, someone has edited my picture. I don't recognize the phone number, but it doesn't take a genius to peg Inara as the one behind the message.

I stare at the words *Fae whore* scrawled above my head. I stare and stare at them, at my half-naked image, at my eyes— which still have a shred of dignity.

I wonder if they'll still manage to retain that spark at the end of the school year, or if Inara will have broken me by then.

I'll never let that happen. Jaw clenched, I delete the photo.

Another text pops up.

Think that's bad? Just wait, Trailer Trash.

Shoving my phone into my pocket, I glance back at Inara and the others. Hate burns in her eyes as she stares over her books at me. Somehow, if it's even possible, the incident earlier today made her despise me even more.

Ignore. Ignore. Ignore.

It takes every bit of my dignity and willpower to turn around without giving her the satisfaction of a response. As much as I would love to tell the snowflake psycho exactly where to stuff her phone, my survival instincts have taken over.

And they inform me that provoking Inara now, after the humiliation she suffered earlier, would end in my blood leaving my body by various routes.

Unfortunately, Ruby has no such filters. Leaping onto my shoulder, she thrusts her tiny fist into the air. I watch, equally horrified and spellbound, as she turns an invisible lever that slowly lifts her middle finger toward the Six.

"Sit on this and spin, Evermore scum," Ruby cackles.

Someone just kill me.

Thank the Shimmer class is dismissed before Inara has time to retaliate. But by the glares both the Six and Prince Hellebore throw me on their way out, I know both will fight for the right to stamp me out of existence.

Pinching the bridge of my nose, I wait until everyone files out to gather my things. This day just keeps getting worse and worse.

Now, more than ever, I'm determined to win the first gauntlet and prove to everyone I deserve to be here.

8

I wake up thrashing and clawing at my throat. Blood wets my fingertips. *Crap. Not again.*

Pressing my hand lightly to the broken skin where my neck meets my collarbone, I staunch the bleeding as I focus on dragging air into my lungs.

That was . . . awful. The nightmare still clings to my skull like the cloying aftertaste of store-bought tea. Blinking up at the metal rungs of the bunk above me where Mack sleeps like the dead, I count the metal slats.

One, two, three . . . see, you're fine. Fine.

The bobble-head Eclipsa gave me—an alarmingly realistic version of her right down to the silver braid and dagger dripping blood—watches me from my nightstand.

"The nightmares are getting worse," I inform the bobble-head assassin. "And considering how bad they were to start with, that's not good."

Bobble-head Eclipsa openly judges me with her silence.

Groaning, I jackknife to a sitting position. *Goodbye, sleep.*

It's the third night this week that I've slipped into Valerian's dreams, which aren't really dreams but fragmented memories that make most horror movies look tame. Wiping at the sweaty strands of my hair pasted to my forehead, I try to make sense of this new vision.

Valerian is young, not much older than twelve. He's tied to a post in the Winter palace courtyard. The air is crisp, cold. Enough that his ragged breath spills from his lips in crystalline clouds.

It's the middle of the night, the moon, a swollen ivory globe, hung low in a dark winter sky. The entire palace had been dragged from their beds and gathered around the courtyard.

Even dreaming, I had enough sentience to understand it wasn't real. And yet, I still felt everything.

The light breeze that lifted the hair from the nape of his neck. The sting of the magic-infused rope cutting into his wrists, breaking open the scabs from only a few days ago.

A dark shadow emerges from the crowd. Up until that moment, Valerian has felt nothing. His emotions schooled into a hard wall of granite, unbreakable.

The coldness, the emptiness . . . it's horrible. An all-consuming ache of nothingness.

But the second his grandfather stalks toward him, Valerian goes rigid. Desperate for anything to block the swell of emotion raging inside him, he shoves his face into the ragged ashwood post he's tied to, the one embedded with shards of iron.

Two mortal poisons—iron and ash. Both meant to hurt him. Break him open.

Splinters of the lethal wood cut into his cheek. White-hot pain flares. He shudders, welcoming the feeling. Grasping onto it. Trying to drive it deeper inside him to purge his emotions.

But he fails, and a tiny sliver of fear pierces his heart. He recoils from the feeling, but he knows—he *knows* his grandfather has felt it.

Just like all the other times, he tries to force the word down into his chest. Tries to choke on it rather than let it escape his lips.

If he could, he would rip out his own throat rather than say it.

"Mother. Please, Mother."

Three words. Three fricking words that undo me. He's never talked about his mom. Not once. And yet the ferocity with which he longs for her in this dark moment . . .

She isn't coming. She never does. And the betrayal of it wounds him to the very core. Not the end of the whip. Not the ash splinters or the iron fragments that tear at his flesh.

The pain from his mother's absence is the torture he can't endure—the weapon he can't fight.

I want to scream, to punch someone as I feel him sag against the ashwood pole, defeated. Rage like I've never felt before splits me open, matching the agony that crashes over him as the wood burns every inch of flesh it touches.

His heart stutters into a weak, unsustainable rhythm; the air wheezes in his throat.

The poison from the ashwood and the iron is slowly killing him. And still. *Still.* He thrusts his body against it, giving the poison more and more access. Using it to drive his mother from his heart.

The pain becomes a touchstone. A fiery inferno that eats away at every part of him, so that when the first strike of the whip cracks open the skin of his back—it's swallowed by the miasma of writhing agony claiming every cell in his body.

Willingly inflicted agony.

Bile tickles my throat. He was twelve. *Twelve.* And he purposefully brought himself to the brink of death as a giant eff you to his grandfather, King Oberon.

I press my knuckles into my damp temples, trying to chase away an oncoming headache. Not for the first time, it comes to me that there is so much more to Valerian than what he reveals to me. Maybe he's smart to hide the darker side of himself.

Because, quite frankly, that part of him terrifies me.

I kick off the light gray sheets, slide from bed, and cross the floor, desperate to purge the memory from my brain. Phantom needles of pain still prick my skin. As unnerving as the memory-dreams are, once my horror fades, the pity takes hold.

If Valerian knew I was reliving his most painful memories every night, he would feel violated. I still haven't figured out if we're actually sharing a dream, which is just another layer of fuckery in this whole effed up situation—because that would mean he also relives that agony every night—or if I'm somehow receiving his memories.

Wonderful. I'm a radio set to the *Valerian's Soul-Crushing Memories* frequency.

Same as the last few nights, I pluck my phone from where it's charging on the dresser, check the screen for a text from him, and sigh.

Nothing.

My blurry-eyed focus slides to the date on the glowing screen. Three days—it's been three days since Hellebore announced the gauntlets, and I don't feel any more prepared than I did then.

Maybe less, considering the nightmares and my lack of sleep.

After school combat training doesn't start until week two. Meanwhile, Eclipsa canceled our last few morning training sessions.

I double-check our text chat, relieved to see this morning's session in four hours is still on.

Four hours. I wipe at my groggy eyes. Just thinking about the first gauntlet sends my adrenaline into overdrive. If there was a shot in hell of waking Ruby from her snorefest, I would force her to use one of her calming spells—which she's aptly named sleepy-sleep magic—to lull me into my dreams.

If the past two nights are any indication, I'd have more luck talking the moon from the sky than rousing her.

I shoot a longing glance at my bed. *It's not you, buddy. It's me.*

Now fully committed to getting up, I run through a short list of ways to use my time. Study. Finish the pile of laundry in the corner. Write out my weekly email to my aunts . . .

I exhale. Too restless. My body feels jacked, my legs twitchy and wired.

Only one activity cures my increasingly anxious moods.

As quietly as I can, I slip on my last clean pair of gray jogging pants, my sports bra, which is still a bit damp after last night's handwashing, and my Nike trainers. My phone goes into my handy pants pocket—a luxury only brands you can't find at the dollar store employ.

After brushing my teeth, slapping my tangled hair into a ponytail, and grabbing one of my new AirPods—Mack's other birthday present—I slide out the door.

When I get to the bottom of the first floor stairwell, I freeze.

Oops. I forgot about the new dorm monitors.

Each mortal dormitory now has a lower Fae guard who ensures shadows aren't sneaking out at night. After what happened with Evelyn, they're being extra cautious.

Lucky for me, our nighttime chaperone is an ancient gnome who sleeps—and snores—all night long.

Must be nice, I think as I tiptoe past the lime green club chair she's sunk into.

The second the brisk morning air meets my sweat-damp

skin, I set my music to my favorite new band and burst into a sprint. From Eclipsa's torture sessions, I know the track around the lake is three and a half miles.

Three and a half freaking miles. That I'm going to run *willingly*. With no one chasing me.

Why do I hate myself?

But as my shoes pound the springy grass, still wet with dew, and my lungs draw in huge gulps of fragrant air, the nightmare falls away. The pixie punk band *The Wailing Shadows* helps. Valerian introduced me to them three weeks ago, and I haven't tired of their playlist yet.

The pixie wails build up to the crescendo, and I align my rhythm with their haunting voices. I focus on my breathing. The smooth, mechanical movements of my limbs.

My mind begins to wander . . .

And runs straight to Valerian. He's like the awful pop single you swear you hate yet play over and over. I keep waiting for the day my mind gets tired of him, but so far, that hasn't happened.

Stupid how much I miss seeing him. The last text he sent said he'd be back in a few days, by Friday morning.

Which sucks major orc balls.

I desperately need to train with Valerian so we can smooth out any issues before the first gauntlet. We haven't physically been around each other. At least, not closely. Not in the way protecting him demands.

What if the tension from not solidifying our bond hinders my focus somehow?

Just the thought of Valerian in tight sweatpants and no shirt—because of course my imagination insists he be half-naked and glinting with sweat—lights the smoldering ember of desire in my belly I can never quite extinguish.

A sudden, terrifyingly powerful ache shivers through my core—

Dammit, Summer! Control your inner thirsty-ass self.

I push into a hard sprint, punishing my flesh for being so weak. The silver glimmer of the lake streaks by to my left. Colorful wooden rowboats dot the shore, turned upside down, the weathered paint flaking from their hulls.

Maybe Mack is right. I need to somehow get that boy out of my system without doing the deed, if that's even possible.

Is it? Oh, boy . . . I can think of several ways . . . several creative, wonderful ways . . .

Groaning, I drag myself from my lurid fantasy and focus on the burn in my lungs, my thighs as I push harder than ever before.

Zen. Find your zen.

It's here. Somewhere.

I drag my focus to the imposing forest beyond. The giant, gnarled trees stretch to the horizon, their branches weighted down with hand-sized reddish-violet and pewter leaves that appear nearly gold in the breaking dawn.

Dawn. The Fae won't drag their lazy butts from bed for another six hours, but shadows will be up soon. Deciding to trade the beauty of the lake for the solitude of the trees, I break for the forest. The soft thud of thick grass beneath my shoes becomes the dull swish of rotting leaves.

If there's zen anywhere to be found, surely it's inside an ancient, magical Fae forest?

I'm nearly five songs deep into the woods when I spy the glint of iron through the trees. A gamey scent rides along the breeze, mingling with the dank smells of moldy undergrowth, rich soil, and mushrooms.

That smell—

It takes my mind a second to identify what the scent is, but my body reacts instinctively. My loose muscles tighten painfully, cramps threatening in my calves, and sweat slicks my palms.

Any scrap of zen I might have found is ripped cruelly away.

Professor Balefire's menagerie. I'd nearly forgotten the outdoor cages from the enormous housing facility the school uses in the warmer seasons stretches into the woods. In the Mythological Creatures class yesterday, the teacher said the most dangerous of the beasts were housed deep in the forest.

Something about being near the forest calms them. When housed too close to the campus, the mortal scents drive the predatory animals into a frenzy.

Mortal scents. I glance over my very mortal body, dripping with sweat. My gaze falls on the painted red signs that line the path.

Danger. Wild creatures. Do not enter. Turn back.

I hit pause on *The Wailing Shadows* and frown. When did those get there?

A screech erupts from the other side of the cage.

My throat spasms shut.

I stumble back, nearly tripping on a tree root the size of my arm. Another beastly snarl rumbles so loudly that the iron cage trembles, followed by the unmistakable sound of sniffing. Something hard and sharp swipes across the enclosure, like talons scraping over metal.

Calm down. It can't reach you.

There are fences. Lovely iron fences imbued with spells to keep them in and me safe. Smoothing my damp palms down the side of my shirt, I pivot and break into a soft, controlled jog.

Predators are attracted to running things, right? I should probably walk.

I think of Chatty-Cat, who surprise-assassinates my ankles every morning when I'm half asleep, his inner psychopath awakened by my jerky movement as I half hop half stumble to the toilet. But when his adorable murder mittens bat my feet, the worst that happens is I trip, loose a barrage of curse words, and owe penance to the swear jar.

Whatever lurks behind that fence promises a much bloodier end.

Walk. You should definitely walk. But fear overrides my good sense, and I find myself slamming through branches as I hurtle down the path. Mud and leaves fly in my wake. I'm mid-leaping over a moss-covered log when I hear what sounds like the squeaking of a metal gate.

My heart punches into my throat. *Screw my life.* My brain tries to rationalize what I heard. There *are* gates that open to the forest, but they're to let the nice, cute, less murderous creatures roam.

The fluffy ones, Summer. Fluffy.

But the piercing cry that splits the morning air isn't fluffy, nor is it *behind* the cage.

Blind panic sears my vision. My arms pump the air. I'm running so fast my feet hardly touch the ground.

Light trickles from up ahead. The lake shimmers in the distance, students dotting the campus behind it. A quick check behind me reveals nothing but trees.

I slow a little, feeling beyond foolish. Nothing is chasing me. I overreacted.

I'm ten feet from the tree line when something darts across the path, causing me to freeze. Frick! Hands on my knees, I peer through sweat-burning eyes at the black shape slithering across the forest floor.

Shadow. It's a shadow—a really freaking big shadow. Which means—

I whip my gaze up to see something that at first glance, doesn't make sense. The spread of ginormous white wings flares from what looks like the muscled body of a lion. Taloned claws similar to a bird of prey cut through the tree-tops, raining the forest floor with branches.

Another predatory shriek bursts from its golden beak, and then I watch in complete shock as the beast turns its eagle-like head to look down.

Shrewd golden eyes hone in on me.

Griffin. I barely have time to congratulate myself on recognizing the creature before my legs propel me down the path.

Above, the crack of entire tree trunks being snapped in half shakes the forest as the griffin shoots straight for me.

9

My first thought as I burst from the woods is that I'm going to die a very public death. The shoreline around the lake mills with students who had the same bright idea I did about extra training. They're just far enough away that I won't put them in danger, at least.

I fling a look over my shoulder, and my stomach hollows out. The griffin smashes through trees like they're made from dust, the sword-length talons protruding from its paws shredding everything in its path.

The closest tree groans as it plunges forward. Cursing, I leap out of the way a split second before it would have flattened me.

Weapon! I spin around, scouring the grass for anything—

A broken branch rests near my feet. Plucking the crooked limb from the ground, I sprint toward the lake. Dizziness sends me careening sideways, and I gulp the air like its ice-cold Mountain Dew in a heat wave.

I hardly make it five feet before a whoosh of air slams into me, blowing my pale hair around my face. Brandishing the limb high above my head, I whip to face the beast.

Ebony claws swipe from the air—

I duck, swinging the branch like a baseball bat. My arms nearly pull from their sockets as the griffin jerks the weapon from my hands and snaps it like a twig.

Well, that went well.

He circles away, his high-pitched cries growing softer. I dart across the ankle-high grass to the lake's shoreline, my shoes sinking into the ivory sand, and glance up. The smell of lake water fills my nose as I shield my eyes from the morning sun.

There. The griffin soars a hundred feet or so above me, riding the air like waves. If not for the situation, I would find the sight indescribably beautiful.

Focus, Summer. Focus!

I glance across the lake to the other side where onlookers have already gathered to watch.

If I run like hell, I can make it. Safety in numbers and all that.

My body tenses, prepared to flee. But, no. My shoulders sag. I can't save myself by sacrificing others, even if most of them are already probably gunning to get me kicked out.

Besides, I've watched enough hawks to know he'll strike like lightning before I reach the other side. His speed from such a height will knock me into a stupor.

Incapacitated, I won't even struggle as he lifts me hundreds of feet into the air. Then, if the textbooks are true, when he's high enough to ensure the fall will crack me open like a piñata, he'll loosen his hold and drop me to my death.

Afterward, he'll take me to his mate for first dibs.

Smart *and* a gentleman. Is it weird to be a fangirl of the thing that's about to kill you?

Think, you clever bitch. What else do you know about a griffin? They're elusive creatures. They mate for life. Most die within a year in captivity. And they're quite terrifying in person.

For some reason, I revisit Chatty-Cat. What does *he* hate more than anything? Belly rubs, me, and . . . the baths Jane tries to give him.

By the way he howls and fights, you would think she was trying to drown the poor bastard—

That's it!

A gut-curdling cry shivers across the lake as the griffin makes its move.

Roaring my own war cry, I make mine. The lake water hits my body like ice. I gasp, pushing past the needles of cold, forcing myself deeper into the emerald green depths.

When the water laps at my neck, I tilt my face to the sky and wait.

"Here, kitty kitty," I croon, praying the griffin is in touch with its feline side and not the eagle one. Crap. Eagle's hunt in water.

Why am I only now making that connection?

The griffin's shadow skips across the lake's rippled surface, tinged coral-pink by the rising sun, toward me. Craning my neck, I watch its white underbelly grow larger. Larger. It's front talons stretch wide, ready to claim their mortal prize.

Perhaps this was a bad idea.

Instinctively, I shut my eyes and prepare to dive. But the sound of wings flapping stops me. I snap my eyes open to see the creature veering away from the water—and me. Sand sprays in all directions as it lands hard on the shore.

It shakes out its massive wings, cocks its avian head in my direction, and belts out a plaintive shriek of displeasure.

Yes! I grin idiotically at the beast, my triumph at outsmarting it overriding my nerves. "You don't like water, do you, buddy?"

At my voice, the griffin tilts its head even more, the way a dog does.

"It's really nice." I splash water toward the shore, sending the griffin hopping back as it squawks. "Sure you don't want to join me?"

Its deep golden eyes peer at me with a surprising intelligence.

As if it understands my words . . .

I remember how animals around the farmhouse sometimes did the same. Responding in uncanny ways to my words. I chalked it up to an overactive imagination.

But now—well, it couldn't hurt.

"I'm sorry," I say. "Truly. I know how frustrating it is to think you're about to eat the best cheeseburger of your life and then, bam, nothing. But you can't eat me because I'm actually really nice."

The griffin makes a low cooing sound and hops closer, just short of the waterline. It eyes the foamy waves lapping at its curved toes, the black talons sunk halfway into the sand, then flicks its cunning gaze to me. The breeze ruffles the feathers that lift on either side of its white head to give him the appearance of pointed ears.

"God you're beautiful." I talk slowly, calmly, trying to will the predator away with my voice, my mind. "You don't deserve to waste away in a cage . . . but you can't hurt anyone else, so you have to go back."

I hate sending this majestic creature to live in a tiny enclosure. It feels wrong deep in my gut, a travesty just as unjust as when the Fae abuse and hurt us.

Low cooing noises rumble from the creature's deep chest. I find myself moving closer to it. Slowly. Hand held out.

The water is thigh-deep. Only seven feet stand between the savage, beautiful animal and me. Something forms between us, a bond so real I can almost touch it in the air. A torrent of emotions floods through me, nearly doubling me over.

The griffin's agony is overwhelming. I see bars. I see a muddy floor and dirty water bowl. I see it throwing itself against its cage over and over as it tries to reach its mate, still somewhere in the wild. I feel its spirit shriveling smaller and smaller every day it lives in captivity.

The few hours I spent locked in a cage come flooding back. The terror. The panic.

I'm sorry, I think, willing him to hear me. *I'm sorry they put you in a cage, and I'm sorry they took you from your mate. It isn't right. Nothing should be forced to live that way.*

Pulling its ivory wings tightly to its feline body, the griffin drops its head, bends down, and . . . bows.

I'm so focused on what the griffin's doing that I barely register the churning water near my legs. Another swish drags my attention to the lake just as something moves beneath the emerald surface.

Fish?

A slick, heavy *something* brushes against my thigh.

So probably not a fish. Because this day hasn't been bad enough.

Dragging my gaze from the griffin, I blink down into the murky depths. Something nags at me. Something important. A warning that prickles my spine with alarming intensity.

The griffin's wings flare as its golden eyes shift to the water. Behind me. Then it screeches so loudly I can feel it in my bones and begins dragging its talons through the sand.

"Don't move!" a female voice commands.

I follow the familiar voice to the embankment twenty yards away. Eclipsa! We were supposed to meet by the lake for sunrise yoga before our session. A crowd forms behind her, including Professor Balefire, the Mythological Creatures professor.

Standing alone, the Spring Prince watches from the other

side of the lake. Unlike the others, his face isn't the least bit concerned for my welfare.

If his lazy smirk is any indication, he's rather amused by the whole affair.

I face Eclipsa. "It's okay. It won't go in the water."

Oh crap—why does Eclipsa look like she wants to murder me? "Summer, did you forget why no one swims in the Lake of Sorrows?"

And . . . just like that, I remember there are selkies in this water. Hungry, flesh-eating selkies.

My heart flails into a mad gallop as I glance left and right. Heads poke just above the surface. Heads with inhumanly large, curious eyes, bright flowing hair that pools around the water like kelp, and rows of glittering teeth perfectly capable of sheering flesh from bone.

There's a ravenous look in their alien faces that steals my breath.

"You don't want anything to do with me," I say, trying to reach out with my mind the same way I did with the griffin. "I taste horrible. Worse than my Aunt Zinnia's cornbread."

Thank God Zinnia can't hear my blasphemous statement. She'd never forgive me.

A pang of regret nearly doubles me over. Shimmer save me, if I die in the Everwilde, Zinnia would never recover. Not after losing her first daughter to the Fae.

I have to fight my way out of this no matter what it takes. But my voice only seems to draw the selkies closer.

Should I make a dash for the shore? The griffin blocks my way . . . but right now he seems like the lesser of the two evils.

I lift my arms, ready to make a break for it—

"Freeze, girl!" Professor Balefire slides down the side of the embankment, pebbles disturbing the pond below. "They're attracted to movement."

The selkies turn their hungry gazes on the professor in unison and then slowly back to me.

He holds up a wooden bucket and pours the entire disgusting contents into the water. It looks like some type of . . . raw meat. Bleck.

Dark red blood blooms along the foamy waves.

A few selkies dart beneath the water, their silky fins churning the lake as they scramble for the food.

But most don't give the bait a second glance.

"It's troll meat meant for the harpies," the professor calls, tapping the bucket like it's a dinner bell. "Best I could do short notice."

Hellebore's chuckle carries on the soft breeze. "Selkies prefer their food live so they can play with it first."

Fae-freaking-tastic.

Eclipsa leaps to the shore. Her sharp focus darts between the selkies, Hellebore, and the griffin, making it clear that she sees all *three* as equal threats.

Her favorite jeweled dagger glints from her hand. I frown at the thin, delicate blade. It's her favorite because it can be easily hidden, and when used by someone with her particular set of skills, can end someone's life quickly, without much blood or mess.

But I'm not sure how finesse will help in this situation. Against selkies and larger, winged predators like the griffin, it's way too small to do much damage . . . but, no. She's bending the blade so that the sapphire in the middle of the hilt catches the sun and sends blue jewels of light skipping across the lake.

Do selkies like shiny things? I get my answer when the rest of the slippery creatures turn their terrifying hunger from me to the sparkly shards dancing around them.

The water vibrates with their strange purring sounds as they slowly begin to circle this new temptation. They pounce on the lights, snarling their frustration when the sparkles move just out of reach.

The trick works. Slowly, Eclipsa draws them away from me.

While Eclipsa and the professor work to keep the selkies' attention, Hellebore has meandered his way around the other side. He stops a healthy distance from the griffin. I can tell by the way he stares at the beast that he feels the same admiration for it that I do.

Which is why, when he tosses the loaded crossbow at me, I stare at the weapon in confusion. "What am I supposed to do with this?"

He lifts a honey-gold eyebrow, that lazy irreverence oozing from his every move. "Whatever you want. Pick your teeth with it, for all I care. But if you desire to actually leave the watery grave you stand in, you'll send a bolt through that glorious creature's heart."

"The hell I will," I snap, glaring at him.

Hellebore flashes his teeth in a bored smile. "Fine. Watching a griffin slaughter you or one of your classmates will be entertaining, at least."

"I'll swim to the other side."

His focus slides to the selkies and back to me; the arrogance inside those turquoise depths make me want to carve them out and feed them to the selkies. "You will be dead before you make it ten feet, but good luck with that."

I flick a sideways glance at the griffin, relieved to see its focus is still very much on me. "And how do you know it won't kill *you*?"

"Griffins are highly intelligent creatures. They don't prey on other apex predators unless defending themselves."

Other apex predators? This guy takes the arrogant Fae stereotype to a whole new level of douchery.

He runs a hand over the cropped side of his silky blond

hair. Probably habit from staring into the mirror for hours on end. "Besides, last I checked, I can fly. Can you? How about any of your mortal friends?"

Fly? I briefly wonder what shifter type allows him that ability before honing in on his statement. My friends.

Clutching the handle of the crossbow, I glance at the shadows on the embankment. Like the idiot tourists at the game parks that leave the safety of their cars to take selfies with grizzly bears, the mortal students keep coming. Drawn in by the promise of watching my humiliation unfold, they've completely ignored the wild griffin's presence.

A few extra-special ones throw pebbles at the griffin, trying to agitate it.

"Ladies and gentlemen," I mutter. "This is Darwinism at its finest."

The griffin's head jerks to stare at the crowd. That's when I spot Mack running across the lawn, Ruby in tow.

Oh, hell. A fresh wave of panic grips me. My brain supplies unhelpful images of her being dropped from hundreds of feet above.

"Order them to leave," I plead. I hate how whiny my voice sounds, how weak, but I'm out of options.

"Why? There's a lesson here."

"A lesson? On what? Asshole Fae princes?"

"No, natural selection." His lips are still curved upward, but his blue eyes darken to storm clouds. "Although, I am beginning to think you need a lesson on how to behave when speaking to an Evermore, little pet."

This is going nowhere, and any minute, the selkies will tire of chasing Eclipsa's sparkles and turn their attention back to me.

I pivot to face the griffin. *Don't eat them*, I silently command, but the certainty from before is gone.

Am I really going to risk lives over an imagined connection with a wild predator? Any moment, he could pick one of them off. Maybe Mack.

Nausea heats my belly at the thought of having to explain to her dads why I hesitated.

My hands tremble as I lift the crossbow. I rest a finger on the trigger.

Please, I mentally whisper. *Don't make me hurt you.*

The griffin's wings unfurl, sending sprays of sand and water into the air. The air shrivels in my chest. I stumble back, tracking the center of its thick white chest as it lifts into the air—

And comes straight for me.

Shoot it. My trigger finger tenses, the wicked bolt tip glittering in front of my face. *Pull the trigger!*

I can't. I just can't kill it.

Shielding my face with my free hand, I lurch sideways, expecting those long talons to close around me any second.

Only . . . with an ear-splitting shriek, the griffin slams into the lake behind me. I whirl in time to see it lifting back into the air. Water droplets explode around the creature's legs.

Caught inside its merciless talons, writhing and screaming, is a selkie.

The selkie's fishlike lower end thrashes, its dark green and teal scales catching the light and refracting rainbow sparkles. The water creature's too-large eyes are dark and filled with ravenous hunger, and they're directed at me.

Me.

The griffin saved me. And I almost killed it.

Three powerful flaps of its huge wings and its arcing through the air and into the clouds. The caught selkie's enraged screech grows dimmer and dimmer before abruptly cutting off.

Still clenching the crossbow, I slog to the shore, grateful I listened to my heart and didn't release my projectile.

In the distance, Eclipsa sheaths her dagger and sprints toward us.

Water pours from my clothes and darkens the white sand as I march to the Spring Prince and toss the weapon at his feet. "You can have this back."

He doesn't even glance at the crossbow. His eyes are riveted to mine. One look at his intense expression and my triumph fades, although I can't determine why.

I shift on my feet. "What? Aren't you glad I didn't have to hurt it? Now it's free. It can find its mate—"

I don't see him create the portal until it's too late.

The dark hole warbles in front of me. He twists his fingers, drawing a sudden wind that slams into my back, and I careen head-first into the portal.

Hellebore follows me through the portal and snaps it closed before I can move. Panicked, I glance around. We're inside what looks to be an over-grown garden. Climbing roses, clematis, and wisteria run wild over a splash of hedges. A family of centaur sculptures rise from the middle, their life-sized bodies entangled in vines.

Something about the air here, or perhaps the magic, feels wrong—twisted, even. Just beneath the sweet spring breeze lurks the stench of decay. Black moldy dust clings to sculptures and fringes the ends of the plants.

"Where are we?" I breathe as I spin around, searching for an escape.

"Welcome to the Spring Court gardens, once the most beautiful place in all the lands, before the scourge took it."

"What? Take me back."

He laughs. Laughs, for Shimmer's sake. "How have you not been punished with a mouth like that?"

"Fuck. You."

A lethal stillness overtakes him, the act so unnatural, so

predatory that I'm frozen with terror. "Why did one of the most dangerous creatures in the entire academy not kill you?"

Just like the air here, there's something in his voice that makes me recoil. Something unhinged.

I try to retreat—only I'm stuck. Too late, I feel his magic glide around my thighs, my stomach, invisible vines imprisoning me in place. The scent of tulips and lilies fill the air, their cloying sweetness causing me to choke.

"Let me go," I snarl, but it's hard to feel intimidating when you can't move. I try another tactic. "They'll notice I'm missing."

"No, they won't. These statues were a gift from Queen Titania herself. They have the marvelous ability to slow down time. I could hold you here for days and on the other side, an hour will have passed."

I swallow. He takes yet another step. And another. His head cocked sideways as he examines me. I'm reminded of the animalistic way the griffin did the same, only I can't control Prince Hellebore.

"Why did it not hurt you?" he asks again, this time softer, his voice almost melodic.

My pendant heats between my breasts; he's trying to use compulsion to make me answer.

Frick. Gritting my teeth, I struggle against his voice, against the seductive power trying to invade my mind and override my will. The invisible vines keep wrapping tighter around me, growing thicker by the second.

"The water protected me," I grind out, glaring murder at him.

"Someone found a way to protect you from compulsion." He shakes his head in disappointment.

"Sorry to ruin your fun, psycho."

Yes, keep taunting him, Summer. See how that works out for you.

The air wheezes from my throat as he cords his magic so tightly over my chest that my ribs crack. "Clever, guessing it hated water. And yet, when that selkie snuck up behind you, the beast braved its aversion and protected you. Why?"

My eyes widen with rage. "You saw the selkie about to eat me and you didn't tell me?"

"I'm an Evermore. Did you expect me to care one way or the other if you die?"

Fury sends searing heat bubbling over my chest. "If that's true then why did you save me this morning?"

"Save you? Is that what you think I did?"

Oh, God. When did he take another step closer? I strain harder as a sense of doom starts to set in. The magic feels just like real binds, and my body is starting to freak out.

"Do you know what we do at Whitehall to mortal shadows who break our rules?"

"Drag them to creepy time-warped gardens and bore them with questions?"

"We drop them in the middle of Ranth Forest and then watch as the predators hunt them down."

"Stop. Please. I don't want to hear this."

"When the predators draw close, they have to fight for the right to claim their prize."

I shudder as his meaning becomes apparent. "I'm that prize?"

"Prize isn't quite the right word, but yes. No one plays with my toys until I'm done with them."

For frick's sake, somebody needs to punch this guy in the pretty mouth. Take him down a peg or ten. "Why me?"

He shrugs, as if my selection was completely arbitrary. But the burning hatred in his eyes says otherwise. "Because you represent everything I despise about mortals. You're soft. Weak. You don't belong here."

"Unbind me and I'll show you weak," I growl.

He tsks. "Now. I'm only going to ask you this one more time, and then you won't like what happens next. Why did that creature protect you?"

"I don't know. Maybe it wasn't protecting me. Maybe it thought I looked too stringy and the selkie would taste better."

His heavy-lidded eyes make a point of looking me up and down, and then his turquoise blue irises go scary-dark, the ominous shade of raging storm clouds.

Fuck buckets. This guy is horrifying when he's mad. A tremble starts deep in my core. I can't breathe. From my fear or his invasive magic constricting my chest, it's a toss-up.

I flinch, shivering against his touch as he closes the distance between us. Strange golden light swirls inside his dark eyes, and something about the molten light fills me with innate fear.

He can't touch you.

His eyes suddenly shift behind me just as the ripping sound of a portal fills the air. A wolfish grin plays over his face. "Are you following me, E? I thought we already discussed appropriate boundaries—"

Eclipsa flies through the air, smashes her knee into his chest, and connects her elbow with his sharp jaw.

Hell. Fucking. Yes!

The magical binds snap from around me as Hellebore rockets backward. A human male would have dropped, but Hellebore barely flinches as he finds his balance and rights himself.

"Get behind me, Summer," Eclipsa growls, her eyes never leaving the Spring Prince's. A part of me hesitates. I've never seen Eclipsa turn full Fae assassin. Even when we were fighting the darklings, she was lethal—but calm.

This Eclipsa could make the Darken her bitch.

Deciding to take my chances with the monster I know, I

scramble to her side as Hellebore circles us. "That was uncalled for, E."

"Screw you and your twisted aunt," Eclipsa snarls.

He chuckles. "I don't seem to remember you wanting to bring my aunt to bed when we—"

Twin daggers slice toward him, spinning end over end. Last second before they sink into his chest, he turns sideways and they *thunk* into the haunch of the closest centaur statue behind him.

Hellebore has the audacity to look wounded by the attack. "If I'd known breaking your heart would have made you this exciting, I would have done it sooner."

Her voice is cold and terrifying as she snarls, "Next one won't miss, Hel."

He sighs. "Hey, it's not my fault she stumbled into my portal. You know the rules. Once she enters my court's territory without permission, she belongs to me."

"Screw your permission. Summer belongs to the Winter Prince, so unless you fancy kicking off a war with the Unseelie Court, back the fuck off."

Her words are like a punch to the gut. I know in Everwilde, everything is fair game to be stolen, like some cruel game of Monopoly, which makes the Fae possessive with everything they own. But to hear Eclipsa talk about me like a possession—

Ugh. I try to make excuses for her words. She's pissed, not thinking straight. But stupid tears prickle my eyes.

No. I will not cry. Straightening my shoulders, I blink the tears away before either Fae can notice.

"I see the Winter Prince still hasn't given you your freedom. Although after owning you myself, I don't blame him."

The balls on this guy. An emotion too brief to name passes over Eclipsa's face, and then rage takes over. A deep, alarming rage that only ends with someone dead.

This idiot should be terrified. Instead, Hellebore laughs like this is all a game. "The Winter Court might be formidable now, but I predict a time in the near future when that will change."

"Keep dreaming, asswipe." Eclipsa bares her teeth in a vicious snarl.

Hellebore's focus shifts to Valerian's brand winding up my bicep. His stare lingers, as if he's taking the time to trace every line, and then he lifts his hands in surrender.

A grin curls his lips as he backs away.

"My mistake." Something flickers behind his eyes as they meet mine. "Don't get too used to that brand, little pet."

A growl rumbles deep in Eclipsa's chest. "She's not for sale, Hel."

The portal he creates is a beautiful, shimmering teal, the edges a soft blush-pink. The glow catches in his pale honey-gold hair as he tsks. "Stop lying to the poor girl, E. You know as well as I that in Everwilde, everything has a price. Just like you once did."

The moment he's gone, Eclipsa whips to face me. "You okay?"

"Yes, but—"

"What the Fae hells were you doing, Summer?"

I stumble back from the anger in Eclipsa's voice. "Me? Someone let the griffin out on purpose."

"Stop making excuses. Don't you understand? You cannot slip up now, not even once. This year is different. There are things happening beyond our control."

"What things?" I cross my arms over my chest. "Does it involve whatever Valerian is doing in the Winter Court?"

She sighs through her teeth. "I can't talk about that. Just stop drawing attention to yourself. Especially now . . ."

I glean the last part of her sentence that she omitted. *Especially now that Hellebore's here.*

"Can we please discuss the fact that the Spring Court Prince just kidnapped me and turned full-bore psycho?"

"What's to discuss? He was toying with you, Summer. Because he can. Because his sadistic urges needed quenching. Because he wanted to see what your fear smells like. Who freaking knows? It doesn't matter why. You don't want someone like him taking an *interest* in you, believe me. So no more mistakes."

Behind the fury in her eyes, I make out expertly hidden pain. The kind that scars the soul and never quite goes away, no matter how deep you bury it. The need to comfort my friend wars with the instinct to lash out at the unfairness of blaming me for Hellebore's actions.

In the end, this shitshow of a morning wins out, and my frustration boils over. "Eclipsa, I'm trying, okay? This year is so much harder than I thought it would be. I can't sleep. Every night I have these horrible nightmares. Valerian's nightmares, I think. Or his memories, I don't know."

She blinks. My heart sinks at the pity in her eyes. "What you're experiencing, I think it's because of the soulbond."

"Is that normal?"

"Not for most mates, no. But the strength of the soulbond is directly related to a couple's combined magic. Considering both you and Valerian possess powers only rivaled by the Darken . . . we have no idea how the bond will react. Especially the longer you resist it."

"So I could potentially relive his memories for a lifetime?"

Eclipsa's face softens. "Something happened recently that has brought some of Valerian's past traumas back to the surface. I wouldn't be surprised if, as his mate, you were subconsciously taking those resurfaced memories from him somehow. Bearing them so he doesn't have to. I doubt he's even aware that you're doing it."

For some reason, just knowing that I'm purposefully

taking on those traumas—even if it's a subconscious decision —makes the nightmares easier to stomach.

"I know you don't see it this way, but the bond you share with the Winter Prince is precious, something most Fae would kill for. You should cherish it."

As we leave the ruined garden, I wonder if I'll ever view the soulbond tying me to Valerian the way Eclipsa does, or if it will always feel like the brand tattooed into my flesh: a mark of my complete powerlessness in this wild and beautiful world.

Headmistress Luna Lepidonis's office is exactly like I remember. Small, orderly, filled with filing cabinets and dust. A mahogany desk basks in the red and blue light of the three stained-glass windows behind it.

The headmistress has her back turned to me. The edges of her powdery beige wings furl and unfurl. I notice the tips are fringed with black, as are the outside of the pale green dots at the apex of her wings.

She turns, clicking her tongue as she stares down her long nose at me. "Summer Solstice, how is it you're already here in my office on the second day of school?"

I shrug where I sit cross-legged in the comfy club chair in front of her desk. My clothes are mostly dry, but I stink like lake water.

Yet another day arriving late to class a hot mess and a half.

"I was clear, was I not, about the rules of your reinstatement as a shadow?"

My hands are balled into fists on my thighs. From the time I left Eclipsa to get changed, only to be called here, I've been reliving this morning and the encounter with douche-face.

Every time his smug, too-pretty face pops into my mind, my anger mounts.

Heaving out a ragged breath, I force my hands to relax. "You were clear, but this morning wasn't my fault. Someone released the griffin."

She absentmindedly strokes the edge of one of her wings. "Fault is a mortal construct."

"That hardly seems fair."

"Fair? Do you need a lesson on our race, Miss Solstice? Neither fault nor fairness are qualities we give much credence to. I would have assumed you understood that by now."

I sigh, letting my head fall back against the chair. "I do, believe me, and . . . it won't happen again."

"We both know that's a lie. Predators instinctively attack those they perceive to be weak or . . . different, and you are both. It will happen again, *and* again, until your luck runs out and you die."

"I'm willing to take that risk."

Eyes narrowed, she taps the end of a long fingernail against her bottom lip as she studies me. "Professor Balefire said you acted cleverly by entering the water. He also said when they found you, the scent of a portal lingered in the air. Care to explain how the two go together?"

"If I said a certain prince abducted me against my will, would he be punished?"

Her lips curl at the corners. "Can you prove this abduction?"

Dammit. She knows I can't. On the academy side, I was only gone for a few seconds at most. Eclipsa must have seen the abduction happen and leapt in after us.

Tugging at my ponytail, I slide from the chair and stand. "I deserve to be here and I'll prove that, if you let me."

"Things are different this year." I could swear her mouth

softens around the corners. "The Winter Prince is no longer the ruling Evermore student."

"I'm aware." I rub my arms as I remember the way it felt having Hellebore's power slide over my flesh. "Why would the academy let someone like the Spring Court Prince in? Especially when you're being investigated by the CMH? You know how shadows are treated at Whitehall, right?"

She scowls, covering up the flicker of surprise in her eyes. Then she turns to stare out the window once. "You will never begin to comprehend Faerie politics. The Spring Court Queen, Prince Hellebore's aunt, doesn't ask for permission from anyone."

The pit that's been forming in my belly since I was attacked this morning feels like it weighs a hundred pounds as I say, "So does this mean I'm . . . expelled?"

Silence. I watch her delicate wings as they move, the tips gently stretching and curling inward. Up close, beneath the stained-glass light, the velvety material is shimmery and beautiful.

Her wings aren't as vibrant or as lively as a pixie's wings, but something about their softness, the graceful way they dance in the air, makes them entrancing to watch.

Finally, she tucks her wings in tight and squares to face me. "Expelling you would be a mercy, but not one I am able to make. If Queen Titania has any blessings left to give, you'll fail the first gauntlet and never step foot in this academy again."

The tension bleeds from my shoulders as those two wonderful words sink in. Not expelled.

Thank the Shimmer!

Valerian must have pulled some strings like he promised. Oh, boy. I'm going to have to find a way to pay him back, and I know exactly how he'll expect payment.

I wink at the headmistress, dizzy with relief. "I'm going to pass the first gauntlet, you'll see."

She wrinkles her nose as if she can't quite figure out why I'm not more scared. I guess I should be, but screw that. "Yes, I suppose we will see. Rather soon."

A flick of her hand is my dismissal.

As I stand, a question comes to mind. "What will happen to the griffin?"

She arches an eyebrow. "The creature who tried to kill you? Why, it will return to its cage. Every beast in the menagerie wears a tag that's spelled to draw them back, if they ever should escape."

The thought of that majestic creature being forced back into a cage makes me sick, and I can't help thinking how our tragic stories are similar. Both of us pulled inexorably toward the place that will ultimately be our ruin.

Only the academy is worse than any cage. At least, in the menagerie, no one tortures the creatures.

As I leave, my focus drifts over her desk again and snags on a file. Evelyn Cantrell.

I quickly scan the other files next to it—all mortal female students, by the names and same red color coding.

My curiosity flares to life. Why are those files together? Have there been more students who turned?

But Valerian said preventing mortal females from bearing Fae children was simple.

If that's true, why didn't the Fae who slept with Evelyn make sure she was taking precautions? Or maybe it's entertainment? It's not enough to seduce mortal shadows just to humiliate them, now someone is turning them into darklings for fun?

That seems rather stupid, considering how dangerous darklings can be. Then again, in my experience so far, the Fae have proven their mindless cruelty trumps their cleverness.

The headmistress clears her throat. Dragging my eyes from the files, I scramble from the room just as Mr. Willis enters. He gives me a kind nod before shutting the door. A lock clicks behind me.

Which of course immediately piques my curiosity. As quietly as possible, I press my ear to the door crack.

Muffled voices filter through. "Should have expelled her anyway," Mr. Willis is saying.

Thanks a lot, buddy.

"The prince expressly forbade it!" the headmistress snaps. From the soft footsteps, she's pacing.

Valerian intervened. I knew it.

Their voices grow dimmer. I press harder into the door, side-eyeing the top of the stairs in case someone appears.

I catch Mr. Willis's gruff voice as he says, "You know why. He wants to torture her. I've heard the rumors about White-hall, so have you. By letting him into the academy, I fear we've let a fox into the henhouse."

Okay, they're not talking about Valerian anymore.

The pacing stops. "I couldn't say no, you know that. Without the Spring Court's influence, they would have shut down the academy."

"Yes," Mr. Willis growls before lowering his voice. "But we still haven't determined why Prince Hellebore is really here. The scourge has invaded the Spring lands, but the academy has enough wards that it would have been protected."

Prince Hellebore? They're talking about that inflated prick? What the heck? Which means . . . he's the one respon-sible for me not being expelled.

Because he's not done toying with me yet.

A small grunt slips from my throat. The room goes quiet. *Stupid Fae hearing!*

Footsteps pound toward the door. My heart slams into my

throat as I leap down the stairs four at a time, nearly crippling myself in the process. I don't stop running until I'm in the familiar halls of the mortal floors.

My mind is all over the place as I rush to my locker where Mack left my school bag. I keep going over this morning. Nearly dying. Mack and Ruby being put in danger along with the entire school. Being abducted and probably almost murdered by the Spring Court douchebag. Eclipsa's hurtful words.

All of it swirls around my skull, a depressing reminder of how screwed I am.

I was determined to fight back and win my place here, no matter the cost, so I can protect humans from the Fae. But what if by being here, I'm putting mortals in more danger?

"Stop attacking your dress and let it do its job," Mack orders.

"Which is what, exactly?" I ask as I halt, mid-yanking down the hem of the offending baby blue dress. It's Mack's, and I didn't figure in our height difference when I asked to borrow it for the Selection ceremony. Even when I'm standing perfectly straight, the light, flowy fabric barely covers my ass. "To show off my hoo-ha?"

"No, to show off your long, gorgeous legs."

"And stop walking like you've got a brownie wand stuck up your ass," Ruby scolds, alighting on my shoulder.

I sigh. I'm one bend away from flashing the school my lady bits. "Guess I won't be sitting down anytime soon."

Mack gouges her elbow into my side. "Aren't you glad I insisted we do laundry last night? Otherwise, you wouldn't be wearing underwear."

Yesterday, after Reina cracked some joke in class about Mack only passing because her dads donate generously to the school and spoil her rotten, Mack flipped. She swore for the rest of the year, she's not relying on any of their money to get by.

Which, unfortunately, means no more laundry service. Both of us spent a good hour washing our clothes in the bathroom sink.

Ruby cackles. "Who knew that bizarre mortal contraption you insist on wearing would come in handy?"

And . . . I was today years old when I discovered my sprite doesn't wear underwear.

I follow behind Mack as she joins a group of students entering the courtyard. On instinct, I scour the yard, searching for huddled groups whispering in my direction.

Tonight, though, I'm not even a blip on people's radar. The entire school thrums with excitement as they wait to see what the new Selection ceremony will be like.

Forcing my shoulders back, I push my paranoia aside. Maybe people have forgotten about me. Since the incident with the griffin, I've managed to remain low-key. I train with Eclipsa, go to class, and then return to our dorms to study.

Soft fluttering lights draw my attention to the courtyard. Butterflies swoop from the air, their wings glowing pale pink and yellow. Refreshments in crystal flutes are laid out on crisp linen tables. After the last incident, no one actually drinks the beverages, but still.

As much as I despise Hellebore, this year's Selection ceremony is way better than last year's. At least, so far.

No one's forced us into a cage and then tried to drown us, so that's something, right?

Mack chews her bottom lip as she spins around, the crisp white empire dress she wears nipping at her ankles. Her sprite weaved miniature pink and yellow roses in her french-braided hair. "Where are all the Evermore students?"

Ruby flits annoyingly around my face before settling on

top of my head. We're definitely having a chat about personal space later.

"Probably on the other side of that giant portal they're herding you through," Ruby says casually.

Portal? Not another one. Cool sweat streaks down my shoulder blades and plasters my dress to my back as I follow the others through the magical doorway. It's only after I enter the other side that I recall the fences used to slowly force cattle into smaller and smaller chutes until they're trapped.

A burst of colors, heady floral scents, and birdsong assault my senses. Dragging in a lungful of the sticky-sweet air, I turn in a slow circle as Mack whispers, "We're in the Spring Court."

I blink against this too-vibrant world. The clear blue sky, the same unnervingly turquoise shade as Hellebore's eyes, crowns a verdant landscape of hills and lakes. Every inch of land bursts with greenery and flowers—a kaleidoscope of tulips, irises, and lilies.

Dusk is fast approaching, its pink and gold tendrils slithering over the land.

They march us down a worn path lined with hyacinth and cherry trees, their soft white petals swirling around us like snow. At the bottom of the sloping meadow rises a palace made from rose-quartz, the domed structure veined with every manner of flowering vine.

"The Spring Court Palace," Ruby announces, as if we haven't already figured that out. "I hear Prince Hellebore has a red room of pain deep inside the palace."

"A what?" I mutter, following the shadows in front of me up the wide marble stairs to a courtyard with four huge ivory gazebos on opposite corners. Evermore mill about beneath the shaded structures.

"You know." Ruby launches in front of my face, her

eyebrows waggling suggestively as she rocks her hips in the air. "The place where he keeps his toys."

I blink, swallow. Hoping toys doesn't refer to mortals.

"Ask that Lunar assassin you train with, Kid," Ruby adds. "She'll explain."

Oh, geez. How involved were Hellebore and Eclipsa?

Magus and the others begin separating us into three groups. The second year and beyond mortals who already have keepers are placed into Seelie or Unseelie sides. The first year shadows without keepers go in the middle. My heart tugs as I watch the first years nervously clump together, their huge eyes darting over the Evermore.

I throw Mack one last fleeting look before we part. She joins our friends on the Seelie side, while I'm forced to squeeze into the Unseelie crowd.

I make sure I'm on opposite sides of Reina and her crew before returning my focus to the gazebos. Clematis the size of my hands adorn the structures. The blooms are different colors for each quadrant: pink, ice-blue, an unusual green, and burnt orange.

"They're grouped by seasonal courts," I say aloud. Inside each gazebo, luxuriously dressed Evermore sit on . . . thrones.

"Oh, crap," I hiss, halting so abruptly a boy runs into me from behind. "Is that—"

"The Winter King," Ruby finishes.

My blood goes cold as I scan the Fae inside. The Winter King and Queen occupy frosty thrones of ice. Inara stands with her parents beside them. And next to her—

A spike of excitement slams through my heart as I take in Valerian. His thick ink-blue hair has that familiar just-stum-bled-from-bed messiness, his sensual lips tilted in a lazy smile that doesn't quite reach his silver eyes.

My body reacts with such fervor at his presence that I bite

my cheek to tamp it down. As if he can feel my reaction, his bored gaze slides to me. Catches.

I thought I couldn't want him any more. But the moment our eyes meet, a chasm of need breaks open inside me—

I rip my gaze away and focus on my toes. The black lacquer Mack insisted on applying sparkles softly.

Yes, focus on your toes. Toes aren't sexy. They're weird, that's why we paint them.

Images of Valerian's bare feet from our one night together pop uninvited into my head . . . except they're not weird at all, but masculine and beautiful.

Get a hold of yourself, Summer!

I drag my attention away from Valerian, looking for something else—anything else to focus on. Beneath the Spring Court pavilion, Hellebore leans casually against a throne made of thick, tangled wisteria vines, obviously too cool to sit in the thing. The giant lavender buds match his silky purple shirt. Spring insects hover around their gazebo. Giant jewel-toned dragonflies, blue and yellow butterflies, and fat bumblebees.

His sister, Freesia, is dressed in similar colors. Beside her, their aunt, the Spring Court Queen, sits erect in a throne made from an enormous buttery-gold daffodil.

The sun seems to set all at once, bathing the courtyard in delicate champagne light. As if on cue, Cronus takes the stage that's been erected in the center of the platform.

"Welcome to the Evermore Academy Selection ceremony," the Master of Ceremonies drones. "This time-honored tradition spans centuries and features mortals from the finest stock. Each one hails from the wealthiest, most powerful echelons of human society. And each match benefits not only the Evermore they're paired with to protect, but your court as well. With the right shadow, you gain access to their invaluable connections in the mortal world."

I fight the urge to duck as a few shadows cut their eyes at me, snickering beneath their breath. They know what I know: My connections include a barren farm in the Tainted Zone, a group of orphans, and two stubborn, tough-as-nails aunts.

Not exactly invaluable, unless one needs to know how to make the perfect pitcher of sweet tea or sew a hem.

Don't worry about that. You're Valerian's shadow. This is all for show.

A low thrum of applause stirs the courtyard as Cronus beckons Hellebore to the stage.

The Spring Court Prince seems to grow taller with every step he takes toward the microphone. If he were mortal, he'd undoubtedly be a politician or an actor. He feeds off the adoration of the crowd. Devouring it in greedy gulps.

"At Whitehall Academy," he begins, "the Selection ceremony is one of our proudest traditions. It's also one of the most dangerous. We believe that to properly claim something, the prize must be won with violence and power."

My stomach hollows out as his words take hold, each one burrowing deep inside my chest and triggering alarm bells.

Violence and power.

The bloody Nocturus battle between Valerian and Rhaegar comes to mind. When I thought Rhaegar was going to kill Valerian—

I drag in a calming breath, but it does little to ease my growing fear. I can't go through that again. What if Valerian is hurt? What if whoever knows his true name is here?

The Winter Prince would be powerless.

"And what better way to test those powers than hold a Wild Hunt?" Hellebore continues, his smug gaze lingering on me. "I know that's what your academy called the final trial you all passed last year, but the true, ancient Wild Hunt of our ancestors is very different."

He lifts something up. Wrapped in purple velvet, the item

is roughly the size of a basketball. Gasps slip from the crowd as he removes the cover.

It takes a moment to realize the smooth, spiraling item is a horn. My body reacts viscerally, every muscle tensing as one word echoes through my skull.

Run.

"When I blow this horn, the hunt begins. The hellhounds will rise from the depths of the Fae underworld, as they've done since the beginning of time, and stalk any mortal not wearing this mark."

He summons one of the mortal attendants serving inside the pavilion. She doesn't even blink as he drags down the neckline of her blouse to reveal the strange symbol scrawled across her chest in . . . blood.

A jolt of panic constricts my vision.

Valerian's head whips in my direction. He mouths, *I'll find you.*

I give a brief nod, trying to look brave. But I know he can hear the heartbeat roaring in my ears, can probably feel the blood rush making my limbs feel heavy and my head spin.

Everything's happening too fast.

The tinkle of delicate metal clinking fills the courtyard. I claw to the surface of my panic just in time to make out the golden chains being passed around to the Evermore students.

Mother-freaking chains.

"The rules are simple." Hellebore holds up his chain to show off the two thick circlets of metal on either end, one small enough to fit a wrist, the other just large enough to go around a neck. "Once you have a shadow chained into submission, they are yours. Finders keepers."

"And the hounds?" someone questions from the Summer Court tent to my left.

Drugged nearly stupid by the cocktail of panic and fear poisoning my blood, I nearly don't recognize the Fae female speaking. Nearly—until the picture Valerian gifted me breaks through my desperate haze.

The Summer Queen . . . and my mother. Sort of. Not that I feel even a sliver of emotion looking at this regal Fae Queen.

Hellebore glances over at her in a way that makes me instantly think they would be enemies, if not for the alliance between Spring and Summer. "The hounds are ravenous, Queen Larkspur. By the ancient law of the hunt, they are allowed three mortals."

The wave of panic I've been drowning under lets up as another emotion takes over: fury. Once again, the Fae are proving just how dangerous they are to our world, our *survival*.

I glance over at the new shadow recruits in the middle. They look horrified, a few crying quietly.

Screw this. Shoving past the others, I step out from our group and lock eyes with Hellebore. Ruby hisses in my ear and tries to yank me back into the crowd, but I ignore her. "This is bullshit and you know it."

I swear the Fae-hole grins, as if this whole thing was a game to get me to react. "Excuse me?"

Ruby has resorted to pinching the back of my neck and cursing. Valerian and Eclipsa are glaring at me, both trying to force me to stay quiet, but right now, I'm so pissed, I despise them just for being a part of this deranged system. "No, you're not excused. We're not here for your entertainment. We're human beings with families and hopes and dreams . . ."

Silence. Frick. As if they care about any of that. I suddenly see myself through their eyes. Hands on my hips, dress barely covering my ass. My sprite attacking the back of my head like it wronged her in another life.

I thought it was quiet before, but when the Spring Queen rises from her throne, even the insects stop chirping. Her hair is the same delicate pale rose color of the castle, elaborately braided and pinned atop her head. Bile warms the back of my throat as I spot the live butterflies impaled on the pins.

"Who sponsored this mortal's enrollment?" The Spring Queen's voice is lazy and soft, like a sluggish breeze, but something about it makes my skin crawl.

I'm screwed. I learned from Mack that all mortals who apply to Evermore Academy have to have one Evermore sponsor. Nick's old keeper, a Summer Evermore high in the Summer Queen's inner circle, sponsored Mack.

But I have none of that.

Murmurs and gasps break the stillness, including my own, as the Summer Queen calls out, "I did."

Why is she protecting me?

Hellebores chuckles, obviously enjoying this. "Sponsoring insolent shadows and questioning our customs? Careful, Queen Larkspur, or one might think you've gone soft toward mortals."

"Soft? Questioning the deaths of mortals when our very survival may rest upon peace between our worlds isn't soft, it's clever. You should try it sometime."

I might not recognize the bond I shared with my Fae mother, but damn if I don't feel some sort of kinsmanship already.

My dead-beat Fae dad, on the other hand, has a lot to live up to. The Summer King's mouth tightens as he glances over at his wife, not bothering to hide his annoyance.

Hellebore grins. "True, most mortals flinch from our rules, yet still, the greedy amongst them willingly give us their children and strike bargains with us, all for the sake of power. I would suggest our kind and theirs are more similar than they'd like to admit."

Liar. If Mack's dads knew how dangerous the academy was, they would have found a way to buy out her contract.

"Still," the Summer Queen stubbornly argues, gaining my

immediate respect. "Forcing the shadows of the academy to endure the primal savagery of the Wild Hunt seems rather . . . cruel, even for Faerie. The hunt will drive every Evermore student to their primal state. Many will be crazed by the excitement of the hunt and the dark magic conjured. I fear, beyond what the hounds inflict, more shadows will be injured."

"The shadows of Evermore Academy have been allowed to forget what we truly are. They're too comfortable around us, too"—the mofo's gaze slides to mine—"insolent. This little lesson will be a lasting reminder. But, so that you can't say the Spring Court isn't clever, the hounds may only take one mortal. Satisfied?"

The Summer Queen nods.

My gut clenches as Hellebore raises the horn. All the shadows quietly look around, wondering which one of us the hounds will take.

My lips wrench back in a snarl that's every bit Fae. If they try to hurt Mack, I'll rip their throats out.

I steal one last look with Valerian. Something dark and predatory glints in his eyes, making him almost unrecognizable. That raw, animalistic savagery pours from every single Evermore, the alarming prickle of danger permeating the air.

Some have already begun to shift. Wings of every kind beat the night. White fangs glisten in place of normal teeth, voices become the snarl of beasts, and footsteps become claws scraping against stone.

The feline glow of nocturnal eyes blink around the courtyard.

"Don't look at them," Ruby hisses into my ear. "They're not your friends right now. When that mofo blows that horn, you run. And you don't stop running until I tell you it's safe."

Oh, hell. As if on cue, Hellebore presses the magical horn to his lips just as the last golden rays of sunlight begin to fade. The haunting wail of the horn blasts across the lush grounds.

The ancient song worms deep into my core, eliciting a mindless, instinctual terror.

Birds startle from the woods in the distance, the noisy swarm darkening the face of the rising moon as they take to the night sky. Heavy mist seeps from the velvety lawn like a thousand angry ghosts awakened from their graves.

My head whips to the sound of baying, the frenzied call of the hellhounds seeming to come from every direction.

Crap. My back and chest are suddenly damp, coated with sweat. *Sweat.* Aren't hounds attracted to smell? Did my stupid tendency to perspire when I'm nervous just mark me as the sacrifice?

I work to calm my mind, but it has the opposite effect. The chaotic din of my hammering pulse and wheezing breaths drowns out the world, my own personal soundtrack of horror —because being hunted by hellhounds and chained by frenzied Fae wasn't fricking terrifying enough.

Shimmer save me, I'm like a giant dog toy that's been stuffed with peanut butter and a squeaker. My body is basically screaming *eat me please.*

A shout drags my focus to the north just in time to spot the first hound. The giant ebony beast bursts from the churning sea of mist blanketing the hills. The size of a truck, the creature appears more wolf than hound.

Frozen, I take in the glowing red eyes and snarling snout, lined with jagged fangs and slobber.

Then I'm sprinting with the others as we run for our lives.

13

Despite being gripped by absolute, blind panic, my mind somehow decides it's helpful to remind myself this is the second time this week I've had to literally run for my life.

Gazelle. You're a mother-freaking gazelle.

Just like a gazelle, I fight and claw my way to the inside of the pack. National Geographic taught me the animals on the outside get picked off first.

Strength in numbers. I leap over a falling girl just before she disappears into the mist. My sandals are long gone, my dress riding up my thighs.

Maybe my pasty white ass will scare away the hounds. Either that or act as a beacon that draws them to me.

"That's it, Kid!" Ruby roars where she clings to the top of my head, her tiny fists clumped into my hair. I don't even have the mental capacity right now to be affronted by her riding my skull like a jockey.

Shouldering my way to the front, I scan the faces of the terrified shadows, desperate to find Mack.

"Leave her," Ruby demands. "Dragon boy will keep her safe."

I don't care what Ruby says. I'm not leaving my friend until I see her with Asher.

Mist swirls around our waists, so thick I can't make out the ground. The baying of the hounds is growing louder.

Four shadows go down ahead, tripped by something.

"Jump!" Ruby shrieks just as the top few inches of a hedge appear in front of me.

Fueled on adrenaline, I leap, clearing the bush like an Olympic hurdler.

"Again!"

My heart pounds in rhythm to my feet as I sprint, leap. Sprint, leap. My need to find Mack overrides my urge to help those who have fallen.

As I'm forced to block out their cries, my hatred for the Fae surges into a searing inferno.

The garden gives way to a sloping lawn, and the crowd spreads out. Someone calls my name behind me and to my right. Mack! She's trapped behind a trio of three girls who keep tripping.

"No!" Ruby yells as I swerve to meet Mack.

Ignoring the enraged sprite digging her toes into my temples, I swoop next to Mack, grab her arm, and drag her around the trio.

Mack's eyes are wide as she pumps her arms, struggling to catch up. "Summer! I thought—"

A roar splits the night. We both look to see one of the girls from the tree get taken down by a dark, hulking beast. My fear ratchets up a notch as I see how the wolfish creature tosses her around like a rag doll, too overcome with its predatory instinct to remember she's mortal and therefore breakable.

"Lycan," Mack hisses.

The shaggy creature is about to slip its chain around the girl's neck when another fully shifted lycan slams into the beast. They explode into a violent brawl over the girl.

"Asher will find me," Mack pants. "We just need to not get taken until then."

The mist is growing thicker. The shadows are slowing, disoriented by the chaotic crush of bodies and fog. Screams pepper the air all around us as the Evermore begin picking off the stragglers.

"Ditch this herd of bumbling idiots," Ruby orders.

I'm not sure when my drunken sprite became the de facto leader of this shitshow, but she's right. I spot a path into the woods up ahead on the left. Grabbing Mack's hand, I cut sideways, my bare feet pounding the lawn. Mack struggles to keep up with my pace, but I drag her along with sheer willpower.

The mist lessens inside the forest, enough that I can pick out the path. Moonlight filters down softly. The horrifying din of growls and cries fade until I can almost pretend it's coming from some bad horror movie and not real life.

This isn't happening. We're not being chased by crazed half-shifted Fae and hellhounds on a Wild Hunt with chains.

That delusion gets ripped to shreds as the forest explodes behind us, followed by a howl so loud it shakes the trees.

"Faster!" Ruby orders, kicking her heels into my head.

A few other shadows followed us, and we all sprint down the trail as the hound gains on us. Branches scratch at my face and arms, brambles gouging my bare legs and tearing my dress. My bare feet slip and slide over mud and moss and rocks.

A sudden clearing opens up. A few feet in the distance, the earth gives way. A churning river burbles below the cliffs, the dark blue ribbon cutting through the canyon. The river ends abruptly . . .

A waterfall. A really high waterfall, from the loud roar of the crashing water.

"We're trapped," Mack pants.

Limbs crack in the woods behind us as the hound closes in. I glance around, desperate for a way to escape, and spot something dark shooting from the sky straight toward us.

Valerian! The figure's wings flare out as he slows his descent to land. As I make out the leathery gray wings and green markings, disappointment fills me.

Not Valerian.

Pushing aside my emotions, I insert myself in front of Mack as the dragon shifter prowls toward us. I scan his face for signs his predatory nature has taken over completely.

Yellow, bestial eyes watch Mack, their pupils slit down the middle. Other than his wings, he's managed to halt his transformation to full dragon.

"Stop right there!" I yell as the others all huddle behind me. Besides Mack and the sprite now attached to my head, three shadows—two girls and a boy—are trapped on the cliff.

Slowly, he drags his intense gaze off Mack. Recognition flares in those eerie dragon eyes—too slow for comfort, but he may be our only hope.

"You're both coming with me," he orders, holding his large hands out in front of him. "I'm taking you both to safety."

"No." I jerk my head toward the woods. "Not until you fly everyone to the other side first."

His nostrils flare, and I see him fighting his inner dragon as his attention keeps gravitating to Mack.

Mack steps forward. "Please, Asher. Take them first and then come back for us. I swear, once we're all safely on the other side, you can have me."

Instead of talking sense into him, the sound of her voice seems to elicit a crazed excitement inside dragon boy, and I prepare myself to fight the giant idiot. Right now, he's the only thing standing between the other students and the approaching hellhound.

Somewhere deep inside, he must know Mack would never forgive him if he let the other students get hurt, because he releases a frustrated snarl before backing down.

"Okay, I'll help them." His voice is gravelly, but at least it sounds like him now, some of the magic from the hunt wearing off.

He flicks another longing gaze at my friend. Then he swoops the first two shadows into his brawny arms, one student literally lodged on either side like footballs, and shoots across the canyon. I hardly take a breath before he's back.

I scour the star-encrusted sky. "Where's the Winter Prince?"

"Eclipsa is fighting him off. He can't be around you yet. Not until the magic of the hunt wears off. That's why I'm here."

"Surely if you can control it, so can he?"

The dragon shifter blinks at me, as if talking while trying to control himself is too much. "Don't let him near you right now, Summer."

He wraps Mack and the final girl into his arms. His wings flare as he prepares to rocket them into the sky.

"No," Mack protests, trying to wiggle from his grasp. "Take Summer first and then return for me."

But I can see by the intensity of his stare that there's no more holding him back from her, which fits right into my plan anyway.

They streak across the canyon to the other side. I watch, relief pouring through me.

"Hurry up, lizard breath," Ruby mutters, pacing anxiously on top of my head.

"The Winter Prince will be here soon," I say. I don't care what Asher says, Valerian won't hurt me.

Ruby tugs on a strand of my hair, hard. "Don't be such a naive human! What do you think will happen with that thing between you and him you pretend isn't real?"

After Inara publicly implied the soulbond was a mistake, I let my friends believe that was the truth.

But the look in Ruby's eyes says there's no hiding the truth, so I don't bother trying.

"He can control it," I insist.

"Maybe before," she remarks. "But when the horn was activated, the magic dredged from the depths of the Fae hells amplified his primal urges a hundred fold, including that. If he finds you before it wears off, he won't be able to control himself."

"You don't know him, Ruby—"

"He's an Evermore, Kid. He may have been able to resist the mating bond before, but only because he spends every second around you fighting the beast that lives inside him. The Fae are tied to nature in a way mortals will never understand, but the Evermore have a direct line to that raw, ancient power. Have you ever seen something in nature not take what it wants?"

Take what it wants? I shiver. "So, you're saying . . .?"

"If he finds you in his present state, nothing in this world will stop him from making you his mate."

I know the power of that bond as is—but amplified a hundred fold? I can't even imagine something that strong.

Before I can respond, a low growl sounds from the forest line.

The hound.

I flick a desperate glance to the other side to see Asher fighting another Evermore, this one nearly completely shifted into a bear. Their roars reverberate through the canyon.

I pivot back to face the hound just as the lupine beast bursts from the trees. As I take in the fiery red eyes, shaggy coal-black fur rippling with muscle, and bared fangs, primal terror takes hold, stripping the air from my lungs.

Warmth blooms from my chest. A green light radiates from my sternum and pulses across the night. The hound sits back on its hindquarters for a moment, shaking its head and seemingly stunned.

What the frick?

Did that come from my pendant? I pull at the chain but . . . no, in the chaos, my pendant got turned around and rests against my back.

That came from inside me.

"Giant hairy orc balls," Ruby hisses. "How did you do that?"

"Do what?" I whisper, slowly walking backward away from the hellhound, who's gotten over his stupor and is approaching, curved incisors bared. Saliva drips from each fang.

My panic grows as I take in its protruding ribs and sharp backbone. *Oh, hell. This thing looks starved.*

"You sent off a distress signal or something." Ruby dives from my head and flits in front of me, hands on her temples, shaking her head back and forth.

"Like the bat signal?" I murmur just as my feet reach the edge of the cliff at my back. Rocks clatter down the cliffside into the raging river.

"I don't know! It was a giant call for help. You know, like a wounded rabbit caught in a trap that screams . . ."

"Only to attract bigger predators," I finish as silhouettes emerge from the shadowy woods.

I scan the Evermore, but I know deep down none of them are Valerian. I would feel his presence if he were close.

The hound halts, its shaggy head whipping to face the Evermore, a low warning snarl spilling from its deep chest.

Whatever it sees, the hellhound's growl becomes a low whine as it ducks back into the woods and flees.

For some reason, I remember Hellebore's words about the predators fighting each other off to claim their prey. Only whoever is stalking this way is so terrifying that the hellhound didn't even try to fight for me.

14

When the approaching Evermore laughs, my worst fears come to life. Inara. At least before, she couldn't outright act on her hatred of me. But now, jacked up on primordial magic straight from the depths of the Fae Hells, she looks like she could eviscerate me and wear my entrails as a necklace without batting an eye.

As she stalks closer, I realize she's mostly still in her non-shifted form, although her eyes have taken on a feline quality, and fangs protrude from her upper lip.

That would seem like a good sign except flanking her are three fully shifted Evermore. The first, a sleek snow leopard with faded silver spots and menacing features, is definitely Bane. The second, a beautiful gray wolf, is probably Lyra, her lycan bestie.

And I recognize the part wolf, part elk creature near the back as Rhaegar. His lupine gaze is near unrecognizable as he watches me with a terrible hunger.

Inara's cruel grin settles low in my stomach. "We heard your cry for help, little lamb. Were you calling for your

Winter Prince?" She makes a show of looking around while the others slowly circle me. "A shame, he's not here. I guess he's finally tired of you."

All the moisture shrivels from my mouth as I scour the area for an escape route. Nothing. I throw a quick glance over my shoulder at Asher—

"Grayscale won't save you either," Inara adds. "He's going to be busy for a while, I think."

Clenching my jaw, I force myself to face her. Something glints from her hand—a golden chain.

I raise an eyebrow. "I'm flattered you want me as your shadow, Inara, but I'll die before you get that metal around my neck."

"If you insist." She swings the chain in little circles as she draws closer. "But I don't want you, idiot. Someone else decided you'd make an entertaining pet. He probably heard how fond you are of your Keepers."

Crap. Only one dickwad prince could make her do his bidding. Hellebore. I eye the chain, heart jackhammering into my ribs. "Are you forgetting what Hellebore did the last time you tried to mess with me?"

Her head falls back as she laughs. "You think he cares if I hurt you? He's watching us right now."

That mofo. Hoping he can hear me, I shout, "What kind of spineless bastard has others do his dirty work?"

"The kind that likes to play twisted little games with lesser creatures like yourself." She grins, lifting the chain. "Now come here, little lamb. It's time to see if we can tame you."

I bolt to my right, but Bane is on me in a flash, his mouth stretched wide, showing off his inch-long fangs. I pivot to my left, only to run up against Lyra as she charges, herding me back to my spot on the cliff.

My heart pounds in my skull, mixing with the sound of the rushing water at my back.

Desperation kicks in. Ruby has taken to the air and is dive bombing the Evermore, trying to take their attention away from me. Bane swipes the air with his claws, barely missing Ruby. Lyra snaps at the air trying to catch her.

The plucky sprite keeps attacking.

Any one of those blows could kill her . . .

"Ruby!" I plead. "Get out of here."

Inara grins as her eyes shift to the stubborn sprite, who refuses to give up her hopeless attack. Refuses to save herself, because she's the best damn sprite in the entire Everwilde.

And now, Inara is going to hurt her.

No. My insides twist as I read the intention in Inara's sneer.

Something inside me snaps. *No more.*

Baring my teeth, I lunge forward before the others can stop me and catch Inara with a roundhouse kick to the face. My bare foot smacks her jaw with a satisfying *crack.*

I'm going to savor that sound for the rest of my undoubtedly short existence.

Her eyes widen. She was expecting me to retreat, to beg and plead. Not to fight back.

If murder had a face, it would be Inara's right now. I'm so going to pay for that.

But not right now. Using her surprise, I snatch Ruby from the air, shoot for the cliff, and leap.

The second my feet push off the rocky side and the ground disappears, the absolute insanity of my decision becomes apparent.

Shitshitshit—

My stomach churns as I careen toward the raging river.

"Kid, you're a badass!" Ruby screams, throwing her arms into the air as if she's on the best rollercoaster ride of her life.

As I release my fingers, sending Ruby to freedom, I can't help but think that's the greatest compliment Ruby could ever give me.

Oh, goody, maybe they can put it on your tombstone.

Frothy waves swallow me.

The force of the river takes my breath away. I claw to the surface, gasping, trying to escape the water's wrath as it slams me into boulders, holds me under, and knocks me in circles until I can't tell which way is up.

By the time I find a log to cling to, the roar of the waterfall is deafening. I catch Ruby darting above me. She's holding a limp willow branch as if she could possibly pull me up.

"Grab ahold, Kid!" Ruby screeches, her voice filled with pure terror.

But it's too late. I hit the edge of the waterfall with just enough time to look over and realize how far down below the water is. Hundreds of feet.

Hundreds. Too high to survive. From this distance, every bone in my body will break.

For some reason, Hellebore's voice slithers into my mind. *I can fly. Can you?*

They won. Inara, Hellebore, the whole evil lot of them. Rage pierces my core. I scramble for a foothold on the rocky bottom. For an indention in one of the nearby boulders to grab. I buck against the river's force, fighting the violent current with all my strength.

I've never wanted to live more than now, just so I can watch the hateful smirk drain from their eyes as they realize I survived. My will to live is a spiteful, burning thing. Greater than anything I've ever felt before.

It's so powerful, so real, that I actually think it could magically change my circumstances.

But that doesn't happen because no matter how much I negotiate and plead with it, gravity's a bitch.

The second the water shoots me into the air, legs churning and dress tangled around my face, I drop like a freaking rock.

A falling feeling hollows out my stomach, and then I'm tumbling down the waterfall to my death.

15

I always assumed in the seconds before my death, some weird type of calm would come over me, like the clarity main characters in movies find right before they pass away. Instead, I'm pissed. Rage-kicking the air as I freefall. Screaming every curse word I can muster.

One second I'm hurtling toward the lake below.

The next, the world around me goes still as my body jerks to a halt. The force knocks the breath from my lungs in a whoosh. The dark silhouette of wings blot out the stars as they beat the air, which has suddenly gone ice cold.

And I know. I just know.

"Valerian?" I breathe, afraid this is some death dream. A final firing of my synapses.

That the sharp ache throbbing inside my chest, the one I only feel when I'm around him, is fear-induced.

The arms around my waist tighten almost . . . possessively. "Don't move. Please."

The low, rasping voice is Valerian's—yet different. Primordial. Almost . . . bestial.

Something about it scrapes down my spine.

I shiver, drowning the urge to face my protector as my instincts warn me into absolute stillness. My belly lurches as we dive beneath the falls.

The curtain of water gives way to darkness. We're inside a cave of sorts. The air damp and cold.

Despite Valerian's warning, as soon as my bare feet feel slippery ground beneath them, I pivot, jerking away from him and—

"Valerian?" I whisper, startled by his face.

"Don't look at me," he growls.

My body tenses, but I refuse his plea. He hasn't provided any magic to chase away the shadows, but the moonlight filtering through the watery curtain illuminates just enough of his features to make me gasp.

Somehow he's even more beautiful than I recall, but in a dark, unnerving way that sends my adrenaline through the roof. His normally cliffed cheekbones are inhumanly jagged, his peaked eyebrows sharper, and his eyes . . . oh, God.

His eyes are wild. Feral. Brimming with ancient, unfathomable power.

His pupils are perhaps the most terrifying of all. Huge black pits anchored inside a sea of molten silver.

It's like it's him—but not.

A low rumble starts in his chest. "Back away slowly, as far away as you can from me."

The breath catches in my throat as I obey, inching backward. My focus snags on the black tee pasted to his body. The muscles of his torso shiver and jerk, his chest heaving, hands clenched at his sides. Water drips from his messy midnight blue hair, the moisture drawing out the waviness.

A few strands have already started to freeze.

That's when I notice the gash in his side. The silver blood dripping from it.

"What happened?" I whisper, struggling to keep the

worry from my tone. Afraid any emotion at all will send him over the edge. "Are you hurt?"

His gaze slowly travels down to his side, back up to me, as if he was unaware of his injury. A muscle in his neck jerks. "I heard you call out, I could feel your fear. They tried to stop me but—"

My foot snags on a rock, and I stumble backward.

I don't even see him move, but before I know what's happening, he's pinned me to the cave wall. His arms post on either side of my head, caging me in.

"Val—"

His hands slip under my wet dress and—

Oh, boy. The moment his fingers touch the bare flesh of my stomach, I know I'm lost. Utterly destroyed. Heat surges in waves through my core as he slides his hands behind my back to cup my ass.

Growling, he lifts me up, using the wall as leverage, and hell if I can't do anything but wrap my legs around his waist and circle my arms around his neck.

Dark excitement flickers inside his eyes. There are no words between us as he holds my stare. Daring me to look at him. To finally accept this thing between us.

I gasp as he slides his hand through my tangled hair, capturing the strands, and tilts my head back slightly.

With his other hand, he brushes the rough pad of his thumb over my lower lip. "When I heard you calling for me, everything faded away but you, and I knew in that moment that I would burn down the entire fucking Everwilde to protect you."

His lips crush mine, his tongue claiming my mouth, making it clear this time is different than the last. There is no gentleness, no holding back. A rush of dizziness overwhelms me.

I melt into him. Wanting more, more, more—

His attention moves on to my throat. I arch my back as his teeth scrape up my neck, nipping, and then when his mouth finds my ear—

The sigh I make is a cross between a moan and a plea. For him to stop or continue, I don't know.

I don't know.

Crap.

"You're mine, Summer." His breath is cold as it tickles my ear, his words clicking something inside me into place, the answer to a forgotten question I'd asked long ago. "Do you understand? Mine, and I will slaughter anyone who tries to take you from me."

Fuck.

My brain is scrambled. I can't find the words to respond. The clarity of mind to articulate why this is a bad idea . . .

Why don't I want this?

How could I not?

Holy mother trucker, the things running through my head right now would make Aunt Vi fall over dead.

Aunt Vi! Focus on Aunt Vi!

But, oh Lordy, there's only a thin, wet tee between Valerian's flesh and my bare thighs, and that shirt is pissing me off. I tug at it, growling like a deranged lunatic, single-mindedly set on murdering the overly expensive piece of fabric.

The rational part of me understands what's happening. We're both reacting to the magical bond between us, just as helpless to escape its grip as I was against the river's immense power.

But the other part of me doesn't want to understand. She doesn't want to think about anything at all except the ache building inside her, begging for release.

When I succeed in twisting his damp shirt high enough that our flesh meets—his skin cool and hard and startling against my feverish thighs—he whips his head back to stare at me.

Our eyes lock, and a new wave of emotions slams into me, eclipsing my physical desires.

I gasp as a current of power blasts through my middle. It's his—or mine. Or maybe both of ours merging into one stream.

The air around us shimmers hot and cold. Either I'm hallucinating or there's butterflies and snowflakes swirling around us, a collision of hot and cold, summer and winter.

Whoa, this is some kinky, crazy stuff.

Muscles feather in his jaw as he murmurs through clenched teeth, "Summer, if you're not ready, tell me now. In a few seconds, neither one of us will be able to stop."

Won't be able to stop. Why would I want to stop?

I blink. This is my choice, right? I know I want this, but . . .

Pale light draws my focus to the golden chain fixed to his wrist—

I throw my hand up, startled by the cold bite of metal circling my neck.

He notices my confusion and says, "I had to claim you before someone else could."

Claim you. You're mine. I'll slaughter anyone else who tries to take you from me.

That's not love, a nagging voice whispers, *that's possession.*

Reality comes crashing in to ruin the party. The butterflies and snowflakes evanesce. My desire drains, leaving me overwhelmingly aware of my other physical needs.

I'm shivering. Half in shock from nearly dying.

"Put me down . . . please."

To his credit, he reacts immediately, gently bracing his hands on my waist as he steps back, guiding my unsteady feet to the ground.

The moment we break apart, our flesh no longer touching,

the predatory sharpness in his features softens, and his stare goes from ravenous, like I'm something to be guarded and devoured, to concerned.

"Summer, you're freezing." He looks around to the frost icing the walls, the waterfall . . . now frozen solid. His gaze drops to the chain pulled nearly taut between us. "Shit. I had no idea—"

Voices draw our attention to the wall of ice just in time to see it explode as Eclipsa and Asher bust through, Ruby a second behind them. They halt when they see us, Ruby slamming into the back of dragon boy's head. I can tell by their silence they're wondering if they're too late.

Eclipsa steps forward carefully. "Summer, are you okay?"

I nod, even as I want to point out the chain around my fricking neck, which is abso-fricking-lutely not okay.

I know it's not Valerian's fault—I *know* that. If he hadn't claimed me, someone else would have, but . . . I'm still pissed and ashamed to be leashed like an animal. And that he did it so stealthily while I was busy grinding over his body like it was a stripper pole and . . . oh, God.

Wait till I tell Mack—Oberon's beard, Mack! "What happened to Mack?"

"She's back at the Selection, safe," Asher assures me.

"And is she . . ." The word claimed sticks in my chest like glass.

"She's my shadow," Asher says carefully.

And for some reason the diplomatic way he says this reminds me of Valerian, who had absolutely zero qualms declaring I was his like a toddler fighting for a toy on the playground.

You're mine.

Eclipsa takes another step—

Valerian lodges himself in front of me, growling low. I guess we're still on the playground.

My stupid leash jerks taut, the metal biting into the back of my neck. Cold blasts through the cave, a blizzard of giant snowflakes pummeling the walls.

Asher growls his annoyance, glaring morosely at the snowflakes, but Eclipsa holds up her hand. "It's me. Eclipsa. Your friend, remember? You're still under the influence of the hunt's magic. We're not going to hurt Summer."

Asher circles around to me, slowly, his eyes on Valerian. Ruby has crept stealthily around the backside of the cave and takes her spot on my shoulder, ready to battle.

"I thought you died, Kid," she murmurs.

"Nope, unless you can die of shame, I'm still very much alive, unfortunately."

Frowning, her gaze slides to my metal collar. Fury settles in her eyes, and I realize that she's also bound to the Evermore, basically a slave.

I wait, expecting some sort of snide remark. Or worse, pity. But she simply holds my stare, a look of solidarity passing between us.

Eclipsa dares another step closer. "Look at Summer. She's freezing. You need to get control of your magic."

Valerian glances back. Whatever he sees breaks through the protective urges driving his actions, and the blizzard abruptly stops.

Asher holds out a hand to me. "Let her go, Prince. I'd hate to have to kick your ass in front of an audience."

I tense as I wait for Valerian to react poorly. But his shoulder's loosen, the violence bleeding from his posture. "You could try, fire lizard."

"There's the cocky prince we know and love," Eclipsa quips, her stance going from primed for fighting to casual indifference. "I thought I was going to have to kill you, idiot."

He chuckles, his voice back to that familiar teasing arrogance. "You tried, remember? You ripped open my side."

"Yeah," Eclipsa says. "And you deserved it, you animal. If you'd gotten to Summer in the beginning, in that state . . ."

Her words hang in the air, their implication clear. The others glance at me, and the pity in their eyes is like the cherry on top of this whole effed up scenario.

Chased by hellhounds on a Wild Hunt. Check.

Nearly tortured and given as a present to the psychopathic Spring Court heir. Check.

Almost drowned in a river and then murdered by a waterfall. Check.

Turned into a horny hooker and nearly bound to an Evermore for eternity against my will.

Check. Check. Frickin check.

All of those things, sprinkled over a lifetime, would mess someone up. But crammed into less than an hour?

I release a ragged breath as Asher rushes over and performs a quick spell for warmth. I didn't realize exactly how cold I was until the heat sinks into my flesh, stinging the more frozen bits like my fingers and toes.

Valerian is still as he watches me, quiet, his face twisted in conflict, as if he wants to help but is afraid I'll hate him.

Do I? As soon as the question comes, I know I could never hate him. Never. And yet, the thing between us that I felt, the thing that made me lose all reason, terrifies me now more than ever.

Eclipsa gives me a knowing look as she approaches. "Prince, we need to get her back to the ceremony to finalize the Selection."

"No," I say. "If I'm going to let myself be traipsed in front of the entire academy like a pet on a leash, I need some answers."

Once again, Valerian's gaze flicks to the chain between us. Just another reminder of his claim over me. Our eyes meet, and I see the apology inside those silver pools—along with that smoldering fire of possessiveness that promises what he said was true.

He would burn the Everwilde to the ground to protect me, to keep me.

Eclipsa raises a silver eyebrow. "Answers about what, exactly?"

"Why the Winter Prince had to leave so suddenly before school started, for starters." My hand hovers over my heart, where the power seemed to come from earlier. "Also, I think I might have used magic somehow."

They share a look, their expressions not matching my surprise. Did they suspect that might happen?

Something passes between Eclipsa and Valerian, and then Eclipsa turns to me. "We'll tell you everything, I promise. But not right now. Your friend is worried, and until you're back at the Selection ceremony, you're fair game. Any Evermore could fight the Winter Prince for you."

My stomach sinks at the thought of Inara or Hellebore claiming me. "Fine, but I want to know by the end of the weekend, especially since I suspect whatever caused him to leave involves me."

I threw that last bit in on a whim, but the way Eclipsa's mouth tightens, I know I hit on the truth.

Crap.

The portal Valerian forms illuminates the air, the silver-blue edges the same color as his eyes. I follow him through the magical disk, resisting the urge to grip the collar around my neck. He's careful to leave enough slack that I don't choke, but I still feel like I'm gasping to breathe.

On the other side, I lift my head high.

The Evermore might have found yet another way to humiliate and demean us, but I won't let it break me.

16

My phone is facedown on my bed next to where I'm sprawled, books open around me.

"ILB?" Mack asks as she hops down from the top bunk and pads to the bar cart in the corner of our room.

I never told her what happened Friday night in the cave, other than that Inara tried to murder me and then Valerian saved me. But my best friend's perceptive—and also stubborn as hell—and she hasn't stopped prying for details.

I check the phone, ignoring the tug of disappointment when I realize it's not Valerian, but Eclipsa. She wants me to meet her at the gym in an hour.

Time to learn why Valerian was in the Winter Court and just how effed my life is about to get. I mean, I assumed it couldn't get much worse—but I forgot the rule while living in the Everwilde.

For mortals, there's always worse.

Today, I'm just a girl technically enslaved to my soulmate and singled out by the Evermore students. Bad . . . sure. But tomorrow I could find myself fighting in the scourge or chained to a stage in a skeevy club owned by Valerian's dad.

"Silver linings," I mutter.

"What?" Mack calls over her shoulder. She's fumbling around with a coffee filter, trying to figure out where to insert it in our new coffee maker. "Hey, how do you foam the milk for the latte?"

I swallow down my chuckle. The expensive espresso machine—named George for George Michael, her favorite singer—is the latest victim of Mack's new resolution to live like regular students.

Whatever that means, since most of the regular students are trust fund babies who pay more for a haircut than I'll spend in a year. But, her dads are a bit . . . generous, especially when it comes to buying her stuff, so I understand her reasoning—even if losing George is a freaking travesty.

"I don't think Fred comes with those options," I say.

Fred, short for Freddie Mercury, is the new twenty dollar Target coffee maker Mack bought from Jace, whose parents run a business ferrying mortal products in the Everwilde. They're the Amazon of the Everwilde and, if the rumors are true, every bit as rich.

I hop from the bed and pocket the phone. "But I think there might be some creamer in the fridge downstairs, if you want me to grab it?"

"Dang. I miss George." She flips to face me, her bottom lip caught between her teeth. "Whatever, we'll make Fred work."

I hate that Reina has made Mack question her rightful place here. Sure, Mack's a legacy, and that helped, but she's also the hardest working student on campus. She's earned her spot like everyone else.

She watches me slip on my sneakers. "Where are you going? Extra training?"

"No," I say too quickly. "Eclipsa wanted to cover some stuff I don't understand, but it's not actual training."

Not a lie, but my face burns with guilt anyway, and I focus on double and triple knotting my laces.

Regular after school guardian training starts this week, but ever since the gauntlets were announced, worried Keepers have already started booking out the gym for private sessions with their shadows.

Mine are mostly in the morning with Eclipsa, but Valerian texted late last night to inform me we have two sessions a week after regular combat class together.

I waited for funny emojis or a clever remark in the message, but that was it. The single text he sent me Saturday morning, after I'd slept off the entire embarrassing ordeal, was just as short.

I'm sorry things got out of hand.

Not sure what I was expecting, but after going full on horny hooker, I expected more than seven measly words in a text.

"Asher said the gym schedule this week is already full," Mack adds, "so he talked the ILB into letting him train me during your appointment. Apparently Instant Lady Boner rented the entire gym out so you two could be alone." She flashes a devilish grin that brings out both cheek dimples. "If you want that—some time alone with him—I'll tell Asher this week is no good."

I look away before she can see the conflicting emotions raging through me. Sometimes I wonder if she suspects that the mating ceremony wasn't a fluke after all. I kind of just let her assume it was after I was expelled because that was easier than trying to explain the truth.

And when I discovered the danger attached to my history . . .

No way will I subject Mack to that hot mess.

"Summer?" Mack says, concern in her eyes.

"What?" I blink as her last question slowly surfaces. "Hell

no. Chicks before dicks, bae before Fae, remember? And you're my only bae. Besides, you deserve extra training time like everyone else to prepare for the gauntlet. If you didn't pass . . ." I shake my head, sending the idea back to the dark hole from whence it came. "That will never happen because A, you're the best student here and B, I need you. Got it? Even if that means training five times a day with dragon boy."

"I mean, if that's what it takes to pass, I'll force myself to do extra sessions with Asher, but I won't like it."

We break into hysterical laughter, earning more than a few weird looks from our dormmates passing by the open door.

Tears of laughter stream down her face as she wraps me in a hug. "I don't deserve you, bae."

I hug her back, knowing the opposite is true: Mackenzie Fairchild is the love of my life, and I'll never understand why she chose me as her best friend. Never.

"Can we please demand George back?" I whisper.

She squeezes me harder. "Shh, Fred will hear you! He's temperamental."

Great. I'm so going to punish Reina for this.

I find Eclipsa wiping down her eggplant purple yoga mat. Her text said to wear comfortable clothes, and I realize why when she pats the pink mat beside hers. I settle next to her, glancing at the two empty mats behind us.

"Someone joining us?" I say, but my heart already knows, and it stutters into a frantic rhythm just as the doors swing open and Valerian enters, followed by Asher.

Both wear black joggers and soft cotton tees that show off

their athletic bodies. Holy hell, they could be models in a sportswear campaign.

This time, I'm prepared for the lightning bolt that spears my middle as our eyes meet. But prepared or not, I still gasp beneath my breath as the raw strength of the connection pulses to life.

Valerian stiffens before dragging his focus away. As they both prowl toward us like the badass predators they are, Asher throws me a wink.

"Princess," dragon boy says by way of greeting as he somehow fits his bulky body onto his mat and falls into a surprisingly graceful pose. He ignores the pink and yellow Hello Kitty mat Eclipsa provided for him, much to Eclipsa's disappointment.

Valerian, at least, hesitates for a hot second as he spots his SpongeBob SquarePants mat. Wrinkling his nose, he peers at the giant image of Patrick, slides his gaze to Asher's Hello Kitty print, and says, "Why did he get the adorable cat and I get the weird . . . whatever this is."

I barely swallow down my chuckle. There's so much about mortal culture he doesn't know still.

Asher draws his muscular body into a bakasana pose with an ease that startles me and mutters, "Because I didn't try to eviscerate her a few nights ago, so I get the cute kitty while you get the pink lumpy creature."

Frowning, Valerian begins to stretch. I do the same, willing my limbs to stop trembling, my breath to even out. The feet between us feel like inches. The aura from his presence seeping across the space and into my bones.

Sweat slicks my palms as I perform a downward dog pose. Sweet Baby Jesus, if I'd known my butt was going to be in his face, I'd have worn my loose sweatpants instead of my skin-tight black leggings.

In my periphery, I catch Eclipsa trying to muffle her

devilish grin. I'm guessing this is a form of punishment for the prince after his behavior during the Wild Hunt.

"I thought we were going to discuss why the prince traveled to the Winter Court?" I mumble just as a bead of sweat slides down my forehead and into my eye.

Eclipsa twists into a spider pose, her face a picture of relaxation despite holding a pose that would break me in half. "We are. But no reason we shouldn't get a session in while we do, right?"

I trade an exasperated look with Asher, who appears just as grumpy as I am right now, despite his flawless form. Ignoring Valerian, who's stare keeps flicking my way like tiny slivers of sleet peppering my skin, I ask, "How, exactly, did you all learn yoga?"

Everyone looks away. Crap. What did I say wrong?

Valerian glares down at poor Patrick as he growls, "Let's get this over with."

His mood shift leaves me feeling dizzy. *Pretend your hands and feet are roots, Summer.* But Eclipsa's trick for balance barely touches me, and it takes all my energy not to land on my face.

"The night before school started," Eclipsa begins, "there was an attack at the old Lunar Court palace."

"Darklings?" I roll into my Warrior II pose.

Eclipsa shakes her head, her silver ponytail whipping back and forth. "There were darklings used in the attack, but we think they acted under the influence of an Evermore. They . . ." Her gaze skips to Valerian and then back to me. "During the attack, someone stole the Darken's soulstone."

I give up on the extended side angle I was trying and sit on my ass. "I'm sorry, the what?"

Valerian's face is emotionless as he explains. "Every Evermore is given one at birth for their first soulmancy rites. I showed you mine, remember?"

The owl pendant.

"My grandfather's soulstone is made from black tourmaline, the only gemstone found in nature that can hold a soul as powerful as his."

"I'm sorry," I say. "Can you back up to the part where the soul of the Evermore responsible for nearly destroying our worlds is stored somewhere?" My voice has gone high and breathy. "You store bacon grease and jam, not souls of evil tyrants intent on mass destruction."

"Remember when I told you all Evermore keep a tiny sliver of their soul in a soulstone they're given at birth?" Eclipsa asks, her voice unusually patient. "And how that soulstone plays an integral part of the soulmancy process?"

My hand flutters to my own soulstone pendant, a ruby held inside a wolf's mouth, and I nod.

"As long as your soulstone survives, your soul cannot be destroyed, only transferred, like energy. The second the wearer dies, their soul automatically returns to their soulstone to await transfer to a new body."

"If a Fae's not an Evermore, where does their soul go?" I ask, trying to remember her lesson on the complicated matter.

"All Fae spirits are tied to Everwilde," Eclipsa says. "If a Fae dies without a soulstone, their spirit rejoins the land."

That definitely rings a bell. I recall Professor Lambert explaining all souls from the lesser Fae not deemed Evermore eventually seep into the land of their ancestors. Their spirits manifest as nature—sometimes in the form of an animal, a tree, even a rock—and contributes to the magic others from their court can draw upon.

There are exceptions. For instance, Mack told me once, if an Evermore runs afoul of the council, they might find their soul imprisoned in the seven Fae hells, a magical Fae prison set in a pocket realm of the Everwilde.

"Why not just send the Darken to the seven Fae hells?"

Eclipsa scowls at my use of King Oberon's other name.

"Because the prison has suffered major breaches over the years, so the Evermore council chose to store his soulstone on Starfall Island."

I raise an eyebrow, and Valerian adds, "Starfall Island used to belong to the Lunar Court, before the Lunar Court was banished for their part in the Darken's war and the island was claimed by the council." Eclipsa goes still at the mention of her banished court, and Valerian flicks his gaze to her before continuing. "Now, the Lunar palace acts as a vault to hold the most dangerous artifacts in Everwilde, including the Darken's soulstone."

I blow out a breath. I'm not even pretending to do yoga now. "I'm assuming the vault was guarded and warded?"

"Heavily." Valerian's brow furrows. "Whoever broke in and stole the stone had been planning the attack for months, possibly years."

Eclipsa sits cross-legged facing me. "Since all the courts distrust each other, they each have their own guards and spells protecting the palace."

"Crap." I massage my temples. "So whoever took the stone has to be powerful."

"Very," Valerian says, and something about his soft tone worries me. "But all the power in the Everwilde couldn't break those defenses unless someone betrayed them from the inside."

"And," I finish proudly, "because every court had a hand in defending the vault, it's near impossible to determine a suspect, and they're all blaming each other."

Asher winks proudly at me, impressed.

"So the prince went home," I continue, working out the angles as I speak, "because someone suspects the Winter Court?"

"Not just suspects," Eclipsa says quietly, her focus shifting to Valerian.

Valerian stretches to a stand, his face near unreadable. "The Summer Queen publicly accused me of the crime. I went home to face the council."

My stomach sinks. "What's the punishment for stealing the stone?" The look Eclipsa gives Asher turns my unease to full on panic. "But why would the Winter Prince steal the Darken's soulstone when he despises his grandfather?"

Silence.

Valerian's mouth hardens as he stares at some invisible spot on the wall. "I didn't always disagree with him. After your death, I had a lot of anger against the Seelie Court. He used that anger to make me an ally, for a time. A part of me thought as long as I stayed close to him, I would know if he ever found you."

He allied with the man who cruelly and methodically tormented him in an effort to protect me? I swallow, my throat bone-dry as I remember the dream I had about the Darken whipping Valerian. The stories I heard about his grandfather torturing him in horrendous ways . . .

Still. *Still.*

The Darken is the reason our world turned upside down. He's the reason we lost almost half our population and land. The reason my aunts both have learned to cry soundlessly in the middle of the night because they don't want to wake us.

"How could you align with someone like him?" I whisper.

A flicker of emotion ripples over his countenance, too quick to make out. "Because I'm not always the good guy, Summer. I'm Fae. In our world, there's not always a good or bad side, only the weak and the powerful."

"But you didn't steal his soulstone, right?"

I don't mean it to come out as an accusation, but it does. His lips twist, my body recoiling from the hurt I see in his eyes before he closes off his emotions behind a hard mask.

"He didn't do it," Asher says, and I can tell by his clipped voice that any points I won with him have been docked severely. "The Winter Prince was the one who turned the tide in the war. He spied against his grandfather, and when it came time, rallied half the Winter Court to the other side. If not for the prince, the Darken would still rule."

"Then why would my—the Summer Queen claim he stole it?"

Eclipsa twists her ponytail around her fingers. "The Summer Queen has had it out for the Winter Prince ever since . . . well, she blames him for your death. Any chance she gets, she tries to turn the council against him. Tries to undermine his court. Anything to hurt him."

I pluck at my soulstone pendant. Over the summer, Eclipsa and I determined that my mother must have taken my soulstone after I died, before my father could find it and destroy it. That's the only way she could have performed the spells necessary to make me jump into another body, rudimentary as they were.

Then, somehow, she got it to me when I visited the half-Fae who erased my memory.

"Wait." I drop the necklace back down into my tank top. "Why not destroy the Darken's soulstone? I know it's possible because Eclipsa said my father almost destroyed mine."

Valerian's eyes harden. "When he created the forbidden weapon that eventually caused both our worlds to collide, he needed something powerful enough to contain that many souls inside the weapon."

I shiver, remembering the dark presence of the forbidden weapons in the vault beneath the academy.

"Most forbidden weapons harness no more than fifty souls," Valerian continues, his jaw clenched. I wonder just how much trauma this whole thing is making him relive— and how much of that I'll take on in my dreams. "A rare few perhaps contain one hundred. But he was desperate to create something so powerful that it could destroy the entire Seelie race. Desperate enough that he melted a fragment of his soul-stone into the iron the axe was forged from. That sacrifice allowed thousands of souls into the axe—but also bound his own soul in the process."

"So, what? This weapon protects his soulstone somehow?"

"Sort of." Eclipsa stands, arching her back. "A soul cannot be destroyed in parts."

"And since a piece of King Oberon's soul was infused in the axe," I finish, head spinning from all the twists, "you need the weapon before you can shatter the soulstone."

"Very good," Eclipsa purrs. "Except, during the final battle that ended the war, the axe was damaged, and a piece went missing." She looks to Valerian, her mouth pressed into a concerned line. "Until we retrieve the missing fragment, and have the axe in its entirety, his soul cannot be extinguished."

"And you have no idea who might have taken the piece?"

Eclipsa shakes her head. "No, but we believe whoever has the piece is somehow able to control the darklings. It was the axe's dark magic, after all, that split our worlds and turned them. It would make sense."

I let Eclipsa help me up, all too aware of Valerian's gaze as he watches me. "Who has the other part of the axe now?"

Valerian scrapes a hand through his messy midnight blue hair, and I fight the unwelcome urge to run the soft strands between my own fingers. "Because the courts didn't know who had stolen the missing piece, they broke the weapon apart. Each court has one piece, stored in a magically hidden location."

I rub the back of my neck. Valerian and the rest talk of the Fae court quarrels and duplicity like it's normal, but I can't

AUDREY GREY

imagine living that way. Being surrounded constantly by potential enemies. Never knowing whom you can trust. Always struggling to stay one step ahead.

My little family back at the farmhouse may not possess wealth or material things, but I see now, in some ways, we have more than Valerian and the others ever will.

Eclipsa thrusts her hydroflask into my hands, even though we hardly broke a sweat. "You okay?"

"Yeah." I shrug. "Par for the course in Everwilde, right?" Boy, my voice came out bitter. I gulp down the cool water and hand it back. "So who do we *think* took it?"

Eclipsa bends down to wipe her mat. "Could be anyone, really."

"But Unseelie, right?"

Valerian gives me a mock-wounded look. "I find that stereotype deeply offensive."

Asher throws his rolled up mat under his arm, Hello Kitty smashed beneath his bulging bicep. "We don't know. We've been following leads to try and locate whoever is allied with the Darken, communing with him somehow. But it seems like he's amassing a following of both Seelie and Unseelie."

"To what end?" I ask.

"We don't know," Valerian says. He's careful never to let our eyes meet for longer than a second.

Frick. If only I could take back my hurtful words from earlier.

Everyone's packing up to leave, but I remember there was one last thing they still haven't told me.

"What does all of this have to do with me?"

The moment I finish speaking, everyone freezes, and the look they share makes me prepare for the worst.

Valerian tugs at the elastic hem of his joggers, taking his time before responding, as if mulling over the best way to explain without freaking me out. "The best spellcasters in

Everwilde layered the soulstone with wards to trap my grandfather's soul inside. Even with all the pieces of the axe, it would take the most powerful Soulmancer in existence to break through those wards."

"And that is . . .?" I raise my eyebrows, wondering if this Soulmancer is famous in the Fae world or something.

Valerian finally meets my stare without looking away. "You."

Sure I misheard the Winter Prince, I say, "Me? A
Soulmancer? No—that doesn't even make sense."

Eclipsa sighs. "This conversation calls for poolside
drinks."

I blink. "Poolside?"

I discover exactly what she means when Valerian creates a
portal that takes us to his penthouse apartment in Evernell,
overlooking the string of his father's nightclubs and bars.

After a lot of arguing, Eclipsa convinces me to throw on a
black string bikini. She frowns at my farmer's tan, practically
scoffing as I find the largest robe possible to cover myself, but
otherwise seems to find me agreeable.

The rooftop pool above Valerian's place is a long,
rectangular slice of crystal blue water. His court sigil, an owl
over two daggers, covers the bottom of the pool.

Fittingly, only Valerian can access this private bit of
heaven. I gawk at the outdoor training mat in the corner. The
couches artfully positioned in various locations, perfect for an
intimate gathering. Lounge chairs line up in neat rows on the

far side of the pool. The water leads to a fully stocked bar where a beautiful Fae male server polishes glasses.

Of course, he's only wearing a speedo. A very tight, very *revealing* blue speedo.

He turns around and . . . my God, is that Valerian's sigil stamped onto his ass?

Valerian and Asher sit at the bar, their stools half-submerged in water. My breath hitches when I realize Valerian is shirtless, wearing dark gray swim trunks.

Duh. This is a pool, Summer. There's going to be skin. And abs. Washboard abs and a little tuft of hair leading down . . .

Heat barrels between my thighs, a wave of dizziness washing over me.

Holy hell. This is a bad idea. I watch my mate, unable to look away. He and Asher are laughing about something, and Valerian is gesturing, the muscles of his back rippling.

Ugh. Get a grip, Summer.

I focus on the tattoos covering his upper torso, the dark silver and black markings sharp against his pale skin.

Just as I start walking toward them, a soft gust of wind whips my robe back. Before I can readjust, Valerian and Asher both whip their heads to stare at me.

For a breath, Valerian's eyes go dark, his expression unapologetically lupine as he devours me with his gaze. That familiar cord between us jerks taut so hard I clutch my belly.

Asher does a double take, earning a low snarl from Valerian.

A mischievous smile lights up the dragon shifter's face.

"Don't do it, idiot," Eclipsa warns beneath her breath.

Asher lets out a low whistle.

Eclipsa steps in front of me. "Crap."

Before Asher can finish his catcall, Valerian attacks. The two explode into the pool, sending water flying everywhere.

They fight so fast I can't even track their movement or what's happening.

"Males," Eclipsa mutters. She must notice the horror on my face because she adds, "They won't mortally wound each other, if that's what you're thinking."

"Do they do this all the time?" I ask, frowning as Asher bellows, either in pain or rage, I can't tell.

"Since you arrived, yeah." She takes one look at my face and explains, "They're not fighting over you, Summer. Asher's helping the prince release some of the . . . tension. It's not natural to fight the mating bond, especially one as strong as yours."

I peer at what looks to be blood tinging the water. "They've been doing this since I arrived at the academy?"

"Better Asher suffers the prince's wrath than some poor mortal boy who accidentally touches you when you pass in the hall. Or worse, an Evermore who tries to claim you just to piss him off. We may seem like we all get along at the academy, but the courts are primed for war at any moment. If the Winter Prince kills every Evermore male who looks at you wrong, he would be costing thousands of lives by starting another war."

My tongue shrivels as the moisture flees my mouth. A war?

I startle as both Fae males don their wings and take the fight to the air. "How long does this usually last?"

She shrugs. "Fifteen minutes? An hour, if he's been near you recently. Sometimes, if the prince is really amped up, I join in. And after what happened in the cave and then seeing you like that now"—her eyes sweep down my offending curves—"let's just say, it might be awhile."

I'm in too much shock to protest as she drags me into the warm, inviting water, but I have enough sense to shuck off my robe and grab my phone. I hold it above my head as the water laps at my stomach, thankful for the sun's hot kiss on my flesh.

The last time I was in Evernell, it was miserably cold.

"Why's the weather so much warmer now?" I ask, taking a spot next to Eclipsa on a smooth stone stool, one of countless that circle the bar.

"The legislation that allows mortal tourists to enter certain entertainment areas of Everwilde is close to passing, so the Winter King poured a crap ton of money into spells to make this area more appealing to humans." Her face takes on a haughty look. "Your kind die at the drop of a hat. Couldn't have some drunk dumbass passing out in the alley and freezing to death, could we?"

While I mull over what a terrible idea letting humans into Everwilde is, she orders us two green smoothies.

The server brings the tall glasses over. Mine is topped with whipped cream and a cherry, no doubt to hide the healthy grossness inside.

She winks at him. "Thanks, Gaius."

I've pegged Gaius as a vampire by his pale skin and the fang tips peeking from his upper lip.

Gaius lets his hungry gaze linger on Eclipsa before disappearing for more ice.

I try to swallow down my chuckle but it slips out. "Are you and banana hammock . . .?"

Lips clamped down over her straw, she peers at me over her drink. "Banana hammock?"

"Gaius. Are you two, you know?"

"Screwing?"

I nearly choke on my smoothie. I've always hated that word for sex.

"Look, I know you're mortal, which means your Fae side is mostly masked. But Fae aren't cut off from their true nature like humans."

"True nature?"

"Yeah. Mortals are so weird about everything. Sex is natural, when done responsibly and with consent. Everyone likes shiny things because it makes us happy. It's okay to crave money or power because both equal safety. You guys like all of those things but hate yourself for it. It's like some bizarre self-flagellation thing. And, geez, when it comes to killing—"

"Whoa." I throw up my hands. "How did we escalate from sex with banana hammock to murder?"

She throws back her head in a laugh, her silver ponytail dipping into the water. "They're the same, really. Sex, greed, murder. All part of nature. Look at any predatory animal. The strong procreate and kill to survive, hoarding resources and territory, while the weak—"

"I get it," I say, hoping she'll drop the subject. If the Evermore believe it's only natural for the strongest to take from the weak, then mortals are screwed in the evolutionary chain. "So, what about Hellebore? Was he just to satisfy some urge . . ."

The words die a quick death on my tongue the moment I see the hurt flash across her face. She focuses on the tiny jeweled half-moons on her nails, composing herself.

When her eyes meet mine, there's a practiced callousness there. "Hellebore was a mistake."

"What happened?" I ask softly.

"Most Evermore wouldn't talk about that part of my past and live, Summer. Understand?"

I nod, but the veiled threat in her voice doesn't scare me. I know what hurt looks like. Whatever Hellebore did to Eclipsa, it really messed her up.

A splash draws my eyes to the middle of the pool just as Asher and Valerian land. They're both breathing hard. Blood drips from Asher's nose and Valerian's bottom lip, and deep scratches rake their flesh.

Valerian claps his hand on Asher's massive shoulder, and they chuckle over something I can't hear.

"You totally gave up your flank, Prince," Asher is saying as they swim over.

"Only because you tried to incinerate me," Valerian growls. "Next time, I'm shredding one of your wings, you overstuffed lizard."

"Have fun?" Eclipsa calls.

"Not as much as if you were there, Eclipsa." Valerian's tone is teasing, but his eyes are serious—and totally focused on me.

"Oh, so you enjoy being embarrassed in front of your girl-friend?" Eclipsa grins slyly. "Noted."

His eyes never leave mine as he shakes his hair out like a wet dog, water droplets sprinkling the air.

But Eclipsa was right. Before, Valerian's attention was filled with raw, masculine power.

Now, the pull between us is intense, but manageable. Ish.

Unless he comes any closer—

Oh, hell. Goose bumps ripple over my arms and legs as he stalks toward me. I let out a breath as he takes a seat two stools down, leaving just enough space between us that I can breathe.

My senses are hyper alert, taking in his every move, every sound. I nearly flinch as he orders two elderberry cocktails.

And then I *do* flinch as music fills the air. The others look in horror as my ringtone for Mack—the Bohemian Rhapsody —blares from my cell on the counter.

"Crap," I hiss, grabbing my phone. "What time is it?"

"Dusk," Asher answers. Most Fae don't give specific times —it's considered mortal and rude to do so—but rather, generic terms for whatever part of the day it is.

Dawn. Mid-afternoon.

But I very much care about the specifics, and my heart sinks when I make out the true time: 7:30 PM.

"Oh, no." I check my messages to see several missed texts from Mack. "We were supposed to study tonight with some of the other shadows."

How did I forget? I text where I am with a quick apology, my stomach in knots as I wait to see if she's pissed. I know keeping Mack out of this whole business is for her own good, but I feel terrible not telling her the entire truth.

Relief pours through me as I read her reply. *You lucky bitch. I'd totally ditch studying to chill poolside at the Instant Lady Boner's exclusive pad.*

Another text pops up almost immediately. *Jace doesn't believe me. He said no one gets invited to the Ice Prince's Evernell pad. Send a picture stat or you're dead to me. I might have just bet on Fred's life.*

Grinning, I say, *You're cruel. Fred deserves better. What do you get if you're right?*

Ten boxes of tampons.

Whoa. The best we can buy at the commons are pads, and they're so cheap that toilet paper works better.

I type, *I get half.*

Two boxes, she amends.

Done.

Lifting my phone, I snap a selfie of myself with the pool in the background.

A few seconds later, she responds. *Holy orc balls, you're hawt. Is Instant Lady Boner a walking hard on right now?*

"What does Instant Lady Boner mean?" Eclipsa drawls over my shoulder, knowing exactly what it means.

Against my wishes, my chest turns blotchy red, and I slam my phone facedown on the marble counter so hard it nearly cracks. "Nothing. So, I have to meet Mack back at the academy. Can we get back to the earlier conversation?"

The levity in the air disappears, any traces of humor gone from their faces, and I mentally prepare myself for whatever comes next.

Valerian tips the last of his drink back and then turns to face me. "The extent of most Evermore's powers don't show up for thousands of years, which is why we wait to enter the academy until typically around the middle of our third millennium of life. But we're tested every five hundred years."

"Okay." I twirl my straw nervously inside my empty glass.

"You were a mystery to all of us," Eclipsa says. "The only true power you ever consistently showed was an affinity for creatures."

"That explains the griffin," I mutter.

"Most Fae claim two or three major powers not reliant on spells or outside magic, and perhaps one shifter form. But you . . . every new testing you showed something different."

"What does that mean?" I've given up pretending I'm not nervous and am chewing the crap out of my poor straw.

"The final time you were tested, I was there. You performed the most remarkable soulmancer spell I've ever witnessed—and I hated you for it. Afterward, your father pulled strings to keep you from testing publicly ever again."

"So my powers are soulmancy and talking to animals?" My mind is spinning, sweat from my palms coating my smoothie glass.

Valerian shakes his head. "No. We don't think your major power is soulmancy. We think it's something else, something so rare that it's either never been recorded or been lost to time. An ability to somehow . . . borrow magical abilities from other Evermore. That would explain how you continuously showed different powers. We think you accidentally took Eclipsa's soulmancy powers during your last test, but amplified it somehow."

I'm nodding. Just nodding and nodding like I'm not freaking the eff out. "Makes sense . . . uh, huh. Totally. And now the big D wants me because I can channel a soulmancer's powers, but stronger somehow?"

Eclipsa shifts on her stool. "Soulmancers have been going missing recently. A lot of them. We think whoever took the soulstone is responsible. If someone could act as a conduit for all those powers, could merge them somehow—they could break through the wards on the Darken's soulstone and . . ."

"Bring him back to life," I whisper. My heart is racing, clammy sweat wetting my palms.

"They would need all the pieces of the axe, first," Eclipsa adds.

Valerian frowns. "Summer, do you need a break?"

Realizing that they're all staring at me, and that I've nearly chewed my straw in half, I stop attacking the poor disposable utensil and force out a shaky breath. "I'm fine. I need to know the truth. So the public SOS call I sent out somehow during the Wild Hunt? What power is that?"

"It could be part of your ability to talk to animals. Perhaps that power to mentally communicate isn't limited to animals, but Fae also. We don't know yet."

Yet. My mind is spinning with everything they've just told me. I have magic. Strange, rare magic that I mainly steal from other Fae. Magic that could bring back the mad ruler who nearly broke our world.

Steadying my voice, I ask, "Does the Darken or his collaborator know about me?"

They share another grim look. "We don't think they know who you are yet," Valerian admits. "But they may still be looking for you. Last year, we believe someone paid the orc to kidnap you because they suspected, but didn't know for sure. That person could be the Darken's collaborator or simply someone who was hoping to sell you to them. With a bounty as high as yours, hundreds of mortals and Fae have been kidnapped over the years and passed off as you."

Oh, God. The thought makes me sick. "But the basilisk . . . it tried to kill me," I remind them.

Valerian's eyes darken with barely veiled rage. "We now think the basilisk was compelled to kill you and retrieve your soulstone. Whoever has that controls your soul."

"And could put me into a new, compliant body." I shiver at the thought of being owned by the Darken, body and soul.

"If they knew for sure," Valerian says, his voice soft, "they would already have you. But they don't know . . . yet."

Yet. There's that dang word again.

My fingers flutter over my chest as I work to drag air into my lungs. My body is both hot and cold. My belly twists. I have no idea why, after everything that's happened recently, this is what's sending me into a full-blown panic attack.

But the one thing I know for sure is that I would die before I brought the Darken back. Even without my memories, something inside me must still remember him, and icy dread slithers through my insides at the thought of him returning.

I clutch my neck as bile slams into my throat.

Valerian growls, the sound a low warning rattle . . . and also an order to leave seeing how everyone flees at once. Even poor banana hammock Gaius.

Valerian is suddenly in front of my stool, calling my name. I try to meet his worried face but darkness swirls around my vision.

I can't breathe. The air—it's so thin. My heart pounding into my skull.

"Summer." His voice warbles in my ears from the end of a

tunnel. I feel his cool hand press into my chest, just above my heart. The other slips under my chin and lifts my face to his. "Summer, look at me."

The second our eyes meet, a surge of crisp white stillness spears through my core, driving back the mindless fear, the sticky black cloud of desperation. The brilliant light grows brighter. Clearing my spirit of darkness and hopelessness.

A delicious warmth blossoms, filling my limbs, my torso, my toes with a hollow, throbbing ache.

Just as that ache begins to center between my thighs, he jerks his hands away and steps back until we're no longer touching.

The light vanishes, sending me crashing back to reality. I fight the stab of disappointment, grateful that my panic is gone. "What was that?"

His jaw clenches. "It's called melding, and only soulbound mates can use it. Usually, it's done the first time the soulbond is . . . consummated, but in a less intimate situation, it can be used to calm."

Shimmer save me, I can't imagine the intimacy required to look someone in the eye the entire time you make love to them. My body can, though, and it shivers with delight at the idea.

Crossing my thighs, I say, "Thank you."

He forces his focus to a spot just over my shoulder. "Summer, I've been thinking about what happened during the hunt. If I had forced you into becoming permanently mated to me against your will before you were ready—" He scrapes a hand through his hair, sending droplets flying, before meeting my eyes. "When we consummate our bond, it will be both our decisions."

I focus on the way the last of the fading sunlight dances across the pool's surface rather than see the intense desire brimming inside his eyes. "And what if I decide I never want to consummate the bond?"

He goes still, but when I finally look up, there's no anger inside his face, only amusement. "I promise you, there will come a time when you realize we're meant to be together for eternity, Princess. And when you do, when you finally accept what you know is true, I'm going to lock you away and spend a full week proving you made the right decision."

Holy hell. Heat floods my chest all the way to my ears. But instead of backing down, the hooker inside me pops her head out and teases, "A whole week? Are you sure you don't mean more like five minutes?"

His wicked grin is a thing of beauty. "On second thought, perhaps I'll make you beg first."

Okay, dangerous territory. I cross my arms over my chest. "That will never happen."

"Challenge accepted." He rakes his gaze over my stomach before dragging his focus back to my face. "You said that you want to know me before you commit your soul to me. So I propose a trial where we can do just that. One night a week, after our training session, we spend thirty minutes together just . . . talking." He frowns at that but continues. "You can ask me questions about my life or whatever you want to know. No physical touching beyond what's needed for training and such—at least"—a devilish look sparks in his eyes—"not until you tell me otherwise."

I swallow. He's giving me exactly what I wanted, but the idea of being so close to him all the time . . .

I exhale. "Deal. But the sessions don't start until after I pass the first gauntlet, and I can veto the dates at any time if they conflict with schoolwork or otherwise . . . distract me."

"Done. But I get an extra day working with you on testing your powers. Once we can pinpoint them down exactly, we can use spells to help you control them."

I narrow my eyes at his amendment, but it does make sense that we would need an extra day a week, if only so I can learn how to not use my magic on accident. "Fine."

He grins, and something about the gesture makes my stomach flutter. "Game on, Princess. But you should know, I'm cutthroat when it comes to getting what I want."

I don't doubt that for a second. Only this time, what he wants is me.

All of me.

Forever.

18

I poke at the salad on my tray, eyeing the now empty spot where the roll sat moments ago. I've never liked salad unless it's drowned in cheese and dressing, but both items were gone by the time I made it back from changing at the dorms.

"So, the blood just exploded from your locker when you opened it?" Kyler asks. She's a first year and is too new to know I'm a social pariah, which is why she keeps asking questions about the incident earlier instead of pretending like the others that it didn't happen.

I nod, half looking at her as I search for just one tiny crumb of goat's cheese to add to the limp kale impaled on my fork. "Yep. Like in those cheap horror flicks."

"And it was real blood?" she presses, biting her lip.

Giving up on my salad, I settle my attention on her. She's pretty, in a naive, wholesome, girl next door kind of way. Fine shoulder-length dirty blonde hair. Bright brown eyes that glow from within. A smattering of freckles.

Mack says her grandparents have deep ties with the Fall

Court King, but she seems too oblivious to the Evermore's cruelty to have ever truly been around them.

"Probably not," I lie before instantly regretting it. Letting someone like her continue their make-believe fantasy that the Fae are decent is cruel and dangerous. Kyler is soft spoken and kind, two personality traits that don't benefit mortals here.

"Good." Kyler's eyes brighten as she leans forward on her elbows. "Hey, does anyone know what happened to the girl who used to live in my room? I found some of her stuff still in the drawers. Expensive makeup, that kind of thing."

Mack and I share a look. A few seats down, Richard and Jace whip their heads in our direction.

Thank the Shimmer, Kyler doesn't seem to notice as she adds, "I think her name is Evelyn? I found some of her old school papers too."

Mack gives a careful shrug and makes some excuse about Evelyn leaving before shifting the conversation to our upcoming exams today. Only our tight circle knows the truth about how she turned, and we've all been asked to keep that inconvenient detail quiet.

As Mack opens her teal folder and pulls out the study guide, any appetite I had left vanishes. At this point, I've studied enough that I know the answers to each study guide question, but . . . still.

I can't shake the feeling that I have to be perfect this semester.

Other than the locker incident and a few other juvenile pranks—like someone setting deranged brownies loose in our dorm room one night while we slept—nothing serious has happened. Yet.

But I can't afford one single mistake.

Mack pulls out her Poisons and Potions quiz sheet, color

coded like the obsessive overachiever she is, and begins rattling off questions.

"What species of mushroom is used to reduce anxiety?"

"Bisporos tranquaire," I answer.

"What type of moss is used as a stabilizer in elixirs?"

"Ash moss, which is actually a liverwort, not a true moss."

"What is the uncommon name for the rare monkshood plant?"

"Dragonsbane," I say. "It was declared an illegal substance by the council after the last war, along with a host of other poisonous plants, after it was used to nearly eradicate the entire dragon clans of the Winter and Fall courts."

Kyler frowns down at her notes, scribbled in bubbly pink cursive. "I don't remember learning that."

Mack and I exchange yet another look. Kyler is a first year, but someone pulled enough strings so that she skipped straight to the more advanced classes.

"The Dark—I mean, King Oberon's grandmother was a descendant of the Ice Dragon Lord who claimed the northern half of the Winter Court's territories. Although King Oberon was only a quarter dragon, his magic chose that creature as his shifter form. During the last war, some of the Seelie took out their rage on the dragon clans. It nearly wiped them out."

"Oh." Her frown deepens, and I feel a stab of sympathy for her. I remember that same drowning feeling I had last year trying to learn thousands of years of Fae knowledge in a few weeks.

"Don't worry," I reassure her. "I doubt that will be on any test this year. I read ahead."

I've been doing that lately, desperate to learn more about the Darken and my own history.

"Translation," Mack adds, "she's being a showoff."

Oh, boy. If Mack's calling me a showoff . . . I open my mouth to reply, but think better of it when I catch the tense line of her shoulders, her forced smile. My gaze slides to her tray, where she's portioned out an apple into tiny cubes.

When was the last time I saw her actually eat more than a few bites of something?

My phone buzzes in my pocket, dragging my attention away from my bestie. As soon as I see the initials ILB, my heart leaps into my throat.

What are you wearing to training tonight?

A blush sweeps over my chest as I take in his question. I can practically hear his teasing voice inside my head, thick with amusement.

Shielding my phone from Mack's curious gaze, I quickly send back a reply.

Baggy joggers and a sweatshirt.

The dots blink forever, and then . . .

Tease. You wouldn't dare.

I tamp down my stupid grin. We've been doing this—whatever this is—ever since the night at his penthouse. Harmless flirting over text. In person, he's kept to his word. Only touching me during training. Not mentioning the soul-bond or pressuring me for anything beyond the light, flirtatious relationship we've established.

Which is wonderful because the first gauntlet is in two days.

Two fricking days.

And we still have no clue what my powers are, how they're activated, or how to stop them.

"Ready to go slay this test?" Mack asks as she gathers her stuff, a strand of her brown hair escaping her ear and falling forward.

"Mackenzie Fairchild, I was born ready," I declare, loud enough to draw weird stares from the rest of the lunchroom.

Grinning, Mack high fives me. "Damn right you were."

Everyone's definitely gawking now, but I don't care. As long as Mack's by my side, I can take on the Everwilde.

---

*L*ast minute, I remember I left my iPad in my locker. Because Whitehall Academy uses all modern technology for lessons, note-taking, and tests, the Spring Court sponsored new iPads for all the students and made online test taking mandatory. Mack said they probably did that just to piss off the Winter Court, whose stance on mortal technology is less favorable.

I grab my iPad, thankful the battery is at seventy-five percent, sling my backpack over my shoulder, and sprint down the corridor toward the lecture hall. My tennis shoes squeak across the marble floor.

When I round the top of the stairs, I spot the closed door. Crap. I still have five minutes before the professor locks the door.

Breathing hard, I wrench the door open and shuffle down the aisle—

Everything goes dark. What the frick? I freeze in confusion. As I take in the black sea of nothingness, cold dread seeps into my veins.

"Hello?" I call, my voice ringing in the absolute silence. As my eyes adjust, I slowly start to pick out shapes from the shadows. Tall, slender shapes.

Trees.

Okay, this is beyond weird. Could it be part of the test? I've heard that some professors hold their exams in the field, but wouldn't they prepare us for that?

"It's okay," I whisper, searching the forest for a clue on where to go. "Don't panic."

Besides the unnerving quiet, the landscape is gray, lifeless, like a three-dimensional painting of a world that has yet to be colored. Everything is monochromatic and covered in—I swipe my finger across the trunk of a tree—ash?

I find a path. It doesn't take very long until it hits me. I know this place.

My heart lurches sideways. This isn't the Everwilde.

Even covered in ash, I recognize the type of trees, honey oak and Texas ash. A familiar path opens up. It zigzags through the forest as it leads to the . . .

Farmhouse. My farmhouse. My *home.*

A prickle of unease trails down my spine as I make out the humming carried on the light breeze, the same song Zinnia sings every day as she hangs the laundry on the line.

Something is wrong.

I jolt into a sprint toward the farmhouse, terror woven into every cell of my being. Movement catches my eye in my periphery. Shadows flicker strangely, almost like—

The shadow of the tree to my right peels from the ash-covered forest floor and lifts, changing shape as it does. Transforming into a—a—

The creature is so grotesque that I reel back in horror, almost falling on my butt. Spider-like legs stab the ground as the thing scrambles past me. A humanoid head with sunken, eyeless sockets and a withered lipless mouth turns to look at me. Two huge arachnoid fangs flash.

The forest fills with chittering as more spider-like monsters rise from the ash. I'm frozen with terror. Afraid if I move, they'll notice me. That if I can just be so very still, all of this will go away.

But it's like I'm not here. Like they're moving past me, more interested in—

Oh, God.

I start to run, but I'm too late. Hundreds of monsters scurry across the forest toward the farmhouse.

No, please no. Horror curdles in my gut. I'm gagging on warm bile, struggling to drag air into my lungs enough to scream, to warn them.

This can't be happening.

As I clear the tree line and the white two-story house comes into view, my world shrinks to the scene in front of me. Everyone is outside. Zinnia, Jane, and Tanner hanging up the laundry on the clothesline, Aunt Vi sipping a glass of iced tea on the porch. The twins are riding their bikes in circles around the well.

They don't even have a chance to scream before the monsters descend. They swarm over my family, decimating the people I love most in this world before I can utter a gasp.

I collapse to my knees as the gurgle of blood, the sharp puncturing sound of fangs sinking through flesh, fills my mind.

Blood—so much blood. It's everywhere. Sprayed in arcs over the white bed sheets swaying in the light breeze. And the smell—it's choking me. Coating my throat and my mouth and oh God, I can't take this—

Thrashing forward, I vomit. Heaving over and over until I can't breathe.

This can't be real. But I see the creatures feasting on my family. Snapping their bones. Drinking their blood. Doing things so terrible my brain can't process it.

Something inside me splits open, a wail spilling from my chest . . .

19

I come to seemingly floating in the air. There's no more sky. No more farmhouse or clothes stained red or pieces of my family strewn over the ground. Instead of the metallic scent of blood, the familiar scent of pine and juniper fills my nose.

Arms—there are arms beneath me. I'm pressed into someone's chest, held like a child, the feeling so comforting and protective that I nearly sigh with relief. By the way my body presses into the cool flesh, I know without looking that it's Valerian.

"My family," I croak, trying to shift to look at his face, but agony follows the simple movement.

"Fine." Valerian's voice soothes the jagged wound inside my chest. "Whatever you saw, it wasn't real."

Wasn't real. Wasn't real. Wasn't real.

I repeat the phrase over and over, each cleansing breath I take clearing more of the horrifying images from my mind until I can finally, finally convince myself what I experienced truly didn't happen.

He lays me down on a bed—his bed—and that's when I

remember what I was doing before I fell into that living nightmare.

"The test!" I lift up, the sudden movement sending tiny nails driving into my skull. "Ow." Groaning, I shut my eyes and clutch my head, gouging my knuckles into my temples. "Is there, by chance, a tiny man hammering into my head?"

His cool breath brushes my cheek as he leans down, easing me onto the bed. "You're going to feel like death for a few minutes until the tormentor spell you walked into clears your system."

Of course it's called a tormentor spell. I sigh, some of the tension bleeding from my shoulders and neck. "So all of that was . . . a hallucination?"

"Yes. That particular spell takes your worst fears and brings them to life in macabre ways."

Wonderful. "Please don't tell me I vomited in front of everyone."

Damning silence. Crap. I open my eyes only to slap a hand over them as the light sears into my brain.

"Was it Inara? I'm going to murder her and then have Eclipsa transfer her soul just so I can murder her again."

He chuckles, the throaty sound hinting that he's still right next to me. "Whoever set that spell in the doorway hid their mark, so there's no way to tell, but I'm absolutely going to have a chat with her about it."

"No, please. I need to deal with her on my own."

I can hear the hesitation in his silence. I begged the same thing after the incident at the Wild Hunt, too. As much as I would love to see Valerian handle Inara, I can't let him fight my battles.

My eyes are still squeezed shut, which is unnerving considering I can feel Valerian watching me. "Wait, why am I in your room?"

"I was running late to class, so I only discovered you were

hurt when Eclipsa and Asher were already sprinting down the hall with you. The quickest way to break a tormentor spell is to remove the victim from the original spell's location. When I saw you, Summer, wailing in Asher's arms, your face contorted in pain—I freaked out. My need to protect you made me see everyone as a potential threat, even Asher and Eclipsa."

"Did you hurt them?" I ask, startled.

"Hurt isn't the right word. It takes a lot to injure a dragon shifter and Lunar assassin. But they'll be sore for a few days and rightfully pissed." He exhales. "I might have also set up wards to keep everyone out."

I'm alone. With Valerian. In his bed. The bond between us tugging low in my belly, growing more and more insistent with every second that passes. Flooding my body with a startling, feverish heat.

This feels . . . dangerous.

My eyes pop open as I feel cool wetness on my cheeks. Valerian meets my stare, a gray washcloth bunched in his hand. Without a word, he cleans the puke from my face. My hair. Gently. The act so caring, so intimate that I have to look away.

Once he's done, I struggle to my elbows once again. "I need to get up. The test—"

"I've already arranged a new time for you to take it in the morning. The spell should leave your system soon, but until then, you're going to rest."

"If I don't?"

"Then the link between the spell and your psyche will reactivate from the stress and you'll experience the same thing over again." He stares down at me, daring me to argue.

I kind of want to just because he's being so bossy, and also because he looks hot when he's mothering me, but there's no way in the Fae hells I'd survive another hallucination watching freakish arachnid creatures slaughter my entire family.

So I peer through my lashes at him and say, "Fine, but I'm not missing training tonight."

"Good." He flashes a wolfish grin. "Because I'm not going to take it easy on you."

"And I need a shower," I add.

"Done." His sharp eyebrows arch devilishly. "Let me know if you need any help with that."

Oh, boy. The horny hooker inside me takes his suggestion and runs with it like a quarterback near the end zone—

Get a grip, Summer. This is all physical, a reaction to the magic, not your heart.

Blowing out a steadying breath, I say, "I think I can manage that alone."

His face is emotionless as he watches me a moment longer before turning to go.

"Are you leaving?" I blurt. I should be relieved, but I'm still raw from watching spider-creatures massacre my family and I don't want to be by myself right now.

He glances back over his shoulder. When I see the dark intent in his eyes, my stomach flutters wildly.

"Princess, you're in my bed. Alone. And I'm already overwhelmed by the primal need to make you mine so I can protect you properly. So unless you want that to happen, I should probably go. Besides, I need to reassure your friends that you're okay."

"Mack?"

"The one and only. She and your sprite are currently making a scene at my front door."

My heart sinks. She must be so worried. Is she done with the test already?

"I'll let them in and tell them you'll come down in thirty minutes."

After he leaves, I fire off a million texts to Zinnia's new phone, a gift from Nick. Once she replies with pictures of the kids plus a rant about Aunt Vi, I go for that shower.

True to Valerian's word, exactly thirty minutes later, after I've washed the puke from my body, voices trickle from below. I trail down the stairs in one of his steel-gray tees, a pair of thin black joggers hugging my hips, to see the dining table filled with my favorite people: Mack, Eclipsa, and Asher.

Ruby streaks over the ceiling above them, taunting Valerian's snow-white owl with a piece of shaved ham.

Valerian is posted against a counter in the kitchen, sipping a cup of tea as he frowns at the noisy intrusion.

Our eyes meet, and I reward him with a grateful smile. I know how much he likes his privacy. Definitely going to thank him later for this.

Surprise flickers over his handsome features, followed by a vulnerable, intimate look that sets my heart on fire and jerks the bond between us taut.

Thank the Shimmer the others are here or that unexpectedly sweet exchange would be enough to undo me completely.

Eclipsa whistles, drawing my mind away from Valerian. "The prince wasn't lying. You survived your first tormentor spell. Impressive. Not everyone does."

Holy frick. Valerian didn't tell me that. No wonder he freaked out.

Mack's chair scrapes across the floor as she jumps to her feet and wraps her arms around me. Ruby screeches and dive bombs my shoulder, her tiny arms choking me as she joins the hug.

"What about your test?" I ask as I gently extricate my overexuberant sprite.

Something passes over Mack's face, too quick to read. "It's

fine. After all that studying, I finished in like five minutes. I'm just glad you're okay."

Relief pours through me, followed by hot, sweeping anger. No matter who actually performed the spell, I know in my gut Inara's responsible.

And she's never going to stop. Not unless I make her.

A few hours later, I get my revenge during combat class. Valerian must know I need to punish Inara because after he puts all of us through a brutal session, he pairs me with Reina for another version of the baton game we played last year.

Except this time is different. My months of extra training paired with my seething fury turn me into some badass murder machine.

Whatever Reina sees in my face, she backpedals in terror.

Any other time, I would feel remorse. I hate the idea of anyone being afraid, even my enemies.

But not today. Not when I can close my eyes and still picture Aunt Zinnia and Jane and all the others lying bloody in the grass like a movie playing over in my head. Not when the sounds of those . . . those *things* feasting on them still echo in my ears.

Screw every one of you Fae-holes.

I stalk Reina. Toying with her. Making her feel the horror I felt. Desperation flickers inside her eyes as she makes sloppy attacks.

Attacks I repel with ease.

I'm faster than I was last year by a landslide. I strike out. The end of my baton connects with her again and again.

When I know she's almost done, I drop the baton, ram the heel of my palm into her nose, and finish her off with a knee to her belly.

She collapses to the mat, writhing and gasping for air.

Eclipsa is grinning. A few feet away, Hellebore watches me lord over Reina, his eyes bored slits. I think I catch a hint of amusement inside those turquoise depths, but I barely register it.

My mind is fixated on one person.

I find Inara's shocked gaze. Then, without looking away, I lean down and whisper in Reina's ear, "I don't care how much money and influence you have, if you ever screw with my family again, real or imaginary, I'll end you."

Reina's twin boy toys help her to her feet, blood pouring from her nose and splattering on the mat. The shadows and Evermore are quiet as I let my furious gaze sweep over them, daring whoever was responsible to own up to it.

Deep down, I know this isn't enough to deter them completely. But maybe they'll think twice before involving my family.

Afterward, Valerian whispers in my ear, "That was sexy as hell."

"Darn right it was," I respond, grinning ear to ear.

A few shadows even clap me on the back, and Mack can't stop talking about the fight on the way back to the dorms.

But my high only lasts until I see the flyer plastered to our door announcing the Lammas festival this weekend celebrating the victors of the first gauntlet.

Kicking Reina's ass might have been easy, but whatever Hellebore has in store for us won't be.

20

Friday comes way too fast. Instead of combat class in the evening, we're taken to the gym, ordered to change into our Shadow Guardian uniforms, and each allowed to choose two weapons to wield in the gauntlet.

Wired with nerves, I fidget near the back of the line, toying with the metal zipper at the front of my outfit. When it's my turn to choose my weapon, I stare at the table full of options before choosing a wrist-mounted crossbow and a standard issue iron infused sword.

Both are two of the most badass weapons I've ever been allowed to use—not counting the forbidden bow I stole last school year or Aunt Vi's shotgun—but now, in my clammy hands, they feel about as lethal as twigs.

Mrs. Richter presides over the table of offerings, and she gives me a grim smile before handing me a metal sleeve with iron-tipped bolts and a back scabbard to carry the sword.

"Thank you," I say, grateful for the extra supplies.

All of the students own personal scabbards and other equipment, many handed down for generations. Everyone but me. Mrs. Richter kindly promised I could borrow the shared equipment we use in class.

Most also had their own spandex Guardian uniforms made for the occasion. Even Mack finally gave in and let her dads order a beautiful, custom fitted outfit that fits her curves like a glove, a metallic sheen making the supple onyx fabric seem to ripple as she moves.

Mine, on the other hand, is a faded loaner uniform that's stained with Titania knows what, is a size too big, and sags in the crotch.

Ruby already made a joke about me being happy to see her before I sent her off on a fake errand.

Reina snickers from nearby. "Aw, look. Puke Face is wearing hand-me-downs. How adorable."

The nearest twin laughs on cue. Despite Reina's beatdown —or perhaps because of it—she's graced me with another nickname.

Mack rolls her eyes. "While you're handing out clever nicknames, you might want to create your own. I was thinking Busted Nose or Shiner, but that might be too literal."

Reina's eyes flash with rage. Inara must have refused to let her be healed after the fight because her nose is still very much broken, and deep reddish-purple bruises circle each eye.

Mrs. Richter blows a whistle, announcing five minutes to finish dressing, and we all switch our focus to the upcoming task.

My nervous fingers fumble with the clasp of my back scabbard, and when it comes to clipping the sleeve to my belt, it's like my fingers are made of Jell-O. Finally Kyler comes over and helps me, even though she looks as nervous as I am.

I give her a kind smile despite my anxiety. "Thanks."

She just nods without making eye contact.

Afterward, we all don leather armor to cover our forearms

and deflect blows, and light vests woven with special material to protect our vulnerable torso and stomach.

I've never felt more like a Shadow Guardian than now, wearing the standard uniform, nor have I ever felt more unworthy of that title.

I crack my neck. Why am I so nervous?

I've trained with the crossbow and sword a million times by now. Besides, the last two sessions, Valerian and I synchronized like we've been fighting in tandem for years.

Breathe, Summer. You've got this.

Adjusting my high ponytail for the millionth time, I follow Mack, Kyler, Layla, and Jace to wait with the others until everyone has chosen their two weapons.

Mack's fingers shake as she tries to pin the Seelie symbol to the front of her suit, just above where her protective vest stops.

"Let me," I insist.

The pin was a gift from her dads for luck. Most of the students wear something to champion their side—Seelie or Unseelie—on their uniform somewhere.

Once it's pinned above her breast, I straighten her fancy leather sword belt. "There. Now you look like a badass ninja."

Her smile is closer to a grimace. "I think I'm going to vomit."

I squeeze her arm. "If you do, at least we can have matching nicknames."

"Reina really pulled out all the brain cells for that one," Mack mutters, still clutching her belly.

"Don't worry, I'm here now!" Ruby calls as she zooms over our heads, her little arms clenched around a small device. She tosses the item at me, and it nearly smacks into my face before I manage to catch it.

Mack side-eyes me with a look that says, *Ruby? Really?*

Because of the way sprites are technically considered a shadow's possession—and in some translations of the old Fae laws, an actual part of their owner, like an arm or a leg—sprites are allowed to assist their shadows in the gauntlet.

Most students, however, like Mack, opted not to bring theirs.

"I told Ruby no a thousand times," I whisper, "yet here she is."

"Have you ever heard of discipline?"

Mack swears I'm too soft on Ruby. That I don't provide enough rules and consequences when she disobeys me—which is basically all the time.

"Maybe she'll be helpful?" I nearly choke on my words as we watch Ruby flit over to another shadow's sleeve and steal an arrow.

Cringing, I force my attention to the device she brought me earlier. It's a digital map, although I don't have time to determine the location before they order us out into the night. I clip the GPS onto my belt next to the metal quiver as I walk.

On the other side of the lawn, I spot a massive crowd around the courtyard. Tall torches line the gravel path, illuminating the night.

My breath hitches when we begin to pass through the mass of people. I found out a few days ago parents and close family of both the Evermore and the shadows are allowed to attend the gauntlet celebrations. But I didn't dare ask Aunt Zinnia or Vi for fear they'd say no.

"Dad!" Mack screams as Nick and Sebastian shove to the front. They're waving Seelie flags and blowing kisses at Mack. Sebastian holds a sign he had printed with her full name on it.

I go to wave at them and then freeze.

Is that . . . I take in the short plump woman with the mess

of wild curls sticking out from beneath a cowboy hat in the middle of Mack's dads.

How is that possible?

"Zinnia?" I cry. My words are lost to the cheers of the audience, but just seeing her here fills me with unexpected hope.

Her eyes shimmer with pride as she mouths, *You can do this.*

Mack leans into my ear. "Nick invited your aunts. Sorry, I would have told you but my dads wanted it to be a surprise. Everything has to be dramatic with them."

Both aunts? Which means . . .

I exhale. *Vi didn't come.*

Pushing aside my disappointment, I focus on Zinnia as a sudden calm descends. Win or lose, she'll be here to comfort me. I feel like I'm nine again, kidnapped and about to be trafficked to the Fae, looking into her kind face through my cage bars as she promises me everything will work out.

Back then, I was too broken to trust what she said was true.

This time, I allow myself to believe her.

I can do this.

The cheers of the crowd grow softer as we near the fiery ring of portals. The flames stoke something inside me, not quite true fear—more like a bizarre mixture of adrenaline, dread, and excitement.

"Get ready for whatever dark, twisted games the Spring Prince concocted," Mack warns as I approach the nearest portal, waiting for the girl in front of me to jump through. "Our Keepers will be on the other side."

They've already explained the rules, which didn't take long because there's only three.

One, Keepers can't use magic.

Two, protect our Keeper at all cost.

Three, make it to the safe zone unscathed by sunrise.

"Oh, God," Kyler whispers behind her. "This is really happening."

Damn right it is. And I'm going to make sure I don't just survive, but win.

Whatever it takes.

21

As soon as we land on the other side, the portals flame out, trapping us here—wherever that is. A quick glance around shows we're on some sort of small island surrounded by a huge urban city.

Professor Crenshaw is here, and she and Mr. Willis go around checking our equipment and GPS devices while Mrs. Richter gives us a speech. "As a shadow, one of the scenarios you might find yourself in is an extraction situation where your Keeper is injured inside an area taken by darklings. Your Keepers are positioned around the city. You have until sunrise to find yours and escort them to the safety zone on the map."

Kyler raises her hand. "What are the glowing red dots on our GPS devices?"

I glance down at mine, startled to discover clusters of bright red specks moving around the city.

Mrs. Richter's eyes narrow. "Those are darklings." She waits until the crowd quiets and adds, "Each of you will see a white circle to indicate the location of your Keeper. The faint green dots are special weapons imbued with magic."

Disappointment hits when I see there are only ten or so magical weapons available—not nearly enough for even half of us—and they're all stashed in the most heavily infested darkling clusters.

"Remember," she continues, "Keepers and sprites must not use even a hint of magic. Any caught doing so will result in their shadow's immediate expulsion, and permanent marks will go on your Keeper's record."

Mr. Willis addresses us next. "The gauntlet will push all of you to your breaking point, but I believe every one of you are capable of passing if you stay calm and remember your training. Don't forget, this isn't simply about your skill with a weapon. You're being tested on strategy, thinking under pressure, and, most importantly, your ability to work with your Keeper—which all mortals know can be like dealing with a child sometimes."

Nervous laughter ripples through the group. We've never heard any instructor dare to openly criticize the Fae like this, but these are special circumstances.

"Years of successfully guarding the Fae have shown me that the most successful shadows are experts at reading their Keeper. You have to know when to take over control of the situation to protect your Keeper, and when it's safe to let them join the fight. At least, just enough to smooth over that fragile ego they all have."

More chuckles.

"It's a dance," he finishes. "A skillful shadow can find the right balance to sync with their Keepers—and when that happens, let me tell you, it possesses a magic of its own." His eyes turn serious, and he sweeps his kind but firm gaze over all of us in turn. "May the luck of Queen Titania be with you all."

As soon as both instructors leave, I scour the island. It's

night here as well, the sky veiled in ominous gray clouds that block out the stars and moon. Around us, high rise marble buildings the Fae prefer stand next to older brick complexes that look more like apartments.

So we're in a turned city, like Evernell, which used to be Las Vegas and is now some Frankenstein of both Fae and mortal worlds. A tug on my belt draws my eye to Ruby, who's trying to lift the GPS.

Mack already has her own out, and she gasps. "No, we're in . . . Lumeria."

Ruby hisses. "Orc balls, we won't last the night."

Some of the others must have already figured out the same because gasps fill the air.

"What's Lumeria?" I ask, praying it's not as bad as they're making it.

Mack slips her GPS back onto her belt and fixes me with a determined stare. "Only the most modern and famous city in the Spring Court territories. Or it used to be . . . before the wards fell and darklings infested the place, driving out all the residents. Now it's scourge-touched, infected with basically everything that can and will kill us. Darklings, orcs, trolls, dark magic."

I nod, forcing the fear from my chest. "Okay, we knew it was going to be tough. Let's not panic."

Ruby snorts, but I ignore her as I look over my own map. The landmarks dredge up a sense of familiarity.

The Washington Monument. United States Capitol. The old White House . . .

"Holy Fae hells," I murmur. "This is . . . ."

"Welcome to the former capital of the United States of America," Mack says, sweeping her arm out to indicate the rising skyline in the distance.

Washington freaking D.C. Just being here, witnessing the

city that used to represent the height of our world's power before the Lightmare, is enough to make me feel lightheaded. Out of all the territories affected by the Lightmare, it was losing Capitol Hill and most of our regulatory body that nearly destroyed our country.

And now the Fae have lost it as well. A part of me is bitterly glad about that.

At least, until we set off as a group toward the shadowy city.

Mack immediately designated herself the map reader, and she spouts off directions as we all jog across the metal bridge connecting the island to the mainland. Thankfully, most of the darkling clusters are concentrated south of where the Keepers are stashed. A few dark shapes flicker in the distance, scuttling across empty highways and over guardrails.

As long as we're quiet, the darklings won't be attracted to us. Once we're with our Fae Keepers, though, things will change.

"Asher and the Winter Prince are together," Mack pants as we halt near the end of the bridge. "But we'll have to break off from the group."

I swallow, not loving that idea.

Cruel laughter draws my attention to Reina. She's with the twin boys and a few other Unseelie shadows. "Careful, Puke Breath. I hear orcs are attracted to certain types of stench."

I turn around, not even bothering with a response.

"Afraid?" Reina taunts.

Without turning, I say, "No, I just have a policy not to feed trolls."

Mack grins as we break into a jog down the closest street on our left, headed deep into a residential block of condos and luxury townhomes. I flick my gaze over the dark landscape, taking everything in. I imagine this place was gorgeous before the darklings overran it.

Just like the Spring Court palace, wisteria and jasmine drape the buildings in veils of bright colors. The homes are a mishmash of mortal and Fae architecture, the contrasting styles a collision of cultures that somehow works.

But there's something . . . off about the air. A whisper of death and decay woven into the fabric of this place.

Even worse than the stench is the unnatural quiet.

Cities are loud, thriving organisms. Even in the residential areas, the sounds of car engines revving, children playing in the streets, and birds singing hint at life.

This place hints at the opposite, and I shudder at the thought that someday, if we don't find a way to stop it, the scourge could completely infest our world.

Mack and I jog silently down an alleyway and burst out into the final street that leads to Asher and Valerian. They're stashed in a collection of overpriced high-rises centered around a circular park.

As we prepare to take the concrete stairs to the third floor where the map says they are, Mack points at the churning red mass in the gardens on the other side of us.

Holy. Frick.

Finger to my lips, we pad to the door and—

The door cracks, and Asher's handsome mug grins down at us. "Ladies." Someone managed to find a protective gray vest that fits his giant frame, and it hangs over a black long-sleeved shirt that barely contains his bulging muscles.

His too-bright dragon eyes instantly slide to Mack as he opens the door for us. "Welcome to darkling hell."

I follow Mack inside the dim apartment, lit only by a single flickering bulb on a side table in the living room. The place is small but gorgeous, all white stone and steel fixtures and giant windows overlooking the park.

That's where I find Valerian. Like Asher, he's clad in dark clothes and a vest, his midnight blue hair nearly the same black shade beneath the meager light.

As my eyes adjust, I realize he's watching me quietly with that smoldering look I find so unnerving.

His eyes soften as something passes between us. Something more substantial and terrifying than the simple jerk of the physical bond. I fight my gut reaction, which is to smile like a maniac at him.

Summer, stop with the mushy crap and save this beautiful fucker's life.

I stroll over like I haven't just spent the last ten minutes in controlled terror, plant my hands on my hips, and toss him a wink. "Ready for me to rescue you, Prince?"

His lips twitch with what I assume is some smart remark, but then he simply says, "I can hardly wait."

We gather around the kitchen island. Mack shoves a spice rack out of the way, pushes a button on the GPS device, and projects a live map of the city onto the gold-flecked ivory countertop.

"We're here," she says, poking a finger at the residential buildings labeled Foggy Bottom. "And we need to get *here* by sunrise."

I watch her metallic blue-lacquered fingertip trail down to a swath of parks and ponds before settling on the tall obelisk on the map titled, *Washington Monument.*

A golden bubble of magic surrounds the obelisk. I stare longingly at the shield that keeps darklings out.

Once we reach that point, we'll be safe.

Unfortunately, we have miles between us and safety, and hundreds of red dots swarm the streets in between.

Screw you and the centaur you rode in on, Spring Prince.

Gulping noises draw my focus to Ruby. She's sitting above us on the copper light fixture, legs dangling, in the process of emptying a crystal decanter of some dark purple liquid.

"Ruby!" I scold, using my mom-voice. "Bad!"

Crap, why did I let her come?

She finishes off the bottle, belches, and throws me an innocent look. "What? You saw the map. We're all going to die; I'm just making sure I die in my happy place."

Asher growls under his breath, glaring at Ruby. "Why is she here again?"

All dragons have a deep hatred of sprites. Supposedly, during the last war when dragons were nearly eradicated, the sprites were the ones who carried out the poisoning with dragonsbane.

Rubbing my temples, I desperately study the map for a plan. We don't have enough time to go around the clusters of darklings to reach our goal.

If only Asher and Valerian could both fly us out of here, but . . . no. Our Keepers can't use any of their powers, including shifting.

Nor can they help us plan in any way, which would be super helpful right now.

No! You can do this without their help. Think. I tap my finger against the churning mass of darklings on the projected map.

"Too bad we can't go under the city somehow," I murmur. "If only . . . wait." I study the tangled meshwork of streets as my pulse quickens. "I thought all major Fae cities have emergency tunnels in case of a surprise darkling attack? If true, the wards that repel darklings could still be intact."

Valerian runs a finger over the sharp edge of his jaw. "You're right. Emergency tunnels were constructed beneath the residential areas for a quick evacuation, but they typically lead to a large, centrally-located portal. That portal could be anywhere."

"Okay," I press, "so where is this one?"

Mack fiddles with the device, and then another image flashes over the counter. The map is still shown, but the tunnels are superimposed in faint blue. They crisscross the parts of the city where the houses are concentrated and then merge into one thick blue line that leads to . . .

I blow out a disappointed breath. The tunnels end beneath the Lincoln Memorial. Technically, the distance between the memorial and the safe zone surrounding the Washington Monument isn't that terribly far—we could run it in ten minutes—but it's teeming with so many darklings that the area is a giant ball of red.

"They're probably attracted to the remnants of the old portal's magic," Asher explains, his voice softening as he takes in Mack's frustration.

"Dang-it." Gritting her teeth, Mack glares at the map, as if she can somehow force it to show us what we need. "It was a good idea, Summer. But with that many darklings . . ."

Frowning, I once again scour the maze of streets between here and the safe zone, each one lit up with darklings. If we try to run directly there aboveground, that leaves miles and miles of ground to cover.

All out in the open, unprotected.

And every second outside this apartment will draw more darklings to our Keepers.

My gut says we wouldn't make it halfway before the darklings overwhelmed us or we ran out of time.

"We could go for one of the weapons," I add, thinking aloud. "Just in case of emergency but . . . if we have to use it, I worry the magic would only draw more darklings to us . . ." My heart skips a beat as an idea slaps me across the face. "Draw them to us," I repeat.

Mack arches an eyebrow.

"We need to move that giant herd of darklings near the portal, right?" Excitement makes me talk fast, and I force myself to slow down and think this through. "What if we used one of the weapons to draw them away?"

Mack's eyes slowly light up. "We activate the weapon, draw the darklings obstructing the path to something— maybe the water in the reflecting pool?—and sprint to the safe zone while they're still fixated on the weapon's magic."

A giant grin stretches my face. Our Keepers can't help us plan the mission, but one look at Valerian's upturned lips and I know we're on to something.

If he thought my plan would end in his death, surely he would be frowning instead.

The closest magical weapon is three blocks away, stored inside a three-story home that at one time probably cost millions of dollars.

Once Valerian and Asher leave the safety of the warded apartment, the darklings will be attracted to their Fae magic, so I order Valerian and Asher to stay while we get the weapon.

At first, Valerian bristles at my command, his bowed lips tugging into a frown.

Well, someone doesn't handle not being in charge.

Breathing hard with excitement, I turn to Ruby, who's zipping through the air in wobbly circles, singing some terrible song in her native tongue. "Ruby, ready to distract some darklings?"

Ruby's eyes are crossed as she nods her head.

Mack frowns. "She has no idea what you're saying."

I grin. "Not a problem. All she has to do is fly around and make any darklings around the house chase her while we steal the weapon. Easy."

"And not get eaten," Mack pointedly adds. "Because that's important."

I grimace before throwing Ruby a thumbs up. "Piece of cake, right, Ruby?"

"Cake?" she screeches before lurching happily into the side of the stainless steel refrigerator door.

Dear Baby Jesus, please, please let this work.

As soon as we near the home where the magical weapon is stashed, a pack of darklings descend. Ruby distracts them while Mack and I rush into the basement, grab the glowing crimson weapon's case, and make it back to find Ruby miraculously unharmed.

Turns out, Baby Jesus was listening, after all.

When Valerian opens the door and spots the crimson case in my hand, Ruby passed out *unharmed* on my shoulder, a flash of pride sparks inside his silver eyes.

Damn, if I wouldn't scale the world's largest mountain just to see that look again.

Get a grip.

I jerk my head in the direction of the city. "Don't be scared, Prince. Mack and I will protect you."

Asher bites down a chuckle as he steps out into the unlit corridor.

Valerian just watches me for a moment. His mouth is teased into an amused half-smile, but his eyes dance with an emotion that makes my toes curl and my breath hitch.

"Enjoying this?" he asks.

"Maybe," I admit. After months of having to take his orders, it feels good to have the roles reversed.

His lips finally commit to a full smile, and it's glorious. "Someday," he whispers into my ear as he passes, "I'm going to find a really, *really* creative way to punish you for that smart mouth."

Oberon's beard. Even trapped in a scourge city and surrounded by darkling zombies, the attraction between us is so thick it's practically a living, breathing thing.

But the moment the door clicks shut behind him and we

break into a quiet jog toward the tunnel entrance a block away, I go straight into badass Guardian mode.

And when the first darkling screech shreds the night, the reality of my situation hits me like a bucket of ice water.

From now until the safe zone, it's up to me to keep the Winter Prince alive. Otherwise, there will be no later flirting, no later negotiating our relationship, no later *anything*.

22

The entrance to the closest tunnel is hidden near an abandoned coffee shop, beneath a wide set of stairs. I don't relax until the iron grate—warded to keep darklings out—senses Valerian and Asher's presence and lights up green before opening for Mack.

As the iron clicks shut behind us, an eerie hissing sound fills the air. On the other side, where we stood just moments ago, countless darklings gather. The warded iron gate does its job, repelling them back a few feet—but it doesn't feel like nearly enough.

Asher's uneasy growl fills the chamber. "Is it just me or are the darklings getting uglier?"

"There's something deeply wrong about being around them and not putting them out of their misery," Valerian murmurs.

I cringe as I study the creatures. Knowing they were once human, a part of me wants to feel sorry for them. But they look so different now, so monstrous, so . . . wrong that it's impossible to find any humanity to connect with.

Their bones are warped and misshapen. Their eyes depthless pits of black. Their faces twisted with hunger and mindless savagery. Any clothes they once possessed are gone, leaving their graying, emaciated flesh exposed.

But it's the way they move—jerky and inhumanly fast, driven by mindless hunger—that puts them squarely in the not-even-remotely-close-to-human camp.

Pushing aside my horror, I fling open the final door to the tunnels . . . perhaps a bit too quickly. Damp air clogs my lungs as we file into the wet darkness. The sound of water trickling down the stone walls rushes over me.

Gaelic symbols are woven into the stone, their meager glow just enough to illuminate the winding, mazelike burrows.

"Do you see any darklings?" I ask Mack, who's peering down at her GPS, her bottom lip caught between her teeth.

"Not that I can tell." She stares at the screen a moment longer before declaring, "It's clear."

I exhale. It's working.

But it's still too early to celebrate.

Adjusting the spear case strapped to my backstrap, I check my wrist-mounted crossbow one more time. "Let's go."

Before I can move a step, Valerian presses the flat palm of his hand against my lower back. Just for a second—long enough to remind me he's here by my side.

A sense of purpose swells in my chest. As Guardian and Keeper, we share a different kind of bond than the one created by magic. A bond of tentative trust between two people from completely different races, born of promise and forged by blood, sweat, tears, and the singular need not to die.

Which is pretty freaking motivating right now.

For the first time since I entered the academy, I understand the deep pride some Guardians take in protecting their Fae Keepers.

Without a word, we break into a sprint. Just like we've been taught, Mack and I position ourselves on the outside of the group, a few meters ahead. Technically, Valerian and Asher could run ten times faster than our breakneck pace, but they keep time with us.

In a real situation, the most powerful Evermore like Valerian and Asher could create a portal to whisk us away, but most Evermore aren't that powerful.

Especially when it comes to portals strong enough to transport more than one person.

The minutes drag by, the walls a blur of shadows and glowing symbols. Our footfalls are soft, the quiet broken only by the rush of our breathing and the occasional splash of a puddle.

All too soon, the final tunnel comes into view. A lattice-work of symbols lights up the other side. Eternal flames of light green magic gutter from giant torches placed on either end.

A single ladder crawls up to the streets above.

As we near the torches, Mack and I go over the map.

She taps a finger over a spot on the GPS screen. "We're here—I think. It"—she zooms in—"looks like the tunnel will come up right at the feet of Abe himself."

My brain, fuzzy from adrenaline and fear, conjures an image of a giant statue.

"It was easier to erect portals near places where hundreds of humans passed through," Asher says. "The residual energy amplifies the power of the portal."

A portal large enough to funnel thousands of fleeing Fae souls would have to be massive, and would require a butt-load of magic. I'm almost disappointed it's no longer active. That would have been an impressive sight.

"Makes sense," I say as I take hold of the first bar on the ladder.

As Shadow Guardian for the highest ranking Evermore in the group, it's my job to go first. I'm not exactly thrilled about it, but at least if anything's waiting on the other side, it will be me the darklings shred to bits, not Mack.

Valerian's gaze snaps to my hand on the ladder. In a flash, his primal urge to protect me takes over and he's rushing toward me.

I bristle, fully prepared to argue. I can do this. I *have* to do this to prove I deserve to be a Shadow guardian.

"Summer—"

"Stop," I order, lifting an eyebrow in challenge as I glare over my shoulder at him. "I can handle it."

He halts, jaw clenched and nostrils flared. Asher stiffens, looking from Valerian to me.

This is what I've been worried about all along. The bond's raw power forcing him to resist my role as his Guardian, which requires serious risk.

"Please," I add.

His snarl echoes through the tunnels, but he retreats a step. "If anything happens to you . . . I'll destroy this entire Shimmer-forsaken city. Do you understand?"

I swallow. Nod.

"Good." He draws a shortsword, his face transforming to the Valerian that terrifies me—the one I have absolutely no doubt would murder every person here, darkling, Fae, and mortal, if I was hurt. "After you, Princess."

"Such a gentleman," I mutter as I clamber up the rungs. A large manhole cover awaits. I hold my breath as I twist, praying the iron in the door has repelled the darklings from this spot.

Panic tears through me as I scramble over the side and onto a . . . a . . . where the frick am I?

The others pour through the hole, but I'm too busy looking around to say much. The enormous columns are just like I remember from the picture. But where I remember seeing the enormous statue of Abraham Lincoln now sits a statue of—

"Is that Maub, the Spring Court Queen?" Mack whispers.

"The one and only," Asher says as we regroup into a defensive circle, Mack and I once again in the front.

Tip of the spear, Summer, I think, repeating Mr. Willis's words from school. *You're the mother-freaking tip of the spear.*

A wide set of stairs leads down into a park, where a swarm of darklings mill around the lawn. Some seem dazed, stumbling and careening, their bones so deformed they can barely walk. Others zip around on all fours so fast they blur into a churning mass of bones and hisses.

As we watch, a few darklings attack one of their brethren. The poor creature doesn't last long, disappearing beneath a swarming mass of its friends.

Cannibal darklings. Wonderful—and so not surprising.

Some have taken to the water of the reflecting pool, which is even more beautiful than I imagined. Lily pads the size of watermelons float across the surface, the pale white flowers sprouting from them infested with iridescent water sprites.

Oh, God. I flinch as I see a darkling snatch one hiding in a lily and bite off the poor creature's wings before—

I look away before I can see the rest, nausea clenching my gut. Thank the Shimmer, Ruby is still passed out on my shoulder, so she didn't have to witness that barbaric—

"Did that creature just bite the head off a flying frog?" Ruby slurs, sitting up on my shoulder.

Holding a finger to my lips, I nod and whisper, "Yes, frogs. Flying frogs."

"Good." She rubs her head, totally ignoring my signal for silence. "Frogs are vile, disgusting creatures. Toads are worse. Some even eat sprites, can you imagine?"

In the hopes that she'll stop talking, I ignore her as we pad on silent feet down the stairs. Any minute now, the breeze will carry the whiff of Valerian and Asher's scent to the creatures.

Mack jerks her chin at the rectangular pool. Go time.

Reaching behind my head, I carefully grab the magical spear's case, grimacing as I unclick the clasp. It pops open with a soft hiss.

Red, fiery light spills from the velvet-lined inside like fog, rolling away from me faster than I expected.

Well, crap.

A collective snarl splits the night as countless darklings all whip their heads in the direction of the magic . . . and us.

My fingers curl around the iron handle of the spear, a tingling sensation driving up my forearm. A single dark red garnet pulses from the hammered spear tip.

Ruby coos as she spots the jewel. "Hello, you pretty little sparkly thing."

Ripping the weapon from its case, I jerk the spear back, find a spot in the water that seems to have the least amount of sprites, and throw it.

Thankfully, the magic inside the weapon improves my terrible aim, and the spear lands exactly where I wanted it to go—in the middle of the reflecting pool.

"My pretty!" Ruby cries.

Ignoring Ruby's furious shrieks, I watch it sink noiselessly into the water and then—

A jolt rocks the steps beneath our feet as crimson magic ripples out into the water. Any darkling within fifteen feet turns to ash immediately. The explosion causes all the water sprites to take to the air like stars shaken free from the sky.

Even Ruby startles, tumbling from my shoulder and nearly face-planting on the stairs before remembering she can fly.

Doubt creeps in; I frown. Did we just waste a valuable weapon that we might need in a few minutes?

All at once, the darklings freeze. As the water stills, the crimson magic can be seen roiling out in waves beneath the surface.

With a collective shriek, the creatures surge across the lawn toward the pool.

23

The reflecting pool teems with darklings. "The magic tainted the water," Mack remarks as we race to the right, following a line of slender trees toward the safe zone. Ruby swerves and dips above us, cackling like this is all some game.

The monument rises in the distance, so close yet still so freaking far away. The golden shield of magic floats around it like a corona of light in a sea of shadows.

I glance to my left at the water as we sprint. Mack's right. The magic seeped into the pond, creating an even larger target and making the entire thing a magnet for the creatures.

A few darklings still remain in our path, torn between the powerful Evermore they smell and the magic in the water.

One leaps in my direction.

I hear Valerian snarl, can feel him tense, ready to destroy anything that tries to touch me.

Before he can react, I put an iron bolt into the darkling's eye. It drops with an ear-splitting screech just as another leaps from the bushes toward Valerian—

My sword cleaves its head from its neck with an ease I

find frightening—but also really fricking awesome. I cut two more down before Valerian can so much as react, dark blood flicking from my blade.

Remembering Mr. Willis's speech, I whip my head back to face Valerian and wink. "You can have the ones I don't kill."

Translation—here's my sloppy seconds. Probably not the best way to force him to accept my leadership position while also keeping his ego intact. But the look on his face—which I'm pretending is respect, not smoldering fury—is worth it.

He begrudgingly falls into place behind me, although I know he'll make me pay for that comment later during training. Staying true to my word, I throw him a few darklings to finish, enough to hopefully sate his bloated ego.

To my right, Mack does the same. Cutting through the straggler darklings like a pro. She's chosen twin katanas, and they sing through the night as she strikes, never missing her mark.

Snarling shapes streak between the trees toward us. The scent of the Evermore has driven them into a frenzy; their black eyes are nearly rolled back in their head with an all-consuming hunger; their inhumanly sharp teeth gnash the air.

Mack and I make sure they never get close enough to endanger our Keepers. I release bolt after bolt of my crossbow, surprised by how different—how *amazing*—it feels to use the weapon against real darklings.

Even Ruby makes herself useful, bringing me back the used bolts. She's convinced herself we made a bargain and I'll be giving her an apple Jolly Rancher for each one.

The landscape slopes slightly upward as we near the end of the pool. My heart sings with pride as Valerian and I fall into a lethal rhythm, our movements synced almost like they're choreographed.

Mr. Willis once said some Keepers and shadows form such

tight bonds that, during battle, they become of one mind, an unstoppable force.

At this moment, I feel like Valerian and I could take down the entire world.

The obelisk looms close, the protective golden shield's glow a beacon of hope that cuts through the darkness around us.

"Almost there!" I call, driving the group forward.

We're past the reflecting pool and racing across open ground. More darklings begin bleeding from my periphery, but we're so close that I push aside the whisper of panic tingling between my shoulder blades.

Across the lawn, figures move toward the monument. I make out a few other shadows I recognize and their Evermore Keepers fighting their way toward safety.

In the distance, the first tendrils of silver hint at dawn's approach.

But it doesn't matter because we're nearly there. Twenty feet separate us from victory. We're so close to the structure that I can see the Spring Court flags whipping from their posts circling the monument.

Ten feet.

Five.

Yes! The golden shield undulates so close I can touch it. Pivoting so my back is to the shield, I catch Valerian's eye and jerk my chin at the safety zone. "Go!"

He hesitates, torn between keeping me safe and letting me do my job. But he must know how important this moment is, with everyone watching us, and he leaps into the protective circle. Asher does the same.

"Summer, get your beautiful ass inside this circle!" Mack orders.

I wink. "After you."

I watch her barrel through the translucent shield, ready to leap after her—

Where's Ruby?

Heart racing, I scour the darkness. There. She's standing on top of a dead darkling, struggling to reclaim the bolt and completely oblivious to the two darklings scuttling on all fours toward her.

My first bolt takes out the closest creature. I wound the second, but my aim is off and my bolt hits its shoulder, hardly making a dent.

Crap. I lunge for the creature, sword drawn, and take it out with a downward strike seconds before it reaches Ruby.

Blood splatters my face, oddly cool and sticky. Fighting the urge to retch, I grab Ruby and toss her onto my back.

Singing and completely oblivious to the danger around us, she dives to add another bolt to the quiver resting on my waist as I rush to the safety zone.

"Ooh, what's this?" she coos, like when she discovers a piece of half-eaten candy she hid and forgot about. "So pretty."

A foul stench reaches my nose.

I turn to go, but Ruby flutters in front of me, dangling a silver, bell shaped device. Rotten air reeks from the tiny holes in the side.

"Why is there orc bait attached to your belt?" Ruby asks.

"Orc what?" I hiss as I snatch her mid-air and begin to run toward the others. Mack, Asher, and Valerian are pressed against the magical curtain . . .

Why are they yelling?

The shield must cut off sound because I can't hear them. I can, however, feel the ground trembling, as if something impossibly large is running straight for me.

Crap.

The second I whip around and take in the huge creature

lumbering toward me, my heart slams into my throat. Pale green skin. Boulder-sized muscles and giant hands capable of crushing my skull. Two thick yellow tusk-like teeth rise from an underbite . . .

Orc.

Oblivious to the oncoming mountain of death rushing toward us, Ruby wiggles from my hand and begins tossing the ball of stench into the air.

Orc.

Orc bait.

Orc. *Bait.*

That was *tied* to my waist.

"Ruby!" I scream before throwing a desperate look back at the safety zone. Everyone inside the protected zone is watching. Mrs. Richter is waving her hands at me while Professor Crayburn works what looks like some type of spell on the shield, possibly one that allows them to cross back over into this world.

Mack is yelling her head off. Beside her, Asher is gesturing for me to run and Valerian is slamming against the magic wall trying to get to me.

But he can't.

Run.

God, I want to, every inch of me consumed by fear. But that's not going to happen. Not without Ruby.

The world slows to a crawl. The orc's beady black eyes, hooded by an enormous overhanging brow, fixate on the bait Ruby dangles back and forth. A bellow shatters the night as three darklings attack his thick legs, but they might as well be flies for all the orc notices.

His platter-sized hand closes around Ruby, who's still holding the bait, the idiot. Her eyes widen as she finally breaks out of her drunken stupor, and the squeal of fear she emits as he shoves her toward his hideous mouth—

A blast of bone-shattering cold ripples through the air, blowing my pale hair forward and turning my breath cloudy white. The grass around us has crystallized, everything in a hundred foot radius transformed from Spring to Winter. Like statues after a blizzard, darklings and the orc are frozen, covered in a deep layer of ice.

The world seems to still, as if time has stopped. But then I hear Ruby's curses and realize what's happened.

Valerian—he broke the rule and saved me. Saved us. Ruby would have died, but still, disappointment fills me as I realize what this means.

I'm going to be expelled.

But I'd ask him to do it again in a heartbeat to save Ruby.

Ruby!

My boots crunch the frosted grass as I rush to her side. Only her feet are visible, and they kick and flail as she works to break free. I reach onto my tiptoes, wrap my fingers around each tiny leg, and tug.

She pops free from the orc's thick icy fingers and dives straight into my vest, trembling. "Thank you," she whispers.

"Don't thank me," I protest as I stumble toward the safety zone, nearly colliding with a darkling frozen in a crouch. "That was compliments of the Winter Prince."

Ruby peeks her head from my shirt. "Kid, I don't know how you did it, but I know magic. And that savage display of power came from *you*."

Me? Crap. I must have stolen the magic from Valerian. Did anyone else see?

"This is bad, Ruby," I mutter as I approach the waiting circle of shadows and Evermore.

Fingers of orange reach across the sky. Sunrise. If I'm not inside that protective shield when the sun rises—

I lunge to where Valerian and the others are waiting, ignoring the tense looks on their faces. I'm trying to think up a way to explain the display when I spot the figure in front of me, blocking my way to safety.

As I see Prince Hellebore's smarmy visage, my frustration overrides my survival instincts. I've been chased by flesh-eating humans turned zombie, covered in their bloody gore, faced down an orc, and now this giant douche face isn't going to stand in my way.

"Move," I growl, my hand going for my sword hilt, "or you'll lose your favorite tiny appendage."

I ignore Ruby's gasp from inside my vest.

He laughs. "Why is it with humans, the weakest ones have the loudest bark?"

Screw this pointy-eared dickwad. I move to brush past him into the safety zone—

A sudden gust of wind slams into me, smashing me flat against the shield—which is now as hard as a pane of glass. He's careful not to touch me—Mack said something about him asking for permission.

But the force of the wind is so strong that I can't move.

And I know—I just know that none of the dangers I survived in the night compare to the situation I'm in now.

24

The shield smells like lilies. I'm not sure why that's the first thing I think when my face is flattened against the magical wall, probably looking as smooshed as when the twins do the same to our screen door back home.

The only difference is they have a choice. I do not.

Valerian roars as he batters the shield trying to get to me, his eyes gleaming with murderous intent. Burst after burst of his magic slams against the thin partition separating him from me, but the shield's power feeds from the entire academy, and it refuses to break.

Asher joins him, their combined magic rolling outward in waves of pale blue and orange, one frosting the shield and the other scorching it.

But I already know the divide between us cannot be breached, and I might as well be in another realm entirely. Unreachable and . . . alone.

With a psychopath.

"What are you . . . doing?" I demand.

Ruby is freaking out, squirming where she's trapped inside my vest. I can't even reach my hand in to protect her because the force of the wind has them pinned against the magical wall.

Hellebore chuckles, an arrogant, lazy laugh that's much closer than I anticipated. Adrenaline floods my veins as I feel his breath warm against my ear.

He still has yet to touch me. Yet to do anything but taunt me with this stupid, impossible wind.

"One touch," he murmurs. "That's all it would take and you would beg me in front of your Winter Prince and the entire school to take you."

I snort, wild laughter bursting from my throat. "To take me? Yeah, to a bookstore so I can buy you a book on better pickup lines."

"You're cheerful, for someone who no longer has a future."

"Bullshit, you can't touch me without permission."

"You're right. I can't physically touch you." His voice is softer now, teasing, like he's my lover and not a wacko forcing me into a weird roleplay game.

Ignoring his insane voice, I focus on Valerian. The teachers are working now to try and undo the spell, but Valerian has stopped, his eyes holding mine, willing me to be brave as he mouths, *I'll come for you.*

Oh, God, that means . . .

I don't even see the portal open up, but suddenly, Valerian and the others just disappear. I'm in a . . . garden. The same one Hellebore took me to last time.

The cloying scent of magic fills the air and then vines of jasmine, honeysuckle, and ivy shoot from the cobblestone path, sprouting and twisting into an elaborate cage that walls us off from the rest of the world.

And then, just to show off, I assume, the flowery cage lifts into the air, drawn by a swarm of thousands upon thousands of monarch butterflies.

Meaning no one can see us. Meaning I'm now alone and defenseless against this raging sociopath, who's obviously decided he no longer cares if I'm protected.

Weapon! Before I can so much as turn around or go for my sword, tendrils of ivy wrap around my wrists and waist, and I'm jerked around to face Hellebore. The vines wind tighter and tighter around my flesh until I'm immobilized against the cage, unable to move. Pinned like a butterfly to a board.

I open my mouth to fling an insult his way, but he shakes his head, a stupid little smile on his face. "Say one more thing I don't like and I'll gag you, understood?"

His eyes flick down as Ruby bursts from my vest, a war cry on her lips. Something flashes to my right, and Hellebore's sprite appears from seemingly mid-air.

I watch the two tumble through the spaces between our cage of jasmine and ivy and disappear.

"Now, where were we?" he asks smugly, knowing he has all the time in the world to torture me. This is his land. It might be infected with the scourge, but it still gives him incredibly strong powers. "Oh, yes. Touching you. I may not be able to physically touch you without your permission, but, as you can see, that doesn't really matter. Besides, I find everyone gives me permission eventually . . . when asked the right way."

I thought I hated Inara. I thought between the loathing I felt for her and Cal, I would never despise someone more than I do them.

But the murderous, blinding rage I feel for Hellebore in this moment burns so hot that I fear I'll burst into flames.

He takes one look at the wild fury in my eyes and draws closer, a moth to my fiery hatred.

My heart jackknifes into my sternum as, slowly, intentionally, he plants his hands on either side of my head. He's so close I can smell his scent over the sweet perfume of jasmine and honeysuckle, a mix of verbena, lilies, and fresh rain.

When he's so close that I'm sure he's going to brush against me, his body halts mere millimeters from mine. "There's that fire I see burning inside you, that raw, untamed pride that flashes in your eyes whenever they tease you, begging to be stamped out."

I strain against the vines circling up my arms like the elaborate cuffs some Evermore wear. If only I could reach my sword, I would eviscerate this jackass.

My knee, on the other hand, is free—

As soon as the thought comes, I go to drive it up into his man goods and then—crap.

I almost touched him. I jerk my leg back, embarrassed at my rash stupidity.

The bastard actually has the audacity to laugh, his sweet breath spilling over my face. "Go ahead. No?"

Twisting sideways, he drives his leg between mine, forming another type of cage around me, one of flesh and bone and poisonous magic.

If I struggle or move at all, I'll accidentally make contact with him.

Bad—this is bad. The moisture shrivels from my mouth. I can almost feel the carnal magic seeping from his skin, begging me to invite it inside me.

If I don't do something, I'll lose control.

"They all saw you take me," I breathe. "They'll be coming for me."

"Who will? Your Ice Prince? The idiot professors who tremble when I merely pass by them in the halls?"

"He'll come for me," I stupidly insist, as if repeating it will make it true.

His eyes slowly trail down my body, his devouring gaze burning where it lingers, just as real as if it were his fingers. "I can see why he wants to keep you as his pet. You're decently made, for a mortal, and your fiery temper coupled with that strange doe-eyed innocence would make taming you a rather enjoyable endeavor—but you're hardly worth a war."

"A war?" I swallow, remembering Eclipsa's words—but no, she also said I was Valerian's property, and as much as I hate that term, it means I'm off limits. "You're the one causing a war."

He runs a finger down the outline of my arm, almost—but not quite—making contact with my flesh. The tangled vine wall I'm pressed against shivers at his touch, as does my skin. "You are so out of your depth at this school, Summer, that you don't even realize you're already caught in my web. You were the moment the Winter Prince used his magic to save you."

My relief that he thinks the magic came from Valerian gives way to panic as I realize what he means.

"So he used his magic and now . . . I'm expelled." My throat tightens with emotion as that disappointment sinks in, but I lift my chin, determined to not let him see my pain. "But I still belong to the Winter Prince."

"Actually, that's not entirely true. Did you know if an Evermore is caught cheating in the gauntlet, it's seen as an affront to the hosting court? By the law of Fae and the academy, I can demand recompense of my choosing equal to or less than the value of such an affront. And the value of a Fae slave isn't very much, just below, say, a well-made pair of shoes."

Lying bastard!

If my hands were free, I'd gouge out his eyes. Instead, I desperately scan his face for hints that he's bluffing, but the horrible smile on his face confirms he's telling the truth.

No. Being owned by Hellebore would be its own special hell. The red room of pain Ruby mentioned flashes in my mind. And Zinnia, oh, God, she's back at the academy waiting for me.

If I don't show up . . .

A wave of nausea hits as I imagine her trying to find out what happened to me. Imagine her reliving her daughter's disappearance as she mourns mine. She'll never forgive herself for not stopping me from coming back here.

Never.

Knowing my panic would only feed his depravity, I manage to hide my anguish behind a hard smile. "The Winter Prince would never let you take me."

The vines around my arm tighten, cutting off my circulation.

"Which is exactly why I would. I could drag you away to my home in the Spring Court and no one would bat an eye . . . but the Winter Prince, I see now that he would go to battle for you. Unfortunately for him, his court's influence is already waning. If he dragged his kingdom to war over one trivial mortal slave . . . well, he would lose everything."

I know what he says is true. The Fae courts are brutal, and power between them is a delicate, volatile thing. Being too attached to something without inherent value would be seen as weak.

In the Everwilde, weakness is blood in the water.

Think. Hellebore might technically be able to kidnap me, but he hasn't done it yet. Instead, he's toying with me. There has to be a reason why.

I glare at him, building up the courage to goad him and call his bluff. "Fine. Throw me in your red room of pain or whatever the frick it's called, you pervert."

Amusement sparks inside his vibrant blue eyes. Eyes too bright, too *unnatural* to be human. "If I wanted you in my red room of pain, as you call it, you'd already be there. But you're right. As much fun as keeping you locked away at my private disposal would be, I enjoy watching you squirm at the academy more. You're like a baby rabbit trapped in a cage full of wolves, hoping that if you just stay really still, no one will eat you."

Wow. This freaking guy. I would make some wisecrack about his poor use of metaphors, but he's dead serious, which is only kind of alarming. "Then all of this . . .?" A chill scrapes down my spine as his true intentions become clear. "You want to make a bargain."

As soon as the words leave my lips, I know I'm screwed.

So *unbelievably* screwed.

Fae bargains are notoriously one sided. There's an entire third year course dedicated to teaching mortals how to navigate them, and shadows that major in Fae law and specialize in bargains are a burgeoning field in New York and other Fae hotspots.

True Fae bargains are bound by powerful magic that cannot be undone. Ever.

Which is why more than one mortal has gone to a bar near the Shimmer and woken up hungover and bound to the Fae for a lifetime, and there's nothing anyone can do about it.

"Just a trivial one," he assures me, his voice slow and rich and seductive, a trick the Fae use to mesmerize us into complacency. "Agree and I will convince the school that another Winter Court Evermore used their powers to save you. You won't be expelled. You'll still be property of the Winter Prince, and he won't go to war over you. All in all, you will gain more than I in this deal."

Liar. Everything inside me screams to deny him immediately. But if his bargain means I can stay at the school and Valerian doesn't suffer . . .

"What would you require in return?" A heavy feeling settles over me as soon as I ask the question.

"A small thing, really." His lips curl at the edges, but my

focus is riveted to his eyes and the darkness that simmers there, a kind of cold cruelty that burrows deep into my core. "Let me touch you."

My throat shudders as I try to swallow, everything inside me—*everything*—recoiling from his suggestion. "What? Now?"

"No, not now, Summer." His intense gaze slides to my traitorous lower lip, which I'm shocked to discover is trembling. "What fun would that be? But there will come a time when I demand you give me permission. This agreement will guarantee you do."

My thoughts race as I try to understand his game. I know allowing him to touch me gives him some sort of power over me—and that all of this is probably just some twisted Fae possessive crap. Two boys in a sandbox who are surrounded by toys but only want the same one.

It doesn't matter that the shovel is broken and doesn't even hold sand. It doesn't matter that the shovel doesn't want to be played with. It doesn't matter that there are a million newer shovels.

All that matters is that Hellebore wants to take something from Valerian.

Of course I'm going to say hell to the no.

Hellebore gives an impatient sigh, and then a tendril of ivy slides along the edge of my jaw, curls over my chin, and forcibly turns my head to look into his strange eyes.

"Do not think for a moment that denying me permission to touch you will somehow make your life easier. You're already trapped in my web, struggling will only make it worse. You can either make it fun for the both of us or simply fun for me."

I grit my teeth as the end of the vine drags across my bottom lip, but deep down I know he speaks some truth.

Valerian would absolutely, without a doubt, drag his court and kingdom to war for me.

The thought makes me sick. And yet, as much as I want to give in and stop this madness, I know I will never willingly let someone gain that kind of control over me.

Ever.

He might make me his slave, but he can't control me unless I let him.

I sink against my ivy prison, ready to deny his request and screw the consequences, when Ruby zips toward us with her teeth bared. She's holding a stick bigger than she is and promising Hellebore's death.

Behind her, Hellebore's beaten up sprite tries to follow. One of his iridescent wings is shredded, his face a bloody pulp where I'm assuming Ruby hit him with her stick. Repeatedly.

My heart swells with pride as she wedges herself between Hellebore and me, a mouse facing off against a lion.

"Take one more step toward my master," she cries, "and I'll cast a spell that will make your shriveled up little sausage limp for a century."

Despite facing mortal peril, I choke out a laugh.

It can't be coincidence that both Ruby and I both threatened his junk, because guys—and Fae—like him think that's what makes them a man.

Hellebore appraises her with a curious expression. "You would die for this mortal?"

"I would," Ruby declares, and I make a mental note to give her all the candy in the world if we survive this. "She's claimed me, which means I belong to her and she to me."

Hellebore turns to look at his loyal sprite, still wavering in the air beside his master looking seconds from falling over dead. "Nerium, I see you met your match."

Nerium says something to Hellebore in one of the old

languages, and then Hellebore lifts him from the air and settles him on his shoulder.

The act almost makes Hellebore seem, if not kind, then decent. Until he turns to me, at least, and his face is anything but kind. "Your choice, mortal. Make the bargain or lose your spot in the academy and become a slave of the Spring Court."

I look from him to Ruby . . . and, slowly, an idea forms. One that, if worded just right, might let me make this bargain on my own terms.

Without being controlled like a puppet by a flower-tatted BDSM serial killer.

"I'll bargain with you . . ." I wait until his lips part with expectation, his eyes gloating, and then add, "on one condition. Actually, no, two conditions. First, you tell Inara and her friends to call off the attacks. No more pranks, no more trying to make me fail. Unless you can't make her listen to you—"

"Done. And the other?"

"Second . . . I choose the part of me you touch."

His eyes narrow.

Shoot. I gave in too easily. I should have protested more. "Or not. If you don't want to bargain—"

"Yes," he says too quickly before he regains his lazy composure, his mouth twitching into that arrogant grin that makes him so throat-punchable. "Now, say it. What are you agreeing to?"

I pull in huge amounts of air, trying to chase away the feeling that I'm drowning.

Talk slowly. Think before you speak.

After I've gathered my thoughts and have my statement ready, I say, "I agree that, when the time comes, I'll give you permission to touch a part of me that will be specified right before the act itself." I peer up at him, terrified he'll hear the pounding of my duplicitous heart and know I'm tricking him. "Your turn."

"I agree to my part of the bargain. You will remain at the academy, and Inara won't touch you."

A wave of magic rolls over us as the bargain is struck, leaving a metallic taste in my mouth and doubt in my heart.

His eyes glitter with dark intent as he adds, "No one will touch you until it's my turn." I flinch as he suddenly leans so close I can feel the heat of his lips against my ear. "And then, Summer, I promise you, it won't matter *where* I touch you, do you understand? You'll be ruined, utterly, completely, permanently destroyed, and the Winter Prince will watch."

I force my eyes downcast. Let him believe I'm cowed into submission. That he forced me into a terrible bargain I now regret. Whatever it takes to feed his demented soul long enough to keep my spot in the academy.

Once he fulfills his end of the deal, I know he'll wait before demanding I fulfill mine. Savoring the secret, shared knowledge that he can touch me whenever he wants. Have me whenever he wants.

Typical Evermore, using a mortal as an unwitting pawn in a game where we couldn't begin to fathom the rules.

But I'm not a mortal—not technically, anyway—and if my hunch was correct, I'll beat him at his own twisted game.

If not, I'm so very, *very* screwed.

25

"**A**gain," Valerian orders. He's posted on the far side of the gym, arms crossed and legs spread wide. When Eclipsa hesitates, he repeats, "Again, Eclipsa."

I flash her a panicked look, and she mouths, *sorry*, before sending a wave of magic rolling across the mat toward me. Taking a deep breath, I square off to face the churning darkness as it rises, transforming into a hulking troll.

It's an illusion spell. I know the troll isn't real. I know it can't hurt me.

And yet, my mind and body freak out as if it were real. I scream and duck, searching for a weapon. Pleading with them for anything to fight this monster. The troll barrels closer, and I can actually smell its rotten egg stench and feel the mat shake beneath its large, hairy feet.

Sweat pours from my body. I'm terrified, helpless to do anything but watch as it swings its huge, spiky club at my face—

"Enough!" Eclipsa snaps.

I must have closed my eyes, and when I open them, everything is sideways. Oh—that's because I'm curled in the fetal position on my side, arms hugging my legs, trembling so hard my thigh slaps softly against the padded mat.

Relaxing, I stare up at the ceiling. The troll is gone and once again, I produced no magic.

None. Not even a tiny little whisper of the stuff.

Both Valerian and Eclipsa rush over to help me up, but when Valerian gets close, Eclipsa checks him with her elbow. "She needs space."

He freezes, his face twisted with emotion. Agony and rage swirl inside his silver eyes as he slowly meets my stare.

It's been two weeks since Hellebore kidnapped me in front of Valerian and my class. Two agonizing weeks of working every night to coax out my magic. Two weeks of looking into Valerian's face and seeing his gut-wrenching guilt for not being able to stop Hellebore.

That plus the seething fury buried beneath the shame convinces me that I made the right choice.

If I'd let Hellebore take me to the Spring Court, Valerian would have burned the Everwilde to the ground, no matter the cost.

"It's okay, Eclipsa," I protest, even though my heart still races and my body is weak from doing this same thing for the last four hours. A nightmarish, never-ending game called let's-scare-Summer-until-she-uses-magic or pees her pants.

My sanity isn't the only victim. The nights after training that were supposed to go toward operation-get-to-know-Valerian are now horror-filled scenarios that leave me sweaty and shaking.

Not exactly *how* I envisioned getting to know Valerian better.

But Eclipsa's wrong. I don't blame Valerian for trying to help me control my powers. Control means I can keep my identity safe and—if needed—can protect myself from psychopaths like Inara and Hellebore.

I'm just convinced it's a waste of time. I'm broken. My mortal body unable to harness the power tethered to my soulstone.

They've tried everything. Orcs. Lycans. Trolls. I even agreed to using the spider creatures from my hallucination, which ended disastrously with me dry-heaving on the ground.

At this point, I'd let Eclipsa conjure Satan himself if it helped draw out my magic so I can learn how to control it.

Valerian's hand is cool as he pulls me to a stand. "I'm sorry, Princess. I—" Frowning, he looks away. "It's well past midnight. We'll try again next session."

"No," I protest, willing my legs to stop shaking. "I want to go again."

"Not happening." His voice is gentle now, like I might break apart any second, and that's almost worse than his frustration. "You need to rest."

"Prince," Eclipsa says, toying with the pigtail braid over her left shoulder. "There's something I want to try with her . . . alone."

"We've pushed her too hard already."

"Trust me."

He stiffens, prepared to argue, but she holds up a hand. "We have no idea how the bond between you is affecting everything. Perhaps if you're not right here . . ."

Her voice trails away, but I can see her implication take hold in his face. His mouth softens, and he looks at me. "Okay, but I'm leaving Phalanx."

He jerks his chin at the huge snowy white owl sitting on the railing above, watching us with those sentient amber eyes. I have no idea how lethal his owl familiar is, but considering how much Valerian trusts Phalanx to watch me, I'd say very.

"I'm fully capable of defending her," Eclipsa assures him. "As you're well aware."

He runs a hand through his tousled blue locks, his hair settling over one eye, before he slides his gaze to me. "If anything happens, I'll know and I'll portal straight here, okay?"

I yawn through my forced grin. "We'll be fine."

I watch him leave and fall into a defensive stance, feet spread shoulder width apart, ready for another try. I'm beyond tired, and my body instinctively tenses, terrified of what new horror Eclipsa will come up with. "What is it this time?" I mutter. "A horde of deranged water sprites?"

Instead of laughing—although, admittedly, my joke was lame—she just shakes her head. "I'm not going to torture you more tonight, Summer. There's no point."

"Because I'm broken?"

"Because I think we're going about this all wrong." She reaches out her hand. "Come with me."

I look around, confused. "Where?"

"Don't ruin the surprise. Just go with it."

I glance at my gym bag, not even trying to hide my longing to go back to my dorm, take the world's longest, hottest shower, and then pass out.

With an annoyed yawn, I slip my hand in hers. "Who needs sleep anyway?"

The familiar scent of the portal barely hits before the white gym walls and high ceilings transform into a brilliant midnight sky splattered with stars. The moon is swollen and luminous, nestled between two ivory mountain peaks.

Its delicate light illuminates the most beautiful garden I've ever seen.

I gasp, and Eclipsa releases my hand. "Welcome to the renowned poison gardens of the Lunar Court."

I know from my classes that days and nights don't exist here, only a perpetual in-between, where the moon shines nearly as bright as the sun. A variety of lethal plants thrive under these conditions, producing the highest concentrations of poison in all the Everwilde.

Curious now, I take in our surroundings. Everything emanates with a faint glow, from the crooked trees to the pools of dark amethyst water to the silver night-blooming roses intertwined over nearly every structure.

Eclipsa and I sit on the edge of a crescent shaped fountain. A rare form of glowing moss clings to the three nymph statues in the center, and moon sprites ignore us as they dip tiny buckets into the amethyst water to take to the plants.

The outer edges of their wings reflect the moonlight so that they look like a thousand tiny stars dancing across the garden.

If the textbooks are correct, the male moon sprites hide in the surrounding trees, guarding the garden from thieves intent on stealing the poisonous plants.

One sting from a male moon sprite can leave an Evermore paralyzed for weeks, and can kill a mortal in less than a minute.

This entire place oozes a quiet lethality, which begs the question . . .

"Eclipsa, why are we here?"

"Because in our world, Summer, knowledge is power. And you deserve to understand why Valerian is terrified of losing you—and why Hellebore is singling you out. Once you understand both, perhaps this all won't be so frightening. As to the *why* we're in the Lunar poison gardens, it's because this is my favorite place in the world."

I tangle my hands together in my lap, trying to still my

thundering heart. In my short but traumatic time in the Ever-wilde, I've learned that revelations are always bad.

"You asked a while ago who taught us the art of yoga, remember?"

I nod.

"It was the Winter Prince's mother, Calista. She was a beautiful soul, kind and generous, which is a rarity for Ever-more. She also loved the prince in a way that was considered too maternal, too human for many of those in the Winter Court, who expected royal Evermore children to be separated at a young age from their parents and honed into cold, cunning future rulers."

I shake my head, wishing I was surprised by the Fae's callousness. "That's horrible."

"Out of all the courts, the Winter Court was the cruelest. The prince's mother couldn't take it. She started visiting the human world. She fell in love with the mortal culture; your food and technology and strange lands." Eclipsa laughs suddenly, her eyes distant. "I remember once she visited a place—I think it's called a monastery—and brought the prince a tiny, smiling fat man made of gold. He has no idea that I know this—and if you tell him, I'll murder you—but the prince slept with that fat, smiling man clutched in his arms every night for years."

I'm fairly certain Eclipsa is talking about a Buddha. Under any other circumstance, I would laugh at the idea. But I've felt Valerian's pain. Heard him calling out for his mother. And there's nothing even remotely funny about any of this.

"Calista's fascination with the mortal world was a scan-dal, especially for the Unseelie Courts, who despise the modern mortal world and cling to the ancient laws. But she always came back, and the Winter Prince's father always forgave her. Then King Oberon recognized the Winter Prince's powers and began grooming him for succession, and everything changed. Calista started to disappear for longer and longer, unable to bear watching him tortured and turned cruel."

Bitter anger takes root inside me as I remember the dream. Remember King Oberon whipping Valerian, and Valerian crying out for his mother.

"After a while, she only came back every few years. Some Evermore children would be used to that type of parental detachment, but the prince's mother had showered him with affection, and when she took that away . . ." Eclipsa sighs, her eyes focused on some distant star in the sky. "Every time she came back, she promised the next visit she would take him back with her. The prince hated King Oberon and wanted nothing to do with his twisted ideology. He truly believed she would rescue him someday from that fate."

I focus on a moon sprite on the edge of the fountain, watching the delicate creature preen its light-gilded wings rather than see the pain in Eclipsa's face.

"When you and the Winter Prince decided to flee, Calista promised to help you and the prince hide in the mortal world together. Then you were discovered fleeing the Summer palace and killed."

My body sags into itself. Lately, whenever I even think about my death at the hands of my father, it leaves me feeling down for days. "What happened to his mother?"

"That's the thing." Eclipsa runs her fingers idly through the deep purple pool of iridescent water. "We think . . . you see, Calista was the only one who could have told the Summer King of your plans."

I straighten in surprise. "Why would she do that?"

"Because she had a daughter, and she knew there was never any chance that the prince could hide from King Oberon—not as the heir apparent. Not with that much power. So she bargained one child's life for another."

Valerian had a sister? "I don't understand."

"The prince's sister, Wynter, had been a hostage of the Summer Court for years. In exchange for the information about your planned escape with the prince, your father not only gave Calista her daughter back, but used his strong magic to hide them in the human world."

"Are you sure she betrayed him?"

Eclipsa's eyes glitter with violence. "All we know is the day you died, they both disappeared, and no one has seen them since."

Oh, God. I press a fist just above my heart. "How can a mother do that? Destroy one child to save another?"

"I don't know but it would have been better if she'd never shown him kindness at all. The day his mother betrayed him and caused your death, something inside him broke. He stopped feeling anything." Eclipsa's voice is so soft I barely hear it as she says, "If my spies ever discover where Calista is hiding, I have a special dagger with her name on it."

I don't doubt that one bit. A part of me feels the same way, especially knowing the pain I felt from the nightmare is nothing compared to what Valerian must have felt when she betrayed him.

A mother's rejection is its own special kind of injury that never heals.

"He won't talk about it, at least, not to me." Eclipsa holds out her finger, watching as a moon sprite lands on the end. "But I thought you deserved to know why he acts the way he does."

"Because he's afraid I'll abandon him like she did?"

"Because you gave him the one thing that could hurt him again—the burden of caring. And that terrifies him more than anything."

Oh, boy. As an Evermore, I suspected Valerian had a mountain of emotional baggage that would take the good part of a lifetime to unpack. But I see now that mountain is unscalable.

There's no unpacking it, only living in its shadow.

Can someone used to countless lifetimes of pain ever learn to fully trust? Fully love in the way that I want—no, that I *need*?

I look to Eclipsa to discover she's watching me intently, probably trying to determine just how freaked out I am. "You knew me then, right?" I ask. "When I was one of you?"

"I did." She grins. "I hated your guts at first, by the way. He actually made me swear an oath of magic not to assassinate you."

For some reason, I laugh. "Why? Was I a raging bitch?"

Her grin fades. "No, you were really kind and funny. But by then, between his mother constantly abandoning him and King Oberon's torture, I knew he couldn't take any more heartbreak."

I tug at my ponytail. "Was it love? Between us?"

Her eyes widen. "Love? Don't be ridiculous. No Evermore uses that word."

"He did before I left school, when he told me who I really was."

She arches a dubious silver eyebrow. "If he did, it's because he knew using it would make you understand, but don't kid yourself. What you and the prince had then was powerful, but only because the bond between you is so strong. That's magic, not love."

"That seems . . . I don't know. Like I'm being tricked into the relationship."

She snorts. "Tricked? What your kind calls love is really just a pretty word for a rush of chemicals to your brain. Love is a drug. An elixir that makes normally rational people do really stupid things. And in the Everwilde, people who do stupid things don't live long."

"Wow," I quip, trying to hide my disappointment. "That's touching. You should put that on a Hallmark card."

But Eclipsa isn't fooled, and her expression softens. "Summer, I understand why you want to believe in love. Despite everything I know about my kind, everything I know about how our world works, I came close to believing it was real once, too."

Hellebore. Just thinking his name feels wrong, as if somehow it's a betrayal of Valerian. Whenever I see Hellebore in class or across campus, or even outside school events, the secret, gloating look he gives me feels like a blunt dagger being slowly driven into my heart.

One only I can see. Which is the point, of course.

I convinced Valerian and the others that the Spring Court heir teased me for a while, but after he grew bored, all it took was reminding him of my brand, and he let me go. Valerian suspects the Winter Evermore that came forward to take the blame for the ice magic did so to gain favor in the Winter Court by protecting its heir.

I thought about telling them the truth a thousand times. I've typed the words in a text message to Valerian every night since, only to delete it before I hit send.

I just can't overlook what happens if I tell them. Valerian would kill Hellebore. And the bargain I made to keep Valerian from doing just that would be for nothing.

It's scary just how much I'm starting to think like a Fae, weighing the truth like something that can be bartered with and manipulated.

I refocus on Eclipsa, determined to discover as much about the Spring Court heir as possible. If I understand him, maybe I can use that to my advantage. "I know you said you don't want to talk about it, but since you brought it up . . ." I scan her face for anger before continuing. "What happened between you two?"

She goes still; the small silver hairs the wind blows around her face are the only part of her that moves. "We met here, actually," she finally says, her gaze roaming the garden until she finds a spot beneath a copse of enormous yew trees. "He was to the right of that tree collecting the buds of a rare night-blooming foxglove flower for his renowned collection of poisons."

Of course Hellebore collects rare poisons instead of doing what normal rich people do and hoarding overpriced wine or vintage cars. I bet he keeps them in his red room of pain. "And then what?" I prod carefully. "And don't say you two *did it* over there because, vomit."

She laughs. "Summer, males like him don't just 'do it.' Not immediately. Sometimes not for years, centuries. They live for the chase beforehand. They only want what they can't have, and once they have you, they've won and the game is over."

"And he couldn't have you?"

My question is supposed to be teasing, but I catch the way her mouth tightens. "I belong to the Winter Court. No one can *have* me—not unless they buy my contract."

The air seems to thin around us. I imagine the pain I feel wearing Valerian's brand and being treated like property is nothing to what she's endured for years.

"I knew the moment I saw him that he was his own type of poison, just like the foxglove blossoms he was so lovingly collecting. I knew he would try to break me, that he would destroy me if he could, but I didn't care."

"Why?"

"Because a part of me wanted him to do it. To break me into a thousand pieces so that no one could own me, not him, not the Winter King, not anyone." She blinks as if coming out of a trance. "I suspected he was only interested in me to hurt the Winter Prince, but when he told me he would buy my freedom . . ." She stands suddenly, wiping at the corners of her eyes. "It's late. Are you ready?"

As I slide to my feet, I ask, "Why does he hate the prince?"

She cuts her eyes at me, any emotion I thought I saw in her face gone. "You mean, besides the prince's arrogance and penchant for pissing off other courts?" Her hand waves over the silvery air, her fingers tracing the pale blue outline of a portal. "Hellebore blames the prince for his parents' death."

And . . . now it all makes sense. Why Hellebore wants to publicly take me from the prince and then humiliate me. Some Evermore vendetta. I'm not even surprised.

"*Is* the prince to blame?" I prod.

She shrugs, and I find her non-committal attitude over whether my possible future mate caused the death of two people rather alarming. "All I know is Hellebore blames the prince for something that happened that ended the alliance between his parents and the Summer King. Without the king's support, his aunt, Queen Maub, could finally have them killed and take the Spring Court throne."

After that, I don't ask any questions, afraid my brain will explode if I learn one more thing about the horrible Evermore Courts. Eclipsa portals me straight to my dorms, and I stumble to the room I share with Mack to find her curled up asleep on the ancient moth-eaten loveseat, surrounded by textbooks.

Cool night air blows in through the open window, stippling her bare arms and legs.

After helping her to her bed, I close the window.

Something catches my eye.

Frowning, I pluck the trinket from the windowsill and hold it up to the moonlight, taking in the rounded shape and smooth petals. The rose is carved from amber, the golden material translucent. Half asleep, I look inside . . .

As soon as I make out the long, thin legs and hourglass

marking on the spider suspended in the amber, a chill runs through me.

It's a black widow, perfectly preserved and so lifelike I nearly throw the stupid thing.

You don't even know you're trapped in my web yet.

Prince Hellebore's words reverberate inside my skull, and I know—I just know, this is from him. He's watching me to see how I respond. Hardly daring to breathe as he waits for me to realize it was him, for me to become afraid.

"Get off on this, you sick pervert!" I hiss, throwing up my middle finger.

Grunting, I yank back open the window and toss the gift to the ground below. Then I slam the window down again, the force rattling the glass, and march to bed.

I have to keep this deranged foreplay going just long enough to get through school. By the time he asks for me to perform my part of the bargain and realizes I've tricked him, it will be too late. School will be almost over. Then he'll go back to his inbred academy and I'll never have to see him again.

I tell myself this over and over until I fall into a restless sleep.

26

"Why did you never tell me the city in the fall is this beautiful?" I ask Mack as we stroll down Fulton Street in Brooklyn, past rows of orange and gold trees. Valerian and Asher walk beside us, their heads on a swivel as they take it all in.

We're on a field trip for our Modern Mortal World class. Professor Lochlan set us free in Manhattan this morning, and we've spent the day traversing the city. The point is to immerse our Keepers in human culture while teaching how to do human things like buy something with a credit card, follow the pedestrian crossing signs, and flag a taxi.

When it came to using the subway line, which we took after visiting the Museum of Modern Art, Mack had to teach all of us, including me.

I sneak a glance at Valerian. He's dressed in a long sleeved gray *Beastie Boy's* shirt we found at a flea market earlier, dark skinny jeans, and a navy blazer. His mess of similarly colored wavy blue hair is tousled artfully to the side. If not for the sharp prick of his ears jutting from his hair, or his inhumanly gorgeous features, he looks just like all the other hipsters milling around Brooklyn.

A pigeon flutters near his feet, pecking at a piece of trash, and Valerian looks ready to slay the poor creature. The pigeon hops away as Phalanx streaks overhead—as if being tailed by a giant owl in Manhattan isn't conspicuous in the least.

I've already warned Valerian twice that Phalanx can't eat the tiny dogs New Yorkers seem to all own.

Valerian agreed, but begrudgingly. He's been on high alert after an adorable golden retriever tried to bite him.

Apparently, dogs can sense the Fae, something I didn't know.

Asher is similarly shell-shocked. He was doing fine until he entered the crosswalk too soon and was nearly flattened by a red Miata. Valerian, used to negotiating for every service in the Everwilde, offended a cab driver when he claimed the driver's rate was tantamount to thievery and got us thrown out.

All in all, it's been an eye-opening experience. Especially learning how much Valerian and Asher don't know about our world. The Seelie Courts have been acclimating their Evermore since they were children, but the Unseelie have done the opposite.

Which is how two of the most powerful Evermore in existence got trapped inside a revolving door for three whole minutes. When Asher freaked out on the escalator, we decided it was best to stay outdoors for a while.

As we moved away from the traffic and stores, both Evermore chilled a bit. Mack insists our final spot should be Owl's Head Park, so she grabs us four salty hotdogs from a food truck, and we find a grassy spot near the water to eat.

Despite it being nearly October, the weather is unseasonably warm, and the park is crowded.

Asher downs his hotdog, and Mack graciously offers him hers. He's interested in the ships gliding along the New York Harbor, so she takes the dragon shifter to see them.

I watch them go and then turn my attention to Valerian. He sits cross-legged, sniffing the sauerkraut on his hotdog and looking incredibly disdainful.

"You don't have to eat it," I finally say.

He sets it on the grass for Phalanx, looking relieved. "Thank Titania, that's quite possibly the foulest thing I've ever encountered."

"Fouler than the mushroom meatloaf the academy makes?"

"Fair point." He smiles, and a part of me celebrates. Things have been strained between us after the gauntlet, and we've both been too busy with school and my extra training to hang out.

On a whim, I say, "Hey, why don't we do the truths game you promised me?"

"Now?" He pointedly glances over the crowded park.

I shrug. "No one's listening."

"But they are staring."

He's right. That's the other thing I wasn't expecting. How much people stare at Valerian and Asher. The men mostly glare, while the women don't even try to hide their attraction to them. I nearly tackled a middle-aged woman on the subway after she tried to grab a handful of Valerian's ass.

Thankfully, Asher wasn't too overwhelmed by the New York subway experience to protect the prince, and he sent the woman scrambling back.

But everywhere we go, women throw themselves at both men, especially Valerian.

I also wasn't expecting how much that would bother me.

"They're staring because you're different," I insist.

"Different? They're drawn to me for evolutionary reasons.

Deep down, the men recognize what I am, an ancient predator who once snuck into their lands and stole their women."

"And the females?"

He flashes me a lazy grin. "Oh, they simply want to sleep with me."

I roll my eyes. "Not everyone wants to sleep with you."

"No?" He turns his head, making eye contact with a pretty brunette walking two Yorkies. The brunette's eyes light up, and she makes a beeline for us.

Lord help us all. I catch her eye, glaring until her perky smile fades and she storms in the other direction.

"That was cruel," Valerian says, resting on his elbow, his eyes sparkling with amusement.

"No, that was a mercy. Now stop trying to distract me and get ready for my inquisition."

His eyes go dark and all liquidy and then he crawls over and lays his head in my lap.

His lips twitch mischievously as he stares at me, one hundred percent aware of how irresistible he is. "I'm ready now, Princess. But beware, this truth thing goes both ways."

Valerian Sylverfrost, Prince of the Winter Court and possibly the most lethal Evermore I know, just crawled over and laid his head in my lap.

Whoa. A thrill of . . . something shivers down my spine. We could be two college lovers enjoying the park after work. The thought dredges a sharp pain in my chest as I realize how much I want that.

A normal, easy, human relationship defined by mundane things like the first time we meet each other's families or share an apartment key.

That's the opposite of what's happening here but . . . against my better judgement, I run my fingers through his dark blue hair, startled by its silkiness.

A puff of air escapes his lips at the contact, and then he closes his eyes.

"You smell divine," he murmurs.

Dangerous territory, I remind myself, but I don't remove my hand, and he doesn't remove his head. Both of us testing how far we can take this new form of intimacy and still control ourselves.

"So," I begin, carefully weighing my questions. We only get four apiece. "You hate hotdogs, you hated the gourmet mac 'n' cheese we found at the flea market—"

"That vile yellow stuff?"

I tug on a strand of his hair. "No interrupting while I have the question leaf."

"The what?" he demands, his eyes flashing open.

I grab a golden leaf and wave it over his eyes. "This. Just go with it."

"Fine. You have the dead leaf, now please. Ask your question."

"So, you hate our food, even the amazing stuff. What do you like?"

Relaxing, he closes his eyes again. "Are you asking what my favorite meal is?"

"Yes, I guess I am." I can't stop staring at the dark blue curtain of lashes resting against his ivory cheeks. The swell of his bowed lips, parted slightly.

"Every year in the Winter Court, we celebrated the ice maiden with a festival. There's this treat called snow candy made from maple syrup. I rather like it."

"Wait? That's your favorite food? You won't touch a taco or deep dish pizza but you'll eat candy?"

He shrugs. "My father never let me have any, so I'd sneak away from the royal entourage and eat so many I was sick."

Whoa. "So you rage ate candy to piss your dad off? That doesn't count as your favorite food. Okay, that's it. I'm making it my mission to find something from the mortal world that you love."

"Never going to happen. Now, my turn." He opens his eyes, those silver irises like trapped mercury as he holds my stare, and takes the leaf from my hand. "What did you want to do with your life, before I dragged you to the Everwilde?"

Okay, he went serious right off the bat. I chew my lip, trying to remember my dreams before all this started. "I don't know, I was so focused on keeping everyone fed and safe that I didn't have time to think about much else. College, maybe? So I could do something that helps people."

"That's very noble of you."

"What?" I bristle at the hefty dose of sarcasm in his voice. "You think helping people is naive?"

"No, I think it's very human, and also useless in the Everwilde."

This guy. I'm so tired of the Fae using the Everwilde as an excuse for their bad behavior. But I don't want to argue, not when he's being truthful, so I blow out a breath, snatch the leaf away, and continue. "What was the first thing that drew you to me, before?"

"Your smile," he says immediately. "You were always grinning like you knew a secret, and I wanted desperately to know what that secret was."

"And did you?"

"Yes, you're deeply obsessed with me. Now, my turn." He takes the leaf before I can argue, twirling it above his head. "Have you ever had a boyfriend, Summer?"

I nearly choke on air. "In the human world? No, I mean— no. A few guys asked me out, but I was too busy for that." I reclaim the leaf. "When we were together before, did we, you know . . ."

As understanding dawns, a devilish smile overtakes his face. Slowly, he arches an eyebrow. "Did we make love?"

Holy crap, his voice just lowered two octaves, and he's doing that magnetic thing where he looks me in the eye like I'm the most important person in the world.

Heat stings my cheeks, but I refuse to avert my eyes from his simmering stare. "Yeah."

"No, we never had the chance. You wanted to get married first."

"I did? That doesn't sound like me at all."

He reaches up, toying with an errant strand of my blonde hair. "What can I say? You wanted to lock me down as quickly as possible."

Snorting, I almost smack his head and then think better of it, trailing a finger over the tip of his ear.

He freezes, a tremor wracking his body as a low groan slips from his lips. "You fight dirty."

"And you're a bastard."

A wolfish grin curls his lips, showing off those perfect white teeth. "But you wanted to marry this bastard."

Shimmer save me, I'm torn between strangling him and kissing him right now.

He chuckles, and we continue like that, interrogating and teasing one another until the sun sets. By the time Mack returns with Asher, we've gone well beyond the four questions.

Mack's eyes widen when she spots Valerian's head in my lap. "What the heck are you guys up to?"

Valerian glances up at me. "She doesn't have the question leaf. Should we let it slide?"

We burst into laughter as Mack and Asher exchange puzzled looks, and I have the sudden, alarming realization that I could fall helplessly in love with this Valerian.

Not the Winter Court Prince. Not the heir to the Winter Throne. Not the Evermore I'm bound to by magic.

The beautiful, sarcastic, funny Valerian who bites his lip

when he's about to say something vulnerable and beams when I laugh at his jokes.

I don't care what Eclipsa said, this Valerian could dare to love me.

And I him.

27

After the field trip, the weeks fly by, and Valerian finally agrees to using some of the time trying to conjure my magic to just hanging out. We ask questions. We flirt but never go far enough to lose control. We tease but don't judge. And slowly, like flowers that only bloom in full sun, we open up to each other.

I learn things about him. Like that he prefers dark chocolate, cats over dogs, and books over movies. That he adores fashion week in New York City and tries to sneak away every year to attend. I discover he watched a forbidden Marvel movie once in the Winter Court on a bootleg iPad and was afraid to enter the mortal lands because he thought the Hulk was real.

Apparently, the prince has a dark sense of humor. He named his owl familiar Phalanx after a finger bone because the creature kept biting off the digits of Valerian's tutors.

His favorite color is black. Not because he's trying to be cool, but because his first memory in life is tugging on the striking onyx strands of his mother's hair and then watching her laugh.

Slowly, the divide between us begins to disappear. It's funny how learning little things about someone makes them more real, more imperfect . . . yet somehow that's attractive.

Like finding out Valerian hates cheese. I should see that as a red flag, because only a psychopath would hate cheese—but instead I find it weirdly adorable.

The closer Valerian and I grow, the further the bargain with Hellebore gets pushed back in my mind. Sometimes I can feel his stare across campus, or during the classes we share after lunch. But he never engages, and true to his word, the pranks have stopped.

A part of me knows his inattention is meant to lull me into a false sense of security. That the minute I truly think I'm safe, Hellebore will strike. But that part of me grows quieter as the days pass in a blur of classes, training, and tests.

Next weekend is Samhain. This year, they're making all the shadows stay in the main hall instead of the gym, with cots set up in the lecture halls and guards posted outside.

We're all camped out on the roof, watching the huge projector screen as an Adam Sandler movie plays. Even with the movie speakers turned all the way up, the wild, animalistic snarls from the campus below pierce the night. A bonfire rages in the distance, the smoke tinging the air and stinging the back of my throat.

I've been restless all day, as if I can feel the Evermore changing. Or maybe my inner Fae is reacting somehow.

I check my phone, scrolling down to my last message with Valerian. I sent him a picture of me holding up a falafel plate that I had Ruby fly over. I've been ordering new foods for him to try, and, so far, he hasn't loved a single one.

His reply: *Delicious. I can't wait to devour it.*

Me: *Really? So I've finally won?*

Him: *Oh, did you think I was talking about the food?*

Me: *You're the worst.*

Ruby took him the food hours ago, and I haven't heard anything since. Not that I'm surprised. Samhain is the one night a year the Evermore's primal instincts turn them half-wild, unable to control their animalistic impulses.

And Ruby probably ate most of it before she arrived anyway.

Mack elbows me, nearly waking the sprite, who's nestled in the front pouch of the onesie Mack insisted I wear. I'm pretending there aren't cats riding burritos on the front. "Stop checking your phone every five minutes."

I tuck my phone into my pocket. "Says the girl who just sent lizard breath ten dragon gifs in a row."

"That was funny," she insists. "And there are so many dragon gifs to choose from."

I glance over at my bestie. She's taken this whole slumber party thing just a bit too far. Her pink-streaked chocolate hair is pulled into pigtails, and she wears a unicorn onesie with a horned hood.

"I'm sorry, what?" I tease. "I can't hear you over the unicorns farting rainbows on your outfit."

"Hey, can I sit with you guys?"

We both look up to see Kyler standing by our row of chairs. She wears a fuzzy green robe over a nightgown, and she's clutching a bag of burnt popcorn.

Mack goes full-fledged protective mode before I can say a word. "Um, do you plan on planting orc bait on us?"

Kyler flinches, her eyes staring down at her cow slippers. "I didn't have a choice. My Keeper said if I didn't—"

"Shh," Reina hisses from two rows ahead. "Shut up or I'll make you, first year."

Immediate, blinding rage pours through me, and I shoot Reina a murderous look until she reluctantly turns around.

I was hurt when I figured out it was Kyler who planted the orc bait on me, but after a few days I had calmed down enough to realize she didn't have a choice. That day, Rhaegar had somehow forced her Keeper to trade her to him, no doubt for that very reason.

Kyler is an easy target. Soft spoken, way out of her depth here, and kind. No way can she stand up to cunning Evermore like Rhaegar and Hellebore.

But Mack hasn't forgiven her, and she tells Kyler exactly where to stick it.

My heart clenches as I watch Kyler try to find a place to sit on the crowded rooftop before slinking back down the stairs.

Mack takes a look at my crestfallen expression and shakes her head. "No. You will not feel sorry for her. I don't care what Rhaegar threatened her with, she still had a choice."

I nod, trying to focus on the movie, but all I can see is her crestfallen expression. The desperation in her face.

Without friends, no one survives this academy. And I won't be responsible for hurting someone, even if they hurt me first.

"I know that look, Summer," Mack groans. "Kyler isn't a wounded puppy, she's a grown-ass adult who chose to almost get you killed."

"I know," I whisper as two Fall Court shadows shush us. "I'll be back. Hold our seats?"

Pouting, Mack pulls her unicorn hood down low over her narrowed eyes and slumps into the metal chair. "Fine. But I'm not sharing my Sour Patch Kids with her."

As I wave goodbye, I smartly decide that now isn't the time to inform Mack that Ruby already demolished her candy.

Once I'm down the stairs and inside the academy, I realize I have no idea where Kyler would have gone. Back to her assigned cot, maybe? Most first years are located in the basement, near the anatomy labs.

My sneakers are quiet as I slip down the steps, suddenly

all too aware of the silence. The academy is almost always full of students and staff, even during the evening. It's weird not hearing anything.

I can't access the basement from this stairwell, so I duck into the halls, searching for the doorway that leads down.

I make it maybe five feet when a flash of motion catches my eye near a glass door that leads outside. Kyler stands in the small courtyard, surrounded by—

Frick.

Three half-shifted lycans. Where are the Guardians protecting the door?

I burst outside without even thinking, prepared to drag her to safety. Kyler whips around to face me, eyes huge and swollen from crying. "Summer? Tell them. Tell them they're not allowed to touch us."

One look at the three hulking lycan males and I know that plea is off the table. Black snouts protrude from their faces, their eyes an eerie gold.

The alpha stands in front of the others. He's grinning.

But not the nice kind of grin.

My flesh prickles with fear. "Kyler, get behind me." As soon as she does, I whisper, "Now open the door slowly and back inside."

The alpha shakes his head. "Why would we let you two go when we're ready to party?"

The other two begin to circle us.

I hold up my brand. "Know what this is, dickwad?"

His lupine eyes flick to Valerian's brand, and a hint of fear ripples over his countenance. But, surprisingly, he doesn't back down. "The Winter Prince doesn't run this place anymore."

"No?" I hiss. "Touch either of us and I assure you, you'll be dead by morning."

Kyler tugs on my hood. "What is that?"

"What?" I follow her finger to shadowy shapes near picnic tables.

Something about the inhumanly fast way the shapes move sends alarm jolting down my spine. The alpha freezes, sniffs the air, and then growls.

On some silent signal, they all bolt.

But they're not fast enough. I watch in horror as the dark shapes converge on the lycans. They snarl as they try to fight back, but they're quickly overwhelmed by the surge of shadows swarming the courtyard, and their snarls soon become whimpers of pain.

"Darklings," I whisper as I drag Kyler back inside. My sweaty, shaking fingers fumble with the lock. A moment later, I stumble backward, trying to collect myself. I need to alert someone.

What's the fastest way? I think there's a darkling switch by the doors . . .

I run to the red button on the far wall, encased in plexiglass, lift the case, and hit it.

Blue flashes of light pulse from the ceiling as a siren wails to life, its loud scream echoing through the school.

"We're safe," she whispers as we retreat away from the window. "They're too stupid to open doors. We're safe," she repeats.

The door handle jiggles. She yelps, scrambling farther into the hallway.

Glass shatters as a hand snakes through the window next to the door and—

"They're unlocking it," I blurt. I might be able to believe a darkling learned how to open a door, but to have the mental acuity to break a window to unlock that door?

The lock twists to the left with a click, and then the door swings open.

I know even before recognition hits who's on the other

237

side. As I take in the deformed creature, I almost think Evelyn is somehow human again. Unlike the darklings waiting behind her, she stands on two legs. Her bones aren't gnarled and twisted. Her hair hasn't fallen out. And her clothes aren't tattered, which means she found new ones at some point.

But her horrific mouthful of sharp teeth are absolutely darkling, and when her all-black eyes find mine, I know she's still one of them.

A monster—only somehow still in control of her mind.

"Summer." Her raspy, low voice comes out like a faint breeze.

"Oh my God," Kyler whimpers. "She's . . . she's talking."

Grabbing Kyler by the arm, I drag her down the hall.

Don't look back. Just run.

But I do, flinging a desperate gaze over my shoulder just in time to see hundreds of twisted darklings surging inside the academy.

O nce I gather my bearings, my only thought is saving my friends. They're on the roof, but if the darklings make it to them, they'll be trapped. Surely the sirens have alerted them something's wrong?

I head for the same stairwell I took down here, Kyler in tow. Halfway up, the stairwell explodes with the crashing boom of countless feet coming toward us. It takes all my strength not to get trampled in the chaos. Someone slams into my shoulder, whipping me around. My head cracks against the wall. I stumble and nearly drop to my knees, fighting against the bodies, but there's nothing I can do as the crowd pushes me in the other direction.

Toward danger.

"The darklings are downstairs!" I warn, but my voice is lost in the mob.

"Summer!"

I whip around at Mack's voice, desperate to locate her. Relief slams through me as I spot the unicorn horn sticking up a few feet away. She's with Richard and Jace, all three of them locked arm-in-arm.

I grab her hand just as we hit the first floor, and we spill out into the hallway.

Somewhere in the struggle, I lose Kyler.

"Where should we go?" Jace asks. All the blood seems to have drained from his face. He's dressed in striped blue satin pajamas and loafers.

"I don't know." I look around, trying to formulate a plan. "I don't understand. Why are they here? They should be attracted to the Evermore, not mortals."

Oh, God. Valerian. Where is he tonight? At the bonfire? Please, please let Asher and Eclipsa be with him.

Real Guardians rush by us, their guns out. Panic is hewn into their breathy voices as they order us to hide.

"Holy crap," Mack breathes, her hand crushing mine. "This is real."

We find out how real when we pass by the body of a boy clutching a flagpole turned makeshift club. He must have tried to fight them. His head rests at an odd angle, his neck broken, and there's no blood—which again, is strange.

"Weapons," I pant. "We need weapons."

Mack nods solemnly. "The gym's armory is too far away, but we can reach the underground vaults."

Now that we have a plan, my fear gives way to purpose. Our Guardian oath echoes in my mind. The one we pledged at the beginning of school to fight darklings and protect our Keepers no matter the personal risk.

I might not be a true shadow yet, but I refuse to hide while Valerian and his friends are out there, unprotected.

When we're nearing the final landing to the vault, my phone buzzes in the front pouch of my onesie where Ruby sleeps like the dead.

Valerian! A wave of emotion fills me as I press the phone to my ear.

"Summer?" The connection is breaking up, but I can hear

the worry he tries to hide beneath his calm, controlled tone. "Where are you?"

"Inside the main hall on campus," I whisper. The final doorway to the first vault appears in front of us. Class one and two weapons wait on the other side. "We're grabbing weapons. Tell me you're safe."

We all hold our breath as Mack slides the massive double doors open.

"I'm fine, but you need to get out of the building. Something's not right. The darklings only attacked the main hall, nowhere else. I think they're being controlled like before."

Sweat slicks my palms, and I grip the phone harder, afraid it will slip out of my hand. "Why? What could they possibly want here?"

The phone falls away from my ear as I duck into the weapon's room.

Mack is turned to me, motioning for me to—

"Run!" she hisses.

My heart slams into my throat as I glance behind her to the countless darklings swarming the walls. They're sniffing, their heads jerking in animalistic movements. A few shriek, but it's almost like they're calling out to one another. Communicating somehow.

This whole nightmarish experience keeps getting weirder and weirder.

I pivot to flee back up the stairs but darklings are filling the stairwell, blocking our path.

"We're screwed," Richard whispers.

There's no choice but to race to the back of the large weapon's room, the only spot where the darklings aren't yet concentrated.

"Summer!" Valerian bellows into the phone. "What's happening?"

I can't speak for fear of drawing the attention of the darklings. Hardly breathing, I hang up and quickly text him. *Can't talk. Darklings everywhere. In weapons' vault below the main hall.*

My sweat smears the screen. His response is immediate. *I'm coming for you.*

No! My fingers hammer the words. *Don't you dare.*

Nothing. Crap. Fear wraps around my chest, tightening with every labored breath.

Valerian around this many darklings—he wouldn't stand a chance.

Praying Eclipsa has the good sense to stop him, I duck low with the others, hiding behind a row of magic armor.

Mack's eyes are glassy with barely constrained terror as she mouths, *What are they doing?*

I shake my head with a look that screams, *Frick if I know.*

The way they're positioned as if on a grid, spread out equally, sniffing the air at measured turns . . . it's almost as if they're methodically searching for something.

Only darklings don't search for things, and they aren't capable of setting up a refined search grid. They mindlessly attack and munch on the Fae like crazed zombies.

At least, that's what we've been taught. But if Valerian is right, if this is like the attack on Starfall Island, and the attack last year . . . someone is controlling them.

I check my phone but the signal is gone. *Don't panic. Don't think about how you're trapped, alone in a room full of flesh-eating zombies, sweating like a sinner in church.*

I. Need. To. Get. A. Grip. Wetting my bone-dry lips, I whisper, "They know we're down

here. We just need to stay quiet and wait until they come for us."

All at once, the darklings grow frenzied. Somehow, they've broken through the vault doors leading to the forbidden weapon side, and they funnel through the iron doors. The chamber fills with the sounds of violence as the darklings clash with the lovely unlaggin orc that guards the other side.

Then . . . silence. Nerve wracking, gut twisting silence. Never in my life did I think I'd be rooting this hard for a cyclops orc.

When the darklings return from the forbidden vault a few minutes later, there's markedly less of them. The unlaggin, at least, took out a fair number of them.

But not Evelyn. She leads the group, her arm cradling something metallic and small inside her hand. A weapon, maybe?

"Looks like they're leaving," Jace breathes, his voice tinny with relief.

"Thank God." I squeeze Mack's arm, ready to hop up and run as soon as they're gone.

Ruby squirms inside the front pouch of my onesie. The heat from my sweaty body is probably smothering her. Without thinking, I unbutton the top of the pouch.

Before I can so much as put a finger to my lips, she shoots past me into the air.

Crap. "Ruby," I whisper-yell. "Get back here."

Ruby turns around to look in my direction, but she forgets to stop flying, and I watch, horrified, as she slams into a mannequin holding an iridescent breastplate and helmet made of petrified wood.

As if in slow motion, the helmet careens sideways, slips off the mannequin's head, and crashes to the floor.

"Oopsie!" Ruby trills before diving into my pouch.

Thirty darklings rush us at once. Blood hammers in my ears, nearly drowning out their hissing snarls. There's nowhere to go. Nowhere to hide.

I wrench a steel helmet from nearby and widen my stance, prepared to fight to the death.

The first darkling hits so fast I don't even see it coming. Pain crashes over my skull as my head connects with the floor. Dizziness slams into me. Shadows circle my vision.

Where is it? The others are fighting around me. They need my help.

Get up! I stumble to my feet, swinging my makeshift weapon. Ruby zips around my head, casting spell after spell to try and confuse the horde.

Another darkling knocks me off my feet. Fire rockets up my arm. Blood. My blood. The smell hits the darklings instantly, sending them into a wild fervor.

Zombies are about to dine on your flesh, Summer, unless you awaken your inner badass.

"I AM NOT FOOD!" I roar.

I kick out, catching a darkling square in the face. The creature stumbles back, shakes its head, and then crouches low, prepared to lunge.

"This is it," Mack whispers as we press together, shoulder-to-shoulder. "I love you, Summer."

Even though we're seconds from dying, I feel a sense of pride swell to fill me. "Being your best friend was the highlight of my life."

A dark streak in my periphery. An ear-shattering shriek splits the air. The darklings recoil from us, but they don't flee, instead crouching ten feet away, heads cocked . . . like dogs waiting for instruction.

"It can't be," Mack cries, and I follow her gaze to Evelyn. She's standing between us and the darklings, making choppy hissing grunts that the darklings seem to understand.

"Evelyn?" I say, forgetting that she's one of them.

Her head jerks in my direction, and I fight the urge to flinch.

Up close, there is absolutely no illusion that she's anything close to human. Emaciated cheekbones protrude below enlarged black eyes, their depths wild and feral and brimming with an ancient hunger.

The potent stench of corrupted magic seeps from her graying flesh—rotting lilies and copper and old blood.

But unlike the other darklings, her eyes aren't completely black. Rings of white light pulse around the edges of her irises.

"Evelyn," I breathe, trying to sound soothing and not horrified, "why are you here?"

She laughs, a terrible inhuman sound that makes me wince. "No choice," she insists. "No choice."

The darklings mill patiently around us, waiting for their master to tell them what to do. But she just said she doesn't have a choice, which means someone is calling the shots.

The same person who stole the soulstone.

I nod slowly. "Someone else is controlling you?"

Evelyn makes a low, whimpering noise that breaks my heart.

"Oh, God," Mack murmurs. "There has to be a way to help her."

"Who is your master?" I persist. "Can you give us a name?"

"Can't talk," she whines. "It hurts. Can't talk."

Jace shakes his head. "This is pointless. She's been spelled into silence."

But I refuse to give up. If we can figure out who's using her, perhaps we can save her. "Anything, Evelyn. Anything you can think of that might help us so we can help you."

"Did this to me," she snarls. "Did this to me. Did this to me!" The darklings react to her anger, growling and baring their teeth.

"Easy," I whisper as the others press against the wall. "Who did this to you? Who is controlling you?"

"Flower. Flower. Star." She grunts in frustration, beating

and tearing at her skull with her crooked fingers. "Star. Star. Bloody star."

"Evelyn, I . . . I'm trying to understand."

Her head stops jerking and when she meets my stare, my heart breaks at the very human pain in her eyes. The brief flash of sentience. Evelyn is still in there. Trapped.

"Blood . . . star," she moans. "Bloodstar!" As soon as she utters the word, she shrieks, leaping over the others as she flees. The darklings rush after her.

It takes less than two seconds for both Evelyn and the darklings to disappear from the chamber, leaving us shaking and in shock.

"How are we still alive?" Richard asks. He's cradling his right arm. "We should be dead. So dead. Painfully dead and in pieces."

"You don't have to describe it for us," Mack snaps, sagging against me.

Ruby hovers in front of my face. One of her wings doesn't seem to be working properly.

Her eyes widen in alarm as she takes me in. "Kid, you're hurt!"

"What?" I glance over at my shoulder, surprised to see my sleeve is covered in blood. Mack jerks from her stupor and drags down the hem of my onesie.

"This cut is really deep," I hear Mack say, only from far away. When did she move? Her face, too, is vignetting around the edges.

"I've seen this before," Ruby says. "The darkling's magic got into her bloodstream from the cut. We have to get her to the infirmary, now!"

"I'm fine," I insist, growing woozy as I try to both breathe and talk, which is growing harder for some reason. "I don't feel a . . . thing."

Jace limps over to me, frowning. "Should we carry her?"

"No. You're all injured." I try to argue more, but my body is shutting down. Cold seeping into my limbs. As soon as I try to take a step, my world careens dangerously.

A growl fills the air. "Crap," I murmur. "They came back. Just leave me."

"No one's leaving you, Princess." Valerian's voice drags my eyes open in time to see him scoop me into his arms.

"Oh, hi," I say, as if I'm not low-key probably dying. "We couldn't get the weapons, but I kicked one in the face."

"Stay with me, do you understand, Summer? I order you to keep your eyes open."

"Always so dang bossy," I murmur.

And then a tidal wave of darkness crashes over me.

My dreams are strange, surreal. I'm watching myself sleep in a small cot, in a hospital, I think. My ashy-blonde hair spills over the white pillow. Red streaks one half of my head where a nasty gash has mostly healed near my temple. I'm still wearing that hideous cat burrito onesie.

Good Lord, who let me make that terrible fashion choice?

One of the sleeves is cut off, revealing my bandaged shoulder. A spot of blood seeps through the white gauze.

People come and go. Mack. The headmistress with her mesmerizing wings that curl as if alive. I even think I see Zinnia at some point standing over my bed, crying, but whoever's eyes I'm looking through never leaves.

Valerian. I can tell by the emotions raging through him.

Rage. Helplessness. Agony.

A wrenching, searing agony that splits me in two.

At some point, Hellebore shows up. Visceral fury explodes inside Valerian as he slams the Spring Court heir into the hospital wall, hard enough to crack drywall and leave a gaping hole.

Eclipsa comes running from somewhere. After that, a brief period of nothingness follows.

The next thing I know, Valerian is posted at the bottom of the stairs leading up to the second floor of his on campus cottage.

Inara paces in front of him, her claws fully extended and face half-shifted with fury. "She's up there, isn't she?"

"You need to leave, Inara, before I make you." I recognize the steel edge of Valerian's tone. She can't intimidate him and she knows it.

Tears flash in her crystalline eyes, her lower lip shaking. She tries to touch Valerian. Over and over.

Every time, he gently but firmly holds her back using magic.

That only infuriates her.

"You spineless bastard," she hisses. "I won't let you humiliate me like this. You took that mortal slut from the infirmary and are keeping her in your house. Your house! That's not a fling with your shadow. You're infatuated with her and everyone knows. Everyone!"

She tries to slap him, but he catches her wrist. Her other arm rears back but he catches that one too. Even though I can't say a word, I cheer him on.

Take that, Spawn of Satan!

"I hate you," she seethes, fighting his grip—but only enough to be dramatic. "Without my father's support, your claim to the throne is weak. You won't last a month before the other courts pick you apart. Why are you doing this to me? To us? To your future?"

"You wouldn't understand."

The callousness in his voice causes her face to crumple before twisting into a simmering mask of vile hatred. "This is the final warning I'll give you. Screw her. Play house with her. Pretend you actually care about her. Whatever will get her and this mortal fetish out of your system. But by the time this school year is over, if you're not publicly done with her, I will make it my mission to tear your life apart piece by piece."

Then . . . nothing.

When I wake up, I'm in bed. Although I can't be sure whose bed until . . . Sweet Jesus, the silkiest, most luxurious infinity thread count Egyptian cotton sheets wrap around my legs.

Wait. I know this place.

One groggy look at the ice-blue curtains swaying in the honeysuckle breeze from the nearby window, the ivory rug, and my suspicions are confirmed.

Yep. In my old bed again—in the Winter Prince's cottage. My thoughts are slightly derailed as I stretch, the sheets gliding along my skin. *Oh, outrageously expensive sheets, how I've missed you.*

"You're awake!" Mack screeches from the corner where she sits, holding her phone and a book.

Squeaking in surprise, I barely have time to sit up before she's strangling me in a death-hug.

"You scared me," she accuses. "Never, ever do that to me again."

"I'm sorry . . . what am I apologizing for?" I ask through a yawn, my brain scrambling to figure out why I'm waking up in Valerian's on campus house and not my own dorm. *Holy Fae hells, I think something died in my mouth.* "I have the breath of a troll—how long was I asleep?"

When she pulls away, I make note of even more alarming details. Like that I'm in an oversized Evermore Academy T-shirt and someone's very soft silk boxer briefs.

Who the frick put me in this?

A slight ache drags my attention to my left shoulder, poking up from the wide hem of my worn shirt. I touch the jagged red scar that starts at the very end of my collarbone, snakes down my shoulder, and ends mid-bicep.

"Wicked." Or it would be—if I could remember how I got it. A hollow bubble of panic swells beneath my ribs. "What am I forgetting? How did this happen?" I frown as bits and pieces of my memory float to the surface. "Why didn't they heal this?"

Her lips tug into a frown. "You don't remember the darklings?"

Darklings. Right, mindless humans-turned-zombie. They were here . . . inside the main hall.

"Evelyn," I whisper.

At our friend's name, Mack's eyes mist over, but she pulls it together, no doubt for my own benefit. "Do you remember the vault?"

My eyes stretch wide as the image of the darklings swarming over the stone walls flashes with perfect clarity inside my head. "We were looking for weapons to fight them."

"Yes, and during the fight, a darkling bit you, severing an artery, part of the muscle, and some tendons."

"Ouch. So I bled out? That doesn't explain why they couldn't heal my wound."

"The blood loss was bad, but not the thing that nearly killed you. Apparently, sometimes the forbidden magic that infests darklings can enter a human's bloodstream after a deep bite. For Evermore, it's like having a bad case of the flu."

"And for us?"

"For mortals, it's almost always fatal without the antidote. Only a few mortals have ever survived without it . . ." Her mouth tightens, and frown lines etch across her forehead.

"What?"

"Ruby said there's rumors that the humans who *do* survive a bite turn months or even years later from their exposure."

"Oh, God, does that mean—"

"No, you received the antidote in time. There was still a chance you wouldn't wake up, but the antidote stripped all the corrupted magic from your body."

I exhale, trying to breathe out my rising frustration. "Why have they never told us this?"

"Probably because 'Hey, darkling magic is hella poisonous for humans,' isn't good for morale. That and the antidote is incredibly rare and expensive. They only keep one vial in the infirmary, and Jace said they only stocked it recently, to look good in front of the Council for the Mistreatment of Humans."

Just when I thought I couldn't despise the Fae any more. "They could at least educate us in class about the deadly side effect of a darkling bite."

"What, and scare all their ignorant human shields away?" She shakes her head in disgust. "Most humans never survive the attack, so it's easy for the academy to downplay the risk. And the poison has to enter a major artery to take hold."

I rub my head. "Wait. Was anyone else poisoned?"

"Not poisoned but . . . five students were killed, their necks all neatly broken, like . . ."

"Like they were more interested in something else," I finish.

"We think the students tried to fight them or simply got in their way." She pauses, her gaze dropping to the cloud-white duvet cover. "Kyler was one of them."

Oh, no. Horror doubles me over, and I clutch my stomach. "But she was with us until . . ." The final bits of my memory lock into place. I had Kyler's hand and then . . . "How could I forget? I lost her in the crowd. Mack, I should have insisted we go after her first."

Mack squeezes my arm. "Stop. You did everything you could, Summer. We all did."

Tears ache just behind my eyes. "First Evelyn, now Kyler. I thought, I don't know, that this year was going to be better." I wipe my nose on my sleeve, surprised by the utter hopelessness I feel. "What about the CMH?"

"It's been reported. But since this was a darkling attack and not something specifically caused by the academy, it's considered an accident. In fact, it's being spun as just another reason to allow the Evermore to live in our world."

"Of course." I settle back on the pillow, drawing my knees to my chest. "The Fae now have their own PR firms, and who knows better how to spin the truth to their benefit than the Evermore?"

Mack flinches, and I remember a second too late that her dad, Nick works in the PR department of the Summer Queen's law firm. "Forget that. I'm an a-hole. Let's focus on why I'm tucked away in the ILB's house in some Faerie version of Sleeping Beauty."

Mack glances back at the door before lowering her voice. "You were in the infirmary . . . until the Spring Court heir decided to show up."

So that wasn't a dream. Oh, goodie.

"I thought Valerian killed him," Mack continues. "You should have seen—"

Mack's words cut off as Eclipsa flounces into the room

holding a cream-colored flyer. Silver and black zebra print leggings show off her toned thighs while a charcoal halter top flaunts her outrageous abs and cute belly button piercing.

A loose silver bun sticks out atop her head.

She winks. "It would take a lot more than that to kill an heir to one of the seasonal courts, especially Hellebore. I would know—I've tried a time or ten."

Mack jumps back, her cheeks bright red. "Oh, I didn't mean to gossip about your kind. I'm sorry."

Even though Mack and Eclipsa fought together last year to save Valerian's life, Mack is still instinctually terrified of the Lunar assassin.

I can tell Eclipsa wants to mess with Mack, but one scowl from me and Eclipsa flashes my bestie a begrudging smile, putting her at ease. "Don't apologize. As long as you're not talking about me, I won't have grounds to kill you."

I shoot her a look and she responds with an innocent shrug.

"Oh, I wasn't, I would never," Mack protests, talking fast. "It's just—it's all anyone can talk about right now."

Well, fudge.

"It caused a scandal everywhere," Eclipsa confirms, "including the Fae Courts."

I twist the silky sheets between my fingers, making a mental note to *borrow* them before I leave. "So once again I'm the talk of the academy. Surprise, surprise. But why is it such a big scandal when the Winter Prince fights with Hellebore, but it wasn't with Rhaegar?"

Sighing, Eclipsa sits on the end of the bed, reminding me she's the only female in existence who can sit with her midriff bared and not gain a muffin top. "Because the Winter Prince invoked Nocturus when he fought Rhaegar. At the academy, royal Evermore are protected by powerful laws made by the council. Otherwise, age-old feuds between the courts would mean brutal fights and assassinations daily on campus."

My heart feels like it's permanently lodged in my throat as I ask, "And what's the punishment for such an attack?"

"Unprovoked? If Hellebore takes it to the council, he could ask for recompense in slaves and property. If the Winter King decided not to pay that fine . . . there would be a trial."

I exhale. Valerian is already suspected of stealing the Darken's soulstone. He doesn't need more trouble with the Fae council.

Mack's forehead wrinkles, the way it does when she's confused. "But why would the Spring Court heir even show up at the infirmary knowing the Winter Prince hates him . . . oh." Understanding brightens her eyes. "He was trying to make him react."

Eclipsa nods, obviously impressed. "Exactly. Someone's been paying attention in class."

Mack practically melts from the praise, beaming at me with a look-how-smart-I-am smile, the show off.

"But why?" I ask. "What does Hellebore gain from constantly antagonizing the Winter Prince?"

Eclipsa seems to be searching for how to word her answer. "People are starting to notice the Winter Prince's . . . infatuation with you. And now that he's broken Fae law, it makes him appear weak."

Weak?

"If you were another Evermore," Eclipsa adds carefully, "especially a highly sought after female with lands and power, it would still be against the laws—but would be viewed more favorably in the courts."

The hypocrisy boils my blood. I fist the sheets, not even bothering to hide my disgust. "But as a mortal slave with about as much value as a turnip, it makes him look foolish, right?"

"Yes, unfortunately."

"But if they knew . . ."

My words trail away. I look to Mack, the urge to tell my best friend everything hitting me hard. But what would I say?

Hey, bestie. I forgot to mention that I'm a body-hopping Evermore princess who also happens to be mated to the Winter Prince and, oh, the Darken probably wants me for his evil plans.

Also, just knowing this now puts you in grave danger. You're welcome.

"Know what?" Mack asks, but she's only half-listening, her face buried in the cream flyer Eclipsa brought in.

This is so not the time to drag Mack into all my unwanted —and dangerous—drama, so I change the subject. "Have they figured out what the darklings were in the vault for?"

"Not officially, but the prince and I have our suspicions."

I lift an eyebrow. "And those are?"

The Lunar assassin regards Mack for a moment before saying, "Remember the Darken's axe? The weapon that destroyed both our worlds and was broken into pieces after the war?"

A cold shadow of dread falls over me as I nod.

Mack slaps a hand over her mouth. "A piece of the World-slayer was here, at the academy?"

Of course the Darken's evil weapon has a terrifying name. Of course it does.

"We think one of the pieces was stored below the academy," Eclipsa confirms, "inside the vault."

"I think you're right," I murmur. "The thing Evelyn held, it looked like part of the axe's blade. So that means whoever is controlling Evelyn is the same person working for the Darken?"

"It certainly appears that way, but—" Eclipsa pauses, and her head swings to face the door.

A second later, Valerian bursts through, trailed by Asher.

Before I can blink, Valerian is at my side. "How do you feel?"

"Other than the room spinning whenever I so much as breathe? Peachy."

"There's that smart tongue I missed." Valerian's intimate tone sets a fire low in my belly. The others look away as Valerian holds my stare, impervious to anyone but me. "I missed all of you actually, Princess."

O-kay then. We're doing this in front of everyone. "Thanks for coming to help us, even though I ordered you not to."

Asher raises his eyebrows while Eclipsa swallows a laugh and Mack stares open-mouthed.

"Ordered?" A seductive grin dances over his lips as he leans down and whispers, "One, I wasn't coming to help your shadow friends, I was coming for you. Never underestimate your value to me. Two, I'm an Evermore Prince. I don't take orders, especially when they put my mate in danger. Understand?"

I glare at him, stubbornly refusing to back down. "No. I don't. I'm your Shadow Guardian, and you should have listened to me."

I don't know why I'm suddenly furious with him. Maybe because he put himself in direct danger for me, and now, apparently, is in even more danger for showing the world that he cares for me.

A mortal.

His eyes soften. "I'm sorry for worrying you, but I would do it again in a heartbeat."

My scowl melts as I recognize the hurt in his tone. Asher and Eclipsa find something on the wall to stare at. Thank God for mortals' crap hearing because Mack is clueless, her face buried in that flyer.

Despite my annoyance with Valerian, I find myself grinning because I've learned two more truths about him just now. He's shit when it comes to taking orders and the soul-bond is strong enough to make him risk his life to protect me.

Not exactly love, but still significant considering how unapologetically selfish the Evermore are by nature.

"Whoa," Mack blurts, holding up the flyer. "Have you seen this?"

"Just pretend I've been in a semi-coma for the past few days and haven't seen anything," I quip.

Valerian lobs Mack a conspiratorial look that screams, *See what I have to deal with?*

Mack rolls her eyes as she thrusts the paper into my lap. "Just read it, smart ass."

I do, forcing my blurry eyes to focus on the elegant, hand-written words scrolling across the expensive cardstock paper. I only get to the first paragraph before the print becomes too fuzzy to make out, but what I do see surprises me.

The Summer Queen is opening up internships to her law firm, Larkspur and Associates, only the biggest Fae firm in the mortal world. Every lawyer who wants to specialize in Fae law dreams of a position at the firm, but only a select few ever enter its hallowed walls.

Mack's dads both work there, and it's rumored Sebastian is slated to become the first ever mortal partner.

My eyebrows bunch together. This seems too good to be true. "The academy okayed this?"

Eclipsa glances over the flyer, her mouth parting as she nears the bottom. "Apparently. They must be trying to save face after all the recent deaths, that's the only reason they would allow Queen Larkspur to poach students."

Asher frowns. "Are you guys going to actually say what's on the flyer or what?"

"Sorry, Asher. I forgot you only read things with pictures," Eclipsa teases, ignoring his low growl. "Apparently, the Summer Queen is offering up spots at Larkspur and

Associates to second and third year shadows. Shadows that are accepted can forgo their fourth year at the academy for a paid internship. They still have to pass the exams, but they live in Manhattan, in the new Fae district, and also learn about Fae law."

My heart skips a beat. Forgo my fourth year? Paid internship. Right now, both of those things sound like heaven. "What are the requirements to apply?"

"Looks like you have to have straight A's . . ." Eclipsa peers at the flyer. "A recommendation from a professor, and . . . pass the final gauntlet."

Just like that, my dream dies a quick, undignified death. "What? How does that make sense when we're not allowed to participate in the final gauntlet until our fourth year?"

Mack gives me that look—the one that says I should pay more attention. "Anyone is allowed to participate in the final gauntlet, but only the fourth years are required. Second and third years are opting for the less dangerous final exams instead because we really like staying alive."

I would laugh, if she wasn't being completely serious. "Does the invitation to apply open again next year?"

Eclipsa peers at the flyer. "It specifies the application window closes after this year. You must enter and then *pass* the gauntlet to even be considered."

"Maybe she'll reopen the applications again next year?" I say, totally aware of how desperate I sound.

"Those internships are extraordinarily competitive and usually only available to shadow graduates with at least five years of experience. I assume the queen is doing this for the PR, since the recent deaths at the academy have brought bad press for all the Fae, including those pushing hard to expand new businesses in the mortal world."

I pretend there's a spot on my shirt, picking at it to hide my disappointment. Not just that the internship is so far out of reach, but that my mother isn't doing this for altruistic reasons.

I shouldn't be surprised, but a part of me needs to know that she's good. Or, at the very least, that she's marginally good. Like a socialite who goes to fancy charities for the status aspect, but also tips well when no one's looking.

Just enough kindness that I can reasonably not hate her.

With my hopes of skipping fourth year well and thoroughly dashed, the others leave to let me rest. Apparently the antidote to the darklings' corrupted magic inside a mortal is nymph tears, which also happens to make mortals sleep. Like, a lot.

I should be fully back to normal before school tomorrow, and Eclipsa promises an early morning training session—if I'm feeling up to it.

Valerian is the last to go. Before he can slip out the door, I blurt, "Can you stay? Just until I fall asleep?"

It feels childish. I haven't been afraid of the dark in years. But I keep reliving Evelyn in her monstrous form, her eyes pleading for us to end her eternal nightmare, and I don't want to be alone right now.

Especially knowing her fate was also nearly mine.

Valerian Sylverfrost doesn't just stay. No, the beautiful, complicated Evermore male crawls into bed beside me, wraps those gorgeous arms around my body—one cradling my head, the other draped over my waist—and strokes my hair.

Proving once and for all that the Ice Prince has a heart. It may be tiny and shriveled, and black as Aunt Vi's coffee, but it's there.

At some point in the night, I wake up to Valerian asleep in the bed facing me. His eyes pop open. Bathed in a square of starlight, with both of our guards down, we calmly stare at each other.

There are no words.

No assumptions.

No defenses to wade through or truths to dredge out.

Just a Fae and girl, possibly in love—or whatever the frick the Fae want to call it—and trying to find the courage to trust one another.

"Truth," Valerian says, his voice husky with sleep. "Are you scared of what you feel for me?"

"Yes." Maybe it's the lingering antidote or my sleep-drugged mind, but the truth flows from my lips. "Are you?"

"Yes. Terrified."

As I close my eyes, on the threshold of my dreams, an uneasy thought comes.

What if Hellebore is right and I have this all backward? That instead of Valerian endangering my life, I'm the one endangering his?

What if by choosing to love me the way I demand, he ends up losing everything?

Two weeks after Samhain, I'm called to the headmistress's office to give my account of the darkling attack. Mack and the others were interviewed the night after it all happened, but since I was out cold on nymph tears, they had to wait until an officer from the CMH organization could come back to do a proper interview.

The interviewer, a human man with steel-rimmed reading glasses, an auburn combover that does nothing to hide his thinning hair, and yellowing teeth, reads a file on the desk while I yawn, wishing they could have scheduled this interview at any other time than the butt-crack of dawn.

As the interviewer shuffles around some papers, I find myself studying him. I'm so used to the Fae, who are all beautiful, graceful, and ageless. Being confronted with my own species' mortality is a reality check.

Someday, my body will suffer the same effects of time as this man. Someday, my boobs will sag, my flesh will wrinkle and spot, I'll need the same reading glasses, and my hair will turn gray and brittle.

Whereas Valerian will stay his stupidly gorgeous self.

I used to be okay with that. Aging is normal. Natural. A sign of wisdom and badassery. Now . . . I'm not so sure.

The man takes off his reading glasses and asks a series of questions about that night. When did I first see the darklings? Where were the shadow guardians? Who suggested going to the vault for weapons? Was that expected of shadow recruits? Are there drills in place for darkling attacks?

The questions aren't hard, but when the interviewer pauses for a break, I'm exhausted. I eye the man's lukewarm coffee. When I've stared long enough to make even the poor mug feel uncomfortable, the man sighs. "Would you like some?"

"Yes. Please." Sighing again, he goes to stand, but I drag Ruby from my iridescent neon-pink fanny pack Mack swears is coming back in style and set her over the desk. "Don't get up. My sprite can handle it."

After the darkling attack, Ruby's wing healed, but her spirit didn't. She blames herself for my near death and has taken to binging straight packets of sugar she lifts from the comm, wearing all black, listening to Fall Out Boy songs on repeat, and scribbling soliloquies on the meaning of life.

I'm hoping giving her tasks will make her feel useful—and therefore better about herself—again.

The moment the man sets eyes on Ruby, a look of horror transforms his face. He jumps back, sending his combover flopping sideways like a dead beaver and his chair screeching into the wall.

Ruby ducks behind his mug as he emits a shrill little scream. "That thing. That—"

"Sprite?" I add helpfully.

"Yes. That dirty, poisonous creature. They're infested with deliria lice and a whole host of diseases. I—I—I'm going for your coffee and when I return, I ask that you have that creature locked away."

He disappears out the door before I can inform him how ignorant he's being. Sure, deliria lice—the parasites that infest certain types of sprites' wings and lay eggs in human brains —are understandably horrifying. But they only affect sprites in the Fall Court, and sprites at the academy are tested and up to date on their vaccinations.

"I'm a scourge on humanity," Ruby laments, sagging against the coffee mug, her shiny wings drooping. "I'm the cause of all evil and sadness in this world."

"You are not." I go to pick her up, but she falls limp on the desk like the twins used to do when Zinnia tried to make them do chores. "Ruby, I told you I don't blame you."

"Just leave me. Sever our contract so I can die of shame like I deserve. It will be a horrible death. A horrible, noble ending to my pointless existence."

Gently, I pinch my fingers around her waist and pick her up. She's closing her eyes, pretending to sleep, but one eye surreptitiously parts.

"I can see you looking at me," I scold.

"I'm not," she insists.

Settling her floppy little body in my palm, I stroke her greasy magenta hair. "You didn't cause Evelyn to become pregnant and turn darkling, and you are not the one controlling her. None of this is your fault. Do you understand?"

"But I knocked into that helmet. If I hadn't snuck that kid's flask of Faerie wine," she continues, her one eye opening wider, "and my secret stash of brambleberry liquor, and that guard's fermented gourd—"

"Ruby, we can discuss your drinking problem later . . . wait." I glance around.

I'm in the main office. *Alone.*

Evelyn's file is completely unguarded, as are the other ones I saw lumped with hers the other day.

"Want to be of help?" I ask. "Go outside the door and keep that interviewer from coming inside."

Ruby's eyes snap open. "What if I fail you again?"

"You won't, Ruby. Know why? Because I believe in you."

She goes from limp and flat to animated and full of confidence as she zips through the partially open door.

The moment it clicks shut, I rush to the ancient filing cabinet in the back alcove. Red, cobalt, and amber light from the stained-glass window discolor the cabinet's scratched and peeling green paint.

Hardly daring to breathe, I rip open the drawers, searching for . . . what? A file that says students impregnated by Fae? Top secret?

My clumsy fingers leave sweaty fingerprints over the manila file folders as I push each one aside. Finally, in the second to last drawer, I spot an unlabeled file.

Hmm. Given the meticulous way the other folders are named, that seems odd. Curiosity piqued, I yank the folder from the drawer and quickly spread it across the dusty, faded emerald rug. Evelyn's picture is the first one on the top, affixed to her file by a paperclip.

I don't even check the rest. I don't have time. With the blank file's contents spread out on the floor, I snap pictures of each one as fast as humanly possible. First the photo and then the actual paperwork.

There are so, so many. Enough that I start to worry this is a dead end because no way could this many students become pregnant without mortals noticing and raising the alarm. Right?

I'm just finishing with the last file of a beaming girl with bright, hopeful eyes—eyes so sure this academy will change her life and fulfill her dreams—when I hear Ruby belt out *Dance, Dance* by Fall Out Boy.

A scream follows.

Oh, boy. That man has some major issues. Cramming the papers and photos back into the file, I manage to get it back into the drawer and dart to my chair before the interviewer practically falls into the office to get away from Ruby.

The man spins around, his face so red I'm worried he's having a heart attack. I watch in disappointment as all the coffee he brought me flies out of the cup and onto the floor.

He points a shaking finger at me. "You—this . . . you!"

I get to my feet, ignoring Ruby in the open door frame, who's alternating between giving me the thumbs up and high-fiving herself. "Are you okay?"

"Get out," he pants. "This interview is over."

Relieved and a little high on getting away with such a risky and impulsive act, I dart out the door, taking the stairs two at a time. Ruby settles happily on my shoulder. She laughs, the tinkling sound like music to my heart.

"Don't ever say I don't need you, Ruby."

"But you—"

"No." I halt on the stairs and look her in the eyes. "You're my friend. My family. You're not perfect, but neither am I, and the only way we'll survive this academy is together. Do you understand?"

"Family?" She hugs my neck. "You're my human, Kid. The filling to my Oreo. The frosting to my red velvet cake. The cream to my Twinkie."

"Ruby, when did you last eat any real food?"

"Before my hunger strike to highlight the injustice of this world."

Yikes. I veer down the closest hall. "We're going to the comm to get you a whole bag of chips."

"Cheetos?"

"Sun Chips. Remember the Cheetos have that red dye we talked about? The kind that makes you hump things and basically lose your mind?"

"Oh, yeah." She throws a look in the direction of the office. "That man really hates the human Fall Out Boy Court. If I had realized he was from an opposing human court, I would have sang something else."

I grin at Ruby's confusion over bands and courts. And I grin all the way to the comm. Even if the photos I snapped turn out to be a waste of time, they did something even better than uncover Evelyn's master.

They brought back my friend.

And something that precious is worth a thousand expulsions.

The Larkspur and Associates law firm takes up the top four floors of the infamous Magnolia skyscraper, the only office building in the city that caters strictly to Fae businesses. The giant steel and glass high-rise on Madison Ave dominates the Upper East Side, with floor-to-ceiling windows to ensure everyone knows they have the best view of the Jacqueline Kennedy Onassis Reservoir in Central Park. When the surprise field trip was announced today in our Faerie Law and Practices class, I expected to be wowed and probably intimidated by the building my mother owns.

But this place takes wow, changes it to screamy all caps, adds a million exclamation marks, and puts it into gif form with fireworks shooting out of the letters.

"Amazing, right?" Mack whispers as we file quietly down rows of desks partitioned by glass dividers imbued with magic.

"That doesn't even begin to cover this place," I breathe.

Everything is in shades of chartreuse, ivory, or gold. From the paintings to the rug to the modern wing-backed chairs and couches. Gilded statues of fauns and brownies scatter throughout the spacious rooms. The air is infused with something . . . a wondrous scent that can only be described as fresh summer cut grass, loamy soil, and honeycomb.

Sprites flit through the air carrying briefs and files. A centaur pulls a rolling tray of espresso and tea through the room, to cater to their mix of mortal and Fae employees. And instead of light bulbs, luminescent spheres of magic churn inside recessed alcoves along the walls, no doubt ready to flare to life once the sun sets.

The guest relations female leading the tour is a delicate faun with white and brown dappled fur, overly large green eyes, and model features. We just finished our lunch at the state-of-the-art cafeteria, a collection of highly curated four and five star restaurants that serve a mixture of mortal and Fae delicacies.

Accordingly, the mortal students ate at the sushi bar or the overpriced hamburger place, and the Evermore preferred the make-your-own salad bar and smoothie restaurant.

As we pass by a blue-skinned Evermore wearing a blazer over gray skinny jeans, Mack leans in close. "These are the associates."

I glance around. "Where do they put the interns?"

She snorts. "Not here. Interns don't get sunlight or hand-foamed espressos." Her eyes light up. "Did you know, all the desks are spelled to make it look like you're alone in a landscape of your choosing? Both my dads use the oceanic spell that makes it appear like their offices are floating in the middle of the Caribbean."

I've always disapproved of magic in the human world, but that's really cool.

We move on to the rooftop, which doesn't disappoint. It's a park—or, according to the handy brochure the faun passes around, the Fae version of Central Park.

"Need to unwind after a long day of work?" the faun calls, dipping one of her hooves into the nearby pool. "Welcome to the Other Park, as we lovingly call it. This is where all the employees gather for recreation or reflection. We also have tourists from all over the Untouched Zone visit."

"Where's the roofline?" I whisper to Mack as I take in the seemingly never-ending tree line. The building is big, sure—but not this big.

Mack laughs. "You didn't know? This isn't actually on the roof—it's in the Summer Court."

"I'm not following."

"At the top of the stairs, we walked through an invisible portal. It's the largest portal in the Untouched Zone, way larger than the restrictions allow. I remember last year when my dads texted me with the news it was okayed by congress. Everyone was so excited."

"So we're actually in the Summer Court right now?"

"Yep."

I blink at the patchwork of autumn-colored trees in the distance. "What about Faerie law?"

Not long after I joined the academy, I learned that, unless invited or stated otherwise in a contract, mortals who enter the Everwilde for longer than an hour automatically become property of the seasonal court they trespassed.

So even if I hadn't stolen the neverapple, Valerian could have kept me from crossing back to my side of the Shimmer for sixty minutes and still claimed me as his property.

Note to self: Fae law is a steaming pile of dung and when I graduate, I'm going to dismantle it piece by piece.

"Remember the paperwork we signed downstairs when we checked in?" Mack asks. "There was a paper we signed that states by visiting this park, we do not give up our rights, blah, blah."

Wow. I probably should have read those better. Being in the mortal world made me let my guard down.

Second note to self: the Fae are cunning bastards everywhere.

By now, that rule should be stamped into my brain. Especially after the research Mack and I did on the students whose files were with Evelyn's. Each student shared the same rare blood type, AB negative.

And each one seemingly disappeared from the school without a trace. When we called the parents for more information, they all said the same thing: Their children had accepted a prestigious opportunity to train in a seasonal court.

When pressed about the last time they saw or talked with them, the parents seemed confused and repeated the line.

Obviously, the school is massively covering up pregnant students who turn darkling, but that doesn't help determine who's controlling Evelyn.

The class spreads out through the park. Our law professor, Mr. Orenthall, partnered with the professor of Potions and Poisons to set up a scavenger hunt. While this park may loosely resemble Central Park, it's very much Faerie inspired.

The carousel is pulled by centaurs and pegasi, the ponds churn with selkies and water sprites, and the zoo is filled with every Fae creature imaginable.

We're just finishing with Cherry Hill and passing over the Bow Bridge when Valerian messages. The scavenger hunt activated Mack's competitive streak, and she's already way ahead with Richard, Jace, and Layla, searching for the elusive bogle, a warty goblin that lives deep in the Ramble.

Facing out toward the still waters, I rest my arms over the stone balustrade. My lips curl at the edges as I read his text.

I keep replaying this morning.

I text back, *you keep replaying me kicking your Fae ass?*

God, you're adorable when you try to act tough.

This mofo. *Try?* I type. *You must be forgetting when I took you to the mat this morning.*

Believe me, that image of you straddling my waist is indelibly engraved in my mind. Even if I let you take me down.

You're an asshole.

But you adore this asshole. A pause. Those annoying three dots flash and then . . . *Still coming tonight?*

I almost respond with something jerkish about checking my schedule before reining in my inner shrew. Even in text, I can feel the vulnerability behind those three words.

Every year before the Yule holiday, Valerian, Eclipsa, and Asher attend a fancy private dinner at a resort lodge owned by Valerian's family. It's tradition, one that Eclipsa informed me his mother started.

She would have the chefs cook dishes she'd found in the human world that she loved, even though the Winter King would have lost his crap.

At least, before she betrayed Valerian and disappeared.

Last week, Valerian officially invited me.

It's funny how one invitation—formally engraved with a cute little blue ribbon—could make my heart feel like it was leaping right out of my chest. After a little negotiating, he even agreed I could bring Mack.

Ruby's invite wasn't quite as easy to conjure; in the end, I promised to wear a dress of Valerian's choosing.

Shimmer save me, I can only imagine what his devious mind is going to choose.

Yes, I send. *Wouldn't miss it.*

I slip my phone into my jean short's pocket, turn to jog down the bridge to join the others, and walk straight into a wall of the Six.

The new Six. Inara, Kimber, Lyra, Bane, Rhaegar, and poor Basil, who stands off from the crowd, unable to meet my eye.

Nope. I whip around, but Reina, blocks my path. Her twin boy toys stand guard just behind her. Their beefy arms are crossed and faces scowling, just in case Reina's one fingered salute didn't make their intentions clear.

Well, frick.

Hands balled at my sides, I force my chin high as I face off against Inara, the obvious leader. She's super extra today in a pressed baby blue pantsuit and cream-colored Louboutins.

"Did you forget?" I taunt. "You're not on the screw-with-Summer approved list."

Her faux look of disappointment stirs something close to alarm inside my gut. "Aren't I?" She makes a point of looking around. "Do you see anyone who's going to stop me?"

Solid point. They snicker as I glance around, praying to spot a professor or another student. Not that either would actually protect me from Inara.

"Don't bother, idiot," Inara purrs, flicking a speck of something from her lapel. "There's no one here but us and you."

Adrenaline floods my veins. Maybe Hellebore lifted his protection. Maybe he got bored of our little game and decided loosing Inara's inner serial killer on me would liven things up. Maybe I should stop counting on one psychopath to restrain the other and deal with this myself.

Gathering every ounce of courage I possess, I fake running right and dart left, toward Reina and the twins. They're human, so the playing field is leveled a bit.

You can take three on one, Summer. Piece of cake.

But I never get the chance to test that overconfident theory because a wall of ice shoots from the wooden floor of the bridge, trapping me.

Oh, hell no. I pivot a second before slamming into the clear wall and dive for the stone balustrade, prepared to jump off the side and into the water—

A cold shock of pain slams into me, jerking me around to face the threat. Inara has her hand up, a blast of ice magic poised to freeze me solid.

Bane frowns and touches his sister's arm. "You can't. Remember?"

So Hellebore didn't lift his protection. Not that Inara seems to care at this particular moment. I remember her words to Valerian. Her desperation.

This is Inara throwing a tantrum.

"I promise you, Inara, you don't want to do this. We both know Hellebore. You might be tough and scary, but he's a whole different level of monster."

I can see the truth of my statement resonate in her expression, a healthy dose of fear pinching the corners of her lips.

Her chest heaves as she slowly drops her hand. "There will come a day when both princes tire of you. When that happens, I'm going to destroy you."

Sticks and stones, Summer. Sticks. And. Stones.

Her words might not harm me, but the malice pouring from her entire being cuts deep, and I believe every word she says.

"I'm not your enemy," I say, willing her to finally see that. "And I never meant to get between you and the prince."

"Of course you did," she snarls. Both Bane and Kimber hold her back as her lips peel back, revealing fully extended canines. "Stop pretending you're not just like us. If you truly were good, if your goody-two-shoes mortal act was real, you would leave him alone before you ruin his life forever."

Ruin. His. Life. Forever.

I blink at the implication of those words as a hollow feeling swells inside my chest. But before my tongue can form a reply, the new Six leave, laughing as Lyra makes some joke undoubtedly about me.

Kimber's eyes find mine through the veil she wears to ward off the sun. I can't read if the look she gives me is her feeling sorry for me or she's just needing a quick snack. I suppose it doesn't matter, anyway.

She's chosen her side.

Rhaegar is the last to leave. Basil paces nervously near the other end of the bridge, looking between the others and Rhaegar. I try to force my way past the Summer Evermore, but he steps in front of me.

I'd forgotten how big he is, his six-foot-five body practically filling the bridge path.

"Move," I order.

He laughs, but it doesn't reach his dark eyes. "I can make this easier for you. Just say the word and when the Ice Prince tires of you—which he will, Summer—I can hide you away in the Summer Court. I have powerful friends that can protect you from Inara."

"But not from you."

"You did humiliate me in front of everyone. That can't go unpunished. But I'll be gentler than Inara."

I glare at him. "There's always a price with you Evermore. What would I pay for your protection?"

"Do you think your prince is any different? That he doesn't want something from you?" His shoulder-length reddish-gold hair falls into his eyes as he leans in. "I would have treated you like royalty. Now I won't be satisfied until you're on your hands and knees, begging for my help. That's my price."

Mother. Forker. I've worked really hard these last few months on my temper. On rising above and ignoring and increasing my odds of staying alive.

But something inside me snaps. First Inara, then Hellebore, now this douche canoe . . . I'm done.

Smiling, I reach up and grab a firm hold of both his shoulders. Rhaegar is so sure I'm about to beg him for help that he doesn't see my knee until it's ramming between his legs.

A surprised yelp explodes from his throat. He stumbles back, eyes glazed . . . and then, in some cosmic form of poetic justice, falls to his *knees*.

"You first," I snarl.

I'm fairly sure I've just eliminated all future mini-Rhaegars in one go, and I give zero fucks. I do, however, care that he's starting to shift. His wild eyes turn more animal than Fae as his hate-wrenched lips transform into a snout. Claws erupt from his fingers.

Time to bail on this party.

I dart toward the heavily wooded area known as the Ramble, sneakers kicking up dust.

Behind me, an unmistakable howl shivers through the trees.

I make it maybe twenty yards when the snarling behind me goes quiet. A few heartbeats later, I recognize the honeysuckle and jasmine scent that heralds Prince Helle-Douche.

Ugh. Life can suck it. Bracing myself, I turn on the dirt path to face the Spring Court Heir.

Oh, Lordy. He's close—way closer than I expected, wearing a white T-shirt, his hands casually shoved into the pockets of his light wash skinny jeans. His full sleeve tats and tall, lean body make him look like an edgy runway model out for a stroll.

"That was cruel," he murmurs.

"Was it though?" I quip, not even caring at this point.

"So that's what the Winter Prince has been teaching you during all those private lessons in the gym. Who knew he liked it so rough."

"No, actually, Amarillo High taught me that particular move." I fall into a fighting stance, legs wide and arms up in a defensive position. "Look, I'm way beyond my threshold for douches today. If you mess with me, I'm probably going to throat punch you. And while I've really been wanting to do that for a while, I'd rather just call it a day."

His honey-gold brows gather in confusion. "Throat punch?"

"Yeah, another human specialty, reserved for dickheads like yourself."

Whoa, Summer. One perfect knee to an Evermore's man onions and you're Chuck Norris.

But Hellebore seems more confused than anything. His head keeps tilting as if he's trying to make sense of my suicidal threats. "Careful, little pet. Unless you want me to leash you right now."

Right. No punching Hellebore because that counts as touching. The universe really has some explaining to do with that one.

I jerk my chin toward the bridge. "You were watching, weren't you? You get off on all of this sick crap."

"Yes. And . . . yes." There's no apology in his eyes. Nothing but dark amusement. "Evermore live a very long time, which means we have come up with thousands of creative ways to stave off boredom. I've hunted the most dangerous creatures in the Everwilde. When that lost its appeal, I turned to mortals."

"You must be so proud. You chased down and killed a species weaker and slower than you."

"Who said I killed them?" He arches an eyebrow. "There are infinite ways to destroy something without physically harming its flesh."

"Your creativity should be applauded."

Why do I keep goading him?

He must think I'm being serious, because he doesn't bat an eye. "Unfortunately, even toying with your species lost its luster eventually. Do you know what I found is the only kind of prey that captures my interest indefinitely?"

Good God. What else is there? "No, sorry. I'm not caught up on the wacko handbook."

A wolfish grin reveals perfectly white teeth. "Nothing is quite as satisfying as hunting my own kind. Discovering what bait they can't resist. Learning how to plant snares so carefully that they never even notice they're caught. And then, when they finally understand that they're trapped, helpless to my desires, I force them to watch as I slowly dismantle everything they've ever cared about."

Wow. I don't even know how to respond to that. "So, I'm not your prey, I'm just your bait?"

He chuckles. "Oh, you're very much both."

The smarminess in his voice grates on my nerves. I want to hurt him right now. I want to make him feel even a sliver of the pain he causes others.

Brushing the hair back from my face, I say, "Tell me. After you've snared your victims and utterly ruined their lives, does it go away?"

"Does what go away?" He asks this casually, calmly, his hands still inside his pockets, his lips still smiling. As if we're enjoying a pleasant chat.

But the softness of his voice is a warning . . .

Screw it. "That hole inside you. The one you can't fill no matter what you do. When you finally destroy someone's life, I bet that hollow recess inside your soul doesn't go away like you think it will. Like you pray it will. I bet it only grows larger. I bet it's eating you alive."

Holy poopballs, I've gone too far. His eyes go scary-dark, and the twisted emotions I see inside them—

He moves so fast he's a blur. I careen backward, only to smack into the huge trunk of an oak tree.

He pins me, hands on either side of my head. "Little pet, I could call in my bargain right here in these woods."

I can't hide the panic clawing to the surface of my face. If he demands I repay him now, my plan won't work.

"There it is." His nostrils flare delicately. "You can mask the fear on your face, but you can never fully hide the scent. Did you know that every mortal has their own unique pheromones for primal terror? And yours, by far, is the sweetest I've smelled yet."

I don't even have a response to that depravity. His gaze goes to my neck. Shimmer save me, if he sniffs me I'm going to laugh in his face, and then he'll for sure murder me . . .

A flash of movement draws my focus to the full sleeve tats on his right arm. The *moving* tats. One would naturally expect to see bees and butterflies flitting over the exquisite collection of vining flowers . . . but no.

Instead of cheerful creatures, Hellebore chose the kind that inspire fear. Black widows peek from inside bell-shaped magenta foxgloves, the silvery threads of their dew-covered webs weaving throughout the scene. Wicked scorpions bask atop the slender red petals of fire lilies, their barbed tails lifted aggressively. A tarantula's fuzzy black leg can be seen poking from beneath a dogsbane leaf.

Forgetting to be scared, I peer at the elaborate art. Every flower has been painstakingly drawn down to the last detail —and each is devastatingly poisonous. Oleander. Hemlock. Nightshade.

The vines twist over his flesh, the buds blooming as I watch, like they're showing off for me.

One delicate white flower is more prevalent than all the rest, its insidious vines strangling the others.

His piercing gaze follows my stare, softening as it rests on the star-shaped white flower. "That one's my favorite. It only grows on the highest peak of the Lunar Court mountains. A mere two to three flowers bud on the vine once a year, during the Winter Solstice. One petal at auction would go for millions of dollars—if I ever chose to sell them."

I swallow, wondering how many Fae he's poisoned with it.

"They say to force the vine into bloom, the moon sprites feed the plant the blood of heartbroken lovers."

The sudden excitement in his voice as he discusses his creepy hobby, contrasted against his otherwise hard, emotionless tone, is jarring.

"You are possibly the most . . . most twisted being I've ever encountered."

Surprise flickers inside his too bright eyes, followed by . . . curiosity. It's honestly terrifying how easily his mood switches from serial killer to inquisitive to BDSM weirdo.

"You really can't control that mouth of yours, can you?" he murmurs. "Like you have a death wish."

I lift my eyebrows. "It's a habit I can't seem to break."

"I could break it for you."

Hard pass.

Suddenly, he shoves off the tree and prowls down the path. "Tell the Ice Prince I said hello. Or not. He does have a terrible temper."

As soon as he's gone, the birds resume their chirping, the insects come alive, and the air becomes breathable again.

As my adrenaline slows, my fear takes hold. And when it does, every emotion I managed to keep buried during the last half hour rushes to join it, forming one giant pity party.

Frustration. Anger. Worry. The knowledge that I am utterly screwed no matter which way I turn.

I need to find the class, but I'm afraid I'll break down in front of them, and I can't handle that special form of humiliation.

Not right now.

Not with all the epic ways I'm screwed so clear in my mind. There's still a lot I don't understand about Hellebore and Valerian's feud, but there are a few things I know for sure.

Hellebore has been planning Valerian's downfall for years, he's using me as bait, and to survive, I have to find a way to trick Hellebore at his own game.

Except I have no idea how to do that.

I don't even try to find Mack and the others, instead racing to the portal that leads me down the concrete stairs to the firm. Even back inside that perfectly air-conditioned office with its giant windows, calming diffusers, and sublime art, I can't force my legs to stop trembling.

Clutching a plastic cup of water, I collapse in the guest lounge on a slender couch made to look like a leaf. I've only just barely managed to still my trembling when Mack's dad, Nick, walks by with a few employees.

I try to hide, but apparently just putting a hand over your eyes doesn't actually make your face unrecognizable.

"Summer!" He rushes over, a giant smile plastered across his face. "Mackenzie made me promise not to embarrass her today, but she didn't say anything about you."

Clearing my throat, I stand and give him a hug.

"Where is she?" He pulls back and glances over my shoulder. "Have you guys been to the roof? She's been begging me for a pass to visit since the park opened."

"She's still there, actually." I try to plaster on a smile, but my lips catch on my dry teeth.

His brow pinches. "How does she seem to you, Summer? Is she okay? Sebastian and I—"

"And who is this, Nick?" a female voice interrupts.

I look past Nick to the tall, gorgeous woman in the metallic gold Oscar de la Renta pantsuit. Two Summer sprites hover behind her.

My mother. Or ex-mother. Or past life mother. It's a working title.

Nick beams. "This is a second year shadow recruit at Evermore Academy. She's the student from the Tainted Zone, the one who caused quite a stir last year?"

"Yes, I remember."

As she appraises me, I drink in her features. Verdant green eyes. Sun-kissed skin. Long scarlet-red hair the exact hue of a woolflower plume, pulled high into a neat collection of braids.

I'm surprised to see her dressed so . . . human.

"Come." She holds out an arm, causing Nick to blink in surprise. "Let me show you my office."

Pushing past his shock, Nick nods encouragingly.

I don't feel up to being around my past-mother, not alone. Not after the day I just had.

Yet her offer doesn't really feel like something I can refuse. Waving goodbye to Nick, I follow the queen down a hallway to her spacious corner office.

More sprites and a white miniature centaur wait inside, poised to do her bidding. The centaur sneaks a glance my way, obviously decides I'm of no importance, and launches into a speech. "Your afternoon meetings have been pushed back, and city councilwoman—"

She lifts a finger, silencing him without a word, and turns her full attention on me. "Chilled cucumber water or strawberry and mint infused?"

It takes a second to understand she's offering me a drink. "Oh, um, strawberry?"

A sprite dives for a glass tumbler on the bar counter opposite the queen's desk, while another begins shoveling ice into the tumbler. Drink in hand, I follow the queen to the long cream bench lining the floor-to-ceiling glass windows overlooking the reservoir.

And wait. And wait. The queen's silence swells to fill the room.

So in typically me manner, I begin rambling to ease the awkwardness. "This place, it's beautiful. The views. The painting. And, holy crap, the restaurants. They have a fondue fountain with chocolate and—"

She holds up a hand, and my tongue literally stops working.

Yes, Summer. I'm sure she has no idea about the fondue fountain in the restaurant complex she owns.

Her head tilts as she studies me. "You stood up to Prince Hellebore during the Wild Hunt."

It's not a question, but I nod anyway. Where is this going?

She gazes out the window to the park below, showing off her sharp jawline. "Have you applied for my internship?"

Whoa, was not expecting that. "I . . . would love to, but as a second year, I'm afraid the final gauntlet will be beyond my skill level."

"Indeed." Her face remains placid, but her tone drips disappointment, and I'm shocked by how much I suddenly care about her opinion.

"Queen Larkspur, I don't mean to offend when I say this, but the Evermore oppress and abuse us at every turn. The final gauntlet would be designed to ensure most of us die just for trying."

A kind smile lifts her cheeks, and my heart clenches as I wonder how many times I was the recipient of that same smile. "I may be an Evermore, dear, but I cannot take offense to the truth." She taps a long, slender finger against her ear lobe, drawing attention to the gold capping the sharp points—the only jewelry she wears. "After the Light-mare, when the Untouched Zone was just beginning to allow my kind to enter, I was told purchasing land here was a fool's folly. My husband, the king and man who openly murdered my only child, forbade me. The Unseelie Courts mocked me."

My heart skips a beat at the mention of my death.

"And yet," she continues, "despite the risks, the imprisonments and attacks I endured, the attempts on my life by my own husband, I now own more land, businesses, and real estate in your world than any other Evermore. And do you know what that gives me?"

I do know. It's the one thing every Fae in existence thirsts for. "Power."

"Yes. With the darkling attacks affecting more and more cities, I now possess the keys to every court's safety, and no one, not even my husband, can intimidate me."

"Why are you telling me this?"

"Because my firm needs mortals like yourself. Mortals unafraid to stand up to the Fae who still believe in the old ways of doing things. The Fae who believe your kind are nothing more than animals to serve them."

Her speech drags my emotions from earlier to the surface, and I struggle to my feet before she can see my distress. "Thank you for the water and the advice, Queen."

"Don't thank me, Summer. That implies you owe me, and you do not."

"My mistake," I mutter. Stupid Faerie law.

Right before I exit her office, my gaze snags on the exquisite oil painting above her desk, housed in a modern silver frame. The same delicate star-shaped white flower on Hellebore's arm—the one he's weirdly obsessed with—is painted against a black backdrop.

A fat bead of blood drips from one of its slender petals.

"Do you like it?" my quasi-mother asks. "The flower is called a Bloodstar. One drop could fell an entire Fae army. A queen from my line once even demanded her husband buy the rare, expensive flower and have a perfume made from it."

She waves her hand, and the centaur waiting behind her perks up, ready to get back to business. "Now go. And don't disappoint me, Summer. I expect to see your name on that list the next time I check."

I murmur something as I leave, my mind reeling.

Bloodstar. She called the flower a Bloodstar.

Where have I heard that name?

Bloodstar. Bloodstar. Bloodst—

Oberon's beard, I have it. That's the flower Evelyn mentioned. I sag against the wall outside the queen's door.

When asked who was controlling her, Evelyn couldn't say a name. At least, not an Evemore's name. Instead she named a flower, the Bloodstar. The very same flower Hellebore is obsessed with. The one only he owns. The one he prizes above all things.

It doesn't take a genius to make the connection.

Prince Hellebore is her master. He's working for the Darken. He sent the darklings to steal the piece of the World-slayer. Evelyn couldn't say his name, so instead she managed to speak the name of the flower he wears on his body.

She must see it every time he gives her an order.

Holy Fae, I've found something that can hurt him.

I turn the corner just as the class is gathering across the hall. Hellebore and I lock eyes.

He dons that arrogant, asshole-and-proud smile that deserves to be punched from existence. The one that screams, *You can't touch me.*

I return his smile with one of my own.

I know your secret now, dickwad, and I'm going to use it to take you down.

"Stop fidgeting," Mack whispers as we stroll through the tables full of Winter Court diners toward the Sylverfrost's private dining room.

"This dress hates me," I hiss, tugging the velvet hem down as low as it will go—which is shockingly not a great length.

Or *not* shocking, considering Valerian picked it out.

Ruby sticks her head out of the black clutch I'm carrying. "Kid, that dress is doing you—and your glorious ass—a favor."

She finally figured out how to access the dog toy I stuffed with vanilla frosting—the kind made to keep pets busy—and her face is caked with the stuff.

Mack shoots me a scolding look. "I can't believe you brought her."

I might have forgiven Ruby for the darkling mess, but Mack hasn't. "Ruby hasn't been off campus in years."

"Have you ever considered there's a reason for that?" Mack mutters as she follows a willowy hostess with frosted skin, cobalt blue hair, and pillowy white feathered wings up a flight of spiraling stairs to a glass room above.

"Everyone can change."

"Apparently." Mack cuts her eyes at Ruby, who finally figured out the hollow dog toy I filled with vanilla frosting— to keep her busy—and is stuffing her face with it. "Wasn't she emo a few weeks ago?"

I laugh, thankful that Mack gets a night away from the stress of school. She's been stressed lately, studying late into the night. And she's lost weight.

Sometimes when I get up in the morning for my training sessions, she's still awake, highlighter poised over a textbook. I keep meaning to ask her if she's okay, but our schedules are so conflicting right now that it's hard to find the right time.

The hostess waves her hand over the frosted enclosure, which is basically a long rectangle of ice, and a door appears. "Enjoy dinner."

Her crystalline eyes look me up and down before she glides back down the stairs.

So far, we've gotten the same indignant look from every patron we passed. Although I'm starting to suspect the anger is directed at me, not Mack.

The mortal girl rumored to have Valerian Sylverfrost under her spell.

Mack enters first. I smooth down the dress Valerian sent me—the one custom fitted to fit my every curve and dyed the same color as his midnight-blue hair—and enter.

A long marble table veined in silver stretches the length of the room, showing off a stunning centerpiece of frosted roses of ice. Delicate snowflakes drizzle from above.

They melt as soon as they meet my warm skin, leaving a slight iridescent imprint that soon has my entire body glowing.

Head high, I fight the urge to tug down my dress as I scan the seats.

My gaze locks on Valerian at the head. For a choked breath, he doesn't move, doesn't blink as he takes me in.

An emotion too brief to catalogue ripples over his countenance. When he stands, though, it's impossible to miss the approval in his eyes.

Asher and Eclipsa do the same, their mouths parted.

"Holy Fae hells, Summer," Eclipsa murmurs. "Every male below just had a heart attack when you walked by."

Asher lets out a gravelly chuckle. "I think it was a different organ that was affected."

"Careful, dragon," Valerian warns.

Eclipsa rolls her eyes. "Males, always thinking with their least attractive appendage." To drive home her point, she stabs a summer sausage from a platter and deposits it on her plate. "You guys hungry?"

Valerian pulls back the chair next to his, his gaze never leaving mine. "You look . . ." His lips twitch at the corners. "Beautiful."

I never thought one word could nearly undo me. But when Valerian Sylverfrost declared I was beautiful with that rich, deep voice, those intense silver eyes peering into my fricking soul, I'm pretty sure one of my ovaries self-combusted.

Asher does the same with Mack's chair, and we all sit. I'm thankful as an army of waiters descend with drinks and appetizers. As soon as they leave, the room begins to rise.

My stomach flutters—and not just because of the sudden movement.

When the floor settles and the frost clears over the walls of ice, I gasp.

Our room now looks out over the restaurant, which is set into a mountainside. The pale lights of the Winter King's resort twinkle from the basin below. Snow-crusted peaks rise all around us, engraved against a sky brimming with stars.

Eclipsa holds out her crystal glass filled with golden plum wine. "To Yule, the Winter Solstice, new beginnings"—her eyes slide to me—"and new people."

I follow suit, my heart as full as the wine glass I hold. Looking around the room at these people—Fae and human—I know just how lucky I am to have them in my life.

After that, I fall into the banter and camaraderie as Eclipsa, Asher, and Valerian all tease each other and reminisce. Any worries that I would disrupt their tradition somehow float away as the night progresses.

And, oh, does it ever. Ruby entertains us by juggling the candied winter berries on the sweets tray and performing an adorable dance every time she eats something particularly amazing. Mack makes us laugh when she tells us the story of her dads' water sprites, which were finally rehomed to an aquatic Faerie creatures rescue center.

I even share some of my family's Christmas traditions, confusing everyone but Mack when I try to explain Santa.

When the main course is delivered, the waiter hands Valerian an extra plate. Eclipsa winks at me as he studies the bowl. "What's this?"

I grin. "SpaghettiOs with meatballs, aka the poor man's heaven in a can."

I can't say that the expression on his face is blissful after he takes a bite, but he doesn't spit it out like the ramen noodles the other day, so I consider it a win.

Finally, when there's a lull in the conversation, I make sure the room is spelled from eavesdroppers before divulging what I learned on the field trip.

When I finish explaining the link between Hellebore and Evelyn, Eclipsa sets down her wine glass, her eyes livid.

"Why didn't you tell us Evelyn mentioned the Bloodstar flower?"

"Honestly, I forgot about it when I first woke up, and then I assumed Mack had already mentioned it."

I cringe. *Way to throw your bestie under the bus.*

Mack taps her fork against her plate, the food untouched. Has she eaten anything since we arrived? "There was so much going on, and I was worried for Summer."

Eclipsa downs her wine in a single gulp and then pours another glass. She's still raw when it comes to Hellebore.

Valerian jumps in. "Now that we do know this information, we need to find a way to expose him."

Asher growls under his breath. "I've always hated that pretty-boy bastard. Exposing him would be a pleasure."

"But why would someone from the Seelie Court work to bring the Darken back?" Mack asks, toying with the red strap of her dress. "I mean, he basically started a war to destroy the entire Seelie side of the Fae, right?"

The others share a look. They must decide that Mack is trustworthy because Asher turns to her and explains, "The Darken wanted to destroy the Seelie because they stood in his way."

I run a finger over the rim of my water glass. "In his way for what?"

They share yet another tense look, and my appetite dies.

"My grandfather believed land was the key to power." Valerian's voice is low, as if the Darken might hear him. "His continuous wars for territory eventually made my court the most powerful in existence, but he wanted more."

A shiver of cold snakes down my spine as Valerian's gaze slides to me.

Oh, God. "The mortal lands," I whisper.

Valerian nods. "The Seelie opposed his plan to dominate your world. Historically the Seelie Courts were more tolerant of mortals, and they already had an overabundance of mortal slaves without a war. So my grandfather decided to remove the final obstacle to his grand plans."

"Oh my God," Mack breathes through the fingers clamped over her mouth.

A lycan waiter enters with a pitcher of water, and Eclipsa sends him running with a glare.

She turns to me. "The Seelie Courts may have once opposed taking over your world, but now, with the scourge and the darklings destroying their own lands and no end in sight, some wouldn't hesitate to bring the Darken back and finish the job."

My hand shakes around my water glass as I bring it to my lips. The thought of what that could mean for our entire world . . .

I give up on my water and set the glass back down. "I have a plan."

Everyone leans in as I explain the scheme I've been putting together in my mind since I left the Summer Queen's law firm.

When I'm done, I recap. "So, essentially, during the final gauntlet held in the Spring Court, we'll have access to the palace, including the vaults where Hellebore keeps every-thing he considers precious. It may be the only opportunity we have to search inside his home."

Unless he gets his way and enslaves me, but I don't say that.

Mack's mouth gapes open. Asher and Eclipsa have gone disconcertingly still.

And Valerian—he's staring at me as if I've lost my mind. "If you enter the final gauntlet, you would most likely die. Do you think any of us here would let you take that risk?"

I swallow, trying to keep a level head. "If we don't, and

Hellebore manages to raise the Darken, my world will never survive. Are you asking me to do nothing?"

"I'm asking you to think about the people here who care about you."

This is not going as planned. At all. "I appreciate that, but you can't ask me to stand by now that I know how to take Hellebore down."

Valerian gets that stubborn, *I'm royalty* look. "Funny, that's exactly what I'm asking."

On some silent signal, Asher, Eclipsa, and Mack all make bathroom excuses. Ruby tries to protest but Mack grabs her by the waist on her way out.

As soon as the magical ice door freezes behind them, I face Valerian. The pulse in his neck jumps. I can see the conflict inside his eyes. That overwhelming need to protect me. To keep me safe. To keep me his.

No matter the cost. Even if that cost is my free will.

"I can't let you put yourself in harm's way, Princess." His eyes soften as he runs the back of his two fingers down my cheek. "If you've learned anything from the past few months about me, you would know that."

I take his fingers in my hand. I don't want to fight. Not tonight. "And if you've learned anything about me, you'd know I'm not going to cower from the chance to save my species just because it's dangerous."

"You're not mortal, Summer. You're Evermore."

"No, I'm both." Something about the vulnerability in his eyes gets to me. He stiffens as I lean forward, brushing my lips against his. "If you truly care about me," I murmur softly, enjoying the way his breath shudders. "If you truly believe I'm your mate . . ."

My plan was to use my feminine wiles to make him listen. To tease him with the possibility of a kiss. But I underestimated how thirsty my body is for his touch, and my traitorous tongue darts into his mouth.

Oopsie.

A low growl vibrates his chest, and I fight to keep control of my senses as he suddenly drags me into his lap.

Abort! His kiss deepens, the words I had poised and ready sinking into oblivion, along with every thought in my head but how nice this is.

So very, very nice. Like the first bite of cookie dough ice cream I ever had. Granted, I emptied the entire carton in minutes and then licked the inside clean.

Licked. The word makes me think of Valerian's tongue and all the things he can do with it.

The things he *is* doing with it right now.

Moaning, I melt into him, focusing on the absolute pleasure of my body pressed into his. His teeth playfully nipping my bottom lip. His tongue parting my mouth. Claiming me.

His hands stroke my back in slow, lazy circles, reminding me just how thin my dress is—and just how skilled his hands are.

Dangerous territory, Summer. Stop focusing on ice cream and tongues and refocus on your plan.

What was that again?

I squeak in protest as he lifts me by the hips and settles me so I'm straddling him in the chair. My dress rides up my waist, presenting large swaths of bare skin for his fingers to explore. The snowflakes fall heavier now, melting against my arms, my legs, painting me in iridescent flecks that smear beneath his touch.

His hands glide up my thighs, slowly, the pads of his thumbs grazing the sensitive inner portion.

When his thumbs flick at the edge of my panties, I gasp. My mind goes blank. Emptying of everything but those fingers as they tease and tease and—

My back arches violently as a puff of air erupts from my lips.

"Every male below us can sense your racing heartbeat," he purrs. "Let's see if we can give them a crescendo."

He kisses me again, gentler now, as if I'm an exquisite chocolate to be savored one tiny bite at a time. Those thumbs tracing little circles in time with his tongue and my heart and . . .

Holy pixie dust, I want to devour him whole.

Right here. In a box of ice. Surrounded by shimmery snowflakes and wintry mountains cut out against the stars.

One of his hands slips into my hair, undoing the rhinestone pin holding it together and sending the tiny blue roses Ruby weaved around the base raining down over my bare shoulders.

Each one draws shivers over my aching flesh.

How did this backfire? My plan was to get his attention and then make him see my point. But Valerian is a drug, and I'm a shameless addict. Willing to sell everything—even my dignity, even my *choice* to be his mate—for just a taste.

And yet, I'll never be mated to someone who doesn't give me equal say in my life.

He growls as I jerk my head back, my lips swollen and covered in the taste of him—plum wine and juniper. His chest heaves in time with my racing heart.

"Valerian," I whisper, but something about the way I say his name only excites him more. His eyes fix on my lips as his hand slips behind my head, his fingers gently twining in my loose hair.

Any moment he'll press my aching lips back to his, kissing away the last of my willpower.

"Valerian, wait. This went further than I planned."

"Do you have any idea what would happen to me if you were hurt?"

I shake my head. "You don't get it. I refuse to be anything but your equal, Valerian Sylverfrost. And yes, I want it all. I want real, sappy love, the human kind. I want equal say in our relationship and my life without your alpha Fae bullshit. I want to be with you because you respect me, not because you think some stupid magical bond says I'm yours. I'm done being property of the Fae—and that includes you. So if that's what you think our relationship is, then I'll never be your mate."

A muscle beneath his jaw feathers. "You're asking me to be okay with you entering a contest that's notorious for its brutality?"

"No, idiot. I'm asking you to let me decide my fate." Hurt sparks inside his eyes, but he's silent, letting me speak my truth. "I'm asking you to respect my decision and then train me to survive it. I'm asking you to acknowledge that I'm a grown ass adult who has the final say in my life."

A ragged breath escapes his lips. He stares at me, nostrils flared, and I can see that he wants to argue. I can feel his abdominal muscles clench against my belly as he works through his emotions, his jaw grinding.

And then, finally, he nods. "Okay."

"Okay?" I repeat, sure I've misheard because Valerian would never give in that easily.

"You're right. You're a grown ass adult"—his hands slide playfully to my rear—"and I can't forbid you from doing anything, even if I think it's a terrible decision. Eclipsa and I will increase your training, plus there will be more sessions trying to coax out your magic."

The tension in my shoulders eases as I celebrate this small but important victory. It means that Valerian Sylverfrost is capable of compromise.

Huzzah. I feel like I should have a cake made or something.

"There's something else," I say. "Since I'm entering the gauntlet, I'm going to put in my application for the internship at Larkspur and Associates."

His fingers resume their lazy strokes over my thighs, his silver eyes still dark with desire. "Of course you are. I didn't expect otherwise."

"So you're not mad that I might miss fourth year?"

"Mad?" He shakes his head. "What kind of male do you think I am? Actually . . ." His full lips curl around the edges. "Considering how your new tactic is seducing me when you want something, yes. I'm furious, Summer. Now, how do you plan to change my mind?"

I chuckle, running my fingers through his hair. "I think we might melt this room if we go for round two."

"Would that be such a bad thing?"

"Without walls, everyone would see us."

"I think this thing between us is beyond hiding, don't you?"

A hollow bubble of hope swells my chest as I imagine a public life with Valerian. "What about the Darken?"

"Consummate the bond, and together, we'll be powerful enough to go after Hellebore and destroy my grandfather's soul once and for all."

My throat tightens, and the question I've been too afraid to ask tumbles from my lips. "Do you love me?"

His eyes darken. "Truth?"

I nod, my heart pounding strangely in my chest as I await his answer.

"When I watched you walk through the restaurant earlier, pulling down your dress, your lips twisted in that adorable half-smile you get when you're uncomfortable, totally oblivious to how every male Fae was watching you, I realized something. No matter what you look like, no matter whose body you inhabit, the bond between us will never be severed." I'm speechless as he drags his thumb over my wavering bottom lip. "I would do anything for you, Summer Solstice. You have to know that by now. Anything. That has to be better than what you call love."

I blink, trying to mask my disappointment. "Valerian, I told you, I want it all. You said those words once, when you explained our soulbond to me. Why can't you say them again?"

"Because that would be a cruelty, pretending I believe in something I do not." A frustrated sigh escapes his lips. "I've watched humans enough to know that human love is an illusion that fades with time, corrupting into apathy and sometimes even loathing."

"Not always."

"How could you want something so fragile when the magic of the soulbond is unshakeable, growing stronger with time, not weaker?"

I frown, searching for the words to explain why this is important to me. "Yes, mortal love isn't perfect. It's messy and complicated and not driven by magic, but choice. The choice to commit to one another forever. The choice to stay when life gets hard. When the other falls ill or gets fat or depressed or—the point is, it's a choice between two people, not some magical bond."

Something cold and unrecognizable flashes over his countenance. "When my mother lived in your world, she discovered this human love. She was obsessed with it, consuming every book and movie she could find about it. And when she came back to visit me, it was all she could talk about. She recounted in painstaking detail the countless mortal men she fell in love with. How wonderful and magical it all was."

I freeze, trying to determine where he's going with this. He's never spoken of his mother to me before.

"She talked of your mortal love right up until the day she

abandoned me, leaving me alone in the clutches of a mad, violent king and a callous father. So I think I've had my fill of mortal love."

My heart aches for him. "Love isn't what made her leave you, Valerian."

I reach out to touch his cheek, but he catches my wrist. "Don't. Please, Summer."

I look down at his fingers tight around my wrist. Back up at him. Tears wet my eyes. "I can't keep doing this, Valerian. Not if you can't love me."

"You say you want irrational love, but I would give my life for you, my eternal mate. Why is that not enough for you?"

The others burst into the room. They halt for an awkward second, and I think they've picked up on the tension in the air, but then Asher cracks some joke about getting a room and Ruby begins drawing an obscene sketch into the ice wall behind us.

Only Eclipsa and Mack seem to notice Valerian's icy demeanor and the hurt I know is plastered over my face. Sliding from his lap, I wipe my eyes and announce that I'm throwing my name in the gauntlet.

Thankfully, Eclipsa uses that as an excuse to end the dinner.

"Early training tomorrow," she says through a fake yawn. "Summer needs her rest before the torture begins."

Asher scowls at her. "What do I do with the tray of ice shots I just ordered?"

Eclipsa looks from Valerian's emotionless face to Asher and shrugs. "I think you two can figure it out."

Right before Eclipsa portals us to our dorm, I look to Valerian as I leave, hoping for . . . I don't know. A look that says he's come to his senses and realized that he can love me after all. That I'm worth the pain and vulnerability that comes with that.

Instead, he gives me a cold nod that pits in my stomach.

Long after the dinner, when I'm tossing on the lower bunk, reliving everything that happened between Valerian and I, his words play over and over in my head.

I would give my life for you, my eternal mate. Why is that not enough for you?

For a Fae, especially one as dark and broken as Valerian, I know it's probably the closest he'll ever come to real love. That I should accept it and hope that he changes.

But I'm done sacrificing my dreams for the Evermore.

I will graduate from this academy.

I will protect the mortal world from the Fae.

And if I choose to spend the rest of my life with someone, it will be for love.

"Keep going, Summer!" Eclipsa yells. My glove slams into the red heavy bag over and over, making it shudder on its chain. In my periphery, I catch sight of an object flying toward my head and duck just in time.

"That was a ten pound dumbbell!" I pant, glaring at my sadistic torturer where she sits, legs crossed, on the bench opposite the mat.

"This is the last practice before the final gauntlet," Eclipsa snarls. "Stop whining and focus!"

I still don't know how four months flew by so fast, especially considering how brutal they've been. Every moment I wasn't sleeping was dedicated to training, studying with Mack for the upcoming tests, working to unlock my powers, and wondering when Hellebore would call in his part of the bargain.

The only day in the last four months that I took a break was the day Mack and I entered—and passed—the second required gauntlet.

If I hadn't had the smart idea to throw my name in the

final gauntlet, I could have stopped my training then and focused more on studying for my final written exams, like Mack.

Instead, it was back to the grueling practices. Two hours every morning with Eclipsa, testing my accuracy with weapons.

Nights were spent trying to coax out my magic. Even with all of Eclipsa's persistence, I've only used magic once, right after she told me I couldn't stop for a drink. I was frustrated and a little hurt because Valerian had found yet another excuse not to show up to practice *again,* the coward.

Eclipsa and I were both tired and yelling at each other and the next thing I knew, my hydroflask was in my hand.

Apparently, I stole Eclipsa's ability to recall objects close by. But that victory was followed by a series of failures, and today's no different.

The timer goes off, and I lean against the heavy red bag, struggling to catch my breath.

Eclipsa frowns, uncrossing her legs. "Enough. Practice is over."

I don't even bother arguing as I begin stripping off my fingerless gloves, the Velcro ripping loudly. It's the last practice before the final gauntlet next weekend, but I don't feel half as ready as I should.

It's no one's fault but my own, even if I want to blame Valerian just to feel better.

When he's here, he's attentive and thorough. Watching my stance. Helping me with some of the new weapons. Offering suggestions. And Eclipsa doesn't need him to train me.

I realize now he only came to my training because he wanted to be with me, not because he thought Eclipsa couldn't handle it by herself.

So it's not fair to blame him for the sudden incompetence I feel. But I do blame him for leaving the second my sessions are over. For the cold, almost emotionless way he looks at me now.

"I'm not ready," I groan. What was I thinking?

"Your skills are there, Summer. It's your magic that worries me." She chews her lip. "We have to hope that you don't accidentally use it during the gauntlet. After that, we'll hit it hard this summer until we figure it out."

"We could try the water bottle again?" I mutter. But my heart really wants to conjure Valerian. To see his stupid beautiful face, even if his emotions are hidden behind an icy wall. I look to the door, not so secretly wishing he'd walk through.

Eclipsa follows my stare, and a knowing look comes over her. "Summer, I don't know what happened between you two that night, but I know that the Winter Prince cares deeply about you."

Cares deeply. Those two words can suck it.

"That bad, huh?" she presses.

I hop to my feet, fixing my ponytail in the wall mirror. "That night . . . I might have asked him if he's capable of love. Loving me, specifically."

Eclipsa's eyebrows shoot up. "And?"

"And he doesn't. End of story. I also might have mentioned his mom."

"Oof."

I focus on looping my hair tie around my ponytail rather than the hurt I feel. I hate how pouty and juvenile I sound. A relationship with Valerian will complicate my life. I should be relieved that I can finally move on and focus on my goals.

Eclipsa comes up behind me. "I warned you that our kind views that stuff differently."

"You did, and I'm an idiot."

"You're not an idiot, at least, not about this. You and the prince are from two different worlds. I don't think either of you were prepared for how different." She meets my eyes in the mirror. "His mother claimed she loved him and then she left him, while those cruelest to him have been loyal. For him, love will always mean pain."

"Always?"

"I know he would do almost anything for his friends, especially you. And if he's been distant these last few months, it's because he's trying to find a way to give you what you want." She walks over to her gym bag. "Love is just a word, Summer. Why put so much importance on it?"

I grab my gloves, stuff them into my Puma bag, and follow her out into the spring air. Students mill around campus, some already dressed for the evening banquet. "If it's just a word, why can't he say it?"

She laughs. "Remind me not to ever go against you in court once you get that internship and become a lawyer."

"Deal." My phone buzzes, probably Mack. "I gotta go." I give her a quick hug. "Are you coming to the dance later?"

I've been so busy prepping for the final gauntlet that I'd nearly forgotten the spring banquet and formal was tonight. Thank goodness Mack texted me a few hours ago reminding me to make time for a shower.

"I didn't plan on it." She frowns at a few shadows who nearly run into us on the lawn, sending them reeling back.

I can't help but think her reluctance is due to a certain sociopathic prince.

"Please? You can go with Mack and me. We're meeting a few other shadows, but I promise they'll be on their best behavior."

Eclipsa sighs. "You are aware that your friends are terrified of me, right?"

"Then come. Show them you're all puppies and unicorns. And wear something slutty."

"So you want me to be a puppy unicorn slut?"

"Exactly."

She rolls her eyes, but she doesn't say no.

"Um, have you seen yourself in that dress?" Mack asks. She's sitting on the floor. Thornilia has just finished putting Mack's freshly streaked purple hair into magical rollers and is now painting her toenails a dark metallic green to match her dress.

I twirl as I check myself out in the mirror, the long skirt of my gown floating around me, lighter than air. The pink color is a bit too . . . pink. But it favors my tanned skin and pale blonde hair. Giant dandelion heads have been meticulously sewn into the skirt, and they ripple at the slightest movement, making my dress seem alive.

"Have you thanked the ILB yet?"

I run a hand down the lacy corset. "I will tonight."

The dress arrived in a long white box with the name from the most famous Fae tailor emblazoned on the top. I hate how happy that single gesture made me, even if he didn't leave a note.

Perhaps what Eclipsa said is true. Perhaps he's been distant because he's trying to find a way to open his heart to loving me.

"Does that mean you're getting back together?" She doesn't look up from her toes, but the caution in her voice tells me more than her expression ever could.

"I don't know," I answer honestly.

"You know I like the prince, and I know you swear you'll use precautions with him—but there's no pill to protect your heart, Summer."

I glance down at Mack. I can't put my finger on it, but she seems different lately. Distant.

It's probably all the time I've spent preparing for the final gauntlet while she's been studying for the regular second year exam.

The exam! "Oh, shoot. I forgot to ask how your final went this morning?"

"Good, I think." Her normally confident tone when it comes to tests is missing, but with the gauntlets and the exams, the last few months have been hard for all of us.

She looks at the time on her iPhone and then hops up, yanking out her rollers. "Crap. I have to go. I'll be back in a few."

"I'll go with," I chirp, moving to follow her.

Her back is turned, shoulders tight as she shakes her head. "No need. I'll be right back."

"I don't mind." I grab a light cardigan.

She's frowning when she turns to face me, her arms crossed. "I'm going to the gym for our final physicals, okay?"

"Our what?"

"Every quarter, before our tests, second year and above shadows have to pass physicals."

"Physicals?" I repeat, imagining running sprints and being timed.

"Yeah. Remember? They take our measurements and weight, check our BMI. Make sure we're up to certain impossible male standards that set us back like fifty years. You know, important stuff."

Confused lines wrinkle my forehead. "I've never had to do that."

Exhaling, she meets my eye. "That's because you're the special guardian of Prince Sylverfrost, and he demanded you be exempt."

"What? Why doesn't Asher exempt you?"

"Because only the Winter Prince could demand something like that. Besides, I wouldn't ask him to, not when everyone else has to pass the same standards."

My chest tightens. Suddenly all her excuses for not eating, like being too busy or her stomach hurting or having eaten earlier, make sense.

"I didn't ask him to do that," I insist, trying and failing to keep the hurt from my voice.

"I know, okay? I'm not saying you did."

My stupid bottom lip tugs low as tears threaten to fall. I feel so horrible. How could I not have noticed she was starving herself for some ignorant standard? "Why didn't you tell me?"

"I mentioned it at the beginning of the school year, but then . . ." She shrugs. "I didn't want to make you feel bad. You already have so much going on."

"Mack, I didn't know. If I had—"

"See why I didn't tell you?" She wraps me in a quick hug. "And *I* don't think it's unfair, not really."

"But the others do?"

"Some, maybe. But they'll get over it. I tried telling them it wouldn't matter. You're like a weird gazelle who never gains weight."

I smack her arm. "Yeah, especially my boobs. If I could just have half of yours . . ."

Her smile lights up her blue eyes, easing any leftover tension between us. "The ILB likes your boobs, and *these* puppies are not for sale." She stares lovingly at her rack in the mirror. "They're my best asset."

"Wrong," I say, a sudden sappiness coming on. "Your heart is your best asset."

She hugs me again, longer this time. "Hurry and meet me at the banquet. I have a surprise for you."

As I watch her go, I mull over my hurt at being kept in the dark over the physicals. Why didn't she tell me? It's not like I've kept anything from her . . .

Oh, hell.

If this is how I feel knowing she kept a test from me, how will *she* feel when she finds out I've been hiding my past? I thought keeping that from her was for her own protection, but I see now that's not an excuse to lie to a friend.

I have to fix this before she finds out some other way.

After the final gauntlet, I'll tell her the truth.

The entire school attends the spring banquet, from professors to students, a tradition taken directly from Whitehall Academy. I rush to the quad just as dusk approaches. Long tables covered in white linen are spread out across the lawn, beneath the crape myrtle and cherry trees. The magical lanterns strung through their branches glow softly.

The Evermore and their families sit at tables in the middle of the courtyard. Accordingly, they get waiters, fancier chairs with cushions, and their own private bar.

I search the quad. *Where are the second year tables?*

While bumbling around looking for where to go, I stumble across a table laden with sweets. Hellebore's sprite, Nerium, is already terrorizing the gnome Fae in charge of doling out the tiny plates of candied violets and strawberry basil tarts.

Ruby screeches from her perch on my shoulder. "Have you ever seen anything quite so beautiful?"

"Ruby, don't you dare leave my shoulder."

There might have been a rule that specified no sprites

allowed at the banquet . . . and I might have broken said rule. I reach for Ruby, but she slips through my fingers, cackling in delight.

Note to self: some rules are probably there for a reason.

I leave Ruby to fight Hellebore's sprite over a slice of apricot almond tart. As I pass by the group of fourth year tables, Callum spies me and nods, but the gesture is clipped.

Of course. I'm the only underclassmen to enter the final gauntlet. There are twenty passing spots and over forty fourth years.

The day I threw my name in the final gauntlet, I declared myself a threat.

I find the second year group near the courtyard fountain, in the shadow of the Magical Arts building that forms the east wing. Mack spots me immediately and runs to drag me over to where she sits beside her dads and . . .

"Holy orc balls," I blurt as she grabs my hand. "Is that . . .?" My vision blurs with unshed tears as I stare at Aunt Zinnia, Aunt Vi, and Jane all sitting across from Mack's dads. "How?"

I knew parents and family were allowed to attend the banquet, but I didn't bother mentioning it to Aunt Zinnia. After she attended the first gauntlet, I was worried just coming to the Everwilde again would dredge up the old wounds from losing her family, and I didn't want to be responsible for that.

But now, seeing them here . . . I realize just how much I've missed them. How much I've needed their presence, if only for a few hours, to remind me why I'm doing all of this.

"Zinnia was easy to convince," Mack says. "But Vi?" She whistles. "My dads and I have been working on her since Christmas."

"They don't make 'em like Aunt Violet anymore," I admit.

Mack loops her arm around my waist and drags me to my

place at the table. "My dads might have sent her an expensive fruit basket and some insanely expensive Russian vodka to soften her up."

I laugh, nodding to Jane. "And her?"

"She insisted on coming. Said she'd cross the Shimmer on her own if she wasn't invited. She swears you're in trouble. That the Fae have done something to you."

Frick. The last few months have been so crazy that I haven't always responded to Jane's texts. In fairness, they're mainly about ways to kill the Fae—she's been busy researching, apparently—but still. I should have responded.

My heart nearly bursts as I take the seat between Zinnia and Jane. After I let Zinnia bombard me with affection, and sit still for Nick and Sebastian's pictures, I turn my attention to my younger sister. Her reddish-copper hair is pulled into a braid, the freckles on her nose just starting to darken under the summer sun.

Somehow my aunts managed to get her into a blue and green cotton dress.

She looks deceptively sweet and innocent.

"Hey," I say. "I heard you were worried about me."

"You didn't answer. I thought . . ." Her eyes narrow as a sprite flits over carrying a basket of bread. "Doesn't matter. I guess you're fine."

The bitterness in her voice surprises me, and I add her lost youth to the long list of reasons to despise the Fae. "What do you think? About the academy?"

She frowns. "I hate it. The tulips, the chirping birds and perfect weather. It's all fake. To hide how horrible it is here."

I cringe, but she's not wrong.

Her cutting stare drops to my dress, the accusation in her face hard to ignore. "How do you stand being around them?"

"I don't know. I guess you get used to it."

"I wouldn't." She glares down at the linen tablecloth. "I

would rather die than live with them—but not before taking a few of the pointy-eared assholes with me."

"Jane!" Vi snaps, leveling her with a fiery look. "Language."

Jane rolls her eyes where only I can see. "I can't believe you left me with them, Summer. They're the worst."

I sigh. I'd forgotten how hormonal and annoying I was at fifteen too. "Don't say that." I squeeze her thin arm. "You don't exactly make it easy on them. You're lucky Vi hasn't locked you away in the cellar like she did me."

"She would if she could catch me."

After promising Jane the food isn't spelled or designed to enslave her, she turns her attention to a spring pie drizzled with honey and figs. The tension in her bony shoulders eases, but I make sure to watch her anytime she gets up for drinks or food.

The food *offered* to us might be perfectly safe, but I'm just beginning to grasp the complexity of Faerie law. She could steal a roll off an Evermore's plate or thank someone the wrong way and owe them her firstborn.

The banquet drags on well past sunset. Because of where I'm seated, I can't get a good view of the Unseelie royal tables. But I know Valerian is there, his father probably with him. Is he seated next to Inara?

A shock of jealous and rage fills me at the thought. *Murder.* I want to murder the ice bitch with my bare hands.

She would never ask him to love her. *She* would never require anything but his loyalty, which is what he offered me. *She* won't risk his kingdom and his status.

I try to brush off my sudden pang of jealousy as shadows and Evermore are paraded to a podium by Magus to receive awards. There's no way Mack's name won't be called, and after seeing how hard she studied this year, she deserves a standing ovation.

When it comes time to honor the valedictorian of the second year class, Nick and Sebastian lean forward, each dad grabbing one of her hands. For some reason, Mack looks mortified, but then again, so would I if I had to make a speech in front of hundreds.

"Reina Vanderhill," Cronus announces. The Unseelie side of the courtyard erupts in applause. Mack frowns, avoiding her dads' shocked gasps.

But unlike them, she doesn't seem surprised. Only . . . embarrassed.

Sebastian goes immediately into lawyer mode. "There's no way Mackenzie lost to a daughter of the Vanderhill's. They bought her grades, I guarantee. Our girl deserves this award. I've already written it into her application letters to the big five firms. Wait until I file a motion with the school—"

Nick takes Sebastian's hand. "Shh, honey. Don't embarrass Mackenzie. We'll discuss this *later*."

Mack, for her part, seems to shrink, caught in the middle of them. I try to catch her eye for support but her eyes stay glued to her clasped hands.

Thankfully, that was the last award. As we stand to say our goodbyes to our families, Nick pulls me aside.

"Summer, you would tell me, wouldn't you honey? If Mack wasn't okay?"

Okay? "Why wouldn't she be?"

But even as the words leave my mouth, I'm taking in her gaunt cheeks and sharp collarbones, the untouched food on her plate.

He sneaks a look her way. "Sebastian means well, but he puts so much pressure on her. And this year . . . well she won't say as much, but I can tell it's been a struggle. She won't let us help her. The school contacted us about her grades—"

My head snaps back to him. "What about her grades?"

"She didn't tell you?" His auburn eyebrows gather. "Then I shouldn't have said anything." He wipes at the corner of his eye. "Did we do the right thing, bargaining for her life and sending her here?"

The turmoil and uncertainty in his voice pierces my heart. There could hardly be two parents who loved their daughter more.

I shrug. "All I know is you did the best you could."

He nods, as if reassuring himself of this. "She's lucky to have a friend like you."

After that, a pit of unease lodges squarely in my sternum. And it doesn't go away. Not even after we say goodbye to our families—Nick and Sebastian promising to escort my family straight to the mortal guest houses behind the quad—and then rush to the nearest bar, Richard, Layla, and Jace in tow.

Eclipsa joins us in line, oblivious how the other mortal students scatter. She took my advice to heart and wears a metallic silver mini-dress that could be painted on. Actually, I think it might *be* paint.

Annoyed at the line, the Lunar assassin cuts to the front, demanding shots. After a few select words with the deer shifter bartending, she waves us over.

"These are my friends. Make them happy. Got it?"

I watch her jaunt away with the tray of shots, not spilling a single drop.

"You okay?" I ask Mack as we wait for the deer shifter to make our lilac shandies.

"Of course." She throws an indignant look over my shoulder at Reina and her friends. "Everyone knows Reina pays for her grades."

"So everything's good?" I persist.

"Yes, Mom." She rolls her eyes. "It will be after you get stupid drunk and dance with me."

The deer shifter hands us our cocktails. Desperate for alcohol, Mack goes to grab mine, but the shifter shakes his head, his large umber eyes darting to me. "This is for her."

I take my fizzy drink, wondering if I should be flattered or weirded out by his creepy stare.

"Someone's not getting a tip," Mack mutters as we cross the lawn toward the center of the courtyard, where students are gathering. The tables have been moved, the soft glow of the pink and green lanterns strung high above illuminating the pockets of people already dancing.

Halfway across the lawn, I nearly run into the Winter Court entourage. Magus is escorting them to their quarters, which I'm willing to bet are more luxurious than where Zinnia, Vi, and Jane are staying.

Despite the pleasant spring air, the Winter King wears a fur-lined cloak of navy blue velvet. The grass where he's walked is frozen, a trailing path of glittery white.

Before I can remember that he probably hates me—and that I should probably hide—his gaze shifts to our little group.

And fixes on me.

Something reaches through his cold demeanor, a curiosity, and then he nods to my drink as he holds his up.

"Is he . . . toasting you?" Mack whispers.

"I don't know. Maybe?"

Crap, he's definitely toasting me.

I thrust my drink into the air, sending the fizzy lavender liquid sloshing over the side.

When the king takes a sip of his, Mack pokes my ribs. "Drink. You're supposed to drink."

I rush the glass to my lips, the bubbly lilac cocktail tingling all the way down my throat.

Without a word, he dismisses me and continues toward his quarters, the ice crackling in his wake.

What the frick was that?

Before I can ask Mack if what just happened was normal, she drags me into the middle of a group of first and second year shadows. A band famous in the Everwilde called the Deranged Nymphs is on the center stage, the mixture of instruments and beats whipping the crowd into a frenzy.

Eclipsa appears with her tray of shots, somehow still not a drop spilled. She offers me one.

"What are those for?" I yell over the music.

"A few of these and your friends will adore me," she promises.

I decline the shots, but the others down them. It isn't long before Mack, Eclipsa, and Layla surround Jace, who's only happy to be surrounded by three of the hottest girls on the dance floor.

Richard and I are the only ones not actively trying to embalm our livers. At some point, we're paired off together, and we awkwardly shake our hips. Like most people who can't dance, we end up yelling over the music, hoping to use small talk to divert from the fact that we suck at dancing.

"I can't believe it's been over a year," Richard yells.

"What?"

"A year! Since Evelyn turned. The dance reminded me of her."

Oh. That explains why he's not really in a partying mood. That makes two of us.

Between Valerian's recent coldness, Mack's struggles, and waiting for Hellebore to call in his bargain, I just can't muster the energy to celebrate.

I look around for Mack, but she and the others have drifted deeper into the crowd. She's already on her third drink and Titania knows how many shots.

I don't like her drinking with this many Fae around, but we're surrounded by mortals, and she's with Eclipsa. Most of the Evermore have taken up the other side of the dance floor and are ignoring us completely.

She'll be fine. Stop worrying. She's with humans, and she needs the break after finals.

Fanning my face, I shout at Richard that I need another drink and flee before he can offer to go with me. The lanterns above dim, the music slowing.

A love song. Ugh.

Fighting free of the crowd, I find myself searching the other side of the courtyard for a certain Evermore. One with silver eyes, midnight-blue hair, and a devious smile.

And then, as if summoned by my thoughts, Valerian appears a few feet ahead. My chest aches as I take him in. A cerulean blue dinner jacket with silver embroidery shows off his wide shoulders, his wavy hair brushed to one side.

A wry smile plays on his lips. "Care to dance, mortal?"

I've been so mad at him these last few months. I even wrote him a letter only to tear it to pieces. I swore tonight if I saw him I would tell him exactly where to stick it.

But now . . .

Valerian Sylverfrost is asking me to dance, and I don't have a chance in hell of refusing.

I accept his hand, hardly daring to breathe as he guides me to the center of the Fae dance floor. The Evermore stop dancing to stare at us. Their pinched faces make it more than clear what they think about a human in their midst.

With one of their princes, no less.

He rests his free hand on my waist, drawing me to him. "Don't look at them, look at me."

"How do I know you're . . . you?" I whisper, Bane's little trick from last year fresh on my mind.

"I could kiss you and you would know, I promise."

His teasing tone sends a shiver through my torso. "True. But if you're Bane, I would have been tricked into kissing him, and I'd rather not."

A chuckle. "Spoken with the cleverness of a Faerie." His hand moves to the bare skin between my shoulder blades, his fingers tracing my spine as they glide down to the small of my back. "What does your body tell you?"

Heat blossoms from my core, and I swear the air gets thinner with every circle his fingertips make against my flesh.

Only one Evermore has this affect on me.

"They're all staring," I whisper.

"Let them." His breath is cool against my ear. His hair nearly black in the soft lantern light.

God, even with everyone watching . . . this feels so right. And yet, I'm pissed at myself for falling into his arms after months of his coldness. "Why have you been avoiding me?"

He pulls back so that I can see his face, limned in shadows. "After Yule, I thought about what you said. About what you *needed* to understand the depths of my feelings for you."

Depths of feelings. That has promise.

"And?" I press. I don't want to get my hopes up. Not after what Eclipsa said, but . . .

"And I realized I was asking you to give up everything, but not willing to do the same."

I blink. Where is he going with this?

"The last few months, I've been visiting the Winter Court, dealing with some *contractual* issues."

"Contractual?"

"Yes. There was a contract made between my father and Inara's father guaranteeing our marriage. I found a way to sever it."

Whoa, shit just got *real* real. I remember the Winter King's toast.

"So your dad okayed that?"

"Okayed? I'm the heir to the throne. He can't force me to marry her, only strongly advise me to. I agreed to it years ago because an alliance with her father was beneficial, if not necessary."

"And now?"

"And now, it's not. I paid recompense to Inara's father using my mother's jewels, ending Inara's claim over me. The only person who can claim me now is you."

Holy frick. My heart is thundering in my ears, making it

hard to focus. Inara's threats come to mind. "But won't her family retaliate?"

I may not be a true Fae, but I know a woman scorned has nothing on a Fae female scorned, and Inara was already homicidal *before* he publicly shamed her.

He shrugs. "Her father will be angry over the slight. Some in the Winter Court will side with him and leave. But they can be won back eventually." He must see the concern in my eyes because he takes my hand, squeezing it. "I refuse to be ruled by fear. I can deal with losing duplicitous courtiers, but I would never get over losing you."

My mind is spinning, the stars above making lazy pirouettes across the night sky. We've given up any semblance of dancing, making our being together even more conspicuous.

My vision might be blurring, but around me, the hateful stares of the Evermore are perfectly clear, as are their silent accusations.

I stole Valerian from Inara. Me. A lowly, unimportant human. I've bewitched him with magic or my human wiles—whatever the heck those are.

"Doesn't that look bad?" I press. "Choosing a mortal over a powerful Evermore?"

"I'm tired of caring about what the other courts think. In fact, I only care about what one person thinks, and she's standing right in front of me."

He brushes his lips over mine. A part of me wants to kiss him back in front of everyone. A giant eff you to Inara and the entire school. A part of me wants to finally, *finally* give in to what my body wants.

And yet . . .

I pull away.

"You still haven't answered my question from months ago." I place my hand on his chest, just over his heart. The coldness of his body seeps through his jacket into my palm. "Do you love me?"

His fingers stop caressing my back. "What?"

"It's a simple question. Are you in love with me?"

He stares at me as a mixture of shock and confusion play over his features. "I just told you I gave up everything for you, and you want to argue about a word?"

My throat tightens. My chest hurts. I suck in a breath, fighting the sudden ache of disappointment that fills me. "Why can't you say it?"

"Why can't you just let it go?"

"Because I'm human. A silly, irrational human and I need love. I need it professed from the rooftops. I need it whispered to me in bed for no reason at all."

He frowns, unable to mask the hurt in his face. "What I'm offering you is better, Summer. It's a guarantee that I will never hurt you."

"But you are hurting me right now."

His hand drops from my back. He retreats an inch. "What you ask . . . it's too much."

I swallow, clearing the emotion from my throat. I feel like my words are twisting, coming out wrong. "So you'll never be able to love me?" He goes to answer, but I interrupt. "Truth."

Silence. I can see him struggling with what I'm asking. "What would you like to know? That I think love is a poison disguised as a cure? That humans are fools for believing in it? That my mother once said those very words and I would rather cut out my own tongue than utter them?"

I flinch from the bitterness in his voice. The pain. "Here's my truth. I think what you feel for me scares you. I think it terrifies you. So you rely on a bond of magic rather than risk opening your heart to me."

His silence scares me. Infuriates me. I can see him

building a wall between us as real as if it were mortar and brick.

In my desperation, I try to shatter it. "The truth is, I think you're a coward. Afraid to love me. And if that's true . . . you don't deserve me."

His face closes off, and I know—I just know I've lost him. He dons the cruel, impenetrable mask from the first time I saw him. "I think it's clear that I can never give you what you desire."

Words lodge in my throat. Words I imagine saying but can't quite utter. *Wait. That came out wrong. I don't want us to end this way.*

But maybe he isn't a coward. Maybe he's the brave one for finally saying what we both know.

Valerian Sylverfrost will never be able to look me in the eyes and say, "I love you." And perhaps that shouldn't be important. Perhaps what he offered me should be enough.

But it isn't. It never will be.

Laughter and whispering remind me that we're front and center, on display for everyone. I look around at all the Evermore watching us. A few take videos with their phones.

Tears prick the corners of my eyes.

No. I will not give them the satisfaction.

Wiping my nose on my forearm, I dart away from Valerian and through the tangle of Evermore. Some grab at my dress. My hair. They call me horrible names. Laugh at me.

Inara and the new Six sneer as I race past, leaving a trail of dandelion heads floating in the air.

Her hate-filled look promises retribution for Valerian's slight.

Part of me is relieved that he doesn't go after me. But that's when it really hits that we're over. This, us, the whole mate thing, whatever we wanted to call it.

It wasn't enough to make him trust me.

To love me.

When I reach the stone walkway that tunnels beneath the main hall to the other side, I let the tears fall. Let the rush of my emotions from everything that's happened over the school year flood me until I'm choking with quiet sobs.

This entire year can go straight to hell.

Sniffling, I enter the dim tunnel. The sounds of revelry and laughter echo off the walls, growing quieter the farther I press into the darkness.

I quicken my pace. There's no lanterns to chase back the shadows. Only the meager light from a lamppost on the main lawn in the distance. It's yellow glow glistens off the stone walls as I near the end.

A stairwell opens up on my right. It's layered in shadows. On instinct, I press against the wall, recoiling from what I cannot see—but feel. The prickle against my skin that means I'm being watched.

"That was an entertaining show you two put on," comes a soft, lazy voice.

Hellebore.

My gut tightens as fear slowly wends its way through my heart.

The Spring Court heir has finally come to collect his part of the bargain.

I know running is pointless. That's what he wants. But my body screams to flee, my thigh muscles quivering in anticipation. My lungs greedily sucking in air as I prepare to dart toward the light.

"Run, and I'll make this even worse for you." He slips from the shadows, the yellow light from the lamppost reflecting off the buttons on his green vest, embroidered with fuchsia oleanders and tiny gold daggers. "I see you liked my gift."

Panting, I try to retreat, only to feel the rough stone wall scrape my bare back. His eyes travel the length of my dress.

Frick. I pinch the fabric of my skirt, dandelion heads blowing in the faint shafts of lamplight piercing the dimness. "This was you?"

"Fae hells, you're adorable. Of course it was me."

He prowls toward me, and I raise my hands. I already know I'm going to fight. I'm not prepared. I thought there would be some sort of warning before he requested my part of the bargain. Time to enact my plan.

"Why now?" I demand.

He flicks up an eyebrow. "Simple. Your Winter Prince is all but ruined. He's been mired for months in controversy. First stealing his grandfather's soulstone, then attacking me over a mortal servant. And now that he slighted an ally of his own court for you, only to be publicly humiliated after giving up everything for you."

"He didn't steal the soulstone." *You did, you pointy-eared prick.* "And that's not what happened. I didn't humiliate him."

He tsks. "Truth doesn't matter, perception does. But you're clever. You know he's doomed. The other courts smell blood in the water. And once I parade you in front of him and all the courts as mine, once I ruin you and then toss you aside, the prize he gave up everything for—his destruction will be ensured. His reign over."

"Liar," I hiss. "I don't care what your powers are, I will never give in to you."

"I am a liar, but you will submit to me, Summer. You will spend every moment of your existence in my thrall. I'm going to parade you in front of him, forcing him to watch you become what you were always meant to be. A slave."

"Are you absolutely sure about that?" I feel my face twist into a look of pure hatred. "The moment you slip up, the moment your magic wanes, just for a moment, and I'll sink a dagger of iron into your heart."

He laughs, his lips twitching in amusement. "I understand now his obsession with you. He and I both share a taste for poisons, but mortal love is more elusive and deadly than a thousand vials of the toxins I collect. Now, speaking of collecting . . ." He closes the space between us, his eyes burning with excitement. "Where would you like me to touch you?"

I cast a desperate glance toward the party in the distance. *Dammit, Ruby. Where are you?*

"No one can help you," he insists cheerfully.

I swallow, my parched throat convulsing. *Ruby Ricin, if you've ever loved me, get your tiny drunk ass over here.*

I turn my cheek as he places his hands flat on either side of the wall. "If you don't choose, I will for you. I vote for something with meaning. Perhaps your smart mouth, since that's your most offending part."

Crap. This is happening. I close my eyes. Knee poised to do as much damage as possible to his nether-regions the moment he touches me.

. I hear him shift slightly. My eyes flick open—

"Ruby!" I shout as every limb in my body goes numb with relief.

"The one and only," she slurs, bowing mid-air before slamming into my shoulder. Nerium follows behind her, dipping in a way that tells me he's as lit as she is.

"I am going to buy you a year's worth of skittles, you glorious creature," I whisper before facing Hellebore. He's backed up a few inches, obviously displeased that his sadistic party has been crashed. "I'm ready to choose where you may touch me, prick." Plucking Ruby from my shoulder, I hold her out as offering. "Ruby, how would you like to be enthralled to the Spring Court heir?"

Her eyes light up, and she waggles her eyebrows at Hellebore. "Does this mean I finally get an invitation to your red room of pain?"

The smile on his face falters. As realization takes hold, something dark scuttles just beneath the surface of his arrogant facade. "Is this a joke?"

"No joke. You see, I remembered a clause in Faerie law that specifically states once a sprite has declared allegiance to a master, and that master to their sprite, they technically are regarded as one. I also double-checked that theory with a lawyer I know. It's ironclad."

I thought watching Hellebore's expression as he realizes I've outmaneuvered him would be satisfying . . . and it is.

But more than anything, it's frightening. He goes still. Which is scary in its own right. Like a cat right before it pounces. But the black fury brimming inside his eyes—I know with absolute certainty that he will destroy me for this.

Ruby squirms, misreading his swelling hatred for disgust. "What, do you have something against tiny people?"

His sharp gaze switches from her back to me, and I know I've gone too far. He's going to straight up murder me right here.

"Why wasn't I invited to this party?"

I glance over Hellebore's shoulder to the figure behind him. Eclipsa leans against the stairwell, half in shadow. A dagger glitters from her fingers where she rolls it between them, proving that no matter how many shots she had, she's still capable of tossing that dagger straight into Hellebore's heart before he can so much as blink.

Hellebore doesn't turn around. Doesn't even take his eyes off me as he says, "I never pegged you for a human lover, E."

Eclipsa picks her fingers with the dagger. Her casual demeanor so at odds with the tension drowning the air. "I don't love them. She's my prince's property, and I'm sworn to protect what's his. Other than that, I could care less what you do with her."

Property? His? After everything, her words hit me harder than if she'd slapped me in the face. I stare at her as a wound opens inside me. I thought we were friends. I thought . . .

Hellebore takes in my wounded expression and laughs. "Oh, did you assume she actually cared about you? That you were anything more than her master's prize, to be locked away and protected?"

Eclipsa smiles. "Hellebore, if you aren't gone in say, five seconds—to match the number of inches of your favorite body part—I'm going to cut out that quivering organ you call a heart and ram it down your throat."

"That does sound lovely, E, but I'm afraid just like the last countless times, I must rebuff your affections." He winks at me, and if there was ever a way to make a wink say, *Enjoy your upcoming murder*, he just nailed it. "Now, I'm off to visit a certain female whom I know will be overjoyed to see me."

The moment he's gone, I sag against the wall as blood floods back into my legs. Nerium makes an obscene gesture at Ruby before zipping after his master.

Eclipsa glides down the stairs. "Summer—"

"Don't." I shake my head as fresh tears slick my cheeks.

"What I said, it's all a game."

"Not to me." I rub the back of my hand over my eyes. "But Hellebore was right. I'm a fool for thinking the Winter Prince could love me, and I'm an even bigger fool for thinking you and I were friends. It won't happen again."

"Summer, wait!"

But I'm already running toward the dorms, Ruby in tow. My room is empty. After texting Mack to make sure she's safe, I curl up on my bed—still in Hellebore's dress—wrap myself in my sheets, and cry.

39

I wake up to Mack's protests from above, and what sounds like . . . meowing?

"Make it stop, *please*," Mack groans from above. "The sun isn't even awake yet."

Wiping the sleep from my eyes, I slide from bed, change out of my rumpled dress and into leggings and a T-shirt, and throw open the door to . . .

"Chatty Cat?" I squeak.

Chatty Cat sits there in all his mangy glory, yowling his head off. I reach for him but he hisses and scampers into the room, still mewling and doing his best to wake up the entire world.

Another groan comes from the upper bunk. "You made it worse."

I drop to my knees beside the cat, who is sitting on his hindquarters, singing the song of his people. "Chatty, what are you doing here?"

Chatty hisses, his ears drawn back in annoyance. I can't help but feel he's growing impatient. What am I missing?

"Just take him back to your sister," Mack pleads beneath

the pillow over her head. "She was supposed to keep him in a crate."

"Jane?"

At her name, Chatty Cat makes a bloodcurdling scream. His lime-green eyes pleading with me to . . .

"Oh my God, Jane!" Cold dread washes over me. "Is she in trouble?"

I swear, Chatty Cat nods before fleeing under my bed.

Just like that, Hellebore's parting words replay in my mind. *I'm off to visit a certain female whom I know will be overjoyed to see me.*

Mack sits up, rubbing her head. "What? Why are you screeching?"

I don't even bother putting on shoes before I rush out the door. Zinnia and Vi are already in the hallway. They're both still in their long nightgowns.

Zinnia grabs hold of me, the desperation in her eyes confirming my worst fear. "She's missing, Summer. Our girl is missing."

While Zinnia's tight lips are bracketed by grooves of fear, Vi's are twisted with righteous fury. "I knew coming here was a mistake. I warned you, Zinnia. If these Faerie bastards have harmed a hair on that girl's head, there will be hell to pay."

Oh, God. I need to handle this before they make it worse. "I think I know where she is," I reassure them. "This is all a big misunderstanding. I need you to wait for me in my room with Mack while I get her back."

Somehow, Zinnia manages to talk Vi into waiting before she goes on a vengeance spree. Zinnia catches my eye as I sprint down the hall. "Get that poor child back, Summer, whatever it takes."

It's early morning, the academy awash in the silvery predawn glow. A few revelers are still up partying and dancing, while others have passed out on the lawn. The smell of smoke and stale honeybrew drift on the morning breeze.

My bare feet and ankles are covered in dew as I march up to the Spring Court manor where Hellebore stays, behind the Combat Arts building.

Honeysuckle and clematis drape from the overhanging porch, and faded purple irises grow in scattered pots along the deck. The buzz of bees stir the air.

I slam my fist into the heavy oak door, disturbing the peeling green paint. I do that for a few minutes until there's a pile of green flakes on the floral welcome mat. I try the knocker next—a gold fox head with emerald eyes.

When that doesn't work, I scrounge around in the front garden until I find a rock, wind that fucker up like a baseball, and hurtle it at the front window.

The sound of shattering glass is music to my murderous heart.

"Wake up, you kidnapping prick!"

Something stirs behind the sheer white drapes.

I grab one of the pots, dump out the irises, and smash it into the arched entryway window. More breaking glass disturbs the stillness of the morning.

"I'm going to break every single window you own until you march your ass out here and face me!" I warn, grabbing the closest pot—an amaryllis inside a small hammered gold planter—and aiming it for the window to my left.

The door parts. Hellebore leans against the frame, the loose cotton pants he no doubt just threw on hanging low on his hips. His bright blue eyes are heavy-lidded, sleepy and feverish, his honey-gold hair raked to the side, as if he's been up all night doing deplorable things. The colorful tats on his arms are nothing compared to the giant spiderweb tat covering his chest.

A tremor courses through me as I spy the black widow in

the center. The arachnid is hunched over a blue-and-yellow butterfly—

I look away from the macabre art, made all the more disturbing by the way the poor butterfly's wings *moved*.

Hellebore drags his too-bright gaze over me. "You can murder that poor flower and all my windows, but no means no. I will not sleep with you."

"Where is she?" I pant, raising the planter like a weapon.

"Oh, you mean that young fire-cracker with the freckles and the red hair?"

My muscles twitch with rage. "If you hurt her in any way—"

"You'll what? Break another window? Throw something at my head? Yell at me?"

Mother trucker. He doesn't see the amaryllis streaking toward his smug face until it's almost too late. Unfortunately, he ducks just in time and it crashes into something out of sight and hopefully very expensive.

The humor bleeds from his face. "Behave that way one more time, I'll close this door and you will never see your sister again. Now, are you going to be a good little pet?"

My jaw locks, but I manage to grit out, "Yes."

"Wonderful." Hellebore draws the door all the way open to reveal Jane, still in her cotton dress. Her eyes are horrifyingly blank above a stretched out smile. "See? She's fine. Happy as can be. A much improved version of the mortal I found snooping around campus. Now *she* was practically feral."

"She's a child. If you so much as touched her . . ."

"Mortals don't interest me in that way. Not when it comes to *that* sort of pleasure."

Vomit.

He smiles at Jane before turning that predatory grin on me. "You should have taught her not to enter portals. She followed me to the Spring Court territories and I'm afraid now . . . she belongs to me."

My heart plummets. If he had taken her directly from the academy, I could have filed a grievance with the council.

For a moment, I let myself imagine going back to my aunts empty-handed. Explaining how Jane is now a slave of the Spring Court and there's nothing we can do about it.

Except there is.

"What do you want?" I whisper.

"Hmm." He presses a finger to his lips as if pondering my question. "Perhaps I simply want to keep her. Good help is hard to find, and she's remarkably sturdy. She just spent the entire night cleaning my house without a break, and she's still on her feet. Most mortals would have physically broken down before then. That alone makes her worth a hefty sum— if I choose to sell her."

If I could murder anyone with my mind, he would be dead right now. Eviscerated, beheaded, and flayed.

Forcing my furious gaze off him, I look at Jane. She's barefoot, feet dirty, still smiling. Her hands hanging limp at her sides, but I can already see the blisters forming. He's going to work her to death.

Something flickers behind her hazel eyes. Just like Evelyn, she's still in there. I know if I don't rescue her today, she'll find a way to do what she threatened.

End her own life.

I tear my focus from Jane and face him. He's won. I know it and he knows it.

"What do you want?"

"Make another bargain with me."

I clench my jaw. "I'll never give you permission to touch me."

"Maybe I don't want that anymore." He traces a finger over the wisteria vine tattoo spiraling down one forearm, making it curl and tighten. "No, all I ask now is this. Wear something of my choosing."

What the hell? I tug at the hem of my shirt. "That's not a bargain."

"Fine. Win the final gauntlet and you get your sister back. Lose, and you must wear an item of my choosing."

I scoff. "Winning is impossible."

"Precisely."

"I get Jane back now just for making the bargain," I amend. "Win and you forget I exist. Lose and . . . I wear whatever freaky item you specify, but it must be an actual item of clothing or an accessory, and I can wear other items along with it." No way will I let him force me into wearing a crotchless nightie or something equally uncomfortable and gross. "Also, it can't possess magic that controls me somehow."

He stares at me with those heavy-lidded eyes. Weighing my words. After our last bargain, he takes me a little more seriously.

"Deal," he purrs.

I feel the magic of our bargain lock into place, and it's similar to the feel of shackles clicking around my wrists.

Behind him, a figure appears on the wide marble stairs leading to the second floor. Inara's bright blue hair falls around her bare shoulders in waves, an ivory satin sheet wrapped around her otherwise naked body. "Who is it?"

"Go back to bed," he orders.

Her eyes meet mine, and rage flashes across her face. "You aren't letting her sister go, are you? You promised we could keep her."

"And now I've changed my mind."

"But—"

"If I wanted your advice, Inara, I would have asked for it. Now go back to bed and don't get up until I return."

She storms up the stairs, furious.

Hellebore runs an idle finger over his neck. "Tell your prince thank you for breaking her heart, by the way. She's so desperate for affection she'll do nearly anything."

God, if there was ever a male who deserved to lose his member just for being a douche canoe, it's him. But I'm beyond caring about things like Hellebore using and manipulating an emotionally unstable Inara after a breakup.

As far as I'm concerned, they deserve one another.

Jane wobbles slightly on her feet, and I growl, "Fix her or the bargain is off."

He sighs as if I'm the biggest bore in the universe. "Fine. She was horrible at making tea anyway."

He snaps his fingers and the glazed look in Jane's eyes disappears.

Her smile falters. Her body sags. She stumbles, emotions clouding her face. "Where am I?" Her eyes dart to Hellebore, anger and fear seeping into her expression before she looks at me. The terror and accusation in her stare nearly make me flinch. "What happened?"

Wrapping my arms around her, I steer her off Hellebore's porch and toward my dorm. "Shh. You need food and rest. Zinnia and Vi are waiting. It's going to be okay, I promise."

But it's not going to be okay. I've just made a deal with the devil . . . and there's no wiggling out of this one. I don't know what Hellebore's playing at, but I do know I want no part of it.

I have to win the gauntlet or die trying.

40

Aunt Vi is on hold with the main office when I arrive with Jane. They take one look at her disheveled hair, ragged dress, and dirty feet, and jump into action. Zinnia helps me set Jane down on my bunk while Vi pours a glass of water for her.

They don't say a word, but I can feel the accusation in their sideways glances.

I should have protected her. I should have apprised them of the risks. The moment I saw them at the banquet, I should have warned them to flee. Instead, I was selfish. Too overwhelmed with my own needs to think of theirs.

We decide Jane should rest in their quarters for a few hours before making the trek back to the other side of the Shimmer. I was supposed to travel with them. We're on break this week until Friday, when I travel to the Spring Court for the final gauntlet.

But now . . . I think it's best Jane doesn't see me. Not for the next few hours.

After they're gone, I begin packing my things. Mack apparently left to check the courtyard for Jane, just in case she'd snuck back to the party, and she hasn't returned. I finish packing in less than an hour—it's easy to gather your belongings when they literally fit in a small carry-on—and then decide to shower. On the way back from the communal bathrooms, I pass by Kyler's room.

The door is unlocked. Someone's already cleaned out Kyler's stuff. The bed is made. The bathroom's tidy. It's like she and Evelyn never existed. Dropping to my knees, I check beneath the bathroom sink, surprised by the pink crate labeled, "Old Roommate's Stuff."

Kyler must have gathered it up and kept it, perhaps to give to Evelyn's parents.

After deliberating on giving it to the school, I take the crate back to my room. I'll take it home and find a way to mail it to them.

By the time Mack returns, my rolling suitcase and Puma gym back sit by the door, packed and ready. My hair is nearly dried, pulled back into a clip. I want to crumple into a ball and sleep away the last twelve hours, but this is the last time I'll see Mack for months, so I hop up to make us one final cup of coffee instead.

Behind me, Mack is unusually silent, but I chalk it up to her hangover. "Rough night?" I tease as I turn, coffee mugs in hand.

When I see the tears in her eyes, I freeze mid-step, steamy coffee spilling onto my fingers and dripping onto the faded green rug. "Mack?" I rush to set down the cups on the coffee table and settle beside her on the loveseat. "What happened? Who do I need to murder?"

Her eyes are rimmed red, like she's been crying for a while. "I got my final grade back." She drags the back of her hand over her nose. "I failed."

"What?" I blurt, positive I've misheard her. "How is that possible?"

"Remember the first Potions and Poisons test? When you were afflicted by the tormentor spell and got to redo the exam?"

I nod, a ball of dread forming in my belly.

"I was so worried about you that I left midway through the test. After that grade, I was struggling to catch up, and then everything kept happening to you and I couldn't concentrate. I was trying to prove I deserved to be here, so I refused the tutors my parents offered. I thought the final would make up for everything, but—" Tears pour freely down her swollen cheeks. " My dads are going to kill me."

I grab her hands. "Isn't there something we can do? Appeal? Extra credit."

She tugs her hands away, her eyes puffy as they meet mine. "The only way to pass now is to win the final gauntlet."

My eyebrows jerk up in surprise. "No. You can't, Mack."

"I already entered. That's where I was just now."

There's a cold finality in her words. Crap. I replay my bargain with Hellebore in my mind. "Mack, please. I'm begging you to rescind your name. We'll find a way. I'll talk to the Winter Prince. Maybe he can do something."

"I know you guys broke up, Summer. The whole school does." Swiping at her eyes, she stands. "It doesn't matter. If you can't be happy that I have one final chance to stay at the academy—"

"You know it's not that. You're my best friend. If anything happens to you, I would die."

"I supported you when you decided to hook up with the Winter Prince, even though I knew he would break your heart. I supported you when you entered the gauntlet on some crazy mission that's probably going to get you killed. Now, all I'm asking is that you do the same for me." She shakes her head. "Never mind. I have to go. My dads are waiting for me, and I haven't told them yet, so . . ."

As soon as the door shuts behind her, my face crumples, tears streaming freely.

How did everything spiral so out of control so fast? In less than a day, I've lost nearly everyone I ever cared about.

Only Ruby is left, and even she should despise me for offering her up to a sociopath—even if she would have thoroughly enjoyed it, the sicko.

The ache in my chest grows as I open my nightstand drawer. She's made a nest of stolen underwear and socks inside. I kiss my fingertip and press it to her sleeping form. Her little shimmery wings stir, but she doesn't awaken.

"Stay out of trouble, sprite."

But I'm starting to think with me gone, Ruby will be the safest she's been since school started.

I ruined Valerian's standing in court. Endangered Eclipsa just by association. Nearly let Jane be sold into a lifetime of slavery. And now Mack is flunking school, her childhood dream of graduating as a Shadow Guardian shredded, because of me.

Maybe love's not the poison—maybe I am.

41

I stare at the crack in my ceiling above my bed. I haven't left my room in days other than to use the restroom. The tantalizing smell of banana bread fills the air, a pang of hunger twinging my middle, reminding me I should eat. Should keep my strength up for the final gauntlet in two days.

I leave tomorrow to journey to the Spring Court, where I'll stay overnight with all the other finalists.

I should *definitely* eat. But my appetite is gone, and I just don't have the energy to force down food at the moment.

Through the thin walls, I hear the oven ding. A moment later, Zinnia's voice rings through the house. "Summer! I made your favorite!"

Ever since I returned home last Sunday, Zinnia's baked enough to feed half the town. Vi's drank enough to petrify her liver. And Jane's found every excuse there is to disappear into the woods.

As for me, I've held a five day long pity party for one.

God, I miss my friends. I worry about Mack and how

she's holding up. I miss having to hide all my food from Ruby. I miss Eclipsa ordering me around during training.

And Valerian . . .

Ugh. Don't think about him.

Flipping onto my stomach, I reach onto my nightstand and grab my phone. Eclipsa's string of text messages show up first. I flip through them, eyebrows knitted together.

I'm sorry.

I was an asshole.

I shouldn't have said that.

I'm the worst.

Worse than an orc boil. A troll's fart.

Hellebore got to me . . . that's not an excuse but, please just text me back.

I'm worried about you.

And the Winter Prince.

If you don't message me back, I will come to your house and kick your ass.

I blow out a breath, sending my greasy hair flying away from my face, and check my last text message from Valerian. It's from the night at Yule.

I can't wait to see you in that dress.

My throat tightens, and I scroll to my texts with Mack. Her last message was from the night of the party.

Where are you? Jace is hooking up with a satyr and Richard is drunk-crying over Evelyn. Need reinforcements STAT.

Now, I send off a quick, *Hope you're doing okay,* and wait. Nothing.

I sit up in bed as Zinnia's footsteps echo down the hall. A moment later, my door creaks open.

"I come bearing gifts," Zinnia calls, waltzing inside with a tray of goodies. I stare at the sliced and buttered banana bread. The sweaty glass of sweet iced tea.

And burst into tears.

"Oh, darling. Don't cry." She deposits the tray on my desk and rushes over.

I've been trying to keep it together. Trying to focus on the gauntlet and be strong. But the second she wraps her plump arms around me, I can't stem the tide of tears.

I bury my head in her chest and let everything out.

She caresses my hair, the smell of her cheap vanilla perfume from the Dollar General comforting. "Remember when I used to do this?"

I shake my head.

"You were nine going on sixteen, so angry and sad and confused. I used to just hold you and let you cry. Afterward, I'd offer you a plate of cornbread or a slice of homemade apple pie with some sweet tea and you'd be all better."

I lift my head, smiling through my tears. "And here we are again."

"Yes, but I suspect this time, you need more than some bread and tea to fix you up." Her gaze flicks to my facedown phone, back to me. "Friend trouble or boy trouble?"

"Both." I wipe my sleeve over my cheek, collecting the tears.

A knowing look dawns on her face. "Nick said Mack's been struggling this year. He thinks it's his fault, that they've pushed her for so long that she doesn't know what she actually wants."

"He said that?" I forget that Zinnia and Nick have each other on speed dial and gossip about us constantly.

"Yes, he's been worried sick about her. It must be hard for the sweet girl, especially when you know exactly what you want to do after you graduate, while she's . . . confused. I told Nick he should step back and let her make her own choices."

"I always thought she wanted to work at her dads' firms." As soon as the words leave my mouth, I think back on all the times we discussed our majors. While I blabbered on and on about finding a job to help protect mortals from the Fae and make our lives better, she was always strangely quiet.

She's never once said she wants to be a lawyer, and when we discussed Guardian jobs after school, she always changed the subject.

Zinnia reaches over and hands me my glass of iced tea. "Now tell me about this boy. Is he cute? Does he have nice parents?"

Cute? Nice parents? Titania save me, how do I explain Valerian Sylverfrost? I take a long sip of my drink, the tea so sweet my teeth ache, and say, "What if it wasn't a . . . *boy*?"

Surprise flickers in her eyes. I wait for the condemnation I know I would feel in her position, but there's only worry. "He's a Faerie?" I don't even have time to answer before she says, "Are you being safe?"

I nod. "We haven't—didn't get that far, but I was prepared." Eclipsa found me the herbs mortal women need to keep from getting pregnant from a Fae.

"Did he hurt you?" she asks, her voice harder, making it clear she wouldn't hesitate to rain hell on him if he did.

"Does my heart count?"

"Ah, I see. The heart's trickier than flesh." She takes a slice of banana bread, munching it as she thinks. "So you're in love with this Faerie?"

How does she do that? I nod again, wishing I could deny it. The Fae killed her family. Loving one feels like a betrayal.

"But he doesn't love you back?"

"No." My chest aches, and I settle back on the bed. "He wanted to take things to the next level physically, he even pissed off his dad and possibly endangered his life for me, but . . ." I clear emotion from my voice. "But he couldn't love me. Not the way I wanted."

"Ah." Finished with her bread, she dusts her hands off,

still deep in thought. "Did I ever tell you that my daughter had a different father than my late husband?"

I shake my head, glad for the shift in conversation.

"I got pregnant with her right out of high school. Unfortunately, her father wasn't a very nice man. When I fled to Vi's with a shiner and marks around my neck, Vi finally told me if I stayed with him, she'd kill him. The day I left with Grace and a trash bag of my belongings was the best day of my life. A few years later, I met Paul. That kind, quiet man took over as her daddy, even if she never called him that word."

"I wish I could have met Grace." I think of the portrait of the happy girl in equestrian riding gear downstairs. Her vibrant eyes and mischievous smile.

"I do too." Her lips press together, as if torn between pride and anguish over her memory. "When Grace and Paul disappeared, they weren't at a cattle auction with Vi's husband and boys. I tell people that because it's easier than the truth."

I shift on the bed, barely able to hide my surprise.

"The truth is, Grace's deadbeat father had asked to meet her. He hadn't been in her life for five years. I let Grace decide, and she chose to meet him. So my husband, the man who had taken care of another man's little girl knowing she would never call him dad, offered to drive her fifteen hours to meet him. He explained that he would stay as long as it took, because when that man broke his little girl's heart, he was going to be there to pick up the pieces."

"Zinnia, I'm . . . I'm so sorry."

Zinnia's eyes fill with tears. "Paul was a man of few words. I'm not sure he ever told Grace that he loved her, but she knew. Not because of his words, but his actions."

I'm crying again. Both of us a hot mess of tears and snot.

"How do you not hate the Fae?" I ask.

"Child, there's enough hate in this world as is. I won't add to it." She brushes a strand of my hair from my face. "I don't know this Faerie boy you love, but I do know you. You wouldn't give your heart to someone unworthy." She sighs. "Sometimes our minds won't let us say what our heart feels."

"You're saying he might be capable of love?"

"I'm saying, love comes in many different forms. The last time Vi ever told anyone she loved them, her teenage boys and husband were rushing out the door. I don't expect she'll ever say those words again, and if you tried to make her she'd tell you to piss off and die, but that woman loves you. Did you know last year after you were expelled, she marched through the Shimmer and straight to that school and told those Fae pricks where they could stick it?"

I snort-laugh through my tears. "I had no idea."

She mutters, "That woman will be the death of me someday. But while I'm still alive, she's my sister and I love her— just don't ever tell her that."

"Deal." I lean against her soft shoulder. "How did I luck out all those years ago when you saved me?"

Emotion trembles in her voice as she shakes her head, saying, "Summer, we saved each other. I was looking for one child, and God gave me another. Although how he could allow your parents to sell you to Fae traders is beyond me."

My heart spikes in my chest. "What? My parents died, remember?"

Zinnia turns to me, her eyes brimming with agony. "Summer, somewhere along the line, you started believing that, and I let you. But they're alive. They own a pawn shop somewhere in Fort Worth. I look them up every few years, praying God had the decency to strike them with lightning or have them both run over by a semi, but he does work in mysterious ways."

I'm trembling. My memories of them were taken by my soulstone, but I was so sure they had died.

"Why did they sell me?" I whisper.

"The last time I contacted the woman, she said you were a changeling. That you were born with brown eyes and then died. When the doctors revived you, your eyes were a strange greenish hazel. She tried to love you, but you were different than the other children. She said animals reacted strangely around you." Zinnia shakes her head. "The Lightmare had just happened and humans were scared. Every child that had a birthmark or acted different was deemed a changeling back then."

My chest aches, but for some reason, knowing the truth is freeing somehow.

"When I found you in that cage and bought your slave price, you didn't speak to me for months. And when you finally did, you told me your parents gave you away because they couldn't love you." She dabs at the corner of her eyes. "I told you I already loved you. Do you know what you said?" Her voice breaks. "You said I didn't yet, but that you would be so perfect that someday I would, and then I could never leave you."

Tears stream down my face. Those painful memories may be locked away by magic, but the hurt and trauma from being abandoned is still there, imprinted on my heart like wounds that have scarred over.

"My response rings just as true today as it did then." Zinnia pulls a tissue from her bra and hands it to me. "Sweet girl, you're my daughter and I love you."

We finish off the bread and tea, and then she talks me into a hot shower. Afterwards, right before I fall asleep, I text Mack.

I love you. And whatever happens, that will never, ever change. See you tomorrow night.

4 2

The sound of shouts and cursing wake me. I stare groggily at the low ceiling. Are Jane and Vi fighting already?

A loud boom shakes the drywall.

Frick. That was a gunshot.

I jump from bed, still half asleep, and nearly slam into Zinnia.

Her face is red and flustered. "Your friends from the academy are here."

"What?" I glance at my iPhone to catch the time, only to see I've missed a slew of messages from Eclipsa. "Who, Mack?"

Zinnia rushes out the door, calling over her shoulder. "No. Your pointy-eared friends. I have to get Vi and Jane out of the house before there's a massacre."

I can't tell who she thinks is the danger; my friends or Jane and Vi.

"She's charming," comes a silky smooth female voice.

I whip around to see Eclipsa leaning against the wall nearest the window, arms crossed. She wears a *Pink Pixie*

348

Pirates black crop top and low-riding silver leggings, the jewels across her forehead sparkling in the morning sun.

I look over her belly tats and navel piercing, the elaborate sweep of kohl eyeliner that brings out the otherworldly largeness of her dark eyes.

"Holy hell, my aunt is going to hate you."

"Oh, you mean the leathery mortal woman who tried to take off my head with that shotgun?" She winks. "I like her. Her aim is crap, thank Titania, considering someone thought it was a good idea to arm her with iron buckshot. But it takes balls to try and shoot one of us."

"Why are you here?"

She arches an eyebrow. "You didn't answer any of my messages. I thought you were in trouble."

"No. I'm just angry at you."

Her lips tug into a pout. "Still?"

"Yes, Eclipsa. Still. I thought you were my friend and your words hurt me."

Eyes downcast, she toes a plum purple and orange sneaker into the warped edge of a floorboard. "You are my friend. One of my only friends, in fact. Which is weird because I don't ever remember agreeing to like you, but there it is. I do, against my will."

I snort. "You are absolutely the worst at apologies."

"I'm aware." She glares. "I'm not good at this, okay?"

"Didn't we just establish that?"

"I mean, having friends. *Caring.* It's not natural to me. In the Everwilde, we've been taught from birth how to betray and manipulate our way to power. It's all that matters in our world, and having friends when everyone is a potential enemy is a liability."

"It can be that way in the human world too," I admit. "Too bad there isn't a soulbond for friends. That would make it so much easier."

"But that's what makes friendship so strangely . . . wonderful." Her sneakers are quiet against my floor as she approaches. "It's like the Bloodstar vine. It needs constant watering and care or it withers into dust."

I'm not sure how I feel about Eclipsa comparing our relationship to the most poisonous flower in Everwilde, but I'll take it.

"What I said in front of Hellebore," she continues, her silver brows gathered. "He is an expert at learning what someone cares about and using that against them. If he truly understood how much I like you, he would use that knowledge to destroy both of us—and I can't bear the thought of him taking something I hold precious and turning it into a weapon."

I bounce on my toes, the urge to hug the prickly assassin warring with my pride. "I know, and you're right. I just wasn't expecting what you said to be so harsh or hurt so much."

"Summer, the rules of the courts and power come to me easily, but the rules of friendship are . . . new to me. I'm still learning. Do you forgive me?"

"Yes!" I throw my arms around her. "How else can I ensure you never murder me?"

"Fair point. Now that that's out of the way, we should probably go save the Winter Prince and Asher."

I jerk back, eyes stretched wide. "They're here too?"

But as I jog down the stairs, I recognize the twinge in my belly that I only feel around Valerian. Like a thousand butterflies of ice beating against my ribcage.

The odd scent of blueberry muffins and gunpowder permeates the air downstairs. Valerian and Asher are holed up in the dining room, looking more prisoner than guest as they endure Zinnia's rapid barrage of offers for beverages and food, aka Southern hospitality at its finest. Their massive frames swamp the antique table and chairs, a family heirloom passed down for generations on Vi's husband's side.

Both Evermore wear the faint but unmistakable look of unease.

Perhaps it's the two watermelon-sized groupings of buckshot that pepper the wall just over their heads. Or Vi, who's watching them from the kitchen, and boy, oh boy is she pissed. Evidenced by her beloved shotgun, Betsy, held low at her waist.

Not happening. This is not happening.

Vi's furious stare bounces from the Evermore to Zinnia, as if she can't decide who to blast first. The Fae sitting at her beloved dining table using her precious china and linen placemats reserved for special guests, or the sister who's cheerfully serving them.

Valerian's gaze slides to me, locks. His unease softens, giving way to that startling familiarity we share. My stomach muscles clench, and I fight the way my body reacts.

Softening. Warming. Aching to draw nearer to him as if caught in his physical orbit. I'm suddenly all too aware of my pulse, my breathing, my sensitive skin reacting as the light elastic waistband of my sleep shorts rubs against my hips . . .

Whoa. Panic trills through me at the thought of Vi realizing my feelings for an Evermore—especially a royal one.

Setting my jaw, I drag my stare from my mate and park it on my newly reinstated friend. "Why are they here?"

Considering their freakish supernatural hearing, I don't bother whispering.

"I couldn't reach you, Summer," Eclipsa scolds. "Did you really think they would let me come alone?"

"You could have called my home number. The school has it."

"And you could have answered my one thousand, three hundred and seventy nine texts, but *c'est la vie.* We're here, no one's dead, and it's the perfect time to discuss details on why you entered the gauntlet in the first place."

"Right now?" I demand, still ruffled by the shock of seeing Valerian and Asher in my house.

Eclipsa side-eyes Zinnia, who's marching toward the dining room with a pan of blueberry muffins between her oven mitts. "As soon as we enter the Spring Court, we have to assume every conversation is monitored. So unless you prefer we go there without a plan, which is like charging into battle without a weapon, by the way, and a really stupid, painful way to die, we talk here."

Right. Tucking my hair behind my ears in a failed effort to hide how tangled it is, I slide into the chair farthest from Valerian. Quiet descends as Zinnia offers muffins and coffee to the group, probably for the twentieth time.

"Zinnia, it's fine," I protest, glancing around for signs of Jane. She'll have already found a weapon, no doubt. "They don't like our food."

"I'll have one of those, *please,*" Valerian drawls in that elegant, smooth voice. His impeccable manners grate on me. "And a cup of coffee would be delicious, Zinnia."

Zinnia's face brightens. "How do you take it?"

"However you take it is fine, Ma'am."

Ma'am? Suck-up.

Asher nods. "I'll have the same." Valerian scowls at the dragon shifter, and he adds, "Ma'am."

"Me too." Eclipsa spots my annoyed look and shrugs. "What? We're polite. Mortals like that stuff. It puts them at ease around us."

Hardly. A tiger with fangs and manners is still a tiger. But I don't argue as Zinnia sets a basket of muffins, a little container of butter shaped like a cow, and a pitcher of sweet tea and lemons on the table.

She sweeps a curious look over Valerian before settling her knowing smile on me.

I frown. My two worlds have suddenly collided, and I'm not sure how to feel about that. After what happened to her family, it takes limitless amounts of grace and forgiveness for Zinnia to serve the Evermore in her own home.

I've never been more convinced than now that Zinnia's too good for this jacked up world.

After breakfast is on the table, and Zinnia assures me Vi has been placated and Jane kicked from the house, we get to work. I sip my black coffee, listening to Eclipsa detail what she knows about the Spring Court palace and the magical safeguards while surreptitiously stealing glances at Valerian.

He's picking at the blueberries inside the muffin with his fork, lips twisted into a perplexed frown. I watch him carve off a little chunk, the pastry steaming from the inside, and place it onto his tongue.

Pure joy lights his face, and I stifle a grin.

Valerian Sylverfrost likes blueberry muffins.

He might not be capable of love, but this confirms he does indeed have a soul.

"We strike during the gauntlet," Eclipsa is saying. She stares down at her milky coffee before apparently deciding it's not drinkable. "If Hellebore has the Darken's soulstone or pieces of the Worldslayer, they'll be stashed below, in his private underground chambers. I know from experience he keeps everything he considers valuable or wants to hide there." She pauses, daring Asher to make a quip about how she knows all this, but dragon boy smartly keeps his mouth shut. "I can only confirm three chambers for sure. Besides the vault with poisons and other treasures, there's a torture chamber and . . . an adjoining bedroom."

No one questions why one would have a bedroom adjoining a torture chamber.

I frown. "Are you sure you have to do it while I'm in the gauntlet? Maybe I can help somehow."

"It has to be then, when everyone's distracted." Eclipsa sets her fork down on her plate; she hasn't touched her muffin. "We'll have to disarm Hellebore's spells to gain entry, but I happen to know those already. And the spells on the vault shouldn't be that hard to crack."

A proud smirk dances across her face.

Of course. Assassins have to be able to break into stuff.

The coffee burns my lips as I take a sip, trying to wrap my head around everything. It all sounds so easy, which is a bit alarming considering how very deadly our plan really is. If they're caught, they could be executed.

A flash outside my window draws my attention to Jane. She's armed with my old bow, peering through the glass at our visitors. The twins and Tanner linger near the top of the stairs, watching my friends with curious gazes.

Asher shifts nervously. "Has anyone else noticed we're slowly being surrounded?"

"Afraid of wee little mortals, Asher?" Eclipsa teases.

"The tiny girl keeps sticking her tongue out at me," he points out, obviously disturbed by this. "And the other one picks his nose and then eats it."

"They're children," Valerian comments. "All children are odd, but not particularly dangerous."

Asher stares through narrowed eyes at them. Most Fae rarely encounter children of any kind. Evermore lock their babies away from society, the children raised by lower Fae until they're in their teens and therefore old enough not to be a nuisance.

I actually totally get that policy right now as I watch Tanner load up his homemade slingshot and point it at Asher's head. Asher bares his teeth, and Tanner grins in challenge, ready to let his marble fly.

Sweet Baby Jesus, save me.

Before all hell can break loose, Zinnia threatens the kids with a flyswatter and they scatter, growling like the little monsters they are.

As my friends finish their food, I find myself chuckling under my breath. Asher lifts his delicate china mug to his mouth, the cup tiny in his huge paw. Valerian finishes off his third muffin. He's still eating it with his fork like a psycho— but he gets a pass for now. Even Eclipsa has found something to like; Zinnia brought her an ice-cold glass of sweet tea, and the Lunar assassin took one drink and then downed the entire glass.

I can't help but think that if these Evermore and my family can find a way to co-exist, then there's hope for humanity yet. Now all I have to do is win the final gauntlet, expose Hellebore, find a way to keep Mack in school, nab that internship, get over Valerian Sylverfrost, and change the world.

Easy fricking peasy.

43

I thought the Spring Court Palace and royal estates were overwhelming the last time I visited. But now, with the special event broadcasted to all the courts, the entire place brims with flowers and life.

Daffodils, crocuses, and tulips line the cobblestone paths that weave through the overdone gardens and lush lawns around the estate. Amethyst and butter-yellow wildflowers grow everywhere, and jewel-toned dragonflies flash against a lapis sky so blue it appears fake.

Valerian, Asher, and Eclipsa have already left for the Keepers' tent to register and then join the festivities. Only the shadows entering the final gauntlet, their Keepers, and royalty are allowed inside the main palace for the event.

The rest of the attending Evermore and students will arrive tomorrow to watch the gauntlet live from a special stadium. The shadow entrants' Keepers, however, can watch the gauntlet from a special room inside.

If everything goes according to plan, Valerian and Asher will sneak Eclipsa into the palace during the gauntlet tomorrow. While everyone is distracted watching the shadows try not to die, my friends will search for the stolen soulstone and axe shard.

Either will prove Hellebore's guilt.

As soon as I round a wall of hedges, Magus spots me and trots over. His silky red tail swishes behind him.

Large moss green eyes appraise me. "I heard you entered the gauntlet, Miss Solstice."

"Surprised?" I ask as he begins to lead me past some sort of game being played by Spring Evermore that involves throwing sprites through hoops high in the air.

"Not in the least," he admits. His equine ears twitch back as he smiles. "Once one gets used to you doing the opposite of what one expects, you're entirely predictable."

I still haven't worked out if that's a compliment by the time I reach the group of fourth years standing by a large wading pool shaped like a butterfly. The fourth years cut their gazes at me, not even bothering to hide their disdain.

"Thank you." I scratch Magus behind his ears. "You've always been kinder than all the others. Hopefully we'll see more of each other when I'm a third year."

"Doubtful," he adds, although I can't tell if he means seeing me or that I'll actually pass the final gauntlet to be here next year. "But . . . I would like that."

He leaves just as a Spring Court nymph begins to lead us to a servant's entrance inside the palace.

The nymph is strikingly beautiful. A crown of daisies tangles through her long pink hair, her dress made from a collection of sunflowers, birds' nests, and moss. She could be human, if not for the papery gold wings fluttering from her back and her violet irises, split in the middle only by a tiny humanoid slash.

I look for Mack in the group, but she must have arrived earlier. Callum nods my way. I shoot him a warm smile, refusing to let his coldness get to me.

This place has a way of turning students against one another.

The interior of the Spring Palace is everything I'd expect it to be. Open, airy, with a thousand paneless windows to let in the breeze. The weather here is always pleasant, so there's no need to keep out the elements. The furniture is sparse but comfortable, the rooms large and filled to the brim with flowers, sunlight, and creatures—butterflies, bees, woodland animals.

But beyond the pretty veneer lies a darkness. The air is too sweet. The sunlight too bright. The flowers unnaturally fresh. The butterflies that dance in the rafters of every high ceiling are leashed on tiny strings that keep them from flying away. The squirrels are fat and sluggish from being fed sugary treats by the courtiers.

A small hob darts past us, chasing two plump gray bunnies as they hop down the lilac and gray carpet runner. Another hob pulls on the leash of a white-tailed deer, grumbling as the creature stops to nibble at the frayed edge of the rug.

"Excuse me," a fourth year girl calls out to the nymph. "What are they doing with those cute little animals?"

The nymph blinks her strange eyes. "Here in the Spring Court, we take in all the forest's creatures, petting and feeding them so that when the banquets and festivals come around, they're fatted and docile, primed and ready for the slaughter."

"Oh, God," I whisper, horrified.

No one asks any questions after that.

As we're paraded in front of the Spring Court courtiers, I can't help but feel like the poor deer. Being led to my own slaughter.

The nymph directs us to our rooms, a small section of the

servants' quarters that have been emptied for the occasion. My room is the last on the left.

"Enjoy your beautiful, spacious chamber with its unparalleled views of the meadow," the nymph says blandly. "You will take dinner in here, followed by one turn around the courtyard before bed."

O-kay, then. I glance over my beautiful, spacious room, which is really a tiny broom closet with an open window barely large enough to fit my head through. A metal cot is pushed against one side, and pieces of hay poke from the lumpy mattress.

"Gee, thank you," I murmur. "The Spring Court heir really went all out for our accommodations."

The nymph doesn't speak sarcasm, apparently, because she gives me an odd look before saying, "Yes, the Spring Prince is generous and beautiful. Everyone says so."

I'm fairly sure everyone only says so because they like living. I'm also fairly certain she's serious about locking us in until after dinner.

"What do we do if we need to use the restroom?"

She nods cheerfully to a bucket in the corner.

"You can't be serious?"

"You'll be safe in your chamber," she repeats before closing the door. A click of the lock follows.

By the time dinner rolls around, I'm contemplating trying to shimmy out my tiny window to the ground three stories below. Twilight fell hours ago, and the only light in my room comes from two lanterns filled to the brim with trapped fireflies. Their glow is ethereal, otherworldly, but it comes at a cruel price.

I've just finished setting the second lantern of fireflies free when a garden hob opens my door, blinks curiously at the swarm of free fireflies, hands me a covered plate, and leaves.

I hold my breath, waiting to hear the lock click, but it

never comes. My relief gives way to disappointment as I survey my dinner—a meager portion of elderberries, pistachios, dried mushrooms and beets, a chilled melon soup, and a wheel of some type of soft cheese.

One would think by now the Fae would remember what mortals eat, but I'm too happy about my release to ruminate on it.

A hob with a warty nose leads me outside to an interior courtyard reserved for mortals. Torches of magic line the stone walls. Their glow reveals a small gathering area surrounded by well-kept gardens, a pond, and a hedge maze.

A few other fourth years mill around the pond, while more recline on the benches scattering the courtyard.

"Summer!"

The gravel crunches beneath my sneakers as I turn, my spirits soaring. Mack rushes toward me so fast I think she's going to tackle me. Actually—

The force of her hug sends us sprawling into the nearest azalea bushes.

Ignoring the strange stares from the other students, we sit on our butts, laughing as we pull twigs and petals from our hair.

"I'm so sorry," Mack says when she finally catches her breath. "I—I should have called you."

"It's okay." I find her hand and squeeze. "Really. I understand why you had to enter the final gauntlet, and why you might be mad at me."

"Even if I'm competing with you to win?"

I haven't told her the reason I have to win—my bargain with Helle-Douche—but she assumes I'm motivated by the internship. To apply, I only had to be enrolled in the final gauntlet, and as long as I pass, technically I'll still be considered for the position.

But everyone knows the Summer Queen will likely choose the winner of the gauntlet for the internship spot.

"I can't think of anyone I'd rather compete against," I say.

Mack scoots back until she finds a patch of plush grass to lay back on. "I shouldn't have blamed you for failing school. It wasn't just that one test. This whole year has been an epic fail. I let Reina get in my head. I was so focused on not eating and keeping up with some stupid standard that it was impossible to focus. And then, when you declared you were applying for the internship . . . I just felt lost, you know? Like you were leaving me behind."

"Never. If you had only told me everything you were going through, we could have dealt with it together."

"That's what Asher said. He's surprisingly full of wisdom . . . sometimes." I raise my eyebrow and she adds, "He came to Manhattan to help me train over the break. He and Eclipsa. She didn't tell you?"

I shake my head, stunned.

"She was only helping because I'm your friend, and she straight up admitted she was trying to buy your forgiveness for something, but you should have seen my dads, especially Sebastian. She's a celebrity in their circle." She rests her arms behind her head. "When he took a selfie with her, I thought I was going to die from embarrassment."

"You're wrong. Eclipsa may not know it yet, but she likes you. Just don't expect her to openly admit that."

I join Mack on the lawn. Just like the estate and the palace, the Spring Court sky is overwhelming in its beauty. I stare at the diamond-encrusted canvas above, trying to find the words to tell Mack how I feel. "I'm sorry. I didn't think how hard that would be on you if I'm not here fourth year."

She groans. "Stop. We've already established I was the dickhead. Besides, I guess none of that matters now."

"You stop. You belong at the academy. You're Mackenzie Fucking Fairchild. We're going to figure something out."

"And you're Summer Fucking Solstice, my ride-or-die. If I ever forget that again, I give you permission to punch me. But like, fifty-percent power—I've seen your right hook. And in the stomach or something. If I have to get a nose job, I'll never be able to hold that over Reina again." Mack props up on her elbows, her face twisting as if she tastes something sour. "Did you know she signed up for the gauntlet after you did? She was in my group earlier today."

"Ugh. Which means she applied for the internship."

Mack pops to her feet, and I reluctantly follow, mentally preparing myself for a night on my moldy mattress of hay. People are already drifting back inside. The gauntlet starts at dawn tomorrow. That's like the middle of the night for the Fae, but I assume by the raging party happening on the other side of the palace, most will have never gone to bed in the first place.

I'm dusting off my leggings when a flash of movement draws my eye. A giant white owl swoops near our heads before landing on the lowest branch of a cherry tree.

Phalanx! The haughty creature hoots twice, looks toward the entrance of a hedge maze, and then flies off.

"I think someone wants to give their shadow a pep talk," Mack says, her wistful tone making it clear she would love a pep talk from a certain dragon shifter herself.

"That makes two of us," a gravelly male voice says.

Mack's smile stretches wide as she spots Asher beside a crooked oak tree. Even layered in shadow, the massive shifter is unmistakable.

When he steps into the delicate moonlight, smiling softly back at her . . . it's like they forget I'm even here. Both of them transfixed on the other and doing weird, embarrassing things with their faces.

Whoa. When did that happen?

They barely acknowledge me when I say goodbye, caught in their own bubble of whatever the frick transpired this past week.

They've always been flirty with each other, but this skipped harmless flirting and went straight to reciting sonnets about each other's eyes and crap.

I make a mental note to ask Valerian about Asher's intentions as I duck beneath the entrance into the hedge maze. The starlight softens the shadows, enough that I can make out the wisteria and jasmine clinging to the green walls. Fireflies dance above me.

As I watch, brownies and sprites collect the fireflies in glass jars, their glowing bodies thudding softly against the glass.

I can only hope these aren't the same fireflies I just released. A few alight on my arm, and I watch, transfixed, as they take to the air and begin to form . . .

Letters?

ILB.

Someone's feeling clever. Laughing, I follow the glowing creatures through the maze, thankful for their guidance. When I'm completely lost, with no hope of ever finding my way out, I feel that exquisite little tug deep inside my core.

The one that screams Valerian is near.

A low chuckle drifts from the shadows ahead. The center of the maze is a statue of two naked lovers. They're locked in an embrace steamy enough that heat pricks my cheeks.

Dragging my focus from the scene, I make out the Winter Prince just beyond. The fireflies swirl around him, their ethereal light matching the faint ring of gold circling his silver eyes.

"ILB?" I tease, alarmed at how nervous my voice is.

"Illustrious lover boy?" he guesses. "No, I'm definitely not a boy. Ignominious little bastard?" His eyes twinkle. "We both know *little* is an unfitting description of me." Holy hell, is he trying to make me blush? "Bastard, however, is probably correct."

My lips twitch at the corners. "Impossibly likeable bastard?"

My breath hitches as he closes the distance between us until I can feel the coolness emanating from his body, as if a winter storm rages inside him. He reaches for me, and I go completely still as his hand cups the side of my face, tilting my head to look up at him.

"I'm a bastard, Summer. I'm selfish. I'm haughty. Vain. I can be thoughtlessly cruel when it suits me, and I don't think twice about bartering for the things I want." He drags his thumb along the curve of my cheek. "I thought I could somehow buy you with grand gestures, like a piece of jewelry I coveted."

He drops his hand, and I fight the urge to press my body into his. "Valerian—"

"Let me say this, please."

I nod, steeling my heart for whatever words come next.

"When I was at your home, when I saw you around your family, I realized my mistake. I've been treating you like a Fae, but you're both. You possess the ferocity and boldness of an Evermore, but a mortal's kindness, untarnished by centuries of living in our mercurial world. And you love with abandon, no matter the price, despite the pain you've been dealt." He takes my hand in his, intertwining our fingers. "You're my mate, Summer, and I'll never give up until you're by my side. Your fight is my fight. Your people are my people. I'll do whatever it takes to prove I deserve you . . . even if that means . . . daring to love you."

Holy mother forking shite, did Valerian Sylverfrost just say the L word?

Pushing onto my toes, I brush my lips against his pointed ear, enjoying the way he shivers. "Everything you said was true. You're vain. Selfish. Sometimes a bastard. And Fae to the core." I pull back, just enough that he can see my face. "But you're *my* bastard. *My* Fae. *My* mate. I thought forcing you to say you loved me would mend a wound that wasn't yours to mend."

I think of my parents. How they told me they couldn't love me. But it was their actions that wounded me the deepest, not their words.

"I know, Summer. After the Spring Formal, I somehow took on your dreams. I saw what your mortal parents did to you. I experienced the confusion and pain you felt as your mother watched the slavers force you into a cage." Anger turns his voice soft, lethal. "I felt your heart break as that mortal woman peered through those bars and told you that she tried to love you but couldn't. That no one ever would."

Air lodges in my throat. I don't have the words to respond. My chest feels close to cracking open . . .

Looking into my eyes, Valerian presses his hand just above my heart. Drawing out my pain. Taking it as his own.

"I will never leave you. I will never hurt you. I can't. You're a part of me. I don't know if that's love or something else, something so rare it doesn't have a name."

Warmth trails down my left cheek. He reaches up, pooling the tear on his thumb. "Say it again," he orders, his husky tone warming my belly.

"What?" I tease. "Bastard?"

Excitement flickers inside his silver eyes as they fixate on my lips. "Mate. Say I'm your mate. I want to watch your lips as they form the words. Then I'm going to kiss you, Summer. Hard."

My head spins, a whirlwind of emotions churning inside me as I whisper, "My mate."

His mouth claims mine. True to his word, his kiss is hard, unyielding, his tongue parting my lips over and over until I moan. His fingers tangle in my hair. Holding me still as his kiss deepens and . . . Shimmer save me, I've never been more sure of what I want than right this moment.

I want Valerian Sylverfrost.

All of him.

The bad and the good. The broken and the proud. The arrogant and the occasionally sweet.

"I want to be with you," I murmur, feeling disembodied, as if the voice comes from a stranger. "To consummate the bond."

My lips are swollen and tender as he jerks his head back to look at me. "As much as I would love that, not here. Not in this wretched place. Not when we only have a few short hours."

"Please."

44

Valerian's eyes darken as something sensual and raw takes hold of him. It seeps into the air of the hedge maze, charging it with tension. A predatory intent that should scare me, but doesn't. "Lie down."

"What?" I squeak.

"Princess, I may possess enough willpower to resist claiming you, but you're my mate, and there is zero chance that I'm letting you leave this maze until I've satisfied the restless hunger I feel inside you. Otherwise you'll never sleep tonight." One side of his mouth twitches. "I might also have an ulterior motive. Once I've shown you the perks of being my mate, you won't be able to resist consummating the bond."

I snort. "Arrogant much?"

"I am arrogant because I can be. You'll understand in a moment. Now, lie down."

And . . . this is what it feels like to blush from head to toe. My body manages the feat of feeling both numb and exploding with sensation as I do as commanded, resting on my back, knees bent.

The ground is wonderfully soft, the thick carpet of grass strewn with fallen honeysuckle buds and dew. For a breath, the raw scent of the earth and crushed petals trigger a strange sensation deep inside me, as if my slumbering Fae has woken from a long slumber.

Valerian is quiet. He stares down at me for a moment with that wicked smile and those glittering Fae eyes. "I'm going to undress you now, Princess."

A puff of air flees my lips as he crouches low. When his fingers curl beneath the waistband of my pants, his face softens, becomes almost vulnerable as he hesitates—making sure this is what I want.

It's this very moment, as he lets me beyond the teasing shield to the real Valerian, that I know I'll never doubt his love for me again.

He undresses me slowly. With purpose. As if every item of clothing he removes is a declaration of his love for me. When everything but my underwear is gone, moonlight casting soft shadows along my curves, turning my skin almost iridescent, his lips stretch into a cat-ate-the-canary grin.

Except I'm the canary. And I'm so here for it.

Those same lips crush against mine. As soon as I open my mouth for him, his kiss turns surprisingly gentle. Soft. Teasing. A promise that he can be both wild and tender, savage and kind. A promise to never hurt me.

"Is this what I have to look forward to?" I quip. "A lifetime of kisses?"

A low snarl builds in his throat. "Where would my mate like to be kissed?"

"Surprise me."

He chuckles. "As you command, Princess. But first, a bargain."

I stiffen. I've had my fill of Fae bargains. "What did you have in mind?"

"If I can make you utter a single sound in the next hour, you must tell me what ILB stands for."

"And if I don't?" I challenge.

"Then I will spend the next few weeks learning how to remedy that failing."

Oh, Lordy. He takes my silence as a yes. The stars appear above me as he drags his attention from my mouth to my throat, strands of his silky hair tickling my jaw. He nips his way down to my stomach as his hands slide beneath my thighs, positioning me so that . . .

Sweet mother of Fae and all things holy. The stars momentarily black out. My back arches against his *surprise*. My legs tremble as a live wire of heat shoots through my middle over and over and—

I bite back the rush of sound ripping up my throat. Heat consumes my body. A deep, aching heat that can only be quenched by Valerian. Every laugh Valerian utters as he works to undo me, every stroke of his fingers against my feverish skin, every piercing, consuming, mind-blowing shard of pleasure that swells my center until I'm certain I'll shatter—all of it confirms what I must have known all along.

What some quiet, buried part of me has always known.

Valerian, this imperfectly-perfect Fae prince, is my mate.

As the stars fade in and out of my vision, blurring with the fireflies, and my voice builds in my throat, scrambling for release, I can almost imagine a future for us.

Human and Fae. Mortal and immortal. Summer and Winter.

All at once, the pressure releases, and the air violently explodes from my chest, snapping my lips wide . . .

Damn. My arrogant, smarmy, beautiful mate lifts his head to meet my gaze, eyes victorious, and says, "You lost the bargain, very *loudly* and adorably, I might add."

"You . . . cheated," I pant.

"I never cheat. But you shouldn't feel bad about losing. I am very skilled in certain areas." One arched eyebrow lifts, his tousled hair more messy than usual from where I clawed my fingers through it. "But if you beg, I might give you another chance to prove me wrong."

I suck in a shaky breath. I'm torn between punching him and spending the rest of my life trying to make his lips curl up like that again.

Pouting, I ask, "When is it my turn to test *your* willpower?"

I have no idea what I'm doing in that department—none —so my suggestion startles me. But something about being around Valerian, about his absolute belief that I am the most beautiful woman in the world, fills me with daring confidence.

His eyes grow heavy lidded, lips parting at the thought, but he murmurs, "Another time. When we have weeks to play, not less than an hour." I go to argue but he shakes his head, eyes defiant. "You won't win on this. My mate and her needs will always come first." Tilting his head, he drags his thumb across my inner thigh, watching with lazy satisfaction as my sensitive flesh prickles with goose bumps. "Now, where were we? Oh, right. Proving what a noisy thing you are."

Afterward, when he's *proven* countless times that I'm hopeless at winning this particular bargain, he leads me from the maze and back into the real world. We sneak around the snoring hobs guarding the human quarters, hand in hand, trying not to laugh as I explain what ILB stands for.

I've never seen Valerian so boyish, so hopeful.

It all feels so unexpectedly . . . right.

At my door, he turns me to face him. "Tomorrow, when you enter the gauntlet, remember who you are. Princess of the Summer Court and mate to the Winter Prince and heir.

You deserve to be there. Once you pass—and you will, Summer—find me and we'll travel directly to the Winter Palace."

"What about the Fae law? The one that prohibits Seelie and Unseelie from being together?"

"Once the bond fully clicks into place, we'll be powerful enough that it won't matter. The courts will fall in line."

"It's that easy?"

"You have no idea the power caged inside you. After we prove tomorrow that Hellebore holds the missing soulstone and pieces of the Worldslayer, we can destroy the Darken's soul once and for all and then consummate our bond. You'll be out of danger, free to announce who you really are, and the courts will kneel at our feet."

Consummated. Never has such a banal word sounded so naughty. A shiver of anticipation trills through me.

In response, Valerian kisses me so tenderly that I imagine dragging him into my tiny hovel and onto my mattress of pain.

"Titania save me, you're beautiful." He winks, running two fingers down the brand marking my arm. "If you thought it was hard being quiet before, just wait until I have you spread out before me with days to draw out the consummation of the bond."

My, God. This can't be real life. This can't be *my* life.

Groaning, I drag myself away from him and lurch into my room, slamming the door before I can change my mind. I don't feel his presence leave until after I'm puddled on my lumpy mattress, a hot mess of wobbly limbs and wild thoughts.

Valerian loves me. I love him. We're mates.

Valerian Sylverfrost, the Ice Prince, *loves* me.

The gauntlet tomorrow suddenly feels so easy. I'm going

to win it, Hellebore will be out of the way, and then I'll be with Valerian.

Somehow I manage to fall asleep. I dream of Valerian in the hedge maze, his wicked grin and teasing voice. His vulnerable expression right before he kissed me so gently.

But when I speak his name and say I love him, he bursts into a thousand fireflies. I try to catch them, try to put him back together.

Yet the fireflies all end up trapped in little unbreakable jars.

And I'm helpless to do anything but watch as they smash against the glass, trying to get back to me, their glorious light fading until there's only darkness.

The gauntlet starts at dawn. We're spread out in the sloping meadow behind the palace. Ribbons of pink and orange tangle along the highest branches of the forest in the distance. The Evermore are gathered in wooden stands that flank us on either side, separated by Seelie and Unseelie Courts. Each stand stretches over the length of two football fields.

Even though I know Valerian will be with the other Keepers inside the viewing room of the palace, I search the crowd, last night still fresh in my mind.

It all feels like a dream.

Like a wild, crazy hallucination.

But the tenderness of my lips and the grass in my hair this morning confirms what happened between us was real.

Real.

Instead of Valerian, I spot Eclipsa. She gives me a conspiratorial smile. As soon as we enter the first phase of the gauntlet, she'll slip away to join the others inside the palace.

Boisterous shouts draw my focus to the Seelie stadium on

the right. The lower Fae are positioned in the highest seats while the Evermore fill the coveted lower half of the stadium.

They wave banners and ribbons and sing the songs of their courts.

Rhaegar sits with Basil on the bottom row, marking Rhaegar as a powerful Evermore. But the empty seats around him also mark him as an outcast with his own court.

His head turns to stare at me, and I look away before our eyes can meet, my gaze falling on Mack. My best friend stands a few feet away, the emerald and gray uniform she wears bringing out her bronzed skin. She's braided her hair, ribbons of chartreuse and charcoal weaving through the ensemble.

Her face leaves little doubt that she's going to win this gauntlet or die trying. We've both quietly conceded to the fact that we each plan to win.

Yet I trust without a doubt that she'll do whatever she can to help me succeed until the end—and vice versa.

Cheers explode into applause as a giant portal shimmers to life at the end of the meadow. My heartbeat roars in my ears.

I rub my clammy palms down the thighs of my tight ice-blue uniform they dressed me in, to match my Keeper's court. Dark streaks of sweat stain the stretchy fabric, joining an ever-growing wet spot.

I crack my neck, ready to begin.

Along our waists they've tied a spelled leather sack. We're allowed to conjure two mundane items from it for each phase of the gauntlet to help us, like clothing, food, approved class one and two weapons, or tools.

The Unseelie sigil is pinned just above my heart. Every Unseelie shadow in the meadow wears the same black diamond brooch, a snake consuming its own tail. But it's not just for show. When pressed, the spelled head of the pin shows a magical map.

A murmur stirs the shadows as Hellebore strolls to the front of our group. He's in his element. His honey-blond hair is artfully styled to fall on one side, revealing the other half of his skull. Someone hand-painted a spiderweb over the cropped side. Flowers are trapped inside the delicate web, a winter and a summer rose.

Really original, douchebag.

He exudes the energy of the Spring Court: vitality, beauty, life. But I know that just like the flowers here, spelled to stay fresh indefinitely, a hint of rot and death lurk just below his handsome facade.

His sky-blue eyes sweep over us, lingering on me for a too long moment. "Shadows, welcome to the Spring Court's final gauntlet, a race famous around the world for its ability to cull the weak from the strong. There are forty of you and only twenty victory spots. If you want to pass this year, I suggest you are one of those twenty." He smiles, making no effort to hide his stare as it locks on me. "Like always, those who fail will have their slave contracts put up for immediate auction right here."

The stadiums thrum with excitement at the prospect, and I clench my jaw to hide my disgust.

"You will travel through the four seasonal courts by way of portals," he continues. "If you pay attention, each portal has a clue regarding the season you're about to enter and the obstacles you might face. Use that information to choose your two items from the pouch at your waist."

To demonstrate, a servant holds up a leather pouch. Hellebore puts his hand inside. "Field rabbit."

We all gasp, including me, as he pulls out his hand holding an adorable gray rabbit by the nape of its neck. The creature twitches its nose, oblivious to the monster holding it.

As the bunny goes hopping into the group, a tense hush falls over the meadow. We can all feel the speech coming to an end.

Which means the race is about to begin.

"If you've trained and studied to be the very best," Hellebore continues, "you'll pass. Otherwise, you'll fail or die. Both are undesirable options, I can assure you."

The prick smiles at that. Psycho. I can't wait for Valerian and the others to expose him for the snake he is.

As if he can feel my burning hatred, he meets my glare with a smug look. "Make no mistake. This race will define every single one of your futures for the rest of your brief lives. Now run, little shadows. Run for your lives."

Awed murmurs stir the morning air and quickly turn to shrieks. When I see why, I understand that Hellebore was being literal when he said run for your lives.

A swarm of huge blue butterflies the same color as Hellebore's eyes descend on us from above.

"Caeruleum mortem!" Mack hisses as she shoves me into a sprint. "The blue death!"

Blue death. Blue death. Ominous as heck, but where have I heard that?

I watch one of the delicate blue butterflies land on the arm of the fourth year boy to my right. The fabric of his suit disintegrates as if something eats away at it.

An ungodly scream rips from the boy's chest. He grabs his arm, blood spurting beneath his fingertips as the butterfly flits in the air and lands on his cheek . . .

I jerk my eyes away before I can witness what happens next, but I suddenly recall where I've heard the blue death.

They're butterflies from deep in the Spring Court territories, and their touch is like acid to mortal skin.

The portal looms. Azure fire licks along the portal's rim. Not fire. Magic. Snowflakes drift from the other side . . .

"The first phase is the Winter Court!" I yell to Mack. We push through the stampede of panicked shadows as students scream around us.

I need to figure out the other clue. The face of the portal is a metallic silver, like molten steel. I try to peer through the surface, but it's completely opaque.

The group of shadows in front of us choose their first two items and leap through. I scour the rim, desperate for any clue as to what comes next. As I drag air into my lungs, working to calm my mind, a scent hits me.

"What is that smell?" I blurt. "A flower?"

Mack ducks beneath a butterfly, barely missing its gruesome touch. "What?"

"I think it's mountain laurel." I would know that scent anywhere. After realizing Hellebore's obsession with poisonous plants, I insisted Eclipsa add those to our training. Thank God she made me learn their telltale smells along with their names.

Mack's eyes stretch wide. "Yes! It grows deep in the Vanier Mountains of the Winter Court. That's where we're going."

Someone shoves us from behind. As instructed, I put my hand into the pouch and whisper the two items I need, just loud enough that Mack knows what I conjured.

Axe—for helping climb high mountains and chopping wood.

Waterproof wool-lined gloves—because I really appreciate all ten of my fingers.

Our suits are spelled to protect our bodies from the elements, but our hands are bare. And I learned my lesson about what happens to exposed digits in the freezing Winter Court temperatures.

She conjures gloves as well as a long electric prod, the kind used in the menagerie for the more dangerous animals.

That's when I recall what else resides in the Vanier Mountains. Something way worse than mountain laurel or the biting chill of winter.

Snow leopards. And not the adorable, normal sized mortal ones.

The massive, mythical, eat-entire-villages kind.

46

"**G**od, I hate being right sometimes," I mutter, watching my breath crystallize in front of my face. The snow crunches beneath our boots as we race along a path. Once again, I'm reminded how much I hate the cold.

Will that change when the mating bond is consummated? Gosh, I hope so because this . . . this is miserable.

"I can't feel my face," Mack moans, casting a sidelong glance at my hair, which I've unpinned and am now using like a scarf to keep my face warm.

"Pretend we're inside the smelly sauna from the school gym."

"Oh, warmth. I would give one of my toes for a few minutes of heat—if I have any left. I can't tell."

I slow, frowning. "Should we stop and make a fire?"

"No." She gives a stubborn shake of her head. "Not yet. We should be close."

We've been running nonstop for at least two hours. Footsteps mar the otherwise perfect crust of snow ahead, which tells me we're on the right path, at least.

It also says we're not first.

How many have already passed through the second portal?

According to the map from my sigil pin, the next portal is on the other side of the mountain.

We quicken our pace. By the time we hit the gently sloping range, a soft drizzle of snow falls around us.

When we're halfway up the mountain, I spot little fires drifting from below.

"Guess they didn't bother with gloves," Mack says, teeth chattering against the cold.

The last forty feet of the peak grows steep and treacherous. We take turns using the axe for a handhold, sinking the blade into the dark obsidian of the mountain. After what feels like an eternity, we hit the peak and begin our descent.

Mack's breath clouds the air as she says, "Look."

I glance at the horizon, assuming she means at the portal glowing like a beacon in the drizzly gray air. "I don't think I've ever seen such a beautiful sight."

"No, Summer."

Something about her voice makes me turn, and I follow her gaze to the wide shoeprints below on our left. Whoever it was chose snowshoes as their item.

The wide prints end in a churned mess of earth, snow, and . . . blood. One snowshoe sits broken and abandoned.

"So much blood." She rests a hand on the electric prod tied to her waist. "Should I check for tracks?"

I shake my head, and we fall into a quiet jog down the slope. No need to check for tracks. Only one animal could do that, and with that amount of blood . . .

No one could survive.

A hollow guilt fills my chest as we pass by the scene of the struggle.

Don't think about it, Summer. Compartmentalize and mourn

later. But my mind is a jerk and won't let me get away with feeling nothing.

Who was it? Are their parents waiting for them to call and say they're safe? Did they have a celebration party planned with a cake and everything?

My cold fingers ache as I curl them into fists. Hellebore is responsible for every death in the gauntlet.

Every. Single. One.

Hot anger surges through me, filling the hollow ache of grief for the nameless student and reminding me why I have to win this race.

So I can watch Hellebore's face when he learns he lost the bargain and has to forget me, right before they send that mofo to the Seven Fae Hells for collaborating with the Darken.

"Screw you, ass face!" I yell, turning in a circle as my voice echoes off the mountains.

Mack stares at me like I've lost my mind. "Who are you talking to?"

"Oh, he knows who he is." I thrust my gloved hand in the air, my middle finger on display. Somewhere, Hellebore is watching the gauntlet unfold. I can only hope that he's so intent on watching me fail that he doesn't notice Valerian and Asher are gone.

When the portal is maybe fifty yards away, we break into a sprint. I'm so happy to be done with this place that I actually crack a smile. I'll take anything over freezing my butt off.

We're nearly there when Mack halts. "Do you hear that?"

I pause to listen as the hairs on the back of my neck lift. "Is that a . . .?"

"Growl," Mack finishes, slowly turning toward the low, vibrating sound.

As soon as I do the same, the air flees my lungs. The snow leopard crouches a truck's length away, a distance it can easily cover in one leap. Pale green feline eyes slide from Mack to me, as if trying to decide who's the easiest prey.

Even frozen with fear, I can see that the creature is breathtakingly gorgeous, a mix of black spots, plush tan fur, and cream markings.

It's also twice the size of a normal snow leopard in the human world.

"It's as big as a frickin elephant," Mack whispers.

"A carnivorous elephant with claws and fangs," I amend, holding its stare. The second we blink or look away, it's going to pounce.

Mack slowly pulls the prod from her waist. "Back up slowly toward the portal."

"Wait. Don't turn it on yet." Calming my thoughts, I gently reach out to the cat with my mind. Willing it to hear me. To relax.

Don't hurt us. My thoughts carry over the snow to the animal. *Let us go. You've eaten enough. Let every human that passes your territory live.*

I can feel the creature's disdain. Why would it listen to me? A mortal?

Because I'm not just a mortal, I send over the snow. *I'm the Summer Court Princess.*

Mack and I both jump as the snow leopard lets loose a frustrated roar that turns into a yowl.

"Why isn't it attacking?" she squeaks.

"I think it's full. Now we should go."

The leopard sits on its haunches and watches, only pouting a little as we near the portal.

"I still don't understand," Mack is saying. "It should have killed us. They eat like six goats and deer a day."

I shrug, pointing to the portal's orange rim. Leaves drift from the entrance and blow around us. "Fall Court territories."

A small shape rushes from the portal and across the snow, its stench immediate and nauseating. The cat-sized, moss green creature is covered in warts, and it wields a small, spiked club.

"Moss goblin." Mack wrinkles her nose as we watch the angry little beast run straight toward the leopard, too busy pounding its dumb stick to notice until—

Ew.

The leopard finishes with its unexpected meal, licks its maw, and gives me a look that says, *You didn't say I couldn't eat goblins.*

"Moss goblins only live in two ancient forests inside the Fall Court," Mack explains, reminding me how big and beautiful her brain is. "One is a beautiful place with winding rivers and dire wolves. The other is a decaying wood infested with every manner of troll and orc."

My shoulders sag. "Then of course it's the gross forest with the trolls and orcs. The other would be too easy."

A part of me is thankful, though. I can kill an orc or a troll without batting an eye. They're cruel, greedy creatures that use up the land until it's ruined beyond repair. But hurting an animal, especially a wolf . . . I'm just not made for that sort of thing.

Shaking the thought from my mind, I reach into my magical pouch and conjure a disgusting vial of green troll musk—to hide our scent—and a wrist-mounted crossbow that comes with a sleeve of iron-tipped bolts.

To murder orcs and trolls with, obviously.

Mack chooses a sword and a magical torch that lights on command. Along with being greedy and stupid, orcs and trolls are supposed to be scared of fire.

Choices made, we leap to the other side. The stench hits me first. Sulfur, mud, and rot. Mack drags up the new map, and we quickly plan out the course before surging ahead. The giant oak and elm trees must have been glorious once, and a few still retain their vibrant array of golden and orange leaves.

Most, however, are in various stages of death, their beautiful foliage carpeting the forest floor in wet, decaying piles.

The troll musk was genius, and we manage to sneak nearly all the way to the second portal before our sweat washes the musk away. An orc bellows to my right, the sound coming from a mound of branches and leaves. The orc's nest.

Falling into our positions, we slash and fight our way to safety. The dying forest fills with the sound of our classmates doing the same. We pass a few of them. Little by little, Mack and I gain ground until I spot the flickering gleam of the next portal through the underbrush.

There's no doubt which season awaits us next. The flames of the portal are bright orange and a strong, hot wind blows from the other side.

"Summer Court." I inhale deeply. "It smells like . . . smoke."

"The burning savannah." Mack takes a step back from the portal, brow furrowed.

Just like me, mud splatters her clothes, leaves and twigs caught in her hair. Dark, oily specks of orc blood fleck her face—but I don't dare tell her.

"Is that as bad as it sounds?"

"The weather is hot, windy, and dry, and fire sprites inhabit the grasses, which means wildfires are a constant."

I frown. "Is there any nearby water?"

"There's ponds but—they're spread out. I don't see how those could help us." The hesitation in her voice is alarming.

"Does anything else live in the grassland?"

"Rabbits, maybe a few griffins from the nearby forests. They hunt the rabbits."

Griffins. I remember the last griffin. How it helped me.

She wipes at her face, unknowingly smearing the orc blood. "What are you thinking?"

"Mack, I'm going to ask you to do something that seems, well, suicidal." Voices ring behind us, along with the bellow of an orc. We need to hurry. "But I promise, I'll explain it all later, okay?"

She nods.

"We're going to make the griffins carry us over the fires." Ignoring her alarmed scoff, I press on. "We need a rope and a dagger each. Once your griffin grabs you, tie the rope to its ankle. When we're over the water, we cut the ropes. Got it?"

To her credit, she only gapes at me for a few seconds. "How do we make them drop us over the water?"

"Just . . . trust me."

She nods, if a bit tensely, and we grab our supplies and leap into the Summer Court portal.

The burning savannah is an endless swath of knee-high grasses that stretch across the gently rolling landscape. Smoke engulfs much of the air, and flames move across the hills at will.

What I think at first are sparks are actually fire sprites dancing above the inferno.

Mack checks the map. "There's a body of water near the portal."

"Any landmarks you can give me?" I ask.

She squints. "Looks like . . . an island in the middle."

She shows me the image. Once I'm sure I have it committed to memory, I nod to the long rope coiled in her hand.

"This better work," she whispers, quickly tying it around her waist.

Once my own rope is cinched around my stomach, I put my hands to my mouth. Mack looks at me funny as I perform the rabbit call, a trick learned hunting in the woods by our house.

Almost immediately, two shadows sweep across the burning grassland toward us.

Mack's eyes squeeze shut. "Titania save us."

I clench my dagger between my teeth, grab hold of my rope, and try not to panic as the sound of their huge wings pummeling the air grows louder.

A shadow falls over us. Mack shrieks as the first griffin grabs her by the shoulders and jerks her into the air. A half second later, my griffin strikes. Its claws catch in my uniform as it drags me into the sky like I weigh nothing.

The feel of the ground hurtling away from me is terrifying. My stomach flip-flops all over the place.

The creature's wings buffer the wind around my head, making it hard to hear Mack's yells.

Quickly, I knot the end of my rope to the griffin's leathery black ankle. Just in case the griffin isn't open to my newly discovered powers of gab and would rather just eat me.

When the knot is cinched tight, my griffin turns its head down to look at me.

Good little griffin, I mentally coo, wondering if this is quite possibly the craziest thing I've ever done.

Mack's griffin flies to my left. Her eyes are huge as she secures her rope in between bouts of screaming. Thank the Shimmer, her dagger is secured in her pocket.

I've barely begun sending the creatures images of the pond near the portal before they veer hard to the left. Mack squeals, legs kicking.

I just now recall how she might have once admitted to being afraid of heights. Oops.

Do not drop us, I mentally order, willing both creatures to hear me. *Not yet.*

Dagger still between my teeth, I grasp the rope holding

me to my griffin. All my focus goes to sending the griffins the mental image of the pond. The ground below us grows smaller, blurrier. The dark smoke and bright red of the fires melding into the canvas of green.

"Summer!" Mack cries. "Look below!"

The pond shimmers beneath us. I give a triumphant yell.

I can't believe this worked.

We cut our ropes at the same time. As soon as the knot falls away from my griffin's leg, I mentally command, *Drop us.*

The pressure around my shoulders eases and then we're falling. Warm water envelopes me. It's only when I surface and see the griffins flying away in the distance that I convince myself we're safe.

At least, for the next few minutes.

As we wade to the shore, Mack turns to look at me, her eyes full of questions.

My bestie is sharp. By now, she's put together the snow leopard and the griffins. But she knows now isn't the time for that discussion, so she lets it go.

"I think I might have peed a little," she mumbles.

"Ditto."

Soaked down to our boots, we slog our way to the final portal.

By my powers of deduction, I know the fourth portal leads to the Spring Court. But even if I didn't know that already, the overpoweringly sweet floral scent that emanates from the portal would be a huge hint.

I press my ear close to the portal's surface. The soft hum of bees comes through.

"Flowers and bees?" Mack says, wringing out her braid. "What do those two things have in common?"

"One can be poisonous and the other stings you, so maybe . . . they're both deadly?"

"Deadly. Right." She exhales, sending an errant strand of damp purple hair flying from her face. "The Spring Court wildlands are an overgrown stretch of nature that's the most formidable and dangerous in the world. Their wasps are the size of birds, nearly every plant is poisonous and the ones that aren't are carnivorous and will literally eat you, and the water is drugged with toxins from the surrounding trees." She rolls her shoulders as she squares to face the portal. "Did I mention the Ash Viper lives here?"

"The snake whose bite turns people into statues?"

"The one and only."

Oh, goodie. Hellebore better guard his junk next time I see him.

With that in mind, we both choose bee hats with netting that falls to our ankles. I make my second item a large fly swatter, and Mack conjures a jug of purified water.

As soon as we come out the other side of the portal, our suspicions are confirmed. A tropical world of dense trees, vines, and flowers the size of boulders awaits.

Hundreds of creatures fill the air. Multi-colored sprites. Bees the size of my hand. Hornets with wicked looking red stingers. Butterflies whose wings carry hallucinogenic toxins.

We down the jug of water and then break into a jog. The netting keeps out the smaller creatures like the butterflies, wasps, and bees, and I use my flyswatter on the sprites. Mack points out the plants to avoid, and more than once, we have to leave a path and find another.

But with the netting and my fly swatter, it's actually not so bad. Two hours later, just as we're nearing the portal, a ravine appears in our path.

Mack points out a rickety wooden bridge. Unfortunately a gate bars our entrance. A sprite that looks more flower than human flits from the top of the gate and points to a wooden box.

I bend down and cautiously open the container. Five vials glint beneath the sun.

Mack hisses through her teeth. "Poison."

The sprite claps. "Very good," she says in her tiny voice. "Your antidote waits on the other side."

"It's a test." Mack perks up at that. "We have to match the correct poison with the correct antidote."

Mack goes first. She places a drop of oleander on her tongue. The gate creaks open to let her through. I watch her rush across the bridge, and a moment later, she appears on the other side, giving a thumbs up.

My turn. I choose snowdrops. The poison tastes like pennies on my tongue as I sprint to the antidote, which unfortunately, is frog's piss.

The portal that leads back to the Spring Court is only fifty yards or so ahead. We have no idea if we're even close to first place . . . or last.

"Has anyone else passed through here yet?" I call to the sprite.

She shakes her tiny head, and Mack lets out a whoop. "I knew it!"

"One of us is about to win first place," I breathe, in shock.

Mack's face is a mask of determination as she turns to me. "Ready?"

I nod, a slow grin stretching my lips. "Let the best shadow win."

We both sprint at the same time, leaping over thick vines that could kill us with one prick of their thorns. My netting flies off, followed by Mack's a second later. Twenty feet to go. My heart slams into my breastbone. Sweat pours into my eyes. I swat away a shiny blue wasp as I hurdle the final obstacle, a fallen tree covered in moss and fire-red ants.

Ten feet. Five. I look behind me. Mack's too far back.

I'm going to win.

Something dark flashes in the middle of the path between us. Still running, I glance down—

The snake on the ground in front of her is black as night. It's coiled aggressively, its head lifted knee-high and fanned out in the shape of a hood. An orange teardrop marking rests on the backside of its skull.

Ash Viper.

A split second—that's all it takes to decide whether to win or save my best friend's life. Pivoting, I fling my weight on my back leg, reach for her, and do the only thing I can.

Tug her forward, over the viper and out of its lethal reach.

Her mouth falls open in shock, our eyes locking as her momentum and my strength pull her in front of me . . .

And through the portal to the finish line.

47

The applause back on the other side is so loud that it vibrates the earth. I blink against the sunlight, the throng of Fae on the field around us. Cronus has already grabbed Mack and is herding her toward the palace courtyard, where the winner's stage awaits.

Winner. She won.

A surge of contrasting emotions flood through me. I'm happy she won her place back at the academy. I am. But I can't shake this feeling . . . this heaviness.

As the crowd pushes me toward the stage, I shove the feeling aside. Hellebore will undoubtedly make me wear something awful, something humiliating and cruel.

But I can handle that.

If he isn't already in chains. I glance around as we near the stage. Garlands of yellow aconite and purple and white crocus are hung above us. Monarch butterflies dance in the air. Refreshments are laid out on tables. Four stands have been set up in each corner surrounding the stage, and the royals from each seasonal court watch as Mack is guided to the stage.

AUDREY GREY

Where is Hellebore?

I shove as close to the front as I can. Mack looks bewildered, still in shock from what happened at the end.

Cronus slides a wreath of daffodil and hyacinth over her head. "Mackenzie Fairchild, winner of the first annual Evermore Academy Final Gauntlet."

Once the applause subsides, two hobs guide Mack off the stage. I start to follow—

"Summer Solstice." Cronus's voice rings loud over the courtyard. "Please come to the stage."

Crap. Is there a prize for coming in second place?

For some reason, it's hard to drag in enough air to satisfy my lungs. Wiping my sweaty palms on my suit, I make my way to the stairs leading up to the podium.

Fine. Everything's fine. This is just a formality.

Cronus beckons me to center stage. He doesn't hold a second place wreath. He doesn't hold anything except a strange look that sends my heart into overdrive.

And then I see Hellebore standing just off to the side, hands in his pockets, lips pressed into the softest of smiles . . . and my body goes cold. *No.*

I turn to slip off stage, but two Spring Court guards block my path. More make themselves known surrounding the dais.

Trapped.

Turning, I march toward Hellebore, working to calm my nerves. He doesn't know. This is him humiliating me.

"Surprised to see me?" he asks softly.

He knows. He knows. I clench my jaw, forcing the fear from my face. "What is this?"

He shrugs. "Fulfilling your end of the bargain. Or did you think I'd forgotten?"

I swallow, throat painfully dry. Whatever embarrassment he has in store, I can take it. "Go ahead. I'm ready."

He beckons to a hob in the corner who shuffles over, carrying something on a golden velvet pillow.

A makeshift crown of ivy, poppies, and bellflowers. But the ivy is withered, the leaves brittle and browned along the edges, and the flowers have lost their bloom and lay wilted and limp.

Hellebore regards the crown of flowers before sliding his unreadable gaze to me. "Put it on."

I drag in a shaky breath. What game is he playing? Perhaps the crown is spelled with magic that will make me do silly things like strip off my clothes. Oh, God . . .

The bargain stipulates the item cannot be imbued with magic that would harm me, but not embarrass me. I should have thought of that, but one can't die of embarrassment, right?

Lifting my chin, I reach for the crown. Whatever he has in store, it cannot break me. He hardly seems to breathe as my fingers close around the ivy base. I swear the tangled vine moves beneath my touch.

"Put it on your head," he commands.

I look out into the crowd. They want to see a spectacle? A show? I'll give them one.

Silence descends as I lift the crown and settle it on my head. I stand there, feeling silly and awkward. What's supposed to happen? I feel nothing.

A pink-skinned nymph in the front covers her mouth with a hand. "She wears the Summer Princess's crown!"

Another cries, "The flowers—they're blooming!"

Blooming? A collective gasp shatters the stillness. And then, as if synchronized, every single Fae in the audience drops into a bow.

Oh, no.

A whisper of panic hits me.

Hellebore wasn't trying to humiliate me. He was trying to expose me.

"Nice to see you again, Princess Hyacinth Larkspur," Hellebore whispers in my ear before slipping his arm in mine. I'm frozen, paralyzed with surprise and dread as he addresses the crowd. "Fellow Evermore, I've found the lost Summer Princess, the fiancé promised to me by her father, King Larkspur."

All I hear is, *the fiancé promised to me,* and then my mind goes blank with horror.

Mack is in the crowd. We lock eyes. Her skin has lost all color, her mouth gaping in complete, utter confusion and shock. I spot Inara, Bane, and a few others close by.

Their expressions match Mack's, although their faces have the added tinge of fear as they slowly realize the mortal they've been taunting was actually a Summer Court Princess.

That's right, Fae-holes. Even in my ever-growing desperation, I manage to find a kernel of happiness in their terror.

After that, everything spirals into chaos. My mother springs to her feet, the Summer King rising behind her. Their court breaks into angry shouts while the Spring Court guards surround me. More guards grab me by the arms and drag me from the stage. The crush of bodies is disorienting.

I try to fight, but I might as well be struggling against boulders for all it does.

I kick and buck all the way to the palace. Hellebore laughs at my struggle, as if watching me be manhandled against my will is a delightful game.

"Where are you . . . taking me?" I pant.

He tsks. "Don't be impatient. Can't I surprise my fiancé?"

That word in connection to him makes me want to vomit. My feet drag over the tile floor as the guards push through a set of tall mahogany doors into a throne room. My gaze skips over the massive chandelier made from butterflies, the parquet floor of interlocking tiles in the shape of the Spring Court's sigil, and onto the spectacle in the middle.

Oh, God, no.

Terror spikes my heart. Valerian, Eclipsa, and Asher are caught in the grasp of thick, thorny vines that sprout nearly fifteen feet into the air, held aloft like macabre decorations, and when I see their faces—

A flood of horror makes me nearly double over. "What have you done to them?"

They look . . . dead. Lifeless. Faces drained of blood and tinged a deathly blue. Lips purple. Eyes shut like they're sleeping.

Please be sleeping. Please . . . I swallow down my cry when I realize that I don't feel the bond with Valerian.

I feel . . . nothing.

A cold, dark emptiness that floods me with fear

"They're not dead," Hellebore offers blithely. "*Yet.* That's up to you."

"Poison," I whisper. My insides twist. My skin both hot and cold, almost feverish as reality sinks in.

My mate and friends are poisoned . . . near death. At the mercy of a madman.

"Very good." Hellebore approaches Valerian, held aloft in the middle of Asher and Eclipsa, and reaches out his hand—

I strain against my guards. "If you touch him, I'll rip you apart!"

"Such a feisty thing you are, Princess," Hellebore scolds as something small and black scuttles from the bottom hem of Valerian's pants and onto the Spring Court heir's waiting palm. He does the same with Eclipsa and Asher before crossing to me. "Feisty is good, but useful is better." He holds up his hand. "Like these misunderstood creatures. Their use as silent, stealthy assassins are unparalleled."

I recoil from the three arachnids crawling over his hand.

Small and dark, they resemble black widows with their spindly legs and fat, round bodies. Each horrible little creature wears an iron thimble with a stinger on the end.

"I still had to get the creatures close, of course, but Inara was more than happy to plant them on your friends for me. Seems her love for the Ice Prince has soured."

"The council will—"

"Do nothing. My creatures only pricked the Ice Prince and the others with the Bloodstar poison once they broke into my vault, as is my right, by law."

Bloodstar. No. Panic claws through my chest. "How did you know?"

Footsteps draw my attention to a figure approaching behind me. The Winter King. The air cools around us as he nears, drawing goose bumps over my feverish skin.

"I told him." Valerian's father's pale eyes glitter above a cunning grin.

"What?" My throat clenches. "Why?"

"My son apprised me of his suspicions that Prince Hellebore stole my father's soulstone. When I realized that my son was bringing both the Lunar assassin and Asher Grayscale here . . . well, it wasn't hard to determine his motives. Breaking into the Spring Court palace."

"You had your son poisoned!" I growl as fury builds beneath my sternum, filling the hole that panic has already carved. "You betrayed him."

"No dear." The king shakes his head, as if I couldn't begin to fathom his reasoning. "Betrayal would have been letting him give up everything for you. When my son came to me wanting to end his betrothal to Inara Winterspell, I suspected who you were. The drink you sipped during the ceremony at the academy confirmed it. Only someone with Fae magic could resist the lethal toxin I had the bartender add."

The toast. I shiver, knowing how close Mack came to drinking the spiked cocktail. Fresh, bitter rage builds inside me. If I had talons I would claw the king's eyes out right now, guards or not.

"If you had agreed to mate with my son, things may have been different. After all, your powers are rumored to be wondrous. But, when my spies told me you'd rejected him that night instead, after he'd already made an enemy of half the Winter Court for you, I knew there was only one way to rectify the damage. A deal with Prince Hellebore."

His flippant attitude over his treachery makes my teeth grind. "How does trading me to your enemy, the Fae who is colluding with the Darken and just poisoned your son, benefit you?"

"Besides the generous offer of lands in the Untouched Zones?" His eyes narrow. "Your mortal nature has made you blind to our ways, otherwise you would understand. I'm saving my son and the throne. With you alive, the contract your father made with Hellebore still stands. You will become the Spring Court Prince's wife, and my son will be forced to forget you. He will marry Inara Winterspell, placating her father and preventing a civil war, our court will have lands in the Untouched Zones, and our claim on the throne will once again be ironclad."

"Any powers I possess will be used to raise the Darken."

"Perhaps. Although I have yet to see any evidence that Prince Hellebore is in league with my father."

"That's because you betrayed your son before he could find it!"

He picks at a fleck on his tunic, ignoring me.

"He'll never forgive you," I whisper.

"Forgive?" The Winter King arches a bored brow. "Such a mortal concept, forgiveness. He will be upset . . . but after you marry the Spring Prince and the bond between you and my son withers into a distant memory, he will come around. And if he doesn't, well, perhaps Hellebore can explain."

Hellebore lovingly finishes depositing his spiders into a small silver box lined with black velvet before turning to me. "Do you know why the Bloodstar flower is so effective? Besides being the most lethal poison in existence, it's the most rare, and the cure almost non-existent."

"You bastard."

"There *is* an antidote that will prevent the poison from taking hold for a time, and if the Winter Prince and his friends behave, it will be administered every seven days."

Oh, God. That's how they'll control Valerian and the others. Threatening to withhold the antidote if they don't do as told.

A sick feeling crashes over me. I fight through it, struggling not to drown beneath the unrelenting waves of revulsion and horror. Struggling to be strong for my mate, my friends.

To find a way to save them.

Hellebore waits until the enormity of his meaning flashes over my face before adding the final nail in my coffin. "Only I possess the true cure. Which they will all receive after you formally become my loving, dutiful wife, and all your powers with you."

I suck in a breath as the walls seem to close in around us. I can't breathe. The feeling of being trapped descends, and with it comes a wild sense of desperation. "I'll pay off our marriage arrangement, buy it out somehow."

Hellebore laughs. "Orc's breath, you're adorable. Our future together is going to be so very entertaining. Especially considering that, as my fiancé, I no longer need your permission for anything, including touching you."

Hot nausea simmers below my breastbone. "I'll kill you before I let you touch any part of me."

Hellebore's chuckle echoes over the marble walls, and I want to carve his eyes out. "Behold, king, a rabbit who believes itself a wolf."

I bare my teeth, near-rabid with a seething fury. *This rabbit is going to rip out your throat someday, Prince.*

The Winter King lacks Hellebore's mirth as he regards me. I hate the disinterest in his hard gaze. As if I'm nothing, unworthy of more than a passing glance.

He shifts his attention to Hellebore. "Do what you will with her. My son possesses a misplaced sense of loyalty to his companions. He might gamble with his own life to retrieve his mate, but he won't risk the lives of his trusted friends for her. As long as the poison runs through their veins, he will behave."

In this moment, my hatred for Valerian's father rivals my loathing for Hellebore. The Winter King has to know that, after what happened with Valerian's mother, this final treachery will crush whatever's left of Valerian's wounded heart.

Both Fae males whip their heads to stare behind me—

The mahogany doors explode in a burst of fire, wood splinters slamming into the nearest wall. My mother strides in ready for battle, flames flaring from either side of her open hands.

Her fiery gaze flicks to my friends above, darts to the Winter King, and then settles on Hellebore.

To her credit, her shock barely registers before she composes her face into a fearsome mask. "I will buy off my daughter's marriage contract. What's your price? Land? Jewels?"

Hellebore's lips twitch. "There is no price on love, isn't that what mortals say?"

"The betrothal was never made permanent with magic before she died." My mother stalks toward us until she's close enough that I can smell her exotic perfume. "By Faerie law, we can still buy out the offer."

"Fine, present me with my parents, alive and unharmed, and you may have your daughter back."

My mother blinks, just barely masking her shock. I get the feeling very few Fae ever surprise her. "That was your aunt's doing, not ours."

"No. My aunt was simply being true to our nature as Evermore. She sensed weakness and acted upon it. I don't blame her, but I do blame the Winter Prince for trying to take what was promised to me."

His eyes gleam as he turns my way. "Our future marriage, secret as it was, formed powerful ties between our courts, and when the Summer King was forced to kill you to keep you out of the Winter Prince's hands, my parents lost that alliance. They died all because one petulant, greedy Winter Prince had never been taught not to take what wasn't his."

That's why he hates Valerian. He blames him for his parents' death. "Why are you telling me this?"

"Because I will see the Ice Prince destroyed one way or another. Either by taking what he covets most or watching him die."

A sinking feeling weighs down my middle. "The antidote."

"If you refuse to make our betrothal permanent . . ." His gaze drags over my friends, one by one. "Then your co-conspirators won't get the weekly antidote to slow the Bloodstar poison. They'll become lifeless statues, empty husks. Dead, their bodies preserved for eternity, souls imprisoned in the Seven Fae Hells. You will never see them again in your mortal life."

The panic searing my veins begins to ebb as I slowly look

over my friends. Taking them in. Remembering how alive they'd been just a few hours ago.

I can picture with perfect, painstaking clarity Valerian's face last night outside my door, the vulnerability and hope that had transformed him. I can see Asher as he waited by that tree for Mack, adoration in his eyes. I recall Eclipsa as she admitted to being my friend, to caring for me.

If saving them means shackling myself to a monster for eternity, so be it.

Jaw set, I nod. "Give them the antidote. Once I see that they're alive, I'll do what you want."

"Don't do this," my mother begs. "Once the betrothal is permanent, you're his. He owns you. Controls you as your male fiancé."

"It's worth it to save them." My voice comes out a whisper, but it's strong—frightfully so.

I've made up my mind.

I'm giving away my life to save theirs.

"Once the betrothal vow is finalized by magic, it will eat away at any claim the Winter Prince has on you, including your mating bond, until any trace of your soulbond is erased."

The idea of losing what Valerian and I share nearly makes me refuse. But I know—I *know* without a doubt that what we have goes beyond magic.

Beyond fate.

Love. Hellebore might be able to sever our mating bond eventually, but he'll never be able to make me love anyone but Valerian.

My mother must see that I can't be swayed because she begins to negotiate with Hellebore. "After the betrothal contract is made permanent, my daughter stays with me at my apartment in the mortal world, as is her right before the marriage. And she gets to finish her third year at the academy before the wedding."

Hellebore contemplates that for a moment before shrugging. "Agreed."

"And my friends won't be punished any further for breaking in," I add quickly.

His eyes narrow, but he nods. "What I have in store for you will be more than enough punishment for the prince."

I glare at Hellebore. Funneling every bit of rage and hatred into my eyes, my mouth, my voice as I say, "Do it."

Hellebore gives a signal and three guards leave their places against the wall. The vines lower my friends to the floor, slowly, until they're laid out in a row next to one another.

As soon as the guards administer the antidote, a drop of silver fluid on each of their tongues, the sickly white of their skin begins to fade. Their lips go from bruised purple to pink, their flesh softens, and their chests begin to heave as air enters their lungs once more.

I nearly stagger with relief, hands flexing and unflexing at my sides.

"They will wake up in a few hours, perfectly fine." Hellebore makes another flippant gesture and the guards begin to drag them away. "Throw them into the scourge lands with the darklings."

"You liar!" I try to break free from my guards, fighting with all my strength.

Hellebore's head falls back as he laughs. "Fae Hells, you're going to be fun to play with. I'm teasing. How can I witness the prince's public humiliation if he's been ravaged by darklings?"

The guards halt, looking confused and wary as they try to determine what they're supposed to actually do. I can tell it's a common theme—read my psycho fiancé's moods and try not to die.

Hellebore waves a hand. "Make sure they end up safely in the Winter territories." He lifts his brows in exasperation. "Satisfied, little pet?"

Not nearly. Not until your smarmy head is on a pike, you maniac.

I nod, my entire body stiff as I wait for what comes next.

I don't have long to wait. Hellebore's eyes glitter with malevolence as he saunters over and says, "Summer Solstice, Princess and surviving heir to the Summer Court Throne, do you agree to complete the promise of marriage between us? To become mine after graduation by the law of Faerie forevermore? To become my possession, my ward, and eventually, my wife?"

His words are cruel, jagged things that carve into the ever-growing wound inside me. Words I had once imagined falling from Valerian's lips. Words that were supposed to fill me with anticipation, not hopelessness and despair.

Words that will bind me forever to the Fae in league with the Darken.

I make sure Hellebore can see the hatred seething from my entire being as I say, "I do."

A dull throbbing pain wracks my right arm, where Valerian's brand has claimed me as his for nearly two years. But I don't have the courage to unzip my suit and pull down my sleeve to see what horror it hides.

Not until my Fae mother has dragged me as far away as possible from the Spring Court and I'm ensconced inside her penthouse in Manhattan, near her office skyscraper. A place that makes Mack's top floor apartment look like a pauper's dwelling in comparison.

Only then do I force my gaze over my arm. A single white Bloodstar bud grows between the metallic gold of Valerian's markings. The tight bud has already begun to open. I know with a terrifying certainty that it will bloom, and then another bud will appear, and another.

Until Valerian's brand is choked out and Hellebore's mark is all that remains.

"Do you want to read them or should I trash them?" Mack asks, tipping down her black Ray Bans to reveal her cornflower blue eyes.

We're sitting at one of the several cream-colored couches on my mother's penthouse balcony, breathing in the warm New York air. Fae gossip magazines stolen from the magazine vendors below by Ruby are spread out on the glass coffee table; my face stares out from every single one.

The image of me taken wearing the Summer Princess's crown—the one that would only bloom for her—is the most widely used.

It's also the picture that I despise the most. The wide-eyed girl on the cover didn't know it yet, but her future had just died.

Her hopes, dreams, freedoms, and love story, all destroyed.

I hate her innocence. How she still clings to that wonderful notion that she can be happy with Valerian. That her life is still hers.

"Trash," I finally say. "Definitely."

"Maybe you could make Ruby stop stealing them," Mack suggests before grumbling under her breath, "and force her to wear some clothes while you're at it."

"I can't make Ruby do anything," I protest, glancing over at the sunbathing sprite. She's laid out on the stone railing, completely, unapologetically nude.

"I can hear you, rude human," Ruby calls before snapping her fingers. A brownie appears from thin air with a doll-sized frozen strawberry daiquiri in hand. "They're calling my master the people's princess. She's beloved by all the world. Why not show her proof of that?"

My head falls back as a ragged sigh escapes my lips. But . . . part of what she says is true. I've been presented as both mortal and Fae, a princess for both races.

No doubt, thanks to my mother, who's taken this opportunity to boost the image of her company. Not that I'd expect any less from a Fae.

Mack grins. "I bet Queen Larkspur loves Ruby."

I snort, remembering the horrified way my mother stared at Ruby the first time she caught her in the walk-in pantry, tiny butt sticking out of a jar of honey.

"How is your mother, by the way?" Mack asks. "To be around every day, I mean."

"Beautiful. Imposing. Hard to read." I shrug, hoping Mack doesn't hear the pain in my voice. Even though I called Zinnia my aunt out of respect for her daughter, I always considered her like a mother.

And now . . . it's hard to feel anything for this strange woman when I miss Zinnia so much it physically hurts. When calling the Summer Queen mother feels like a betrayal to the woman who raised me.

Zinnia hardly batted an eye when I revealed the reason I

had to spend the summer here. She must have always suspected I was part Fae somehow—suspected and still loved me.

Yep, there's no way the Summer Queen can take Zinnia's place.

"You don't remember the queen from your life before?" Mack presses.

I take a sip of sweet tea and then lean back against the sofa cushion. "With the Winter Prince, there was a connection immediately. But . . . not with her. The only thing that feels familiar is her perfume. It has this exotic floral aroma I can't place, but remember somehow. It's unmistakable."

"You've been here two weeks and that's all you know about the woman? The scent of her perfume?"

"She works all the time, so I really only see her at dinner."

My mother's one request. That we eat dinner together every night. She seemed offended at first by my preference for mortal food, but now she has her chef provide both.

Mack quickly shuffles the tabloids together. Before she can stand to throw them away, one of the two brownies employed by my mother appears and jerks the magazines from Mack's grip, rushing them to a trash can hidden in the corner.

"I will never get used to them just appearing like that," Mack whispers. "It's creepy."

"Same."

I'm starting to suspect the brownies spy on me for my mother. But at least they're super helpful spies, and once the tabloids are gone, my tension eases.

The news of my appearance—in a mortal body, no less—caused major waves in the Evermore and mortal community. Waves I've mostly been protected from by my mother, who's had the penthouse under locked guard and the Fae news channels turned off.

No one gets into the penthouse but the lesser Fae servants who are sworn to secrecy and Mack.

My mother sends out for everything so I don't have to leave the apartment. The few times I made the mistake of venturing into the Fae communities around the city for groceries or coffee or just to get out of the house, the Fae made it impossible to fly under the radar.

They stared. Took pictures. Whispered. A few even touched me for luck.

I once walked through a Fae market and the Seelie vendors fell over themselves to give me gifts—neverapples, healing crystals, rare and expensive tonics. When I returned my mother freaked out because, inadvertently, I'd accepted favors that I now have to repay.

It's like a strange nightmare I can't wake up from. One where I gained a mother and new life but lost my old life. My friends. My other family. My freedom.

My mate.

The only silver lining to this whole mess is that Mack's apartment is two blocks away. I can literally wave to her from my floor-to-ceiling bedroom window. Or, with the right high-powered flashlight, send her signals.

Which was super helpful when I was trying to get her to forgive me for lying to her.

It took a week of shining my high beam into her bedroom window until she finally returned my calls. But it only took two seconds on the phone for both of us to break down in tears.

Five minutes later, she was on this very balcony, giving me a stern talk about never keeping secrets from each other again.

After that—and an entire carton of Half Baked Ben & Jerry's ice cream, smuggled in by Ruby—all was forgiven.

"Any word from the ILB?" Mack asks softly. She knows

now that he's my mate, and that being away from him is torture for me.

I shake my head, mindlessly running a finger over the Bloodstar that's now half-bloomed on my upper arm. Now that my engagement to Hellebore has been made permanent, he can control almost every aspect of my life. My mother has been using the firm's resources and clout to negotiate for certain freedoms I used to take for granted.

Like whom I'm allowed to see, talk to, even wave at.

So far, the Spring asshat has agreed to me being around Mack for two whole hours a day, allowing a visit to my aunts in the Tainted Zone one weekend a month, and letting Ruby come live with me at the Summer Queen's residence.

He also finally agreed to Eclipsa's request to tutor me once a week, since I'll be attending school in the fall as an Evermore, not a mortal shadow.

Who better than the infamous Lunar assassin to school Hellebore's soon-to-be wife on all things Fae?

But Valerian . . . he's off limits. I haven't been able to reach him since everything happened. All I know is that he's safe.

For now.

As long as he does exactly what his father says.

Forget about me. Get back with Inara. Pretend I don't exist as Hellebore's mark slowly eats away at our bond until there's nothing left between Valerian and me but bitter memories.

"You okay?" Mack asks before her eyes turn dark with fury. "Did Prince Helle-Douche do something? If he did—"

"Nope," I say, pushing away the pain. I've become something of an expert at that over the last two weeks. "Helle-Douche knows if he shows up here, my mother will 'accidentally' cut his tiny balls off, so he's been gloriously absent." I drag a strand of hair from my face and tuck it behind my ear, desperate to change the subject. "Now, ready for *Operation Destroy the Bastard*?"

"Hell, yes."

After I've sent the two brownies on a fake errand to the nearest Fae market, Mack drags out Evelyn's box of stuff. I had it sent over with my things the first week here.

My only hope to escape my new bonds is to expose Helle-bore. The Spring Court Prince may own a spot on my flesh, and he may be able to control who I see—for now. But he can't control what I do in my spare time. And with my access to my mom's law library, I've dedicated every free hour to researching Fae laws that could break my engagement to him.

After nearly two weeks of searching, I still know of only one ironclad way to break his hold over me.

Expose his ties to the Darken.

So that's what Mack and I do. We sit on the balcony, drink entire pitchers of the sweet tea I taught my mother's staff how to make, and search for the key to Hellebore's downfall.

There has to be something in Evelyn's box of random things that points us in the right direction. There *has* to be.

All I need is one clue. One tiny little shred of evidence. And I'll spend the rest of my life following that thread until it leads to my new fiancé's absolute destruction.

When the sun disappears behind the glittering wall of steel high-rises, Mack finally leaves. I'm watching her hurry down the sidewalk from the balcony when the sound of wings rustling the air draws my attention to the sky above.

Phalanx! He lands on the stone railing, flares out his massive ivory wings, and puffs out his soft chest. A tan scroll is clutched inside his dull orange beak.

I use a piece of my leftover turkey sandwich to coax the note from his mouth—carefully, considering how he got his name. Once Valerian's familiar takes to the sky with his deli offering, I flatten out the thin parchment.

My throat tightens as Valerian's elegant handwriting comes into view, scrawled neatly across the paper.

And when I read his words . . .

I'll fight for you, always.

Love,

The ILB

An ache yawns open inside my chest. For a moment, I see his deft fingers writing this note, despite the danger it puts him in. See one side of his lips curl up as he adds *the ILB*, probably hoping to make me smile. Or perhaps hoping to make me remember our last night together.

When he learned what that acronym stood for . . . and I learned that he loved me.

Fighting back the jagged pain in my heart, I read those seven words over and over until they're indelibly engraved in my mind, a touchstone for when the tether between us begins to fray—and a reminder of what I'm fighting for.

Then I roll up the scroll, close my hand around it, and use my magic to set the paper afire inside my palm.

My magic.

As I dump the note over the guardrail and watch the bits of ash spiral into the night air, a slow grin finds my face.

Something happened after the final gauntlet. I don't know if it's being inside my mother's house, or the trauma from what I endured.

Or if it's something else entirely.

But my powers have been unlocked. My Fae side unleashed.

And the one thing I'm certain of is Hellebore is going to regret the day he decided to use me as a pawn against my mate.

The next time I step foot on the academy grounds, I'm coming armed with secrets, lies, and powerful magic. Now that I know the lengths they'll go to hurt me, to manipulate, humiliate, and destroy everyone I love, I'm going to fight back.

And I won't stop until I've beaten the Evermore at their own twisted game.

The End

AFTERWORD

Thank you so much for reading EVERMORE ACADEMY: SPRING. I hope you enjoyed catching up with Summer and her friends as much as I enjoyed writing them.

The next book in the series, EVERMORE ACADEMY: SUMMER, releases sometime in early 2021.

In the meantime, check out my other available books at www.AudreyGrey.com

ABOUT THE AUTHOR

Audrey Grey lives in the charming state of Oklahoma surrounded by animals, books, and little people. You can usually find Audrey hiding out in her office, downing copious amounts of caffeine while dreaming of tacos and holding entire conversations with her friends using gifs. Audrey considers her ability to travel to fantastical worlds a superpower and loves nothing more than bringing her readers with her.

Check out her website at:
www.AudreyGrey.com

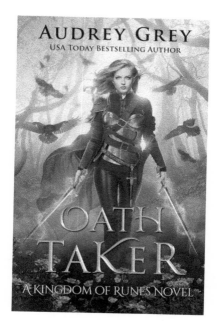

Light magic is forbidden.

Dark magic spells death.

Haven has both.

After the Prince of Penryth saved her from captivity, seventeen-year-old Haven Ashwood spends her days protecting the kind prince and her nights secretly fighting the monsters outside the castle walls.

When one of those monsters kidnaps Prince Bell, Haven must ally with Archeron Halfbane and his band of immortals to rescue her friend.

Her quest takes her deep into the domain of a warped and vicious queen where the rules are simple: break her curse or die.

Lost in a land of twisted magic and fabled creatures, Haven finds herself unprepared, not just for the feelings she develops for Archeron, but for the warring powers raging inside her.

Faced with impossible love, heartbreaking betrayals, and a queen intent on destroying the realm, only one thing remains certain.

Haven must shatter the curse or it will devour everything she loves.

My name is Maia Graystone: prisoner, rebel, and reluctant savior of a dying world.

In exactly 552 hours, an asteroid will end life as we know it. Trapped inside a hellish prison, my chances of survival are dismal at best.

Then a mysterious benefactor offers the impossible: a chance to compete in the Shadow Trials. Win and my brother and I receive a coveted spot on the space station in the stars.

But the opportunity comes at a steep price. Partner with a dashing psychopath, survive the ruthless trials created by my own mother, and kill the Emperor--the very man who's hunting me.

In this cunning game of life and death, nothing is as it seems and everyone expects me to fail. But they forgot one tiny detail.

Never underestimate the girl with nothing left to lose.